I0703878

Coral

Kyla Breene

Copyright © 2024 by Kyla Breene

All rights reserved.

No part of this publication may be reproduced, distributed, or transmitted in any form or by any means, including photocopying, recording, or other electronic or mechanical methods, without the prior written permission of the publisher, except as permitted by U.S. copyright law. For permission requests, contact ky@kylabreene.com

The story, all names, characters, and incidents portrayed in this production are fictitious. No identification with actual persons (living or deceased), places, buildings, and products is intended or should be inferred.

Cover by Kyla Breene

Illustration by Yoingco and Kyla Breene

1st edition 2024

A note on species and politics

There are a lot of alien species in this series. This will help you keep track of which ones you have come across so far.
Manticorid: once empire seeking, now mostly living peacefully. The origin of manticore mythology on Earth.

- **Abstainers**: A sub-sect of manticorids with a strong political presence in Session. They believe venom is dangerous and cut off the tip of male manticorid tails at birth.

Genali: The slimes we all love to hate. Opportunistic, with a specialty in exotic goods, including people of all species.
Braceaaer: The origin of Little Green Men mythology on Earth. Violent, small, and much stronger than they look.
Drakonid: a dragon/dinosaur-like species that was once a servitor race to the manticorid empire.

Kira

"You were hired for your looks, not your opinions."

For a moment I'm speechless, which almost never happens, though in my defense this isn't a time where I can tell someone to shove it. No matter how much I want to.

My usual quick retorts would get me fired. And I need this fucking job.

I have to bite my tongue, in this case hard enough to taste blood, to avoid verbally lashing out at my asshat of a client. I thought Mar did a better job of screening assets.

We're going to have a serious talk about this guy.

He's handsome, I'll give him that, with designer everything and impeccable grooming. He probably has a freaking pedigree sheet or something, if his thick black hair and firm jaw are any indication.

Too bad it's all just shiny gilding around a rotting carcass of terrible personality. Ugh.

After a slow breath to steady myself, I see if I can let off the vice grip I have on my poor abused tongue without throwing verbal knives.

"I was under the impression someone wanted to kill you," I say in a tight voice.

If he gets huffy, it won't phase me, thanks to my time spent around sergeants. Sarge insults are fucking awe-inspiring. I might have a foul mouth, but they are next level.

In fact, compared to most marines, I'm pretty damn tame. Some of them manage to say *fuck* every three words, which is a feat by itself.

See. That wasn't so bad, Kira. Not a single death threat or curse word.

You've got this, I tell myself.

The piece of shit doesn't even answer me, just runs his eyes up and down my body and then looks away. I guess chivalry really is dead amongst the upper classes. Not that I've ever rubbed elbows before this, but I guess I still held out some hopes about human decency.

I curse under my breath when my hand strays over to the dagger at my wrist.

Not allowed, bitch, I chide myself.

Stabbing a client is a great way to no longer be employed. I apparently don't care about that because my hand just keeps on creeping over to it, as I imagine ways I can use it to teach this insolent fucker a few lessons.

Without causing too much damage, of course.

Mar would kill you, the more rational part of my mind points out.

That is a much better deterrent.

I owe her big time for giving me this chance and I can't fuck it up. She's worked hard to build her security business, and I'd never jeopardize that. Not to mention I think she's saved my life a couple more times than I've returned the favor.

I was practically born into the military and without it, I don't know who I am. Working with her feels as close as I can get to still being in the Marines, and I'm clinging to that small lifeline currently keeping my head above the addiction water.

I have a feeling she might want to drop this client after I report in, but for now, I just need to suck it up and get through the night without killing the dickhead.

Tomorrow we can commiserate over the sting of people underestimating us.

He just keeps walking toward the seediest looking warehouse-cum-nightclub possible, completely disregarding my attempts to dissuade him.

Dumbass.

I mean, everyone knows a warehouse party in the middle of a 'hood is sketchy as hell, right? Not that I've ever actually been to one.

I've had far more important things to do with my life.

Like getting shot at in foreign countries.

I'd rather not get shot at here in the States, dammit. Though I guess I should have considered that before taking a job as a personal bodyguard.

My mom always said I was the dumbest genius she ever knew. Usually right after I fell out of a tree or got a beat down when I didn't back down from a fight that was well above my weight class.

If my dad was the one home, then he would just look at me with pride and talk about independence. Moving around a lot while my parents traded off deployments taught me the value of only relying on yourself. Now it's my superpower.

The good ol' days. Long before war wrecked my body, and I had to figure out what other ways a penchant for violence might pay the bills.

And so here I am.

I'd say going into a dodgy-looking nightclub would be a cry for help from this rich scumbag, except he's old enough to know better. I'm old enough to know better too, and yet I still trudge after him, my steel-toed shit-kickers thumping out my rage in the only way currently socially acceptable.

The bouncer at the door eyes me, his gaze clocking most of my hidden weapons. Knives at wrists, boots, and embedded in my belt. Guns under my left breast and the small of my back.

He missed the knives in the collar of my beat-up jacket and the outer stitching of my leather pants. Probably too distracted by how well my ass fills out the leather.

I suppress a smirk.

He takes a glance at my client, and we're waved through. As we move forward, I'm hoping that not being pawed at by the muscle-bound oaf bodes well for the rest of my night.

I dart a look back at the bouncer as we pass and, sure enough, he's ogling my hips. I feel like a genius for asking for the pants to be designed this way.

With a shake of my head, I bring my attention back to my job and scan the club for threats.

The music is pounding, lights are pulsing, and it smells like a barracks, except with the addition of sex, alcohol, and ganja. I'm sure there are plenty of other temptations in here I've been avoiding in my quest to stay sober.

Well, except sex. I haven't been avoiding it. More like men have been avoiding me.

I scare the shit out of them.

Not to mention they want a different kind of woman altogether. Less competitive. Less aggressive. Just... less.

I wish men were my problem, but unfortunately, it's everything else that causes me trouble.

Especially whiskey.

Nothing like immense pain to make you want to feel numb. The ache in my left arm, which still isn't fully functional, is like an insistent thrumming, all but crying out for me to go see who might share or let me buy.

It doesn't help that no one believed me when I told them a cyborg turned my arm into pulp during that fucked up one-way trip they sent my squad on to Antarctica.

I was the only one to come back alive, and my psych eval afterward claimed stress-induced psychosis. Because cyborgs don't fucking exist. I'll admit I turned to some chemical help to deal.

I'm past that, though.

It was more the mix of shame, guilt, and—most damning—relief that I wanted to deaden. I can't avenge any of my squad now and that rage swirling in my belly is all mixed up with relief that I won't have to face something so terrifying.

Then there's that insistent feeling of being unmoored now that I no longer have a long military career in front of me.

Well, as long as any infantry jarhead makes it, at least. Semper Fi, and all that shit.

It's all a jumble, but what I do know is medical retirement doesn't fucking suit me. I'd rather be around my usual type of chuckleheads than protecting Mr. Tall, Dark, and Half-witted.

A job's a job, though, so I follow like a good little bitch, ready to bite anyone who looks sideways at him or his precious designer watch.

I really don't like how so many people are jostling against us as we push through the crowd. I asked repeatedly to be briefed on his plans and our movements, but, of course, he refused. A niggling thought keeps trying to surface about how that seems really fucking suspicious.

Except Mar would never have sent me to him if he hadn't been thoroughly vetted.

And this is also my trial run. You know... since her finding me on a semi-permanent bender and offering me a lifeline didn't exactly inspire a lot of confidence.

I push down my self-loathing as I shove yet another person out of the way.

Plenty of insults comparing me to a dog and reproductive organs are hurled back at me for my efforts. I can't say I blame them.

I would have probably said the same damn things.

Not hurling anything back is the only apology they get from me. Lucky for them, the only person I want to knife right now is my asset.

I can see where he's heading now.

A roped-off section with another bouncer, this one clean cut and with a palpable edge of danger. I don't think I could take him in a fair fight.

It's hot as hell.

Now I'm the one letting my eyes roam over him.

Instinct requires I find his weapons first, but then I get to enjoy the cut of his suit, the corded muscles of his neck, and as I look back up to his face, the completely biteable lips. His eyes are just finishing up their own assessment of me and there's an answering appreciation and heat in his gaze.

It's been far too damn long since I had a hard fuck.

I'm not sure if I'm happy or annoyed that I don't get by this time without a pat down.

Okay, more annoyed. I fucking delight in being armed.

That said, it looks like this job comes with some benefits. He takes his time finding my weapons, being especially careful to ensure there's nothing hiding in my bra, between my legs, or on the plentiful globes of my ass.

As if anything would fit there.

I don't even have to pretend to pant as a distraction; he gets that honest, but he still misses the same weapons the other guy did.

Four whole knives.

I'll be sure to let my tailor know she's a rockstar.

He stores my confiscated weapons in a locker and hands me a key, spending just a moment too long running his fingers over my palm.

It sends a fizzle of pleasure right down to my core, and I clench my thighs in response.

He smirks when he notices, then nods at the woman behind him to move aside the ornate barrier that's keeping the plebs out. It's useless, of course, but few people would make it through the two of them.

He tosses his head toward the VIP area instead of speaking to us, which is a disappointment. I'd really like to know if his voice is as alluring as he looks.

Unfortunately, it's the woman who speaks. "She would eat you alive, Jin."

He grunts and just keeps on looking at me like he wants to eat me.

Please, please do, my gaze tells him.

The woman rolls her eyes and adds more to convince him. "This one doesn't want the picket fence, you idiot. You'd never know where you stand."

Damn, sis. Way to call a girl out. I raise an eyebrow at her, but since I'm not one to lie, I can't say much.

Love is dicey business, and I jump ship at the first glimmer of it in someone's eyes. My mom loved my dad, and where did that lead her? That's right. Dishonorable discharge and the bottom of a bottle.

The woman's not the first person to point out how emotionally stunted I am. In my defense, it's not that I'm completely opposed to settling down. I've just never met a man who could handle me.

I honestly don't think he exists.

In the meantime, there's plenty of man candy in the world. Might as well make them feel appreciated.

I blow the sex god a kiss as I walk by, and he runs his tongue along his upper lip with a wink.

Holy shit balls.

I take it back... This place is definitely worth revisiting.

Unfortunately, I must leave sexual fantasy land to focus on keeping the idiot in front of me in one fancy piece. He heads straight toward a room, pulls out a key card, and opens the door.

Did that fucker have a reservation and couldn't be bothered to tell me jack shit? I bite off a whole litany of curses. Every one of them well-earned.

My fists clench, but I keep my cool, and simply follow him into the room.

It has an exit in the back, and I waste no time ensuring it's locked. There's opulent furniture, a clearly visible camera, and a selection of drinks and drugs. Nothing that looks like a threat.

I put the authoritative growl in my voice that's made plenty of buck privates all but piss themselves, then try to reason with the man again. "Now would be a very good time to tell me why we are here."

He continues ignoring me, helps himself to a line and a drink, and then falls back onto the chair, sprawling out like he owns the place.

Maybe he does. Must be nice being rich.

I don't have to wait long before the mystery is solved about why we're here. Two more men enter the room, clearly also invited because my client remains calm, and they have a key.

Unlike me, they still have the telltale bulges of weapons.

Not good.

I try to get the attention of my client, once again to no effect.

The man in front looks me over. "Really, Chet? A female bodyguard?"

My asset shrugs. "It was the best I could do on short notice."

My eyes narrow at the insult. Guns pretty much even up the...

Oh, right. Sex god has my advantage locked away.

Still, there's no need to be offensive about it. Plus, I have a few tricks they probably don't want me showing them that involve knives in tender places. Imbeciles.

I keep myself loose, and don't let any of my thoughts show on my face. Even with the ache in my arm, I'm confident about my aim. Just because something gets smashed to pieces doesn't mean it can't heal up just as ready to kick ass as the rest of me.

It just requires some adjustment.

And insults? Nothing they can say could be worse than a staff sergeant yelling in your face.

"This won't do much for your debt," the man continues.

What won't?

I glance at my client, but he doesn't have any currency or valuables in his hands. If they wanted money transferred, they wouldn't have needed to meet.

My skin prickles. Nothing about this feels right.

I need to get out of here, preferably with my asset still alive, but after the way he's acted, it's no longer topping my list of priorities. Mar will just have to deal.

"Let's finish this in the back," the man says.

I clear my throat. "I advise against that."

Just like all the other times, he ignores me and gets to his feet.

I hold my hands out toward him as I shift my body to block him. "If you willingly go toward that door, I'm calling this contract void."

Dread spiders down the back of my neck when my client laughs in response. Fuck that, his stupid-ass name is Chet.

He's no longer a client.

"There's only a limited market for this type. Pretty much only the slimes, and that comes with a whole lot of inconvenience. This only gains you a month, at best."

Fuck. They're talking about me. What the hell, Mar? So much for vetting.

When the door opens behind me, I rush the men at front of the room, catching the one who just said I was fucking undesirable with a hard blow to the throat with my elbow.

He collapses to the plush carpet, his hands flying up to his crushed windpipe, his eyes opened wide in shock.

He's unsuccessfully trying to keep living when his companion pulls a gun. I'm not fast enough to knock it away, and so the sound of a silenced weapon firing coincides with a searing pain in my upper thigh.

I let out a screech of pain, but keep moving, pushing the gun to the side as I reach up and yank out a knife from my lapel. A moment later, a darting hand flings it forward, and it's embedded in the man's eye.

Fucking Chet is screaming by that point, pleading with the men who came from the back to kill me. I'm slowed by the weakness in my leg and turn around just in time to take a shot to my left shoulder.

It throws me back and I thump into the door before sliding down it.

I know it's over, but I use the last of my strength to rip another knife from the side of my pants. It takes everything in me, along with a screaming cry, to make myself raise my good arm. I pull it up to my right ear, take aim with my already swimming vision, then let it loose.

Seeing the blood pumping out of Chet's throat makes it all worth it.

I'm laughing manically as I take a boot to the head.

* * *

I'm in and out of consciousness as I'm transported. They really don't like me very much, especially when I share some of the choice insults I learned from my sarge.

I take a few more kicks, but no more bullets, before I wake up with straps holding me down. The room is icy as fuck and I'm shivering, which sends spikes of pain all over my body.

There's too much swelling and blood in my eyes for me to see, but I can feel unyielding, frigid hands all over me. Pain follows wherever they touch.

No, not hands. Metal instruments? Ones that grip and pivot. Robots?

There's this weird hissing, gurgling noise as the robots or instruments, whatever they are, continue to prod me. It has a cadence that my mind wants to associate with something. Almost like... I'm too far gone to figure it out, so I give up.

Another cold touch, this time digging into the bullet wound in my leg, brings me back to wondering about robots. My hands jerk, trying to kill the bastards, but they are held fast.

I scream until they stop digging, then lay there panting.

Whatever it is, it shoves my head to the side next, and I screech as it pushes painfully into the swelling from the repeated battering. Then another agony altogether joins it as they force something into my ear.

A searing pain flows from the canal into my skull and down into my throat. It's all too much and I'm losing my grip on consciousness.

As I fade into the black, I hear someone speaking. Almost like an overlay to the gurgling, in a confusing jumble. "I disagree. The scars will just let a buyer know how they can paint her."

"No. Shentrea sent a new suite to test on this harem. There won't be any star-baked scars."

"Next time say that first, desiccated member. I don't like my time wasted. Just make sure this one's pink."

What the fu...

2

Drasuk

"The famous Drasuk," I hear someone call out in a feminine rumble behind me.

When I turn to look, I see it's Neoval, one of the most battle-hardened females I've ever known. She's crisscrossed with scars, and I note the new ones since I last saw her, my already elevated respect for her cresting higher.

She has sacrificed as much as any of us to protect our citizens. She's just more successful than most.

My spines shift to reflect my feelings, and she sweeps an arm out to accept my show of respect.

"Yet another female was speaking of you," she continues in her needling rumble.

I haven't been able to dredge up any interest in a city female in a very long time. I suppose not in a Maj'Ra warrior either, but it's best to not share that part.

"Were they?" I ask, as if I don't already know what this conversation will be about.

Her spines show her amusement. "Yes. You are still spending all your time outside the city, Drasuk. They would like your strong hatchlings."

She glances up to see that my jutting blue spines are communicating my desire to avoid this conversation, hisses out a laugh, then continues.

"Is it still because of Nkisa? Your hatchlings would have been the best of the generation, but there are plenty more females wanting to continue your line. I'm sick of having them ask me, Drasuk."

"Maybe if you stop asking me, then they will stop asking you."

She snorts out a breath as she shifts her armor and weapons around. "Why do you avoid them? You aren't sentimental like a venom beast, are you?"

She says the last in a teasing tone, and I try to avoid letting my response quiver along the spikes on my forehead.

"I'm busy, Neoval. They have other options."

She gives me a look I don't bother trying to interpret and goes back to preparing for the coming fight, but her words keep running around my skull.

If only Neoval knew how many times my mind strayed to the bond manticorid mates have or how fascinated I am with it. Nkisa never understood my continued interest in her, any more than I did.

It isn't normal to focus on such bonds, and I'm spared the conflicted feelings rising, as they always do, when Neoval speaks again.

"Do you think this time we'll not only have off-worlders to swat out of the way, but a lesser species will somehow have entered?"

I let out a laugh. There's a running joke about how the percentage of easy kills rises each year, with the number of drakonid warriors from our neighboring planet steadily increasing.

She walks away, her spines twitching in amusement.

I shove past Gorak, our resident mountain of a Maj'Ra who complains good-naturedly about the jostling. He's always been my favorite, but I'd never admit it.

I flick my tail at him, and he smacks it out of his face with a huff, eliciting a rumble from my chest as I squint at him.

"Easy there, cave *shoano*," I tease back, feeling a flicker of warmth replace the discomfort of Neoval's prodding.

Laughter bubbles up from another group stepping into the open-air arena.

Tough competition surrounds me, mixed in with the off-worlders looking distinctly out of place and nervous.

We're a motley gathering of drakonids in mismatched armor, some wearing the new high-flex bio-mesh, others bearing the old, scarred leather they swear by.

Today is looking to be yet another generic khufulle. A day-long mock battle where the only objective is to be the last drak standing by the time the red sun lowers to signal the day's end.

An opportunity for the softer draks come from the other planet in the system to play at being elite. Unless they hide to extend the experience, they never last past the morning.

They live in a paradise and it's reflected in their relative weakness, which is stupid beyond belief. There is a thriving market for the various body parts of the more genetically desirable denizens of the universe.

Listening to an itinerant spice trader tell you how much you're worth on the galactic black market is an experience I am still stuck with mixed feelings over.

I laughed at the time, right along with them and their supposed joke. They didn't laugh much longer.

Reaching the battle grounds, I see the simulated zone spread before us. A holographic cityscape sprawled beneath a dark green sky, dotted with crumbling towers and deserted avenues.

Hovering drones buzz overhead, ready to record our performance.

A thrill courses through me.

There's a chill skittering across my thick hide and down my tail, but it is little more than a vague sensation relegated to the back of my mind as I inhale the *xerea* fumes being pumped into the air via chutes buried beneath the start zone.

Nothing like a bit of delirium to make the fighters more sluggish and ensure a drawn-out fight.

The ceremony is part martial skill and part endurance.

Very few still bother to make *xerea* fumes, so the product is expensive, reserved for the more illustrious of our number who can afford the exorbitantly priced canisters of stimulating yet numbing smoke.

For the Darangul Clan to spend this much to douse us, it means some heavy spenders threw their weight behind making this year's event as entertaining as possible. They were always richer than my clan.

We wouldn't agree to the waste.

The stark increase in numbers compared to last year's live audience is telling enough.

From a glance, it seems like the usual mix of civilians, their proto-wing drapings and ornaments clearly marking them as non-combatants. Aside from the occasional disabled veteran, none of them know what it's like to fight for their lives.

My chest swells with pride that my efforts make that possible for them.

The scars on my hide are clear proof.

Our leader, Maj'Rasare Xallen, a grizzled veteran with a cybernetic arm that gleams in the morning sun, bellows the starting signal. The air crackles with the suppressed energy of fifty eager draks.

This year, I plan on lasting until the end.

The mock battle begins. We scatter through the holographic city as the countdown ticks down before we are allowed to fight, using the ruined buildings for cover. The drones whir, mimicking blaster fire as we prepare to engage in our simulated skirmishes.

I slip through an alleyway, navigating the debris with practiced ease. My reflexes, honed by years of patrolling and training, come into play.

A hulking figure rounds the corner. Thorg, another veteran with an axe the size of my torso. I roll out of the way just as the blade whooshes overhead, sparks flying against the stone under us.

"You're getting slow, Drasuk," Thorg booms, his laugh echoing through the alley.

I leap at him as I retort. "Just warming up, old friend."

We lock blades in a mock duel, the training bio-mesh groaning in protest.

We exchange a few playful blows. The temptation to use more lethal tactics is there, spurred on by my already intoxicated mind, but this is a mock battle.

Lethality is frowned upon.

I tail whip the defensive Thorg into a nearby pool marked as poison, a shrill chirp letting me know it counted as a kill. I sheathe my blade in the holder on my under-armor plating and take off on all fours in search of new opponents, my heart pumping out my excitement.

As I do, I feel the *xerea* settle in my lungs and the roof of my mouth like a magnetic cloud that fills me with equal parts thrill and lethargy.

Long moments slide by.

I dispatch three more competitors, feeling a pang of regret each time, even though it is simply a way to sharpen our skills and they aren't harmed. No one wants to imagine the death of a fellow drak. It happens far too often.

A few hours later, the battlefield thins.

The remaining ten are the most formidable, with tricky tactics and strategies used to good effect to stay alive.

I stalk through a deserted plaza, eyes scanning the rooftops. A flicker of movement catches my eye. A figure clad in black armor, wielding twin energy blades, leaps down from a building.

It's Anyla, the youngest in our group, but his agility and ruthlessness make him a formidable opponent.

We lock gazes, then pandemonium breaks loose.

The simulated city flickers, distorting. A high-pitched whine fills the air.

Before I can react, the holographic world dissolves around us, replaced by the harsh glare of a crimson sun.

My stomach lurches.

We're not in the khufulle simulation anymore.

Ships. Dozens of them, sleek and sinister, emblazoned with a sickly pink sigil, descend from the sky.

I feel the growl even before it bubbles past my lips like a rolling storm.

Genali ships. Specifically, genali raid lancers.

Those slime-covered parasites. A guttural bellow escapes my throat.

The void-suckers have periodically harassed us ever since we settled down and renounced our warlike ways. It's been millennia, and they still decide to periodically return.

Back again to pick more at the carcass.

Panic surrounds me.

The civilians, used to the safe confines of their protected cities, scramble for cover. But there's nowhere to hide.

The genali ships launch a volley of energy blasts, painting the sky with streaks of green fire.

I turn my head to the side and instantly regret it as a barrage of energy blasts descend on a group of unsuspecting civilians, eviscerating them with consistent pelting until they are too disassembled for their nanites to overcome.

Chaos erupts.

The simulated battlefield becomes a real one.

A few of my brothers and sisters, caught off guard, are obliterated by the overwhelming firepower. Bellows of pain fill the air, punctuated by the booming explosions.

Fury rises in my chest. These cowardly genali would use this training exercise to attack us?

The mock battle has been completely abandoned.

It's time to crush them.

I scan for the nearest genali ship, a low-flying lancer that seems to be focused on mowing down a Maj'Ras trapped in the quicksand pit.

A roar escapes my throat.

I activate my jump jets, the familiar power surge coursing through my body.

I can see other Ras shaking off their surprise and closing in on other ships. The slimes might have held a momentary advantage, but there are still plenty of us to make them regret such an ill-conceived plan.

The ground rushes away as I propel myself upwards, toward the unsuspecting ship. It spots me at the last moment, its laser cannons pivoting toward me.

I dodge the blasts with a spikes' breadth, adrenaline masking the fear that threatens to cripple me.

I reach the ship, my armor shimmering as the lasers graze past.

With a roar that would make the ground tremble if they tried me in a fair fight planet-side, I slam my armored fist into the cockpit window. The reinforced glass shatters inwards, spraying the pilot with shards.

There's a flash of gray and pink, a glimpse of the genali's grotesque form before rage takes over. I reach in, ignoring the searing pain that shoots up my arm as the genali's protections burn through my gauntlet.

There's no room in my mind to assess that new development, more content to let the rage take over.

Grabbing the gelatinous creature, I rip it from its control console, its amorphous form writhing in my grip as I squeeze a delightful scream out of it before releasing it to plummet down to the unforgiving ground.

I roar again, a challenge to the sky, a promise of retribution burning in my core. The cockpit alarms blare, a cacophony drowned out by the pounding of my heart.

As the lancer arcs downward, I sweep toward another, this time feeling the burn of a laser across my side before I'm able to move inside their guard and send another pilot screaming toward the ground, trying unsuccessfully to engage the jets I was sure to crush as I flung them.

Another quick darting maneuver and I have another slime in my claws, this time holding on to them and their ship for a moment to give my rage an outlet before it overtakes my good sense.

I search for another target, pleased to note that my brothers and sisters have already significantly thinned their numbers.

This won't last much longer.

Before I can even think, another lancer swoops in, firing a thick, dark-green cloud of gas. It engulfs me, the acrid fumes filling my helmet.

Why wouldn't they just simply blow me apart with their advantage?

My vision swims, the world turning into a swirling vortex of green. The crushing grip I had on the genali loosens as it overtakes me, its amorphous form slipping free.

A roar dies in my throat, replaced by a choking cough.

My lungs constrict, and the world turns on itself as the lancer flings me off as it careens downward to its destruction.

I land with a muted plume of dust, coughing up blood and greenish-pink gas as my unfocused eyes take in the world around me.

The simulated battlefield has become a scene of carnage.

Drak bodies litter the barren landscape, some twitching in the throes of genali paralysis gas, others still.

The few remaining genali ships sweep down to scoop up bodies, then flee, their mission complete. Smoke rises from the twisted wreckage of downed lancers, taken out by Maj'Ras bellowing out their victory cries.

The genali weren't here for conquest. Of course not. That would require a goal beyond quick profit.

As a ship scoops me up, my limbs won't respond, and I'm lifted into the air as it continues to pump green gas in my face.

Maybe that spice trader really will get the last laugh.

The last thought that runs through my tapering out consciousness is a white-hot fury that simply won't dissipate even as the world dissolves to black before my eyes.

3

Kira

What shocks me awake is the realization that I'm submerged in molasses.

The ghostly sensation flees the moment my eyes snap open. I am hard-pressed keeping the cringe off my face as I step out of the pod on shaky feet.

It's subtle, barely lasting longer than a few seconds before I school my features. Not that it stops my legs from quaking with strain.

Bits of black begin to stain the edge of my vision from the slowly increasing stench of something both vile and acrid, and then it hits me that I might be a bit screwed, and not in a fun way.

I'm stark naked.

From the periphery of my vision, I spot an equally nude woman quickly moving to the front of my chamber. She dashes in with just enough time to help ease my sudden fall before my lungs are on fire.

The woman rubs her eyes once the gas is vented out and looks around. Her eyes are runny red, though oddly modified so they are fully light blue.

Dammit. Mine are probably the same. She smiles at me despite the maelstrom of emotions I see warring on her features.

She has the prettiest smile I've seen in a while. Then again, all I've had to see for the past who knows how long have been robots, so my two cents on the matter might not really hold much water.

I fucking hate it when people mix metaphors and have to suppress a growl at myself.

There's also the fact that my vision is still blurry from the noxious gas. Multiple blinks later and I can finally see the details of the woman in front of me.

She's a little over five feet tall, with shimmering indigo hair and aquamarine eyes, vaguely Asian features mixed with white, and a slender build.

I retract my earlier disclaimer. The woman is a beauty through and through.

She reaches forward and touches my arm. "I know you're scared. We were abducted. Those are the ones who took us."

My eyes sharpen just in time to turn to the three disgusting beings watching us interact like a trio of goo-covered voyeurs. I immediately shiver at the mental image, then subsequently frown at the warm sensation between my legs.

It brings up vague, chopped up memories. What the fuck did those blobs do to me?

My go-to instinct is rage.

If I wasn't hacking just to catch my breath and if there wasn't a glass wall between us, I could probably take out at least a couple of the gooey fuckers before they subdued me again, naked or not.

Keep it together, hotshot, I warn myself.

I turn my attention away from the slimes back to the smaller woman, and despite my annoyance, I can't help but look at her peculiarly colored hair and eyes.

Luckily, I stop myself from blurting out my thoughts, because even I know better than to tell a kidnapped woman how pretty her captors made her look.

The woman shifts her weight under my scrutiny, and I blink slowly, realizing I've been staring.

"They did that to you?" I offer, in the way of drawing out this conversation.

She nods, figuring out I'm talking about her eyes and hair. "Yours are pale pink."

I scoff on pure instinct at the fucked-up pronouncement before looking down to the sight of soft coral waves tangled up with my naked body.

What the fuck? We've been so excited at the idea of UFOs we didn't stop to think of the possibility of them being intergalactic pervs who turned women into sex Barbies.

They picked the absolute worst color and the absolute worst length.

"Couldn't even get the texture right."

The woman blinks dimly, and I guess she's realizing that I might be just as unhinged as the space mucus keeping watch over us.

"I'd share my name, but they punish us when I try. I've just been calling you Coral and myself Indigo."

"Fuck that, my name's Kira."

The woman cringes, and I resist the urge to chuckle like a maniac. Getting my squad into trouble is a famous pastime of mine...

Was... was a famous pastime of mine.

I squash that thought before it spirals out of my control. A subtle glance to the side tells me the slimes seem to be ignoring us.

The woman continues. "I'm Ree. It's a relief to not think of you as a color anymore."

I let out a muted, dark chuckle.

"Oh, I'm used to that," I croon with a bit more enthusiasm than the situation warrants.

I should probably tone down the intensity, but I've built a social interaction system on the basis of putting my bad habits on display and letting people decide whether to turn tail and run or to lump me in with the rest of the sociopathic community and, you guessed it, turn tail and run.

Two peas in the same decision-making pod.

Oh my god, Kira, enough with the fucking metaphors, I berate myself.

I'm not at my best, but this is ridiculous.

Fortunately, or maybe, unfortunately, the woman is too distracted to appreciate my dark humor.

Her attention is back to the slimes.

My gaze follows her lead, and I pay attention to their conversation as well. They're sharing nasty jokes and I wrinkle my nose.

"They aren't speaking English."

Ree shakes her head. "No, we have translators."

I resist the urge to give her an incredulous stare, at this point, weirder things have happened since the beginning of this whole mess and I need to move past the little stuff.

"What else?"

She turns her attention back to me and takes a deep breath. "We heal faster. Adapt to new environments. We'll keep changing, somehow, depending on who we're around. Who, uh, buys us."

I don't need a mirror to see that I am making a face. Change into what? A giant dripping blob?

Fuck.

I've got an entire crew of choice words sitting on the launch pad that is the tip of my tongue, but the effort would be wasted ranting to the equally-victimized woman.

I'll have to save the vitriol for any of the slugs providence deems fit to leave at my mercy.

A thrill shoots through me at the thought of it.

Ree takes my silence as her cue to go on. "That belt around your waist will expand to clothes, but if you do it, they punish you. You'll be aroused and can't control it. There's a live feed."

I look toward the camera, and she follows my gaze.

The one in the middle moves forward to smash itself against the glass, leaving disgusting pink smudges. I want to kill him for looking at the rest of the women that way, especially since they aren't even fucking conscious.

My hands are itching to hold a knife.

The mucus should make me wretch, but the reflex is gone. Like a gap in my mind that has always been there but has been over-flooded to the point of being useless.

No... not gone, just switched for another impulse.

I feel the outer edges of my labia peel open slightly, like a flower in bloom at the intense look in its, frankly, stupid-looking eyes, and my brain jerks to a stop at a sudden realization.

I'm turned on.

The sight of these pink cum-covered pieces of shit is turning me on.

Motherfuckers.

She said it, but I just dismissed it as not something that would happen to me.

In my simmering rage, I wonder what it will feel like to drag cold metal across their stupid, nearly non-existent necks and watch them bleed out.

The slime on the right seems bored and is picking at the short claws rising from his webbed fingers with a single index claw.

I wonder whether it can come off easily if I pull the adjoining joint in the opposite direction hard enough. The thought of ripping off its claws and seeing if all of them can fit in one eye socket is almost enough to bring a smile to my lips.

Almost.

Bored Slime turns to Stupid Gaze Slime. "We're nearing the hunting grounds."

This causes him to shift his bulbous eyes away from the red-haired woman it was ogling to join the conversation. "I hear they stocked it with a whole new range of species this year."

The one on the left shivers like it just came on itself, like one of those half-crazy anime antagonists I used to see on streaming services back on Earth. And now I want to gag at the mental image I just scarred myself with.

I mostly tune them out for a while, my gaze shifting all around our sleek white cell, taking in the colorful features of all the women, then looking for a way out.

I note when they talk about a manticorid. A bit later it seems to excite and frighten them, which pulls my interest again.

"Won't it just kill all the rest?" Bored Slime asks, his body somehow still matching his name as he puddles closer to the floor.

Pissed off as I am, that sounds like someone to know. Ree and I share a look.

They keep talking, mentioning there are blocks loaded into the prey to keep them from harming each other, but apparently not the hunters. Tricky bastards.

Clearly, organized violence is not a human-exclusive trait.

Of course it isn't, dumbass, I chide myself.

This manticorid thingy sounds very good at it.

The idea that there is something capable of putting the fear of Hades into them is extremely satisfying, though.

I give Ree a cursory glance from the side of my eye and she seems to be engrossed in the conversation.

While I'd much prefer being the one making them shiver in fear like that, it won't be happening unless I find a way out of this cell, so I'll settle for the vicarious pleasure as I keep scanning.

I suppress a laugh when they talk about snack-sized cats, though I can tell it makes Ree sick. She's a cat lover, if I had to guess.

Idiots. With no fancy gadgets and doohickeys, I doubt they'd consider a full-grown adult tiger a harmless little snack.

That alone tells me a lot about their combat experience.

When you survive near-death experiences, it changes your worldview about a lot of things.

I can attest to that.

"Except with venom," scoffs Bored Slime.

I look over to Ree, and she turns to see that I am staring at her. A small smirk forms on my lips, and, as much as she is doing a great job of hiding it from the slimes, I can tell she's thinking violent thoughts.

They keep fanboying about bloodsport as I catalogue the likely places they are vulnerable, though it's hard to tell for sure since they continually change shape.

Eyes, head, neck, and gut are probably a good assumption regardless of species. Maybe?

Stupid Gaze turns back to us. "The pink one is poor entertainment. Ratings are going down. Bring out the red one."

They argue for a while as I share another long look with Ree. Her face is telling me not to resist, which either means she has no spine, or they have done terrible things to her. Or both.

"Go back to your chamber, pink slut."

I just send knives at the fucker with my eyes and refuse to move. A pointless endeavor, but I have a habit of making a point where there's no need to make one.

Bored Slime presses down on the control to punish us and the noxious gas fills the cell once more, eliciting tears and snot to run down my face, before he pushes another button to make it recede.

He gurgles another order, more forcefully this time.

I flip him the bird, and he froths over with anger and pushes buttons on the control in a mad rage.

More gas fills the room.

I wipe the tears from my eyes and almost go back to sassing them before the sound of hacking and coughing beside me reminds me I'm not alone here.

Shit.

I look over at Ree and let out an inaudible sigh. This crap doesn't just affect me. She's a victim as well.

I have no right to let her suffer because my jarhead stubbornness wants to rear its ugly head like it always does if left unchecked.

She catches my stare.

"I'm with you, whatever you decide."

Alright, she has a lot more grit under all that pretty packaging than I would have thought.

I feel respect flood my system and it's a far better feeling than rage.

They send in more gas and when it lets up, I glance at her before turning my attention to look at the slime and their flipper hand hovering over the controls.

Man, fuck this guy, I grumble to myself.

With those cheery words of motivation, I get to my knees easily enough, letting out a long exhale to expunge any remnant gas in my lungs before I wipe my features and get my head in the game.

No clue how, but I am going to make these fuckers squeal.

I turn to Ree. "I'll see you soon."

I turn and sweep my eyes across them, settling on Bored Slime.

"You're dead," I promise.

Then I stand up, climb back in, and stab out at a screen that reads *freeze* in some other language with squiggling, ugly lines before he has time to stop laughing and use his controls.

There is a hiss of gasses and then slowly the world fades out of focus around me.

The last conscious thought I have before darkness takes over is the possibility of spit-roasting a live blob over an open flame as I stare with dispassionate eyes.

This time, I let myself grin.

4

Drasuk

The world flickers back into existence in agonizing waves. A wave of nausea washes over me, forcing a guttural groan out of my throat.

I lay still for what feels like an eternity with the tangy taste of something metallic clinging stubbornly to my tongue.

Slowly, ever so slowly, my body rights itself. A low rumbling gurgle erupts deep in my stomach, accentuated by a stabbing pain in my liver that quickly eases up the longer it hammers on my nerves.

Slowly, like an ancient vehicle slowly stirring to life after years of inactivity, the obnoxious sensations leave me.

The benefits of possessing a drakonid physiology—whilst not as efficient or hardy as a manticorid—can never be overstated.

Bodily functions are returning, and I can still feel my liver efficiently filtering and expelling the genali toxins from my system. At least there's that.

A perverse comfort.

That gas, whatever it was, won't be as potent when next used on me. My body has already begun building immunity.

It has been a while since the pink-covered insects made a toxin that took this long to purge from the body.

It would seem that their scientists weren't avoiding their duty.

Though I suppose no one would with Shentrea cabal in power.

From all accounts, they are just as likely to kill their own as their enemies from other species. It might also explain their newfound interest in us if they are testing out another round of biological weapons.

If they think they've perfected new compounds and weapons, it will make them more reckless. If they can conquer us, then they can subjugate almost any species.

They must feel the need for more efficient tools for their expansionist plans.

I could guess why.

Leave a pest running about your cave long enough and the seemingly helpless creature will develop a system to make sure the actual owner would be hard-pressed to eject the new proprietor.

Perhaps I'll write a feed about it in the future? A compendium of how the various sentient species of the mapped universe exert dominance?

An odd topic to write about, but I hear the reading tastes of the more refined drakonids in the richer systems are vast and diverse.

Too bad my clan wasn't exactly equipped in terms of philosophers and anthropologists.

I mash the errant thought as the last vestiges of my nausea subside and push myself upright to survey my surroundings.

The contrast is clear even before I can take in the finer details.

Gone are the harsh, irradiated plains of the khufulle grounds. Instead, I find myself nestled amongst the thick undergrowth of a lush semi-tropical forest.

The air, thick with humidity, is cleaner than anything I've ever breathed back home.

The sickly pink rays from the waning sun hang high in the sky, casting dappled shadows through the dense canopy overhead.

A lush welcome.

Not a terrible place to wake up in, but even I, placid as my brood-draks have countlessly accused me of being, know not to trust the universe to grant me such a thing as fair providence.

When your last conscious memory is being knocked out by gas via an aerial vehicle, anything fair seems well out of reach and a fool's hope.

This was no accident.

The genali scum has shipped me off-world, most likely to one of their notorious hunting grounds. It's the only explanation for why someone isn't sniffing my dried and ground up cartilage so they can stiffen in places their extravagant lifestyles have left hopelessly soft.

I suppose a hunting ground is the better option.

I've heard of such places in passing from off-worlders. Entire planets terraformed. Or left as they were, entirely dedicated to the commercial hunting of exotic, but lethal creatures.

The bloodier, the better.

Apparently, the mucus bugs decided it was about time a drakonid made his debut.

A low growl rumbles out of my chest, a visceral concoction of anger and an affront so deep it stings sharper than the anger of being captured and shipped off to be hunted against your will.

Hunting me? A Maj'Ra?

A sick amusement flickers in the back of my mind, re-routing my momentary rage.

Jests of being sub-manticorids are common when discussing drakonids in the intergalactic scene, but that's as far as it ever went.

Jokes that remained jokes, because the few who have lived through conflict with a drak know, servitor race or not, there are very few things in the universe as terrifying as facing down a murderous Maj'Ra.

Is genali memory so short? Are there no logicians among them?

I snort, pushing the more complex thought threads I tend to weave in my head aside in favor of the cruder, more basic part of my brain that is my primal instinct.

An intuition that is currently seething at me to avenge this insult by finding and killing the inferior genetic wastes of space that dared think that they could hunt an apex predator.

For daring to think I am their prey.

A sharp prickle at the back of my neck, the kind refined by years of combat, snaps me out of my reverie. I instantly recognize its pungent, sickly-sweet nature.

Genali. Two of them, their grotesque pink forms obscured by the dense foliage a little ways off. The stench of their slime is unmistakable.

Though mixed in is something caustic and unidentified.

It isn't enough to engage my risk aversion.

A roar erupts from my throat at the divinely given opportunity and, sure enough, they spin around, startled, their amorphous frames warbling in surprise.

Before they can react, I am on them.

Gone is the cautious warrior, replaced by a blur of rage and vengeance.

I use my speed to my advantage, propelled forward by the burst of power from immediately going down on all fours and launching at them.

The one in the lead lets out a shrill shriek that pierces the air. It raises a gauntlet-clad hand, intending to swipe at me, but I'm already past it. My claws are out and before the foul thing can properly vocalize its horror, I am already looming over it.

With a single powerful slash, I cleave through the genali's torso.

The creature melts into a puddle of gray slime with an ear-splitting hissing wail. The second genali, smaller and nimbler, dodges my initial attack. It launches itself backward, spraying a thick glob of acidic slime from its mouth.

I twist my body just enough to avoid a full hit, but the corrosive slime hisses briefly as it injures my skin in an acidic cascade.

It burns for a moment, then the sting fades.

With enough exposure, I'll develop an immunity, but for now, it's best to avoid it.

I watch it slide off my tough, slowly healing hide. It bubbles along with harsh hisses that let out acrid smoke on contact with the lush plants.

The stench burns my nostrils, sending my head rearing back as I let out a cough to expel it.

I would happily never smell it again, but unfortunately my immunity doesn't extend to olfactory attacks.

I wasn't aware that there was a class of genali that could spit acid.

Are the insects playing with their own genetics now? Not just their hapless slaves?

The second genali lunges at me, its limbs flailing wildly. I meet its attack head-on, my arms a blur as I deflect its blades. The creature is surprisingly strong for its size, and its movements are erratic and unpredictable.

Usually, a fight with a genali is a straightforward matter of getting close enough and crushing them.

This is a chaotic dance, a constant struggle to avoid its acidic attacks.

A surge of hormones course through me, momentarily masking the ache in my muscles from the earlier genali poison.

The ache makes me realize my error. The green smoke from my capture was poisonous, and I should have taken the time to rest.

When you're death-resistant, such things become afterthoughts.

Unsure of what other surprises to expect, I realize I can't afford to drag this out. I need to take this creature down quickly and find a way off this perverse planet.

Images of my fellow Maj'Ras, their bodies strewn across the mock battlefield, fuel my rage.

Of course, before I head anywhere, I wouldn't deny myself the pleasure of making whatever genali in my path scream for the sins of their species.

With a renewed ferocity, I press my attack.

He might have poison, but I have agility and strength gained from years of brutal fighting.

I disarm the creature, sending the offending slimy appendages flying through the air to land in wet thuds. Before it can recover, I land a devastating blow to its chest cavity, then latch on.

Twisting and turning, I chortle at the struggling insect before I begin to squeeze. The old clan-taught grip designed to crush bones the elders drilled into me years ago comes into play.

I am in no mood to play the merciful drak.

Unlike the first genali, this one doesn't melt into the usual puddle.

Its body palpitates erratically on its way down. It convulses violently for several long moments before it makes one last weak twitch before ultimately going limp.

With a dissatisfied huff, I stand over the fallen creature, the metallic tang of blood mixing with the cloying stench of slime in the air.

The thrill of victory is muted by the spirit-chaffing combination of the irritating sensation of my un-assuaged rage and the grim reality of my situation.

I'm stranded on an alien planet, surrounded by hostile creatures, with no way of contacting my clan.

Nothing I can't handle, but not something I would have chosen. All of this for entertainment?

It's senseless.

I take the time to wrest a blade from the detached arms. It wasn't made for my four opposing digits with their thick claws.

I can hold it, but it shifts around wildly on the thick pads of my hands.

Useless.

I fling it hard enough to make a loud thwack as it embeds into a tree far above my head. A moment later, two more join it, all waving around wildly in a neat row.

Another surge of white-hot rage threatens to make me see blue once more, but before I can let it loose, something catches my eye.

Half-buried in the undergrowth, a glint of metal shows through the dense foliage. Curiosity piqued, I kneel and brush away the surrounding dirt.

5

Kira

I jolt awake, disoriented and gasping for breath, and the first thing I notice is the jarring, pounding headache in my skull.

It throbs from my eyes to the back of my head in jagged spikes that make my stomach roil.

The chamber I am lying in is bathed in an eerie gold, pulsing emergency light that flickers erratically, and beyond that, everything is silent.

Well, silent except for the ominous groaning of metal around me.

A cursory look at the information console that displayed my status when I stepped into the chamber confirms it.

The stasis chamber is offline.

So much for seeing if it would provide any useful information. Such as where the hell I am right now. Or where Ree is.

I don't have the time to fully comprehend what the actual fuck is going on before the tremors hit, sending me bouncing against the padded interior. I slam my fist on the control panel, a futile gesture against the dead tech.

"Great," I mutter, the word thick with sarcasm. "Unhinged jarhead due for routine psych evaluation meets her end in tubes built by pink cum-covered aliens. Just peachy."

I have never been the superstitious sort, but if this little mess really ends in my death, I and whatever deity is in charge of fate are going to have a drawn-out talk.

They'll really need to explain whose parade I fucked up so badly in a past life to warrant having to go through this shit.

I turn my focus toward the glass see-through pane in front of me and feast my eyes on the chaos around me.

If the monumental quantities of red earth I can see is anything to go by, we crash landed.

Tremors start again as the view outside the chamber changes, and I realize it must be sliding down rocks. I have a ridiculous impulse to jump out of it before I remind myself that a metal can is better than nothing.

The slow slide turns into a roll.

The momentum increases within moments, and I bounce off the sides of the chamber like a ping-pong ball. Pain blooms in multiple locations, then the chamber comes to a sudden halt.

The glass slams into a rock, and a moment later, I slam into it.

When I come out of my daze, the first thing I notice is the new webbed pattern of breaks across the glass. The second thing is the burning pain on my forehead.

I lift a shaking hand up to it and it comes away covered in blood.

Must have rung my bell.

My gaze drifts down to my body, the bright pink hair clashing with the stark reality of the situation and I am quick to let a string of curses rip from my lips, a torrent of vitriol aimed at the slime-covered bastards who subjected me to this ridiculous modification.

Afterwards, I feel moderately better.

It's time to get out of this death trap and see where I am.

But not as a sex Barbie.

No way am I wandering around an alien planet with a head full of cotton candy and my ass bared to the fucking wind.

Reaching deep within myself, I focus on the tickling sensation of the band around my stomach.

I have a vague niggling thought about how the thing works, which was in my mind even before Ree brought it up. Strange, because I have no recollection of being awake between being captured and having her in front of me.

I let out a growl at the memory of getting the shit kicked out of me before being sold to aliens.

"Fuck you, Chet!" I yell, causing my head to hammer more, but something in my chest to loosen.

Life's a tradeoff that way.

I make myself focus back on the being-clothed plan.

Why does it feel like I know how to use it?

I guess if the slimes have the tech to modify a body to such drastic levels it isn't too much of a stretch that they might have found some way to insert usage instructions in our heads.

With a mental command, I will the small band of fabric to activate.

A cool sensation spreads across my skin as a sleek black suit materializes, expanding out from my navel to the rest of my body like a black, gooey, semi-solid before molding itself perfectly to my body and solidifying.

It's nowhere near as warm or as comfortable as the thick combat fatigues I am accustomed to, but it'll have to do.

Now to get out of here.

Frustration claws at me as I slam my fist against the chamber door one last time.

Dead. Useless. Good thing I'm well versed in taking care of myself.

Glancing around, I spot the emergency release, complete with a label, tucked away in a corner.

It's still a mind-fuck that I know what the alien writing means.

With a grunt, I rip the panel off, exposing the lever. I reach out with my left arm and pull on it until I hear a click.

I'm just about to push the glass away when I freeze.

My arm doesn't hurt. I rotate it around, then flex the muscle hard. That would have caused spikes of agony before.

I use my newfound control over my clothing to make the fabric recede and inspect it. The surgery scars are gone.

The surgeons were sure to point out all the pins and plates they had to use to get me even that limited amount of movement. The skin at the back of my head prickles as I absorb this new development.

Considering all the weird shit we started to see on deployments and all the rumors that circled around, the whole alien thing isn't exactly a surprise. I just never thought it would impact me, for good or ill.

Stupid thinking.

I mean, I guess a functioning arm is a pretty decent trade for this ridiculous hair.

Too bad it also included slavery and crash-landing.

"Fuck me sideways," I mumble out, tamping down the giddiness that bubbles out of me at the idea of having my fucking arm back.

I will have to save that for some other time when my life isn't in peril.

I eye up the glass cover and leave my mixed feelings about my arm for later. Right now, it'll be really damn useful. Throwing my weight against it, I feel a satisfying crack as the glass pushes out now that it's no longer held fast.

Before I can fully leverage it off, it shatters.

Shards rain down around me, some glancing off my suit. Others cut me as they bounce off.

I hiss at the sting and return to my grumbling. "All their tech and they don't make this shatter-proof? Fucking amateur hour in the universe."

Now that there's no glass to block me, I sit up, raising my head slowly as I look for threats.

I'm at the bottom of a small crater. Nothing but jagged red rocks and grit.

Good, that will give me time to get my shit together.

Ignoring the sting, I grab a shard, the sharp edge reflecting the gold-purple light with an unsettling glint. It's no scalpel, but it'll have to do.

Without so much as taking the time to appreciate not being stuck in an alien transport cell anymore, my fingers find the perfect balance on the shard, and then I go to town across my pink nightmare.

The hair falls away in satisfying chunks and within minutes, the obnoxious bubblegum mane is reduced to a short, curly pixie cut.

Leaving the rest of the hair on the chamber floor, I carefully gather a handful of the longer strands.

With nimble fingers, I braid them together, creating a lumpy handle for the glass shard. The rest I weave into a thick braid, securing it around my waist like a makeshift belt.

It is not ideal, but it will have to do.

As I tuck in the edges, the flickering emergency light dies. I don't need it to see or anything, but a powered pod might have been useful.

I glance around, briefly consider trying to cut out some of the fabric from the pod, but can't think of a good enough use for it to outweigh remaining in such an indefensible location.

Geared up like a post-apocalyptic Joan of Arc, I step out of the chamber.

I check my head wound again, pleased to note that it's no longer gushing blood, then make my protesting body climb out of the crater.

There are few worse places to be caught by an enemy than a glorified hole.

I finally scrabble my way up the side of the crater and come face to face with the gaping opening that must have been part of the larger ship.

The ship's interior is a mess—twisted metal, dangling wires, and scattered debris. My stomach lurches as I take in the sight.

Despite the force of the crash leaving an enormous wave of rocks and sand around it and further denting it, I can still see the jagged outline of warped metal forcibly separated from when it came apart from the main body.

Another chilling realization strikes me.

Somehow, the larger mass didn't crush my pod in the crash.

"Well, shit."

Small blessings, I guess.

I glance back down to my stasis chamber. There are dents and scars all over the admittedly tough pod, evidence of my being thrown around.

Last I remember, I was in a cell with multiple other pods. Plus Ree, of course.

I scan, looking for them as I look for threats.

Nothing.

I'm going to have to go into the broken piece of ship to look.

I chance a peek above to see the alien sky—a swirling mass of purple and green—stretches out above, offering no comfort.

Though, I realize I do feel... better.

Something in me feels more settled than it has in months. This is far more normal than civilian life could ever be. I was dying a slow death. I'm back in the field now, working on a goal, surviving, saving civilians.

I'm terrified and giddy all at once.

Suddenly, a guttural sound echoes through the wreckage, sending shivers down my spine. A pink cum guy—or whatever the hell they are called—lurches out of the debris pile, its bulbous body covered in slime and gray blood, bulging black eyes searching the wreckage.

I freeze, the shard of glass digging into my palm. The gray freak, thankfully, doesn't spot me.

I'm not exactly easy to miss, so it must be disoriented.

It lumbers toward the front of the wreckage, its movements slow and deliberate.

An opportunity.

Taking a deep breath, I stalk toward the creature, moving with the practiced stealth of a seasoned assassin.

Huh. Maybe I should have taken up that profession. Then I could have been killing off the Chets of the world instead of trying to save their traitor asses.

A flash of memory showing the look of surprise on his face pulls a feral grin as I shadow an equally repellent enemy.

Its progression is slow, its senses dulled by the crash, but any slip-up on my part might be fatal.

I close the distance, every fiber of my being screaming with an urge to start running toward him, but I suppress it.

Just as I reach striking distance, I lunge.

My makeshift blade finds its mark, plunging deep into the bastard's slimy side. The creature lets out a surprised screech, a sound that is both wet and high-pitched.

It thrashes around, sending tendrils of slime flying, but the shard of glass holds, doing me the favor of capitalizing on the erratic movement to rip at more mucous-covered flesh.

With a last heave, I push my weight against the creature, sending it crashing back onto the rocky ground. Its thrashing slowly ceases, and a little while later, its body slowly turns a sickly shade of light gray and melts.

Heart hammering in my chest, I kneel beside the creature, my breath ragged. My first nonhuman kill.

The boys are never going to believe it.

I let out a breathy laugh from the remnant adrenaline in my system, and with a smile wide enough to give my military assigned shrink reason enough to write up a report, I pull the glass dagger out of the dead alien puddle with a satisfying squelching sound and gingerly set it aside.

The alien isn't wearing any clothes, but it has a pouch strapped to its back brimming with stuff I can use.

A pouch that is covered with the same viscous pink mucous all over.

Revulsion wars with pragmatism as I reach for it. Sure enough, the bag itself is slick with mucus, but I grit my teeth and unfasten it.

Inside, I find a collection of unfamiliar items—some kind of food bar, a canteen filled with a viscous blue liquid that is hard to look at, even though some unknown instinct tells me that my system should be able to accommodate it now.

My eyes fall on the highlight of this haul.

A weapon. A ridged, bulky, multi-barreled firearm lays nestled at the bottom.

I heft it tentatively; these weren't designed with primates in mind. A clip of metallic cartridges sits beside it.

Not ideal, but it'll have to do.

The slime's melee weapon is a serrated blade dripping with the same sickening ooze, which feels alien and repulsive in my hand.

It goes back into the bag.

I could keep it around as a trophy or maybe even a last-ditch weapon, but it's not a tool I want to use.

With a deep breath, I secure the bag over my shoulder, the weight grounding me.

This isn't the sleek, high-tech ship I'd been on when I talked to Ree.

Was that yesterday? A fucking decade ago?

No clue.

This is a hostile world, one where I am completely alone. That's nothing new. I've been that way since they forced my retirement. Just the same shit show in a new place.

Except...

A faint hum resonates from a control panel behind me, barely perceptible.

My head snaps up, a spark of hope igniting. Maybe there is a way to salvage some information.

Some clues as to where we landed and how this happened.

My heart sinks when the hum dies, but I keep moving through the battered section of the ship, hoping to find something useful.

Rations, maybe? Or more water.

With renewed purpose, I sift through the mangled mess, also searching for any salvageable circuits or data storage devices.

The lack of other pods in the wreck further cements the reality at hand.

We were separated in the crash.

My stomach rumbles, a reminder of my basic needs. The strange ration bar tastes like moldy cardboard, but it does its job of filling the void.

Taking a swig of the blue liquid, I wince at the metallic tang, forcing it down.

With a final, defeated glance at the mangled control panel, I turn my back on the wreckage. The alien landscape stretches out before me, a daunting canvas of red and orange.

In the distance, I see the desert bleed away into lush greenery. The stark coexistence between plenty and drought stuns me for a bit, making me drink in the sight with wonder.

To be fair, such a location wouldn't look out of place on the brochure of an exotic travel destination, but that was civvy talk.

I'd seen enough combat scenarios to know that even the most beautiful locations can hide the deadliest pitfalls.

Taking a deep breath, I adjust the bag on my shoulder, then I bend back to retrieve the makeshift glass shard and flex my digits on its handle.

There's no point in dwelling on what ifs.

I have to get moving, find shelter, and figure out a way to survive.

Plus, find a bunch of civilian women. Who are probably freaking the hell out right now.

Perfect.

6

Drasuk

I brush away the layer of damp leaves, revealing a small metallic box embedded in the soft earth. My claws, still dripping with the genali's gore, click against the smooth surface.

It's a clip of ammunition, likely of braceaaer origin.

Before I can figure out a way to store it, a fresh scent hits me, sharp and alluring, cutting through the metallic tang of blood and the cloying stench of genali slime.

Sure enough, it is the scent of my enemy, the genali, but laced with something else, something tantalizing.

My instincts roar to life, urging me toward the source.

This isn't just another slime. This is something different.

It causes a shifting interest at the junction between my lower gut and pelvis and I take a few steps toward the scent before I am even conscious of the motion.

How could something so discomfort-inducing also smell so good?

I glance around for the clip of ammunition I dropped, but decide it isn't worth sifting through the puddled corpses or displaced flora.

Ignoring the throbbing pain in my muscles, I push forward, drawn by the irresistible aroma.

North, it beckons. The dense foliage brushes against my tough hide, the humid air heavy in my lungs.

The lush grass-covered ground gives way to rocky terrain, the undergrowth thinning out, but still green and lustrous.

With each step, the scent grows stronger, filling my senses with an unknown yearning.

My mind screams at me to stop, to be cautious.

This could be another trap, but danger seems to be a fleeting concept when the smell clinging to my palate like an embrace simply refuses to go away. I pull it deep into my lungs, then ignore my mind's attempts to be reasonable and cautious.

I pad toward the wafting scent.
What else do these insects have in store for me?

7

Kira

The alien sun dips below the horizon, casting long, distorted shadows across the endless red wasteland. Sweat stings my eyes, blurring my vision as I have long abandoned the fruitless task of wiping them off every ten seconds.

Hunger gnaws at my stomach, a constant companion that I could have done without, but it isn't as if I have a say in the matter.

The alien weapon feels heavy and awkward in my hand, a stark contrast to the standard issue slug luggers I am used to wielding back on Earth, but I hold it at the ready, regardless. It's been quiet so far, but every step from the crash site feels like a gamble, a dance with an unknown predator in a hostile environment.

I roll my eyes.

Damn, Kira, way to tempt fate, I chide myself.

Given the fact that I'm heaven knows where on some unknown planet somewhere in the universe, some predator might very well be following me. I don't even know what to look for or what sounds might signal impending doom. This is so stupid.

I halt my advance, frowning.

I don't enjoy complaining. Right from my early days in the academy, it was something I took care to expunge from my system, and with time, it became second nature to ignore uncomfortable situations I had no control over.

Now look at me.

Right from the moment I got entangled in this whole alien nonsense, I seem to have gotten a long list of things to complain about. Am I really all that tough if years of training and built-up fortitude can get wiped away so easily?

It's a vexing thought.

A flicker of movement in the distance catches my eye, rousing me from my thoughts, and I catch a ripple in the endless sea of red sand. I squint, adjusting the makeshift scope on the stolen weapon.

Two figures emerge from the haze, their grotesque forms resolving into a horrifying scene.

One is unmistakably the same pink slime covered three-legged abomination that I've seen more than enough of for a lifetime, its bulbous body pulsating with that same old infuriating shade of pink I am slowly starting to abhor with every fiber of my being.

Luckily, it's a different shade than my new hair or I'd have clear evidence the universe fucking hates me.

The other alien is entirely new, and a cliché that's making it seem like all those conspiracy theories about Area 51 I used to laugh at might not have been as insane as they seemed.

It stands taller than the blob. Slimmer and drier, its gray-green, bulbous form vaguely humanoid except for the spindly arms. Its large black eyes gleam with cold intelligence.

The new creature, this Graylord, I christen it on the spot—and let it be known that my penchant for naming shit is dog water—seems to be aligned with the slime.

I'm not sure how much longer that will last for them. Even though I am some distance away, I can deduce that it isn't a smooth partnership.

It might look like a child, but I am sure it's the one calling the shots, judging by the way it has its small chest puffed out and the decisive gesticulation. The slime doesn't seem to appreciate whatever it's saying.

A sickeningly familiar surge of wanton sensation washes over me as the pink blobs' body modifications do their job and I feel a sickening arousal bubble up in my gut the longer I stare at the slime-covered freakazoid and its Graylord master.

Fury clouds my vision.

Before I can rein it in, I raise the alien weapon, aiming for the slime's pulsing mass. No, that's stupid thinking.

I pause for a moment. Is this wise?

It would be better to test my weapon first, but as soon as I do I'm announcing my presence anyway. I've never met a gun I couldn't figure out within a few shots. I glance around to note what cover I need, then decide to just go with it.

Those two would look a lot better with bullet holes in them.

My finger squeezes the trigger. The unfamiliar weapon coughs, a plume of purple smoke erupting from the barrel.

The shot misses, scorching the sand a few feet away from the surprised blob.

"Dammit."

Both creatures whirl around, their stomach-roiling eyes locking onto me. The dolphin snot slinger lets out a high-pitched screech that sends shivers down my spine. The Graylord hisses, its spindly arms waving vaguely with activity as it points a fixed, bulbous finger in my direction.

Adrenaline surges through my veins, momentarily eclipsing the simmering anger.

I'm not here to pick fights with the dominant species. I need to get out of here before whatever other denizens of the land get curious enough and decide to join the party.

Of course, I should have thought about that before taking a pot shot.

I shrug and take another one. Might as well go all in.

This one flies wildly past the Graylord's head.

Panic threatens to consume me, the unfamiliar weapon feeling like a dead weight in my hand.

Taking a deep, steadying breath, I force myself to focus. I close my eyes briefly, picturing the countless hours spent on the firing range back at base. I think back over how each shot missed and make a quick calculation.

Opening my eyes, I line up the shot, ignoring the part of my brain screaming at me to run. This isn't about revenge anymore. This is about survival.

With a newfound calmness, I squeeze the trigger.

The alien weapon roars, spitting out fire and purple smoke as the slug strikes the slime square in the chest. It lets out a piercing shriek, its bulbous body convulsing before collapsing onto the sand in a heap of glistening goo.

The Graylord screeches in outrage, its spindly arms lashing out in a frenzy.

I take the time to double check my cover. The rock is smaller than I'd like, but hopefully enough.

It pulls a weapon, and I fold in my body as much as possible.

Shards of rock rain over me as it returns fire, clearly much more familiar with its weapon than I am.

There's a moment's hesitation and I take the opportunity to stick my arm out and shoot in its general direction.

A chittering clicking, followed by a muffled thud, inspires me to take a chance at popping my head out.

I'm right, the alien is looking for cover.

Before it can react further, I aim again, this time focusing on the creature's jutting forehead as it tries to sink down behind its own rock.

Another shot erupts from the muzzle, blasting a hole into its egg-like head. The Graylord stumbles back, its eerie eyes flickering with confusion before its entire body crumples to the ground, twitching.

"Fuck yeah," I say in an explosive breath.

It's good to know I can take care of myself just as well here as on Earth. Dad would be proud.

Heart pounding a frantic rhythm against my ribs, I stand there for a moment, the weight of what I've just done settling on my shoulders. I get closer and the metallic tang of alien blood fills the air, and oddly enough, the pungent smell seems to cool the nerves the tension of this little fiasco filled me with.

I've spilled plenty of blood in my life, and now I have the weapons in hand to do it more efficiently. If that's what it takes to survive here, then watch out alien world, Kira has arrived.

Before I can pat myself on the back further, the ground trembles.

Dammit.

I should know better than acting out of rage without thinking things through. I've dressed down plenty of other people for far less.

It's the sort of stupidness that gets you dead real quick. The sort of thing I thought I was immune to as a veteran. Sanity might have come back to me too late.

What fresh horror did I just summon?

"Fuck."

Without a second thought, I turn and sprint, the alien weapon clutched tightly in my hand.

Drasuk

The popping sounds grow louder as I continue my advance, my burning curiosity piquing with each burst of noise. The sound ends as quickly as it begins, signaling the end of whatever conflict arose. With that realization, my claws dig into the soft earth as I lower myself to all fours, picking up speed.

As I sprint through the undergrowth, the forest becomes a blur of green and brown.

The first hint I get is the noticeable shift in the surrounding air, transitioning from its crisp quality to a sharper tone with a drier heat that contrasts with the previous humidity.

As I advance, the reason for the change becomes clear as the lush foliage gradually transitions, giving way to a desert. Dark red soil crunches and puffs up dust motes beneath the thick pads of my limbs, the air noticeably hotter.

I can't help but wonder how long it took them to terraform this planet to such extremes.

The process was refined by the manticorids at the height of their empire. After their decline, it was only a matter of time before the technology was stolen.

Other empires attempted to replicate the methods that ensured environmental variety, but had never done so. These limitations are clearly no longer relevant.

Fanciful thoughts to muse over, Drasuk, but this is not the place.

I trample the errant thoughts and focus on my task.

The scent, that tantalizing blend of enemy and something else, guides me.

Ahead, I spot a crash site. A heap of warped metal juts out from the ground, the remnants of a larger ship. I barely give it a second glance, my attention drawn to the bodies near a makeshift campsite. One braceaaer, one genali.

The corpses are fresh, their ballistic wounds still oozing.

But it's not their scent that draws me. No, there's something else, an eerily pleasant aroma that fills my nostrils.

How had this somehow become even more... exciting?

I move cautiously, scanning the area. A single crack of a gun rings through the air, replaced by an unsettling silence.

My instincts scream at me to be wary, but the scent is too alluring to ignore.

I draw nearer the bodies, examining the scene. The braceaaer's rigid stance suggests it was aware of the threat. Genali puddles don't leave much to analyze, of course, but the cause of death seems clear.

I crouch beside them, inspecting the wounds. Bullet holes, not energy weapons. As expected, I suppose. A vague memory surfaces about a hunting ground where technology ceases to work.

If nothing else, at least that narrows down the possibilities of where I am. Not that I could send out a distress signal or anything.

Focus, Drasuk.

I sniff the air again, trying to pinpoint the source of the enticing scent. It's not from the bodies, nor the campfire remnants. I close my eyes, focusing my senses.

It's strongest to the north.

I move away from the crash site, heading toward it. The ground shifts beneath my pads, the red soil giving way to rocky terrain. The temperature continues to rise, the sun burning along my rough blue skin.

Despite the discomfort, I press on, driven by an inexplicable need to find the source.

As I crest a rocky ridge, the landscape before me is a stark contrast to the lush forest I can still see from afar. A barren expanse stretches out, dotted with jagged rocks and sparse vegetation.

My eyes narrow as I see a tiny figure in the distance, leaving the desert biome and darting into the forest. The scent seems to waft from the direction the small creature took, so I give chase.

I drop to all fours again, feeling the muscles in my limbs coil and release with each powerful stride. This one has a scent designed to trick me, like the carnivorous plants of my world that lure in unsuspecting animals.

Beneath that enticing layer, there's the unmistakable stench of the genali. No doubt a product of their body modification program.

That's enough for me to ignore the temptation the scent stirs in my loins.

Angry with myself for even entertaining such thoughts, I pick up my pace, crashing through the forest after the running creature. The foliage whips past me, branches scratching at my hide.

The chase is exhilarating. My senses heightened by the thrill of the hunt. I force myself to focus, to remember why I'm here.

Vengeance, not some twisted game.

The creature ahead is quick, darting around trees with a speed that belies its size. I am faster. My claws make deep furrows, propelling me forward. The smell grows stronger, filling my flaring nostrils and urging me on.

I push through the fatigue, my eyes locked on the elusive figure ahead. Glimpses of bright pink act like a beacon, drawing me toward it.

The forest thickens, and the undergrowth becomes denser. The creature weaves through the trees, but I am relentless. With a burst of speed, I close the gap, my breath hot and heavy in my throat. The figure glances back, its eyes wide with fear.

It knows it cannot win.

I leap, my claws outstretched, ignoring the impotent bullets the creature sprays me with as I feel the blood rush triumphantly through me.

Kira

Panting with exhaustion, I realize I can't outrun the thing chasing me.

My lungs burn, my legs feel like lead, and each step becomes more laborious than the last. The red wasteland stretches behind me, the alien sun now completely swallowed by the horizon.

Darkness is seeping into the world around me, making everything even more disorienting. The landscape transitions to a forest right ahead of me, but I'm not sure I'll be able to run through it without breaking my neck.

I stumble into a clearing and stop to catch my breath, my heart pounding in my ears. Chancing a look back, I get a glimpse of my pursuer.

Rough blue skin and spikes. A thick, humped neck covered with jagged protrusions. It's bipedal, based on my first sighting of it, but it's giving chase on all fours. The creature's massive hands end in thick, fleshy pads similar to a rhino's, each hand boasting two layers of opposing digits like some chameleonic nightmare.

Then there is the overbite of huge, sharp fangs, right below its billowing nostrils. Like I'm in some sort of fucked up combo of the running of the bulls and all those fantasy books about dragons I never bothered reading.

The sight of it sends a fresh wave of adrenaline through my veins.

"Damn it all to hell," I let out a litany of cuss words between ragged breaths, my voice raw with fear and frustration.

I decide to take a chance in the forest, ignoring the burning pain in my lungs and side. By some miracle, I don't break my neck, but all of my weaving isn't working. The monster is closing in and I'm almost spent.

Deciding that running is futile, I stand my ground.

The alien gun I swiped from the corpse of the pink drool alien is just as unwieldy, except this time I'm trembling in exhaustion and fear. Should have taken the time to grab the Graylord's gun. Fuck.

I aim, trying to steady my breathing. The creature barrels toward me, its blue skin rippling in the low light. With a shaky breath, I squeeze the trigger.

The sharp recoil of the gun going off almost jerks the stock into my gut but rings true regardless, striking the creature's shoulder. It doesn't even flinch. My heart sinks as I realize the bullet barely scorched its thick armor plating.

No, not armor, it's just a thick hide. I try again, squeezing off several more shots.

It's so large I can't really miss, but it won't do much good if it's impervious to bullets.

"Oh, fuck me."

Another shot, then another, each one failing to penetrate its hide. The creature roars, its eyes burning with an unnatural intelligence as it closes the distance between us.

"Shit," I curse, firing wildly.

The shots go wide, missing the creature's eyes.

I can feel panic rising, my grip on the alien weapon slipping as the beast leaps at me. It slams into me with the force of a freight train, sending me sprawling across the ground. My head spins, and pain explodes in my side where it hits me with an out outstretched arm.

With a snarl, I drop the useless weapon and pull out my makeshift glass knife. The blade gleams faintly in the dim light, a desperate weapon against the monstrous creature.

I brace myself, ready to fight to the death.

The creature lunges and I dodge to the side, slashing with the knife. The blade glances off its thick skin, doing little more than annoying it. It roars again, swiping at me with a massive, clawed hand.

I barely duck under the swing, my heart hammering in my chest.

In hindsight, it was probably stupid of me to swing at something that could shrug off slugs with a shard of glass, but the glass has impressed me by not splintering thus far, so I like my chances.

As I prepare to strike again, the creature screams something at me in a guttural language that somehow makes sense to my ears.

"You won't have me as a trophy!" it bellows, its voice echoing with a strange resonance.

I blink, stunned.

Did it just speak? And did I understand it?

The experiments the pink slimes did on me must have messed with my brain more than I thought. Pissed off and not thinking straight, I yell back in the same guttural language.

"No one would want your ugly head as a trophy, hole in rear."

My throat feels raw and ragged after the words leave my mouth. They also sound completely wrong, like the translator fucked it up.

The creature hesitates, its eyes narrowing. It seems momentarily taken aback by my response.

Seizing the opportunity, I lunge forward, aiming for its face. It reacts with surprising speed, knocking the knife from my hand and sending me sprawling once more.

Desperation fuels me as I scramble back to my feet. The creature stands over me, its eyes gleaming with a mix of curiosity and disdain.

It speaks again, this time more softly, almost mockingly. "You fight well for a creature so small. But you are weak."

I glare up at it, defiance burning in my chest. "I'm not done yet."

With a roar, the blue devil swipes at me again.

This time, I'm ready. I dive to the side, snatching up the alien weapon and firing point-blank at its face. The shot only grazes along its cheek, but it's enough to make the creature reel back in surprise.

Taking advantage of the brief respite, I scramble to my feet, snatch the glass blade in my free hand, and prepare to make a last stand. The creature circles me, its movements slow and deliberate. It's toying with me, savoring the hunt.

My anger flares, and I force myself to focus.

I hold the blade up again, with renewed determination. This time around, the monster snorts in what I could swear is amusement.

"So tiny," it rumbles and then charges me again.

Drasuk

The creature slows down, and so do I.

My headlong rush fades into a more cautious approach. This small thing speaks my language. Suspicion gnaws at me, but so does a strange intrigue.

I decide to see how much fun I can have with it. Keep it talking. Maybe I can extract some useful information before I end this. Though, it would be a shame to kill something that smells so intriguing.

Is it anger that makes it smell so enticing? Interesting. Why not find out?

"Is that all you can do?" I taunt, swiping at it with a clawed hand.

It barely manages to dodge, the dagger glinting in its grip. My words seem to infuriate it more than anything else so far.

"Fight me, you overgrown *lizard*!" it screams back, voice trembling with a mix of fear and rage.

I chuckle, a low, rumbling sound. "You're weak. Small. Pathetic. Hardly worth the effort."

My claws strike out again, this time grazing the top of its head before it can dance away from me, adding another injury to slowly bleed it dry.

The pink fur, or whatever it is, feels strange beneath my touch. Smooth brown skin peeks through where the fur recedes.

Intriguing.

The little alien's eyes burn with anger, and it lunges at me with the dagger. I easily evade its clumsy attacks, the scent of its fury intoxicating.

"You call that fighting? I've seen hatchlings with more skill."

Its face contorts with rage, and it attacks again, more recklessly this time. I sidestep, watching as it struggles to keep up. Its movements are wild, desperate. The glass dagger swings through the air, missing me by a spike's width.

"You're wasting your energy, little one," I say, voice dripping with condescension. "Do you really think you can win this?"

The dagger comes at me again, and I deflect it with a casual swipe of my hand. Its frustration is palpable, almost delicious.

We circle each other, the creature's breath coming in ragged gasps. It's tiring, while I am merely warming up. I let it come close again, my eyes locking onto its furious gaze.

"Why do you fight so hard? What are you hoping to achieve?"

"I'm not letting you take me," it growls, swinging the dagger wildly. "Not without a fight."

The determination in its voice is amusing. "You're brave, I'll give you that. But bravery won't save you."

I feint to the left, then swipe at it from the right. The creature yelps as my claws slice through the air, barely missing its arm. It stumbles back, eyes wide with panic.

"Stay still, little one. It'll be over quicker."

Its response is a wordless scream of rage, as it slashes the dagger at me again. I easily sidestep, watching as it loses its balance and nearly falls. The pink fur fluffs out in a comical display of agitation.

I can't help but laugh.

"So much impotent rage. For what goal?" I ask, my voice a mocking purr. "Look at you. You're nothing."

It glares at me, fury etched into every line of its face. "Fornicate that."

It lunges again, and this time, I allow it to graze my arm as I try to figure out what it means. Fornicate what? The pain is minor, but it fuels my amusement.

"See? I can hurt you."

I raise my brow spikes, licking the blood from the shallow wound.

"Impressive," I say dryly. "But not nearly enough."

The scent hits me again, that tantalizing blend of enemy and something else. It's intoxicating, clouding my thoughts. I shake my head, trying to focus, but the scent lingers, pulling at my senses.

The creature takes advantage of my distraction, swinging the dagger with renewed fury. I dodge, but it's closer this time. Too close.

Angry with myself for being so easily swayed, I roar and knock the creature down. It sprawls on the ground, eyes wide with shock and fear. I loom over it, my claws poised for the kill.

"You should have picked better allies," I tell it.

I almost end it there, but I'm curious how it'll reply.

The creature is on its feet in a flash. "Oh, fornicate in your own hole, you... you scale-covered piece of excrement."

It wants me to do what? And can't it see I don't have scales?

It's insane.

I blink and take an involuntary step back at the unhinged look in its eyes.

It yells out in rage, then continues speaking. "I did not fornicating go through literal fornicating hours of DNA-modifying surgery, or whatever the fornicate they actually did, to be hunted down by *lizard*-shaped tree fruit sack stupid enough to hunt me down and fornicating accuse me of what I'm not!"

It's hard to make sense of what it's saying between all the talk of mating, but I think I might have gotten a general sense.

Possibly.

There may be a chance I acted hastily, but I'm still quite certain the small creature is insane.

"Is your whole species as obsessed with mating as you are?"

It's face screws up in some sort of mysterious expression. "What the fornication are you talking about? Damn the thing, should have known I'd get a *lizard* instead of a venom *cat*."

I don't understand all her words, but she piques my interest when she mentions venom, though I quickly dismiss the hopeful surge that there might be a manticorid here.

Still, it seems like she might know more than I do about what's going on.

Kira

I'm just hopeful I can survive, though I'd also like to get some information if I can, since this place is clearly stupid deadly.

That plan goes tits up the moment the creature lunges at me again, sending me backtracking with an unspoken curse on my lips.

Apparently, my penchant for saying *fuck* isn't translating as well as I'd hope.

I'll admit the lizard comparison isn't really on point. If anything, it looks more like a dinosaur dragon, except for no wings. Deadly, and beautiful, but it feels better to denigrate it to the role of skittering lizard.

Its blue coloring transitions to an off-white color on its belly, under its neck and on the underside of its tail, which is the only true resemblance to a reptile.

Judging by the way it moves, its spines are less rigid than they look. I stay away from them, just in case. Images of Bowser from Super Mario rolling over me with his spikes flit through my mind.

Not a great way to go.

It chuckles, a low, rumbling sound as it continues to enumerate the ways I'm inferior.

I can't say I completely disagree, but all it gets from me is more rage.

Its body is surprisingly nimble for its size. The rough blue skin ripples and its spikes seem to convey emotions I haven't learned how to read. I might even call it enchanting, in a completely terrifying way.

If it wasn't such a giant dickhead.

I barely stop myself from falling when I make another hopeless attempt at maiming it. It continues to mock me, now with an almost sexual gravel in its voice.

Of course, it's getting off on this.

A bunch of terrible, oversexed male aliens is all I've seen so far in this terrible place. Talk about a universal fucking issue.

"I have nothing to do with those fornicating wastes of breath," I say by way of emphasis.

It stills, its mouth dropping open. I'm not sure if it's because of how many curse words I've said or if I've finally made sense to it, so I just keep cursing the day it was fucking born.

After a few moments it cuts in. "Repeat that."

"You were born on a—"

"No, not that, what you said about the genali."

Not sure what a genali is, but I assume it means me trying to explain myself, not that it's done much good. "I was kidnapped, too, excrement for brains."

It blinks slowly, then speaks again. "Are you saying..."

I don't see how that wasn't completely fucking clear, but I yell out the shortened version since it is clearly lacking in intelligence, emphasizing every word. "Taken. Against. My. Will."

Talk about lacking basic social skills.

The creature's expression shifts, confusion giving way to realization. It steps back, claws lowering slightly.

"You... you were taken?"

"Yes, you idiot!" I shout, my voice trembling with rage. "Do you think I asked for this? Do you think I wanted to end up here, fighting for my life against some oversized reptile?"

Its eyes soften, just a fraction. "I assumed you were one of them."

"Well, you assumed wrong," I grit out between my teeth, gripping my dagger tighter. "Now, are we going to keep doing this, or are you going to let me go?"

"I might consider it, if you have something of worth to offer in exchange for your life."

I take a deep breath, calming my racing heart.

The fury that drove my initial attacks fades, replaced by a cold, calculating determination. I start to circle it again, eyes locked on it.

I can't think of anything to give it, aside from being lunch, of course, and that possibility seems to have completely overtaken my brain.

"I'm not your meal, lizard breath," I taunt it, wanting to smack myself for not being able to think outside the terms of predator and prey.

It lets out a grumbling sound, which I assume is laughter, judging by the way its eyes are shining. It sounds like rocks grinding together.

"Maybe we both have information to exchange," I point out.

"Then state it," it challenges back.

The conversation I overheard on the ship suddenly pops into my head and I realize I might have something to trade after all.

"We are on a hunting ground," I blurt out as I duck under a swing of its tail.

"I know that."

A surge of rage rises into my throat. "What, because you paid to be here?"

He makes a hissing, rumbling sound that I take to be displeasure. "I would never fall so low."

"Alright, I get it. You are completely honorable, which is why you are currently trying to kill someone a fifth your size."

"Enemies come in all sizes."

He has a point, the bastard. I scour my brain. "I was in a ship with squishy aliens, and they said a manticorid is here."

He is mid-swipe when he suddenly stills.

"How many?"

I gulp, wondering if I'm giving away information to the enemy about a possible ally, but decide to tell the truth.

"Just one."

"Male or female?"

"Male."

He takes a deep breath and then speaks again. "How do you know anything about them?"

"I don't. The slimes woke me up briefly on their ship. I overheard them talking about this place and that they had captured a manticorid for this hunting season."

"Are you positive they said manticorid?"

"Yes. They just said he had venom, and they seemed scared. I liked seeing them scared, so I assume I will like a manticorid. Or die really fast, but at least they will die, too."

"Yes, they will."

I picture an entire field full of dead slime puddles everywhere and a grin spreads across my face.

"I approve," I tell it. "Maybe if we stopped trying to kill each other, we could help make more slime puddles."

I don't admit to myself just how desperate I am that he'll say yes, which he needs to do before I collapse and lose any semblance of advantage.

12

Drasuk

It seems like I made some unfortunate assumptions.

The pink creature may not be as strong or as deadly as I am, but it's not a terrible fighter. For its size. A shudder runs through me at the thought of being so small.

Plus, if there is also a manticorid here, then there may be others who are not my enemy.

If the manticorid male has venom, it's not an Abstainer, which makes me optimistic he won't be a raging idiot. Hopefully, with some mentorship from me, he can cast off his pacifism and we might have a chance of living through this.

I look closer at the small creature that may be my ally in the meantime. I cannot believe something so frail can smell so alluring.

All the whispers behind my back about my strange fixations might have had some merit, after all.

Still, it seems hasty to consider it worthless.

My anger subsides, replaced by a curiosity about this tiny creature—this small ball of violence and rage, that refuses to surrender and still yells out its insolence when clearly outmatched.

Its curse words are strange, a mix of creative and confusing, unlike anything I've heard before.

I am still at a loss to how many times the thing mentioned the word *fornicate*.

It has a peculiar way of speaking.

Still, I'm in a playful mood, so I decide to continue our spar, if only to enjoy how nimble this pink-furred creature is.

"You're fast," I admit, circling it. "But not fast enough to avoid capture. How did someone as agile as you get caught?"

The tiny thing's eyes narrow, and it lunges at me with the dagger. I sidestep easily, chuckling.

"Not a subject you would like to discuss?"

"Close ascend," it snaps, slashing at me. "What the fornicate is wrong with your language? *Shut up.* You got captured, too, didn't you?"

I laugh, a low, rumbling sound. "Yes, but I'm a warrior. I was taken down by an army, not by some petty trick."

My eye twitches at considering a genali raid an army, but it doesn't need to know the details.

"Maybe you're just not as smart as you think," it retorts, its dagger barely grazing my side. "Getting captured isn't exactly a mark of genius."

My spines shift, enjoying this tiny thing's sharp tongue. "I like your spirit," I say, dodging another wild swing. "You've got a fire in you. Not many would dare insult a drakonid in their presence."

It lets out a snort of amusement, though I can't quite tell if it's genuine. "Glad you're entertained," it mutters, its movements quickening as it tries to land a blow.

"You should be," I reply, feinting left before striking from the right. The nimble creature dodges, barely, and I laugh again. "You're fun to play with."

"Play?" it huffs, breathing heavily. "This isn't a game."

"Isn't it?" I counter, swiping at it again. "You're dancing around, trying to avoid my claws. It feels like a game to me."

Pink eyes flash with anger and the creature attacks with renewed vigor. "I'm not your toy."

"No," I agree, parrying its dagger with ease. "You're much more interesting than a toy. You've got a dagger for a tongue and quick reflexes. I like that."

"Good for you," it snarls, its quick movements becoming more desperate. "But I'm not here for your amusement."

I tilt my head, watching it with a mix of curiosity and admiration. "Then why are you here, little one? What do you hope to achieve?"

It gives me a floundering stare. "Are you hopelessly stupid?"

My spines shiver at the unimaginative insult, a retort waiting on the tip of my tongue before it shakes its head and breaks in again.

Its enchanting pink eyes burn with defiance as it lunges at me once more. I easily dodge, this time only allowing my claws to sweep against it to let it know what would have been a death blow.

It stumbles back, glaring at me. "Why do you keep taunting me?"

"Because it's fun," I admit. "And because I want to see how far you'll go. You're a fascinating little creature."

Its stony expression hardens, and it takes a step back, breathing heavily, but arms still raised and ready to fight. "Fine. Let's see how much fun you have when I actually hit you."

A rumble of amusement rises as I prepare for its next move. "I'm looking forward to it."

I dodge the attack, but this time, it's closer. Too close. The annoyingly durable glass dagger grazes me on my more sensitive underside, drawing blood. I hiss in pain, but it's more of an amused hiss than an angry one.

"Another little scratch. It will only take you a tens of tens more to kill me. Will your blood pump explode before then?"

Pink eyes glare at me, the intricate patterned organs opened wide, I assume showing its affront. "I'm not done yet."

"Good. Because neither am I."

It growls at me. "You'll wish you hadn't said that. You little like-a-cock excrement."

I give the creature an incredulous stare. There is nothing small about my anatomy. Not a single thing.

I smooth my features before the outrage shows along my spikes. It was a clever use of words, though, and I can't resist the snort that escapes my nostrils.

"You are very creative with your language." I compliment begrudgingly.

If this were a battle of words, I'd have lost horribly, so it was only fitting I give praise.

13

Kira

The creature snorts at my statement, a sound that's half amusement, half derision. It compliments me, but its eyes gleam with a mixture of interest and malice.

I'm exhausted. I feel it in every muscle, every bone.

My earlier rush of adrenaline is wearing off, leaving me drained. "We could keep doing this all day," I lie.

I try to catch my breath as I continue. "Or we could just walk in opposite directions."

"I'm having too much fun to stop now," it replies, pouncing again with claws extended.

I dodge, barely, the effort making me more exasperated by the second.

"You're wasting your energy," I hiss out, ducking under another swipe. "We'd be better off using it against the aliens hunting us. Besides, you're making too much noise, you idiot."

Not that I've been quiet, but that was when I thought I was about to die.

My words don't deter it.

It keeps after me, relentless and unyielding. Each swipe, each lunge is a fresh challenge.

Desperation fuels my next words.

"We could join forces," I blurt out, hoping to reach whatever part of its brain is capable of reason. I've said it before and was ignored, but my strength is ebbing away.

The thing tilts its head, considering. In that brief moment, I put some space between us, my heart pounding.

It adopts a thoughtful disposition, its claws lowering slightly. "Join forces, you say?"

"Yes," I reply, trying to sound convincing and less like I'm about to collapse. "We can't keep fighting each other and expect to survive."

I might prefer to be alone, but I'm not stupid. A giant blue dino-dragon who likes to pounce on people might be good to have around. Besides, if we create an alliance and it dies, I'm not the least bit attached to the asshole.

No need to go on a month-long bender wallowing in my grief. Perfect.

"Very well, I'll join forces with you," it says, its tone imperious. "You provided useful information when asked. But I should keep you as a pet."

"That's not what I said," I retort, my exhaustion giving way to anger. "I'm no one's pet."

The expletives flow freely now, before I'm able to make them into a useful sentence. "I'm not a fornicating toy for you to play with."

Damn. That did not come out right, especially considering I'm on this planet because of alien sex trafficking.

I don't let the translation error show on my face. Sometimes life is all about bravado.

"Are you female?" it asks suddenly, sniffing the air. "You smell too good to be male."

The absurdity of the question throws me off. "Plenty of males smell good," I respond, irritation clear in my voice. "Males should smell good."

Before I can continue my rant, a whiff of the alien's scent reaches my nose. It's unexpected and heady, and it derails my train of thought entirely. Arousal surges higher within me, unbidden and unwanted, and I clench my fists.

I was aroused from the moment I saw it, just like the other aliens, but this is even worse.

"For fornication's sake."

I stamp a foot, seriously pissed off at the slimes and my own errant body. The lizard just keeps looking at me like I'm a snack.

Or I guess, even worse. A pet.

Focus, damn it, I tell myself.

I shake my head hard to clear it. The creature is watching me closely, amusement dancing in its eyes.

"Are you distracted?" it taunts, taking a step closer.

"No," I snap back, gripping the dagger tighter. "I'm just planning our next move."

My voice is steadier than I feel. "We need to get out of here and find a safe place to regroup."

It studies me for a moment longer before making a low grumble. "Agreed," it says, the amusement fading from its expression. "Lead the way, little one."

It holds out an arm, and I can't help but stare at its odd hands. Four fingers on each hand, each set of two directly opposing each other, so when it walks, they jut out directly to the outside and inside. Each finger is thick enough it looks like two fused together. There is no difference between the ends of its four limbs, so I'm not sure to call them all hands or all feet.

At the tip of each finger are long, curving dark-blue claws that come to a relatively blunt looking tip, but have a sharp, serrated edge on the underside between the end and where it disappears into the flesh of the fingertip.

I move my gaze back up to its face, which is the most dragon-like part of it, with big nostrils that remind me of a horse, teeth that are an over-bite of large fangs in the front of its large mouth, and others that jut up from the bottom jaw as an under-bite of smaller, but just as sharp looking, teeth. It has minimal lip movement, and so I assume most of the way it forms words must be an internal structure.

Its eyes are bright amber-gold orbs with a slitted pupil. Around them is a thick, lighter blue hide that it can pull together over the eye. As it did when I tried to shoot at them before. In a v-pattern from its forehead down to its nose is darker blue hide, with multiple spikes that start small between the broad expanse between its eyes, and then gradually become bigger on its forehead and down its broad back, until transitioning back to smaller down the length of its tail.

The spines shift quite a bit as it communicates, and I wonder what that might mean. I move my gaze back to its face and could swear it looks entertained at my long assessment. Smug and arrogant, too.

I don't trust it, not entirely, but for now we have a common goal.

I take a deep breath and start moving; the creature falling into step beside me. The uneasy truce is better than nothing.

The silence between us is tense, filled with the unspoken threat of violence.

I keep my dagger ready, just in case. Lizard breath might be a temporary ally, but I'm not about to let my guard down. We move through the dense foliage, every sound amplified in the quiet.

I'd much prefer to be alone, even if it was a human here, but a beast that admits it likes playing cat to my mouse? Ugh.

"What's your name?" I ask after a while, trying to break the tension.

It glances at me, its eyes narrowing. "You didn't defeat me to earn that privilege."

I snort. I highly doubt they make their elders fight them for their name.

"Fine, be mysterious. But if we're working together, I need something to call you."

It considers this for a moment.

"My name is Drasuk," it says, voice low and resonant, reverberating through the air between us.

"Fine, Drasuk," I say, rolling the name around in my mouth. "I'm Kira."

"Kira," it repeats. "Interesting."

We keep moving, the tension between us easing slightly. I'm still wary, still on edge, but at least we're not at each other's throats. For now, that's enough.

As we walk, I keep my senses sharp, listening for any sign of the aliens, looking for flashes of silver that might lead me to other women. The forest is dense, and every shadow seems to hide a potential threat. I glance at Drasuk occasionally, watching for any signs of betrayal. But so far, it seems content to follow my lead.

"What's your story?" I ask eventually, unable to keep my curiosity at bay. "Why were you hunting me?"

Drasuk's eyes flicker with something I can't quite read. "I was brought here against my will, it's only fitting I hunted down those foolish enough to hunt me. I simply confused you to be one of them."

"No excrement," I mutter.

"You are right. I didn't smell that. You smell like a genali."

"I didn't mean that's what I smell like. I meant... Forget it. Genali?"

"Gray and covered in mucus. Three legs. Obsessed with all things wet."

I shudder. "Yes, they changed me, so it makes sense I smell like them, not to mention I killed one. But why were you hunting them in the first place?"

It hesitates, its gaze distant. "Revenge, of course," it says finally. "Dying on my side without a fight is not a lifestyle I am accustomed to."

I nod, understanding all too well. "Same here," I say quietly. "They took..."

I almost say *us* and I'm glad I stopped myself. If I come across another woman, then he'll get to know who I'm searching for, but for now I don't want to let him know.

"Me. Took me and experimented on me. I'm not going to let them get away with it."

Drasuk's eyes meet mine, a spark of recognition passing between us. I'm relieved when I see something other than a predator in its gaze. There's a shared pain, a mutual understanding.

It's a small thing, but it's enough to cement our uneasy alliance.

We move through the forest, our pace steady. Every now and then, I catch Drasuk glancing at me, its expression thoughtful. I wonder what it's thinking, but I don't ask. We're both carrying our own burdens and I don't want to shoulder any of those for it.

Eventually, we come to a clearing. I pause, scanning the area for any sign of danger. It seems safe enough, and I motion for Drasuk to follow me. We make our way to the center, and I take a moment to catch my breath.

Drasuk watches me, its eyes sharp. "What's the plan?" it asks.

"We rest," I say simply. "And then we figure out our next move."

It nods, settling down beside me.

The silence between us is companionable, a stark contrast to our earlier hostility. I lean back against a tree, letting my eyes drift shut for a moment. The exhaustion is overwhelming, but I can't afford to let my guard down completely.

As I rest, I think about everything that's happened. The experiments, the escape, and the constant fight for survival. It's a lot to process, and I feel a pang of homesickness. But there's no going back, not now.

All I can do is keep moving.

Beside me, Drasuk shifts, its presence a comforting weight. For all its bluster and aggression, there's a growing sense of camaraderie between us. We're both survivors, both fighting against the odds.

I open my eyes, meeting Drasuk's gaze. "Thank you," I say quietly. "For not killing me, I mean."

It snorts, a sound that's almost a laugh. "Don't thank me yet, little one. We're not out of this place."

I roll my eyes. "No excrement. Damn the thing, that isn't as satisfying in your language."

I let my head flop back again, annoyed that I can't even curse properly.

"I said my name's Kira," I grumble.

All I get is grunt in response.

It's like everything possible has been taken away and I have to push back that surging impulse to complain. Then argue with myself when I want to complain about not being able to fucking complain.

This seems like a good moment for it, if there ever was one.

A sudden draft of wind blows, wafting the creature's distinct scent into my nose and I can neither help the shiver that runs down my back, nor the liquid trail of arousal I know is trailing down my legs, hidden by the thin cloth material of the black suit.

I sneak a look over at it... him and barely have time to regain my composure as Drasuk gives me a curious stare.

There is a rumble building in his chest and the vibration sends spritzes of arousal flowing down my legs at a quicker pace.

Damnable slimes and their body tinkering.

14

Drasuk

I am watching Kira closely, fascinated by the sudden shift in her scent. It's richer, more intoxicating, almost overwhelming.

I've never encountered anything like it before.

I don't know how to interpret her expression, but I think I might know what her scent means.

"Why do you suddenly smell better than before?" I rumble.

Her eyes widen, and a dark flush spreads across her brown cheeks. "What do you mean, smell better?" she retorts, her voice edged with annoyance.

She's delightful when she's angry. Tiny and fierce like a cornered animal. I find my spikes twitching despite the situation.

I like how expressive her face coloring and her thick, brown-red lips are. Judging by how much they move, the patches of black fur above her pink eyes must also communicate her feelings. Her delicate nostrils flare out just like a drak's would when angered, except on a much smaller scale.

So far, I've only seen anger, but I am curious to know what ways her features will shift with other emotions. Such delicate, expressive features that make me want to just keep looking.

"You're too small to not make the perfect pet," I say, unable to resist teasing her.

The anger that flares in her eyes is amusing, her reaction just as entertaining as I had hoped.

"I am not a pet" she snaps, her voice rising. "I'm a person. I'm a fornicating head of a container... damn the thing, you insipid, overgrown..."

I don't understand any of the words that flow out after that.

Eventually she cuts herself off, before looking away with a huff. Her indignation is palpable, and I can't help but be delighted by it.

"Is it because you want to be more than a pet?" I ask, my tone dripping with mock curiosity.

The idea intrigues me more than I'd ever admit, especially to this tiny human with her fierce spirit.

She stares at me, her anger boiling over. "I don't want to be anything to you," she grits out. "I'm my own person, damn the thing. I'm *human*. Not an animal."

That same intoxicating smell of hers waxes stronger, tainting the walls of my nostrils and nuzzling the back of my throat.

I vaguely acknowledge the fact that I have taken a few steps closer to her.

I chuckle, the sound deep and rumbling. "Of course you would like to elevate your status, but you will have to convince me. I'm not sure I see the appeal," I say, leaning closer to her.

Her scent intensifies, and I find it increasingly difficult to maintain my composure.

Her face turns a deep shade of red-brown, which clashes with her bright pink hair, and she erupts in a slew of nonsense words in my language. "Fornicate until finished, scale face. What the fiery pit in the ground... excrement. Fornicate."

She lets out an exasperated sound. "Your language is terrible."

Her attempt at cussing in Drakonid is both hilarious and endearing.

I can't hold back my laugh, the sound echoing around us.

"Fornicate until finished? This really isn't the place," I tease. "First we would have to start, which I haven't agreed to, of course, but then it would be a very long time until I was done. This isn't the time for that."

She grabs a stick from the ground and flings it at me, but I dodge easily. "No. I said *fuck off*. Fornicate until finished. Excrement."

Her frustration is evident, and it only makes me want to keep prodding at her. Before I can, she throws her little arms up in the air, raises a single dainty digit, and stalks away from me.

"That's enough rest for now," she growls as she heads deeper into the forest.

I follow her from a distance. I've never been so entertained.

As we move through the dense foliage, I can't help but feel a growing companionship with this tiny, fierce *human*. Her spirit is indomitable, and it draws me to her.

I watch her closely, my amusement gradually giving way to a grudging respect.

I call out to her after a while, my tone softer than before. "Why do you fight so hard? What drives you?"

She glances back at me, her eyes still blazing with anger, but there's a hint of something else there, too.

"I fight because I have to," she says, her voice also lower. "Because if I don't, they'll win. And I can't let that happen."

Her words resonate with me, stirring something deep within my chest. I let out a rumble of agreement, understanding her more than she might realize.

"We are more alike than you think, *human*," I say. "I too fight because I have no other choice."

She stops walking and turns to face me, her expression thoughtful. "Maybe we are," she admits. "But that doesn't mean you get to treat me like a lesser being."

"You must admit, you are rather pet-like when you're angry."

Her earlier annoyance returns as an exciting glare on her face, crossing her arms over her chest. "You're impossible."

"And you are delightful," I counter, enjoying the banter. "Perhaps this alliance won't be so bad after all."

She rolls her eyes, but there's a hint of amusement on her face, I think. I might be misinterpreting. Her fur doesn't communicate like my spines do, but the movements of her face seem like they might be the equivalent.

"Just don't get any ideas, *iguana* brain. I'm not here for your entertainment."

"A preposterous assertion, little thing," I say, my tone serious now, despite the amused cant of my spines. "We have a common goal, and I respect that. But that doesn't mean I can't have fun along the way."

She sighs, shaking her head. "You're unbelievable."

"I've been called worse. Though I did say my name was Drasuk. Now, let's keep moving. We don't want to disturb the local fauna with our pet play."

She raises her middle digits at me again with lowered eye fur and turns away, leaving me blinking at the mysterious gesture.

An odd creature, this one.

We continue our journey through the dense forest, the canopy above casting a dappled shadow on the path. She is agile, weaving through the underbrush with ease, her movements graceful and precise.

I follow her lead, my larger frame making the journey slightly more cumbersome, but manageable.

As we walk, the silence between us becomes less tense. I find myself watching her, and not just out of curiosity. Her determination and resilience are qualities I respect, and her fierce independence is a refreshing change from the submissiveness I've encountered in civilians.

I assume she must be a human version of a Maj'Ra.

Most species erupt into screams the first time they run afoul a drakonid, after all. Her screams were taunts, expressions of impeding violence, and curses.

I want to hear her yell at me again soon. It's fierce and exciting.

We come across a small stream, the water clear and cool. Kira kneels beside it, cupping her hands to take a drink. I watch her, noticing the way the moonlight catches in her hair, and the way her eyes reflect the light.

She looks up at me, catching me staring.

"What?" she asks, raising the fur above one of her eyes.

"Nothing," I reply.

She takes another sip of water before standing up, brushing the dirt off her knees. "Where exactly should we be going? You haven't been very forthcoming with details."

I hesitate for a moment, considering how much to tell her. "We're on a genali hunting ground. Supposedly, they have outposts stationed at strategic points on the planet where shuttles bring down supplies from orbit."

She narrows her eyes, studying me. "And you're just now telling me this?"

"I didn't think you'd be interested in the details," I say, my spikes taunting her. "But if you are, I can tell you more."

"Spare me the *sarcasm*," she mutters, but there's a hint of a smile on her lips. "Just tell me what we need to do when we get there."

I rasp out a laugh. "Don't get your hopes up, little one. I'm running off speculation here. For one, I have never been to a hunting ground before, so I have no idea how to find these drop points. But I do know that there's a drop point for every biome on a planet, according to the manual on genali methods. But this ground is fully developed, so it's definitely an older one. The design principle should be the same."

"There's a fornicating manual?"

"Every species has thousands of those to appeal to the baser instincts, but that's not what I'm talking about."

"*Porn* isn't what I—"

She just shakes her head instead of finishing. I don't know what it means but assume it is to communicate she is done speaking.

"Secondly, as I said, these are orbital drop points. Basically, it's where hunters head to, to communicate with operatives in the planet's orbit and place orders for weapons, ammunition, medicine, or whatever they need. Of course, I think we also might be on a planet where anything advanced won't work."

That catches her interest. "Tech doesn't work? That lines up with something I overhead on the ship."

"It either doesn't, or they have special rules here, though if they mentioned it, then we should assume it is a tech-suppressed planet. If you've run into any hunters, you'd notice that their weapons of choice are too elementary."

I point to her weapon as an example. "The blaster you're using is an outdated tech from the era of ballistic weaponry. If energy-based weapons don't work here, then communication tech doesn't either, which is what makes this talk of orbital stations questionable at best."

She lets out a sigh. "So basically, we've been charging through dense forests at night like a pair of directionless morons for the past couple hours."

My eyes squint as I hold in laughter. "But that's not why I'm interested, though. Hunters need a way to get off this world. What better place for extraction than such a place? If this planet destroys technology, then no ship can enter this planet's atmosphere and leave. Many have tried even with the most primitive exploration class models on tech suppressing planets. They all lose power and crash. Either way, they always have an orbital station above that steadily needs to drop off supplies. It has to connect somewhere, even if by space elevator."

Kira runs a hand through the choppy pink fur on her head and I resist the urge to stare. "That's a lot of *ifs* and *maybes*."

I grunt out my agreement. "Do you have a better alternative?"

She says nothing for a while before she punches a nearby tree violently, splitting the bark and making me recoil in shock.

"Fornicate me sideways."

I can't resist the rumble of laughter that comes grinding along my chest and up my throat.

"I doubt that would be an effective method of copulation."

"Oh, fornicate off into a pit."

I laugh again.

15

Kira

Drasuk says nothing as I pick the remnants of bark out of the skin of my knuckles with detached annoyance. Its laughter... his laughter, whatever, subsided a while ago, and he has settled for staring at me with his amber-gold eyes.

The silence between us is comforting in its own way. My mind keeps drifting back to his scent and the unexpected reaction it provokes in me. I shake my head, focusing on the task at hand.

We need resources if we're going to survive, and there's only one place I know to find them.

I take a deep breath, steeling myself. "Before we start laying any plans, I say we head back to the crash site," I suggest, keeping my voice steady. "There are supplies there from the aliens I killed. We could use them."

Drasuk makes a rumble of agreement, standing up and stretching his massive frame.

"Lead the way, little one," he says, his tone still carrying a hint of mockery.

I roll my eyes at his continual refusal to use my name and start walking, the dense foliage parting slightly as I move.

Behind me, Drasuk follows, his heavy footsteps crashing through the underbrush. I clench my fists, my irritation rising with each noisy step he takes.

Just as loud as ever with his giant stupid body, I think to myself, a small part of me still irritated that I've picked up such a pushy, insulting stalker.

I'm better off alone.

The silence between us stretches, broken only by the sound of Drasuk barreling through the foliage gracelessly behind me. Eventually, I can't take it anymore.

"If you're going to be that loud," I say over my shoulder, "you better have excellent hearing because you're making it impossible for me to hear anything else."

Drasuk snorts, a sound that's almost a laugh. "Do not worry, weak human. I can keep my pet safe. Besides, if your hearing is that bad, you clearly need me."

I grit my teeth, trying to keep my temper in check. "Not your pet," I snap. "And I don't need you. In fact, you could do us both a favor and go away."

Drasuk's eyes gleam with amusement. "You know, for someone who doesn't need me, you seem awfully keen on having me around."

I stop walking and turn to face him, my fists clenched at my sides. "Listen, lizard face," I say, my voice low and dangerous. "I don't know what you think is going on here, but I'm not interested in playing your games. I'm trying to survive, and your constant noise is going to get us both killed."

Drasuk's forehead spines shift, his expression one of mild curiosity. "You have strong opinions for such a small creature," he says, taking a step closer. "But your anger is misplaced. I'm here to help you."

"Help me?" I scoff. "You've been nothing but a pain in my ass since we met. If you really want to help, then start by being quiet and letting me do what I need to do."

Drasuk chuckles, a deep, rumbling sound. "Very well, little one. I'll try to be quieter. But don't think for a moment that I'm going anywhere, whether you like it or not."

I turn back around, muttering curses under my breath as I continue walking.

Men are exactly the same no matter the species. They want to feel needed.

I don't need them, so there lies the rub.

The banter and insults continue as we make our way through the forest, each comment a fresh spark of irritation. Despite my annoyance, I have to admit he is clever and that my anger with him is a lot easier on my mental health than wallowing in despair.

It's infuriating and confusing, but for now, I push those feelings aside.

Finally, we reach the crash site. The area is still and silent, the bodies of the alien hunters lying where I left them. I glance around, scanning for any signs of danger before approaching the green-skinned one.

Drasuk watches me, his eyes sharp and alert.

I kneel down beside the alien, my fingers deftly searching its body for anything useful. I find food, water, and some medical supplies, stuffing them into my pack. There's ammo, too and I strip the thing of its armor, though it's a ridiculous gold color.

Not to mention my boobs aren't going to fit, but poor fitting armor is better than no armor.

I wipe the green blood off it and my hands on nearby sand before folding the surprisingly flexible material and shoving it into my pack.

Not much, but plenty to keep me going for long enough to find another hunter. I glance over at Drasuk and refuse to include him in my ration calculations. The big idiot can take care of himself, regardless of our truce.

Besides, he doesn't seem concerned and isn't snatching up weapons. I glance down at his claws and over to the tail I'm pretty sure would wreck me if he swung it my way. I guess he's his own weapon.

We can be together and still fend for ourselves. It grates against my training, but he isn't my responsibility.

As I stand up, I feel Drasuk's eyes on me. "What?" I snap, my patience wearing thin.

"You're very resourceful," he says, his tone almost admiring.

I roll my eyes. "Gee, thanks. Now let's get out of here before more of them show up."

We leave the area, transitioning back out of the open desert with almost no cover and back into the trees, where I breathe easier.

Soon, we're moving quickly and quietly through the forest. The uneasy alliance between us holds, but I'm still on edge, my senses sharp and my dagger ready.

As we walk, I'll admit to feeling a sense of relief that his hulking form is here with me, even if I'll never admit it to the annoying jerk. For all his bluster and arrogance, Drasuk seems to be a capable ally.

Maybe once I get my feet under me, I can convince him to beat it.

We walk in silence for a while. The forest is dense, every shadow a potential threat, but with Drasuk by my side, I feel slightly more at ease. His presence, as irritating as it is, is useful.

All my waffling on his utility is another layer of annoyance, this time with myself.

There's also the irritating fact that having him this close is doing things to my lower regions that are making the latex-like material of my pants really irritating to have on at the moment.

My body is telling me all kinds of wicked things that I'd usually be completely on board with, but not with him. I try to think about that bouncer at the club, but I get caught up in wondering if he helped them throw me in a van.

Then I'm right back to thinking about Drasuk and how much I'd like him to say something clever again. I mean, I hate it, but it's hot.

I don't know what the fuck I want right now.

Ridiculous.

Suddenly, Drasuk breaks the silence. "You smell better again. Why is that?" he rumbles, his voice low and curious.

The question throws me off, and I can feel my cheeks heating up. "I don't know what you're talking about," I mutter, trying to sound nonchalant.

The truth is, I do know. The scent, the arousal, is because of him, and it's infuriating.

Drasuk chuckles, a deep, throaty sound that sends another unwanted shiver down my spine. "You can deny it all you want, little one, but I can smell it. Your body betrays you."

I clench my fists, anger flaring. "Just keep your nose to yourself," I mutter, feeling a mix of embarrassment and frustration.

This is the last thing I need right now.

"Very well," Drasuk says, his tone amused. "But if it becomes a problem, do let me know."

I glare at him, but he simply rumbles out a taunting sound and continues walking.

The silence stretches again, but this time it's filled with a different kind of tension. I try to focus on our surroundings, on fucking staying alive, but my mind keeps drifting back to Drasuk and the confusing feelings he stirs within me.

I let out a breath. "Hole in rear."

"As eloquent as always," he deadpans, and I brush past him in a huff.

16

Drasuk

As the night air grows cooler, I continue to follow Kira through the forest, her slender form a dark blur ahead of me.

Her mood is sour, but I have no complaints about the diverting spectacle she's putting on.

Unlike her stealthy steps from before, each step she takes now is fueled by the irritation I provoke in her. It is fascinating how easily she's riled up.

The moon dips lower in the sky, casting long shadows that meld into the creeping darkness. Despite my heavy footsteps crashing through the underbrush, Kira moves with a determined grace, pushing forward as if trying to outrun her anger.

Her scent is impossible to ignore—an intoxicating blend of arousal and irritation that has my senses on high alert.

Kira eventually shoves her way into a thicket, a tight cluster of bushes and low-hanging branches offering a semblance of shelter for the night. She's quick, efficient, and clearly wants nothing more than to be rid of my presence, even if just for a few hours.

My spines shift, amused by her futile attempt to hide from me.

"You can't fit in here," she snaps over her shoulder, her voice tinged with annoyance. "Go away."

Ignoring her, I take a step back and then leap, landing gracefully in the middle of the thicket beside her. Kira lets out a quickly cut-off yelp, her eyes wide with a mixture of surprise and anger.

"You fumbling fornicator," she hisses, her voice low but seething with rage. "Arg, *stupid fuck.*"

Leaning closer to her, my eyes gleaming with mischief, I speak to her in a rumbling whisper. "I fumble at nothing, little one. I would have you trumpeting my name and groveling on your belly for more."

She fidgets, her scent growing stronger with every word.

It's maddening and alluring all at once, but instead of retorting with another biting comment, she turns onto her side, facing away from me.

"Food excrement. *Bullshit*. Fumbling fornicator..." she mutters under her breath, cutting herself off.

She laments softly, almost to herself. "Why do these attempts at cussing you out not have a word-for-word translation?"

Her frustration is palpable, and my spines shift to amusement at the way she's hitting sticks out of her way, rearranging the thicket as if it would somehow ease her anger.

"Fumbling pieces of excrement putting broken tech in me. I'm going to fornicating kill them all," she growls under her breath, her voice a dangerous whisper.

Feeling conversational, I interject with a rumble of amusement. "Now I see how someone so small can survive. You draw them in and fornicate them to death. It sounds messy, but effective."

She whips her head around, glaring at me. "What? No. I don't fornicate to kill. It's— I mean— Just close ascent or leave. *Shut up*. Fornicate. It's like they made sure I would sound as stupid as possible."

She finishes her tirade with a growl, the sound both menacing and appealing to me. I watch her in silence for a moment, my spines shifting to betray how fascinating she is.

She's a fiery one, this little human, and the more time I spend with her, the more I understand why animals get trapped in carnivorous plants. Except the one calling me so strongly with her scent has a barbed tongue, and I love it.

The night deepens around us, the sounds of the forest a symphony of life and danger. Kira's breathing slows, and though she remains tense, her anger seems to dissipate slightly. I lie beside her, feeling the warmth of her body despite the distance she tries to keep.

"Hole in rear," she mutters again, but there's a softness to her voice now, almost as if the fight is leaving her.

"Charming," I reply, earning another huff from her.

The silence between us stretches, filled with the sounds of the night. I can hear her blood pumping, the steady rhythm comforting. She's strong, this human, stronger than she realizes.

And while she may not admit it, I know she needs me as much as I need her.

An image of Nkisa rises, unbidden. I fling it away, but not before making the connection in my mind. Protecting others is my natural role, but this is becoming more. Is this my chance to do better? To provide Kira the protection I failed to give Nkisa?

My mind provides no answers.

As the hours pass, the forest grows quieter, the night creatures settling into their routines. I find myself watching her, her small frame curled up defensively, her expression one of defiance even while resting. There's a vulnerability to her she tries so hard to hide, and it only makes me more determined to protect her.

I've never responded like that to a weaker species.

Strange.

17

Kira

I lay in the thicket, trying to find a comfortable position on the uneven ground. The night air is cool, a welcome change from the stifling heat of the day, but sleep eludes me. Drasuk's presence leaves me unsettled.

I can still feel his eyes on me, and it's infuriating.

I turn onto my side, pulling my knees up to my chest. The scent of earth and vegetation fills my nostrils, grounding me slightly, but my mind refuses to quiet down. Thoughts of Drasuk swirl in my head. A relentless storm of irritation and confusion.

He's arrogant, pushy, and infuriatingly smug. And yet, there's something about him that I can't quite shake off. Something that resonates.

"Fumbling fornicator food excrement," I hiss, echoing my earlier frustration, before almost screaming in annoyance at the realization that I've muttered out another line of word salad.

I take a pause, forcing my throat to remember what it felt like to speak English, and after a few seconds of disconcerting writhing in my throat, I test my lingua once more.

"Stupid fuck? Bullshit?"

Blinking at the realization that I'm back to the default potty-mouthed setting fills me with a bit of relief before I let out a groan once more.

I continue grumbling in English. "Why do these damn translations never get it right?"

Naturally, I get no response, so I switch back to drakonid to keep trying, as bullheaded as always.

I mutter a string of curses that sound like gibberish even to my ears. I should just give it up. Accept that there is no good way to curse in his stupid language, but it just sounds like one too many changes.

I've given up control of how my body looks, my freedom, my home, my language, and now cursing? No.

He'll have to be the one to fucking figure it out. I ignore the part of my brain telling me I'm going to keep sounding like an idiot.

I'm done changing.

The quiet of the wilderness presses in on me, amplifying the sounds of my breathing and the distant rustle of leaves.

It reminds me too much of the early years of my deployment back on Earth—the anxious waiting during hot desert nights, the eerie stillness that only heightened the tension. Except now, instead of the sweltering heat, the cool forest air wraps around me, making the memories feel even more distant and surreal.

I roll onto my back, staring up at the canopy of leaves above. The shadows play tricks on my mind, shapes shifting and merging in the dim light. Sleep tugs at my eyelids, but I refuse to give in.

I don't trust Drasuk, not fully.

He might be a capable ally, but he's still a wildcard.

I wouldn't have these damn conflicted feelings if he would just leave. As requested, hell, demanded, multiple times.

My mind drifts to the events of the day, replaying the battles and the moments of tension. The alien hunters, the crash site, the supplies we scavenged—it all feels like a blur. My body aches from the exertion, every muscle protesting against the hard ground beneath me.

Except the adrenaline still courses through my veins, keeping me on edge. Dammit.

The night is full of distant sounds, but it's the much closer relative silence that gets to me. The wind rustles the leaves, insects chirp, and somewhere in the distance, a night bird calls out mournfully. Despite the sounds, there's an oppressive quiet that makes me feel more alone than ever.

I shift again, trying to find a position that doesn't make my muscles scream in protest. The ground is cold and hard, and every rock and root feel like a personal affront.

"Damn it," I mutter, sitting up and rubbing my face with my hands.

The smooth texture of my black-suit gloves rubs against my skin to generate a bit of heat that does little to stave off the nips of cold on my skin, reminding me of how long it's been since I've had the luxury of simple comforts.

Good thing the suit could extend itself that much, I suppose. I could be stuck with a fucking bathing suit to match my sex Barbie hair.

My mind keeps drifting back to Drasuk.

Why does he have to be so irritatingly powerful? Every move he makes is calculated, every word a challenge. It's like he knows exactly how to get under my skin.

My left eyelid twitches.

Even now. I'm still thinking about the lizard.

It's not just that he's an alien. It's that he's so damn confident, so sure of himself.

I want to scream out again, but I've done enough of that for one day.

My mind wanders to our first encounter. I remember the way he moved, so fluid and precise, like a perfect predator. I didn't doubt for a second that he could have taken me down with a single, well-placed shot.

I hated him for it then, just as much as I hate him now.

I lie back down, staring up at the stars visible through the canopy. They're different here, foreign constellations that don't match the ones I grew up with. It's an uncomfortable reminder of how far from home I am.

I wonder what my family is doing right now, if they're safe, if they even think about me. If they are mourning me like we all mourned our parents. Hopefully not like my mother mourned my father.

Likely, the only thing that brought me out of my own addiction was the realization that I was becoming like her.

I let out a huff through my nose. That's not fair either. She was fucking amazing before he was killed.

The thought brings a pang of homesickness, a dull ache that settles in my chest.

The forest around me is alive with the sounds of nocturnal creatures. I try to focus on them, to use them as a distraction from my thoughts. It's no use.

My mind keeps circling back to Drasuk. To the way he looks at me with that infuriating stare.

I wonder what he's thinking about. Probably nothing good. He's always plotting, always scheming, something tells me. Willing to play with my mind.

It's what makes him so dangerous. He's so focused on me, trying to figure me out.

I'm afraid of what he might find.

My eyelids are growing heavy, but I fight it. I can't afford to sleep, not with Drasuk so close. I need to stay alert, to be ready for whatever he might do, but the exhaustion is overwhelming, a weight pressing down on me.

I close my eyes, just for a moment, telling myself I'll stay awake.

The darkness behind my eyelids is soothing, a welcome respite from the constant vigilance. I let out a long breath, trying to release some of the tension coiled in my muscles.

My thoughts drift, the edges blurring as sleep tugs at me. I think about the mission, about the importance of what we're doing. Survival. Find the others.

It feels like a lifetime ago that I cared about anything other than survival.

I remember the faces of my comrades, those who didn't make it. Their ghosts haunt me, whispering in the quiet of the night. I can see them, their expressions etched in pain and fear. I squeeze my eyes shut, trying to block out the memories. But they're always there, lurking in the shadows of my mind.

A sudden rustle in the bushes nearby snaps me back to full alertness.

My heart pounds as I sit up, scanning the darkness for any sign of movement. Every nerve in my body is on edge, ready to spring into action, but there's nothing. Just the wind and the trees and the distant call of a night creature.

I lie back down, but the moment of near-panic has driven away any lingering drowsiness. I stare up at the stars again, counting them as if it will help me stay awake.

One, two, three...

But there are too many, and my mind wanders back to Drasuk. Always back to Drasuk.

The way he moves, the way he talks, it all grates on my nerves. There's something else there, too, something I don't want to admit.

A grudging respect, maybe. He's good at what he does, and he knows it. He's a survivor, like me. Maybe that's why I can't shake him from my thoughts.

He's a mirror, reflecting parts of myself that I'd rather not see. Just how much of my humanity have I lost in my quest to forget? I haven't let anyone tell me.

He won't hold back pointing out my flaws, I'm sure of it. Am I ready to face them?

I shift again, trying to find a comfortable position. The ground is unyielding, but I force myself to settle. The night is growing colder, and the chill is already working its way into my bones.

It makes it easier for my eyelids to droop over my eyes, and shortly after that, I don't feel much of anything else as the world fades to black.

Drasuk

I spend hours watching her, my eyes tracing the delicate lines of her form against the dim light. The forest around us hums with life, but all I can focus on is Kira. She intrigues me, but there's something else, something deeper, that pulls me toward her.

Something that reminds me of my short-lived obsession with Nkisa in my youth... The one I knew better than to talk about with my broodmates.

As the night wears on, I find my thoughts drifting. I've never spent this much time with a female I was focused on before, especially not one so different from my kind.

Maj'Ras males rarely interact with civilian females unless chosen when they go into heat. It is very bad form to pursue Maj'Ras females, since they chose a warrior's path, and I was never interested in being confined to a city.

Kira's presence stirs something unfamiliar within me. Doubt, that's what it is.

I don't like it.

I remember the way she bristled at my teasing earlier, the flash of anger in her eyes. At the time, it had been amusing, but now I wonder if I crossed a line.

Was my excitement to engage with her overwhelming?

Different species have different ways of expressing amusement and interest. What's entertaining to me might be uncomfortable, even offensive, to her.

Yet, for some inexplicable reason, I did not want to stop. If I'm honest with myself, I don't plan to stop. It's too satisfying.

I just don't know why.

My gaze drifts back to her, curled up defensively in the makeshift shelter.

That sweet scent she carries wafts toward me again, and I inhale deeply, feeling a jolt of energy course through my body.

The realization hits me hard: I want to mate with her.

The thought is as exhilarating as it is terrifying. It has been a long time since I felt this way, and it's both thrilling and confusing. I have no idea how to convince a female to choose me for her heat, which is very inconvenient since this little human seems to be right in the middle of hers.

Suddenly, I can't stand being so close to her. The urge to act on my instincts is overpowering, and I know I need to distance myself before I do something foolish.

With a burst of movement, I spring up, scaling the nearest tree with ease. The rough bark feels grounding under my claws, a needed anchor for the chaotic swirl of my emotions.

Some things aren't meant to be felt, let alone expressed.

As I reach a branch high above, I hear her voice, faint but clear. "Taking the first watch, then?" she mutters, still half asleep from me disturbing her.

I pause, torn between the desire to respond and the need to maintain my distance. "I thought you needed rest more often than me, being of weaker constitution and all," I call down, my tone light but strained.

She doesn't rise to the bait, her silence in contrast to the earlier fire.

Her scent invades my nostrils again, and I hastily continue my ascent, finding a perch where I can keep an eye on her without being too close. The distance helps, but only slightly.

She still consumes my thoughts.

I try to focus on my surroundings, to lose myself in the familiar rhythms of the night, but my mind keeps drifting back to Kira, to the way she challenges me, provokes me, and draws me in.

Maj'Ra females are fierce and commanding, their presence demanding respect, and in some cases outright awe. Kira is different—smaller, more delicate, but with a similar strength of will.

She's a puzzle I can't solve. A challenge I can't resist.

Hours pass, and the night deepens. My thoughts are a tangled mess, a confusing blend of desire, curiosity, and uncertainty. The urge to be close to her, to protect her, to understand her, is overwhelming.

It's not natural, as any drak would tell me.

I know I need to tread carefully, to respect her boundaries and her strength. I can only hope I can navigate this new territory without doing something stupid.

Eventually, exhaustion sets in, and I find myself drifting into a low-level sleep, my senses still attuned to the sounds of the forest and the presence of the human below.

A prickling sensation jolts me awake.

It's not external, no danger lurking in the forest around us. It's internal, a burning ember deep within me that explodes into a roaring furnace the moment my eyes fly open. Desire—raw, primal, and utterly terrifying—slams into me with the force of a charging bull.

I let out a startled sound, a strangled mix of a growl and a choked gasp. The sound, ridiculous in its absurdity, earns a snort from below. I glance down to see Kira, still thankfully curled up in the makeshift shelter, but her eyes are narrowed in suspicion.

"What now, Drasuk?" she mutters, her voice laced with sleep and annoyance.

"Nothing," I grumble, forcing my gaze away from her. "Just... clearing my throat."

Clearing my throat. Right.

Because that's a perfectly normal drakonid activity in the dead of night.

I clench my hands, digging my claws into the rough bark of the branch beneath me. This is unsettling. I've never felt anything like this before, this all-consuming need that sweeps away rational thought.

It's exactly why our ancestors avoided the sorts of bonds manticorids and other species have.

Shame burns in my gut alongside the fire in my loins.

Hours crawl by, each minute an eternity. I spend them perched on the branch, a sentinel consumed by an internal battle. I focus on the forest floor below, the play of moonlight filtering through the leaves.

Finally, with a growl that rumbles deep within my chest, I can't take it anymore. I have to put more distance between us. With a burst of strength, I propel myself farther up the tree, the rough bark reassuring under my claws.

The higher I climb, the cooler the air becomes, carrying a faint scent of sand and something else. Freedom?

I reach a sturdy branch overlooking the vast expanse stretching before us. Below, the forest gives way to a seemingly endless sea of sand dunes, shimmering under the pale moonlight. It's a familiar sight, a stark contrast to the lush greenery surrounding us.

A pang of longing stabs at me, a yearning for the desolate beauty of my home world.

Taking a deep breath, I allow the cool desert breeze to wash over me, clearing my head somewhat. Scanning the horizon, I check for any signs of danger, a habit ingrained in me since I was a hatchling. Seeing nothing but the silent dunes, I turn my attention back to the forest below.

A sharp gasp rips through the night, shattering the fragile peace. My gaze snaps down to Kira's form. She's thrashing violently, her limbs flailing, a strangled cry escaping her lips. Fear, stark and raw, shoots through me. I look around for threats, but don't see any.

She's having a nightmare, I realize.

I recognize the signs all too well. Night terrors are a common affliction among younger draks, especially after witnessing the brutal battles between the various vicious species on my planet and the Maj'Ras.

Even for a species as combat-oriented as us, it still does damage.

It's a visceral experience, one that scars both body and mind. While the effects usually dull with age and are replaced with latent, controlled bloodlust, the vulnerability it exposes is one of the more constant brutalities we are forced to endure.

My first instinct is to descend and pile on top of her, the usual response we use to anchor a thrashing Maj'Ra. But logic slams into me. She's human, fragile, and nowhere near as robust as a drakonid.

That kind of restraint would crush her.

Instead, I launch myself down from the branch, landing beside her with a heavy thud. The noise startles her awake. Her eyes fly open, wide with terror, reflecting the moonlight in an unsettling way.

"Kira!" I call out, my voice gruff with urgency. "Wake up, it's just a dream."

Her scream dies in her throat, replaced by a series of rapid breaths. Her eyes shut again, back to darting around like she's still stuck in a memory. She trembles, but her struggle reduces considerably.

19

Kira

"Keep them back," Hayes shouts, his voice barely audible over the chaos.

I pop up, squeezing off shots at the advancing soldiers. They fall in droves, but more keep coming. It's a desperate, chaotic fight, the air thick with smoke and the acrid smell of gunpowder.

We retreat, regrouping around the biochemicals. The enemy presses in, and I can see the determination in their eyes. They aren't going to let us leave alive.

Suddenly, the lights flicker and go out, plunging the room into darkness. I hear a low, mechanical hum, and my blood runs cold. The sound promises nothing good.

"Cyborgs? What the fuck," someone screams out.

They emerge from the shadows, hulking figures of metal and flesh, patterned off a very different type of biped. Nothing human, which makes them look all the more terrifying. Their giant eyes glow with an eerie, unnatural light, and their movements are fluid.

Panic surges through me as I realize we are outmatched.

"Hold your ground," Hayes shouts, but his voice wavers.

The cyborgs attack with terrifying speed, their strength overwhelming. I watch in horror as one of them grabs Johnson, lifting him off his feet. He screams, a high-pitched, desperate sound that cuts off abruptly as the cyborg crushes him like a rag doll.

"Johnson!" McCready yells, firing wildly at the cyborg.

The bullets ricochet off its metal plating, doing minor damage. The cyborg turns its oversized eyes on McCready, moving with a predator's lithe beauty. Before he can react, it's on him, tearing him apart with its bare hands.

"No!" I shout, my voice breaking.

Chaos erupts around me. Some of the squad breaks ranks, running for their lives. They don't get far. Some sort of odd energy fire cuts them down, reducing them to smoldering heaps. Others fight valiantly, only to be overwhelmed by the cyborgs' sheer strength.

"Fall back!" Hayes screams, but there is nowhere to go.

I fire at a cyborg advancing on Zeke, the bullets sparking off its armor. It barely flinches, its eyes locking on me. I try to back away, but I trip over a fallen soldier, hitting the ground hard.

"Get up!" Zeke yells, but it is too late.

The cyborg reaches me in an instant, its cold metal hand wrapping around my arm. Pain shoots through me as it squeezes, the bones cracking under the pressure. I scream, a primal, animal sound.

"Let her go!" Zeke shouts, firing at the cyborg's head.

The bullets strike true, and the cyborg's head jerks back. It releases me, and I fall to the ground, clutching my pulped-up arm. The pain is blinding, every heartbeat sending waves of agony through my body.

"Come on, we have to move!" Zeke grabs my good arm, pulling me to my feet.

The fall seems endless, the abyss swallowing me whole as I plummet through the darkness. My lungs burn with each breath, the noxious fumes of something toxic scraping at my insides. I scratch and claw with my one good arm, desperate for something to hold on to, but there's nothing. My other arm—where is my other arm? The pain where it should be is a dull throb, a constant reminder of its absence.

The darkness presses in, squeezing my chest until I feel it might collapse around me. I can't breathe, can't think. I'm drowning in this abyss, and there's no escape. My screams are silent, swallowed by the void.

* * *

Suddenly, I feel something warm. It starts at my back, a gentle heat that spreads through my body, soothing the pain and the panic. It wraps around me, a comforting presence that makes the terror fade. It's nice, so very nice. I lean into it, letting the warmth calm me. For a moment, I almost forget where I am.

Then reality comes crashing back. I'm not falling anymore. I'm being held. The warmth is a body, and I'm pressed against it. My cheeks heat up with embarrassment, and I'm grateful for my dark skin hiding the flush.

Sensation returns to the rest of my body, and I realize I'm being spooned against a soft belly with smooth, velvety skin. My heart plummets as I crane my head back and see Drasuk.

"Get the fornicate off me," I yelp, struggling to break free.

Instead, he pulls me closer, cradling me against his underbelly with a tight grip around my waist. His other hand is hovering over my shoulder, as if he's completely fine with dragon-handling me like a jerk but isn't sure if he should touch me there.

My throat is still raw from the dream, and now my chest is filled with my rage at being confined.

20

Drasuk

The sound of her ragged breathing fills the silence. I have her held close, so she doesn't hurt herself as she thrashes out the rest of her fear.

My other hand instinctively reaches out, hovering over her trembling form. It's a strange sensation, the urge to comfort a creature so small and fragile. She's barely the size of my two legs, all sharp edges and delicate bones.

Hesitantly, I lower my hand, placing it gently on her shoulder. The warmth radiating from her skin sends a jolt through me, an urge that clashes with the tenderness I feel for her in this vulnerable state.

There's a morbid fascination in the way I hold her, a creature so easily broken cradled against me. The feeling is... unsettling, yet oddly comforting at the same time.

"Fornicator with mother. I didn't say you could touch me," she yelps, trying, and failing to scramble away from me as fast as her tangled limbs allow.

I can't help but snort, a deep rumbling sound that shakes the leaves around us.

"After so many invitations? You are obsessed with fornication. Are you that desperate for young?" I tease, the absurdity of the situation momentarily pushing aside the burning ember within me.

Her cheeks flare deep red, an interesting counterpoint to the pale moonlight filtering through the leaves onto her bright hair.

"No. Why would you say that? I keep telling you to leave," she grumbles, her voice still laced with a tremor of fear.

"Females only fornicate for young," I state, more to myself than to her.

It's a fact ingrained in my very being, a law as old as time from our early days on our original lava-strewn planet.

"What the fiery pit in the ground. That is complete food excrement. *Bullshit*. Women can fornicate any time they want. As much as they want," she sputters, her voice rising in pitch with every word.

"Fornicate that excrement."

I can't help but raise my forehead spines at her outburst.

Then what she's saying sinks in. The concept of females seeking pleasure for her own sake is certainly an alien concept, though not without precedence, of course.

Drakonid females are majestic creatures, aloof and powerful. They tolerate our advances during breeding cycles, but the act itself is a duty, a means to ensure the continuation of our lineage.

The thought of a female initiating such an act for her own gratification is... well, frankly, absurd.

Something for venom beasts, and, it seems, humans.

"Any time?" I repeat, the question rolling off my tongue before I can stop it.

Part of me is appalled, and another part disturbingly intrigued.

Might this explain my errant arousal? It's suspiciously like my odd obsession with Nkisa, which extended beyond a desire for hatchlings into something I never truly understood, beyond knowing it was unacceptable.

My hide shifts in shame, but I don't let her go.

She throws her hands up in exasperation, an awkward thing to do in her position. "Yes, Drasuk, where did you come from? Some rear-backward cave where females are nothing but walking wombs?"

I bristle at her words, a low growl rumbling in my chest. "Maln'Kril is a proud world, with even prouder females," I retort, offended.

"Well, your world is full of some seriously messed up ideas about women," she shoots back, craning her head back to stare me dead in the eye as her fiery spirit overshadows her earlier fear.

We lock eyes for a long moment, the air crackling with unspoken tension.

This is unlike any interaction I've ever had with a female. Females are either revered and kept at a distance, or they are fighting right alongside you and rarely have an interest in breeding.

Civilian females are the lifeblood of our society, the creators of our offspring, but extended interaction beyond a breeding contact is rare.

Here, with Kira, the lines are blurred.

She challenges me and insults me, yet I find myself drawn to her ferocity.

"Look," I finally say, breaking the silence. "You clearly don't want me here. But you're having nightmares, and this forest is teeming with dangers you can't even imagine."

She hesitates, her defiance flickering momentarily. She mutters something about danger, her voice barely audible.

"Creatures that can tear you limb from limb," I reply vaguely, not wanting to frighten her further.

She bites her lip, her gaze flickering around the forest nervously. Then, with a huff, she stops trying to wriggle out of my hold. It takes all of my control to avoid hissing with laughter at the recalcitrant look that finds its way onto her features.

21

Kira

Drasuk moves his face closer to mine, his voice calm and infuriatingly composed. "Besides, you were thrashing in your sleep. I was only keeping you from hurting yourself."

The shiver his warm breath causes from my head to my toes pisses me off.

"I don't need your help," I snap, my voice shaking with anger and residual fear.

Fuck. I could have done all this alone and not been stuck with trusting this big alien oaf to keep me safe. There's no time, and definitely no interest, in being all warm and fucking snuggly.

"Keep your head and just stay the fornicate alive," I mutter to myself.

"Well, that is always my plan, Kira."

The way he says my name sends another shiver through me and it takes me a beat longer than it should to realize he released his grip.

I scramble away, trying to put more distance between us, my body trembling.

Judging by the look in his eyes, he didn't miss my hesitation. Dammit.

"Why were you watching me?" I demand, glaring at him.

Drasuk tilts his head, his expression unreadable. "You seemed distressed. I was concerned."

"Concerned?" I laugh bitterly, rubbing the spot where his arm had held me. "Since when do you care about anything other than yourself?"

I know as I say it that I'm being unfair. I just met him. How would I even know? It's a low blow insult, even for me.

Something in me is panicking, though, bringing irrationality right along with it.

He doesn't respond immediately, just watches me with those unnervingly calm eyes.

"You're my ally," he finally says. "Your well-being affects my survival."

I snort, turning away from him. "Sure, it's all about survival, right? That's why you were getting all cuddly."

"You were dreaming about a fight gone wrong, weren't you?" he asks, ignoring my jab.

I hesitate, the images from my nightmare flashing through my mind. "Yes," I admit reluctantly. "It's hard to forget."

"I know the feeling," he says quietly.

I look back at him, surprised by the sincerity in his tone. "You? Haunted by anything?"

His eyes meet mine, and for a moment, I see a flicker of something—sorrow, maybe. "We all have our regrets, Kira."

The way he says my name, so soft and serious, makes my heart ache. I want to hate him, to push him away, but there's a part of me that's drawn to his strength, his calm in the face of everything.

It seems like every moment I've been with him I've been reactive.

I hate it.

"Why do you always have to be so infuriatingly perfect?" I mutter, sitting down and wrapping my good arm around my knees.

He raises his brow spines. "Perfect?"

"You're always so composed, so sure of yourself," I say, frustration bubbling up. "It's like nothing ever gets to you."

Drasuk sighs, looking away. "It's not about being perfect. It's about surviving. I've learned to control my emotions because letting them control me would get me killed."

I can't argue with that logic. It's something I've tried to do myself, but it's hard.

"I just... I don't know how to do that," I admit, my voice barely above a whisper.

He turns back to me, his eyes softening. "It's not easy. But you're strong, Kira. Stronger than you realize."

I scowl at him, the annoyance from his grip lingering, but a warmth blossoms in my stomach, too, a feeling I can't quite define. Pushing it aside, I glance up at the sky.

Still dark. Great. Just freaking fantastic.

"Look," I say, trying to keep my voice steady. "It's the middle of the damn night, and I can't sleep anyway. How about I take a second watch while you get some rest?"

Drasuk's spines shift again, his amusement clear. "I already slept."

My jaw clenches. "Already?" I grit out through my teeth. "What's the point of taking turns then, you giant idiot? We're supposed to be alert for threats."

He shrugs, his nonchalance pushing all my buttons. "Threats don't get by me when I sleep. Besides," he adds, a hint of a amusement in his eyes, "aren't you the one who just declared your undying love for taking a second watch? Well, get on with it already. Guard your superior as he rests."

"Undying love?" I sputter. "Don't twist my words, you giant iguana. I'm just saying the whole point of having watches is so everyone gets some damn rest, but also so someone is awake to keep an eye out. How the hell are you this much of a stupid rear?"

I take in a ragged breath, then continue. "Besides, what do you know of love? You seem to survive on pure arrogance."

After a long blink, he responds. "I am certainly aware of it. I have felt it from my brood."

That gives me pause. "Only your brood? Not a female? Or male? A partner, I mean?"

His spines shift in a way I can't interpret yet, but really wish I could. "If you mean a mate bond, then no. That doesn't occur in my species."

For a moment, I'm floored. No romantic love in his species? What the fuck?

Hell, who am I to judge? I never thought love meant anything and now I'll probably never experience it before dying on some fucking alien planet full of misogynists.

Should have taken my chances when I had them, I guess.

As usual, I push that worry down with bravado and deflection. "No wonder you only have room for arrogance. But, still, we need to have a better watch set up."

He lets out a rumbling chuckle that shakes the leaves above us. "Relax, little one. I assure you, I can sense danger even in my sleep. It's a drakonid advantage."

"Oh, great," I mutter sarcastically. "Supernatural senses. Just what I needed all the other threats out there to have on this lovely camping trip through Predatorville."

He wiggles his head, his amusement turning into something that looks suspiciously like... pity?

Ugh. The last thing I need is pity from a huge blue dino-dragon alien. Not all of us can be the size of an Asian elephant.

"Look," I say, my voice rising a notch. "I don't need you coddling me, okay? I can handle myself just fine. In fact, I've been handling myself just fine for the past however-long-it's-been we've been stuck on this stupid planet."

Drasuk opens his mouth to reply, but I cut him off. "And don't even try to tell me you're not sleeping. We all have to sleep. It's a biological necessity. Or are you some kind of mythical creature who thrives on pure conceit?"

He raises his hands in mock surrender. "Point taken. Sleep is important for even the most impatient humans."

I glare at him. Impatient? Is that what I am? Maybe a little. But mostly just frustrated. And terrified.

And maybe, just a tiny bit grateful for his presence despite everything.

Dammit.

"Fine," I grumble, sinking back down onto the makeshift shelter of branches and leaves. "But if anything attacks us while you're snoozing the sleep of the oblivious, I'm blaming you."

What the fuck Kira, I grumble internally.

I'm speaking out of both sides of my mouth. I hate that.

Drasuk lets out another low chuckle. "By all means. Just remember, if you're so helpless while you sleep, what good is a second watch, anyway?"

His words spark a fresh wave of anger. "Helpless?" I leap to my feet. "Who's calling who helpless? I may not have glowing blue scales and razor-sharp claws, but I can fight. I can think. I don't need someone like you telling me how to survive."

He raises the spikes along his forehead, his expression unreadable. Maybe amusement, maybe something else entirely. "Interesting choice of words," he says finally. "And, again, you do realize I don't have scales?"

I feel my cheeks burning, suddenly conscious of how ridiculous I must sound. Especially with all the fancy space-lingo he throws around.

"Close ascend, head of cock," I blurt out, hoping a good curse will shut him up for once.

Silence.

Then, to my horror, Drasuk bursts out laughing, a deep, rumbling sound that shakes the very ground beneath us. Tears of frustration well up in my eyes. Not only did I sound like a complete idiot when I tried to say *shut up*, but even my curse came out wrong in his alien language.

"Oh, fornicate," I mumble, sinking back down onto the leaves with a defeated sigh.

Finally, his laughter subsides. "Close ascend, head of cock?" he repeats, his spines wiggling.

"Yes," I mutter, feeling like I could crawl into a hole and die.

I knew I should have stopped trying to curse.

Nah, fuck that.

He regards me for a moment, then asks, with an almost playful seriousness, "Where do you want it? Actually, it's best if I pick where."

My head snaps up, my cheeks burning. "I wasn't—That didn't mean—" I stammer, completely flustered.

"Curse a thing. How do you insult people in your language?" I ask, my voice barely above a whisper.

Drasuk's amusement fades, replaced by a flicker of something else—curiosity maybe, or the hint of a playful challenge.

"We don't curse," he says simply. "There's no point. We communicate directly and state our observations and disagreements clearly."

I scoff. "Sounds about as exciting as watching paint dry."

"Perhaps," he replies, his gaze unwavering. "But it passes on our intentions well enough. Why leave room for double meaning? Isn't communication supposed to be clear and meaningful?"

I glance away, my cheeks still burning for fuck knows why. "Fine," I mutter. "Maybe your way is better. But it's still boring."

He lets out a soft puff of air, a sound that could almost be a chuckle. "Possibly, but it is effective."

He falls silent then, his gaze shifting back to the forest.

The silence stretches between us, thick and heavy, and with a huff, I put some distance between the two of us, grabbing my backpack as I head deeper into the foliage for some privacy.

I force myself to focus on something other than the infuriating Drasuk, turning my attention to the mess that is my pilfered pack, grateful for the bright moonlight. It contains some ammo for the unwieldy rifle I snagged, a medkit, some rolls of cloth-like materials I figured could come in handy as bandages, some bars of what look like rations.

The haphazard collection I managed to salvage from the soggy bastard and his friends tumbles out in a disorganized heap. Sorting through the mess might not be the most thrilling activity, but it's a job, and those provide a much-needed distraction.

The rustling of leaves from behind me is the first clue that my attempt at peace is about to be shattered.

Drasuk emerges from the undergrowth, his massive form easily navigating the dense foliage. This close, I can see the intricate patterns etched onto his blue hide catching the moonlight in an almost mesmerizing way. I clench my teeth, willing myself not to react.

Of course, silence seems to be my kryptonite, so I mumble some curses at him.

"So," he says, his voice a low rumble, "any plans to approach the glorious day ahead?"

Is he fucking with me here?

Gritting my teeth, I manage a tight smile. "Survival, mostly. Any brilliant ideas from your vast well of drakonid wisdom?"

The amusement playing in his eyes only serves to further irritate me.

"Patience, little one. The forest holds its secrets closely, but they will reveal themselves with time," he finishes in an overly exaggerated manner that I can't help but think is supposed to come off as sage.

Little one. Not my name. That's another thing I hate.

It's condescending, but a fullness flickers in my chest at the sound of it. Heat rises to my cheeks, and I quickly bend down to rummage through my bag again, anything to avoid looking at him.

Is it just the constant fear? The isolation? Maybe being stuck with a giant blue alien is messing with my head in more ways than one.

The thought sends a fresh wave of anger coursing through me. That's it. I'm officially pissed. Pissed at him, at the situation, at myself for feeling so... off-center around him.

Pushing myself to my feet, I grab a handful of dirt and grit from the forest floor. "Look," I say, my voice tight, "I appreciate the advice, but right now I could use some space."

Drasuk opens his mouth to protest, but I cut him off. "Just for a minute, okay? I need to think."

He looks at me for a long moment, his expression unreadable. Finally, he retreats farther into the trees. I let out a shaky breath, the tension draining from my shoulders as he disappears from sight.

With the awkward silence broken, I finally focus on the golden chest plate and bracers in my lap that I salvaged from the Graylord alien I managed to take down with a lucky shot from my not-so-cooperative gun cannon thingy.

The metal, once gleaming and proud, is now marred with scratches and dents from the fight.

A perfect symbol for my current emotional state.

I have a feeling that the gun itself is one bad shot or rough bump away from falling apart, and that does little to calm me down.

Anger spurs me on.

I grab a rock, scraping it across the surface of the armor, dulling the golden sheen with each determined stroke. The metal groans in protest, but I don't let up. Each scrape feels like a cathartic release, a defiance against the chaos this world has thrown me into.

As I work, the first blushes of dawn break. The air hums with the sounds of the forest—the chirping of unseen birds, the buzzing of insects.

Slowly, the rage begins to subside, replaced by a dull ache of exhaustion.

Finally, the armor lies dull and lifeless in my lap, a shadow of its former glory. Collapsing back against a tree trunk, I let out a long sigh. It isn't a solution, but it feels like a small act of rebellion in this messed-up world.

A twig snaps behind me, and I whip around, heart pounding. Drasuk stands there, a thoughtful expression on his face. He gestures toward the armor.

"What are you doing?"

I hesitate, unsure how much vulnerability I want to reveal. But the frustration that still simmers beneath the surface spills over. "Taking back a little control," I say, without putting much thought into it. "It's the only thing I seem to be able to do right now."

He stares at me for a moment, his gaze serious. "Control is an illusion," he says finally. "The only constant in the universe is change."

Is he some sort of closet philosopher under all that menace?

I scoff. "Easy for you to say, Mr. Super-Senses. You can probably smell danger coming from a mile away. All I have is this stupid rock and this hunk of useless metal."

He squints his eyes at me and goes to lean against a nearby tree. "So it would seem."

I scowl.

Yeah, fuck this guy.

Drasuk

I watch Kira as she meticulously cleans the golden armor. Her movements are precise and deliberate. Her clever little hands work with an alluring grace, wiping away the blood and grime that mar the once-gleaming surface.

There's a certain rhythm to her actions, a careful attention to detail that draws my gaze. She's not just going through the motions—she's dedicated to this task as if it's a way for her to reclaim some semblance of control in our chaotic world.

I can respect that. It must be difficult to be so small.

I've never thought of it that way before, just in terms of strength and weakness. I suppose maybe there is a type of strength that might rise from others being physically stronger.

Her fingers deftly untangle the straps, and she begins the process of fitting the armor to her small form. It's fascinating to watch her work. The armor is clearly designed for a braceaaer—a creature much thinner than she is—but she's determined to make it work.

"You look soft," I comment offhandedly, watching her struggle to fasten the last strap. "Soft and squishy."

She glances up at me, her eyes narrowing in irritation. "Do I? And you look like you need an extra hour to turn your giant body around," she retorts hotly. "Slow and stupid, that's what you are. You need more armor to make up for it. Case and point is your giant rear."

I snort, amused by her fiery response. "Slow and stupid, you say? Maybe I take my time because I know I don't need to rush. Unlike some fragile little human who thinks she can hide behind a few pieces of metal when it only takes one hit to crush."

Her eyes flash with defiance as she adjusts the armor's fit. "Fragile? At least I don't lumber around like a clumsy oaf. And for the record, this 'soft and squishy' human has outsmarted plenty of hunters on this planet, including you."

We trade more insults as she keeps trying to readjust the different armor pieces, our banter flowing easily now, each jab met with a quick retort. Eventually she growls out in frustration and seems to concede that the braceaaer armor just doesn't fit, letting it flop onto her lap with narrowed eyes.

It's strange, this weird relationship we've developed.

In my experience, interactions with Maj'Ra females feel no different than how you would interact with a male.

With Kira, there's a sense of companionship that's both unfamiliar in the undercurrents of tension and almost like being back with my battle group.

"Seriously, though," she says after a particularly biting comment about my sense of direction, "what's your deal with always having to hit things just once? You think you're some kind of one-punch wonder?"

I lean back, considering her question. "It's not about hitting things just once. It's about precision. Strength. Knowing exactly where to strike so that one blow is all you need."

She blinks, momentarily taken aback by the seriousness in my tone. But then she recovers, a thoughtful look crossing her face. "I guess that makes sense. You don't waste energy; you just get the job done."

"Exactly. Speed isn't everything. Sometimes, it's about being deliberate. Calculated."

She blinks, thinking over my points. Her gaze meets mine, a question lingering in its depths. Then, with a slow move of her head up and down, she grunts in agreement.

"But speed can be useful," she counters, her voice barely above a whisper. "Dodging attacks, maneuvering, and the like."

"True," I concede. "But for a drakonid, our strength and resilience are our greatest assets. A single well-placed blow can end a fight before it even begins."

We sit in silence for a moment longer, each lost in our thoughts. I can hear the hunter making its way toward us, three wet limbs moving along. It'll take it a while to get here, so I just enjoy the moment with her.

As the silence stretches, I find myself studying her more closely. The way the early morning light glints in her strange eyes, the determination etched into her features. There's something about her—something resilient and unyielding—that draws me in, despite my better judgment.

Suddenly, Kira speaks, her voice hesitant. "Drasuk," she begins, then stops, biting her lip. "Back there... with the nightmare..."

My gaze snaps to her face again, a flicker of concern sparking within me. "What about it?"

She hesitates, then blurts out, "Why did you touch me?"

I understand her apprehension.

Physical contact between draks is a rare occurrence, reserved for mating rituals, when someone needs help, or displays of dominance. Here, with Kira, the urge to reach out, to comfort her in her moment of fear, had been a powerful one, an alien impulse that I didn't fully understand.

Still don't.

"Like I said, you were writhing," I reply, the memory of her frantic movements sending a tremor through me.

Her eyes search mine, a flicker of vulnerability replacing the initial suspicion. "But... why my shoulder? You already had me contained."

"You are fragile," I explain, choosing my words carefully. "A drakonid's grip could easily crush you. A gentle touch was all that was needed."

The truth is more complicated.

The urge to touch her had been overwhelming, a magnetic pull I couldn't explain. The warmth of her skin beneath my rough hand, against the more sensitive skin of my underbelly, the vulnerability in her eyes—it was a sensation entirely new to me, both exhilarating and unsettling.

"Humans aren't that delicate," she scoffs, a hint of defiance returning to her voice. "We're tougher than we look."

I raise my forehead spikes. "Perhaps. But compared to a drakonid warrior..." I trail off, letting the implication hang in the air.

She stares off into nothing for a bit, then makes a noncommittal sound of agreement before turning her attention back to her task.

I blink at her.

Did I say something she didn't like?

Kira

The serene silence settles back around us, thick and comfortable. Drasuk's words hang heavy in the air—a simple statement laced with truth.

I don't have a good retort, and it bothers me. How am I going to survive here if there are more aliens like him?

He probably does hit like a truck.

My gaze drifts down to my lap, where the ruined armor lays discarded. Most of it is useless, but I decide to keep the bracers on and put the chest piece in my pack just in case there is a use for it. The rest just can't be fitted to me and I toss it under a bush with a growl, using my left arm without even having to think about it.

My fingers twitch toward the newly healed bicep, a reminder of the nightmare as I rub at it.

As observant as always, he notices. "Were you injured there during that dream memory?"

I almost ignore him, just like I've ignored anyone who asked. It's classified.

Then I remember where I am and the desire to share some of the misery and possibly expunge it makes my heart thump painfully in my chest.

I clear my throat. "The arm was all but ripped off during a botched operation. It barely worked before I came here. My career was over."

"As a warrior?'

"Yes. That mission was a disaster, and the rest of my original battle group died. The memory of their screams still haunts me."

He makes a low sound that manages to communicate his own shared experience.

That day has been the cause of my persistent nightmares. Despite the trauma, I all but begged to return to active service, but after months of healing and physical therapy, my arm never improved enough.

The familiar phantom ache blooms in my limb, a dull throb that never fully subsided until the genali took me. My squad was taken from me in a few short moments.

It's a memory I lock away most of the time, a gaping hole in my past that still manages to claw its way to the surface in the quiet moments.

And then I just up and dreamed about it. I hadn't had that dream in weeks.

Pushing the memory down, I flex my left hand. Fully functional flesh and bone, the familiar ache of exertion.

I still can't get over how seamlessly it moves. If I'm honest, all of me moves better than I have for years. Maybe better than I ever did.

A marvel of alien biology, a fully functioning limb thanks to those damned pink slime monster genali. It feels strange. Not alien, exactly, but different. Like wearing a well-made, but ill-fitting glove.

They did more than fix a limb, of course. The whole-body modification surgery, or whatever they did, is a mystery. A jumble of fragmented memories and hazy explanations.

The ability to speak alien languages after a single exposure, the persistent low hum of energy that seems to course beneath my skin, and the occasional, unexpected pang of regeneration when I scrape a knee.

What else were they hiding in me, these unwanted upgrades?

Lost in thought, I idly trace the unfamiliar curve of my new arm, the smooth, hairless skin nothing like the scars that used to be etched across it. My fingers brushes down to the tips of my fingers, and a frown mars my face.

Pink nails. The same disconcerting shade as my hair, which, much to my dismay, has somehow grown to midway down my back since yesterday.

I hate the pink. It screams 'alien experiment' louder than any other modification, though I suppose that's because I don't often see my eyes.

A quick look in the reflective glass was nauseating.

Scowling, I run my thumb over one of the newly formed nails. They are different. Thicker than human nails, with a slight, unsettling sheen.

An idea sparks in my mind, a flicker of defiance against the helplessness that gnaws at me. With a determined set to my mouth, I reach into my backpack and retrieve the makeshift glass shard.

So engrossed am I in my task, meticulously scraping and sharpening the pink nail into a point, that I don't notice Drasuk looming over me until his shadow falls across the makeshift workbench of leaves and twigs I created.

"What are you doing?" he rumbles, his voice deep and curious.

I flinch, startled, and nearly stab myself with the blade. "Ugh, you scared the living daylights out of me, Drasuk," I exclaim, tossing the glass shard down in annoyance.

"Do you survive on lights? What an odd form of sustenance."

"What? No."

"Then why—"

"Don't worry about it, lizard brain."

He regards me for a moment, his spines shifting in what might be concern, confusion, or possibly wondering how crazy I am.

"You were sharpening your nails?" he finally asks, the amusement evident in his voice.

Heat floods my cheeks. "Not exactly," I mumble, self-consciously flexing my newly sharpened appendage. "More like, uh, making them into weapons. You know, just in case."

The amusement in his eyes deepens.

"Interesting tactic," he rumbles out, his voice low. "Not very elegant, but perhaps effective for a human."

"Hey," I protest, puffing out my chest in mock indignation. "Don't underestimate the power of a good manicure, lizard man."

He chuckles, a deep, rumbling sound that vibrates through the ground. The sound, surprisingly, isn't unpleasant.

"I'm only guessing at what you mean, but perhaps not," he concedes, his amusement fading. "But is it truly wise to rely on such fragile weaponry?"

I narrow my eyes at him. "Fragile? Have you seen how thick these things are? They're practically claws now, thanks to you scaring the creativity out of me."

The spikes on his head rise, a playful glint in his slitted eyes. "Is that what it is? Creativity?"

"Don't mock me," I grumble, turning my attention back to my makeshift claws.

There is a relaxing silence for a while, broken only by the rasping of the glass against my nail. Then Drasuk speaks again, his voice softer this time.

"Carry on."

I roll my eyes, but don't bother pointing out to him that I don't need his permission. Instead, I get lost in the task of sharpening all of them.

He moves away at one point; I assume to patrol.

Soon after, Drasuk's voice rumbles from behind, causing me to jump and nearly mangle my finger with the makeshift blade. "Those are tiny, but definitely better now. I approve."

How can he move so silently, but then earlier sounded like a bulldozer moving through the trees?

My heart hammers in my chest. "I'm not doing things for your approval," I snap, throwing him a glare. "Fornicate in your own hole."

The words are out before I can filter them. A knee-jerk reaction fueled by frustration and lingering anger over his selective use of stealth. Even though I've tried the same insult and failed miserably at it.

He lets out a soft, amused rock grinding sound. "So you like it that way? Is the goal to list all the ways you like it before we try?"

His voice is laced with a teasing lilt that sends a prickle of heat up my neck and then down from there.

Down low indeed.

"I'm not talking about me," I grumble.

I say it again in English this time, knowing he won't understand, but it makes me feel better.

"See? It wasn't an invitation."

His spikes shift again, and his eyes let me know he is still getting way too much enjoyment out of making me squirm.

"I see," he drawls. "It's a delightfully creative way to express your displeasure."

I clench my jaw. Talking to him is like walking through a minefield—one wrong step and I'll detonate. There is no winning with this alien.

It doesn't help that my go-to method of deflection makes me look like a fool.

Fucking genali tech.

He seems to take my silence as an invitation to continue. "Perhaps a more conventional insult would be better suited to the situation?"

His voice has a mock seriousness that makes me want to throw something at him.

A crack of a twig catches my attention before I can reply, and I snap my head in that direction.

"It is merely a genali, they will be in range in moments."

"What the fornicate, Drasuk? I need some warning about this excrement."

He ignores me and simply stares in the direction of the approaching noise. I pull out my gun, assuming he will go pounce on the thing, but instead he just stares.

I look away from him, shaking my head. I can't figure him out.

A moment later I see the flash of gray, and within a breath I take aim, squeeze the trigger, satisfied when I see the spray of gray blood.

"Well done, Kira."

"You need to tell me if something is coming."

He looks back over to me. "Noted, though it's a poor reflection of your species that it got that close before you knew."

Motherfucker. Instead of engaging this time, I manage to keep my mouth shut. Time to wrap up the chores and get moving. I've got women to save, if I survive all of the verbal sparring with this iguana.

The wind whips past, tugging playfully at the strands of my long hair. It's a reminder of the unexpected changes the aliens inflicted on me.

I set down the makeshift blade and reach for my salvaged military knife.

Drasuk's head tilts as he watches me. "And what might you be planning with that?"

He isn't moving away, so he must know I don't plan to stab him. Or doesn't care.

Yes, probably the latter. Ugh.

"A haircut," I mutter, already sawing at the thick hair cascading down my back. "Then we need to leave."

The alien tinkering may have provided some clear benefits, but it didn't make the hair any easier to manage. The long strands feel like an unwelcome tether, a constant reminder of my captivity.

He chuckles, a low, rumbling sound that vibrates along the ground and sends a pleasant shiver through me. "An unconventional approach, but perhaps effective. Are you sure you wouldn't prefer assistance?"

I snort. "From you? Doubtful. You'd probably cut my head off just to test your skills."

"Possibly. Although," he adds with a mischievous glint in his eyes, "I wouldn't want to deprive you of the opportunity to create your own masterpiece."

His words are laced with a playful undercurrent that makes me suspect he is still messing with me. Is there a goal to it? A way to lower my guard for some unforeseen reason?

It's an unsettling realization—has this alien been toying with me all along, even after we called a truce? Has the teasing, the almost flirtatious banter been a deliberate strategy?

It seems impossible, yet I don't know what his angle is.

Or why he is so damn interested in everything I do.

I ignore him, focusing back on my hair. With a practiced hand, I hack away at the hair, aiming to simply get it as short as possible. It won't be winning any awards, but it is practical and efficient.

As the hair falls away in clumps, a sense of satisfaction washes over me.

It's a small victory, a way of reclaiming a piece of myself. I just hope I don't have to do it three times a fucking day or the good vibes will wear off really damn quick.

Drasuk watches me in silence for a moment, his expression unreadable. Finally, he speaks. "You know, humans are an intriguing species."

"How so?" I mumble, still focused on checking for missed strands of hair from my impromptu haircut.

"Your capacity for both resilience and self-destruction is fascinating," he says, his voice thoughtful.

I give a humorless laugh. "Resilience, huh? Maybe."

It feels like a loaded word given the situation I find myself in.

"Indeed," he continues. "Facing a situation like this, I assume most of your kind would crumble. Yet, here you are, sharpening your nails and cutting off your hair."

"What am I supposed to do?" I grouse, dropping the knife and turning to face him fully. "Just sit here and wait for them to dissect me?"

He takes a step back, a hint of surprise on his big blue face. "Dissect you? No, I highly doubt that was their plan."

"Then what was the plan, Drasuk?" I challenge. "Because so far, everything with you aliens seems to be one big, confusing experiment."

He hums noncommittally. "Actually, I'm being hunted for my skull. You are being hunted for... another body part. I doubt they'd have the facilities to experiment on us here."

It reminds me of the women. I'm going to have to tell him about them. Now that I know him a bit better, I think the risk to them is minimal and if his sense of smell is as good as I think it is, then he is perfect for this task.

I give him the flattest look I can muster, before letting out an explosive sigh and returning to the task of cutting the rest of the stray strands of my hair.

24

Drasuk

My gaze flickers between Kira and the newly diminished length of her hair, the scent of genali blood heavy in the air. Each swipe of the blade sends a shower of vibrant pink cascading down to the forest floor.

It is an undeniably strange sight, this ritualistic shedding of what humans called hair. Threads, perhaps, would be a more accurate term from my perspective. Long, fibrous strands that seem to serve no real purpose other than perhaps rudimentary temperature regulation.

Or maybe mere ornament?

An illogical pang of something akin to disappointment flashes within me as I watch the vibrant pink diminish. It is an illogical sentiment, I know. Why should I care about the color of her hair?

Yet, the sight of it, so different from my leathery hide, holds a certain intrigue I cannot deny.

Curiosity gnaws at the edges of my notoriously overthinking brain.

In one regard, the practicality of her actions is undeniable. Unrestrained, the hair would become a tangled mess, a hindrance in any potential struggle for survival. Yet, a small, illogical part of me mourns the loss of the softness it brought to her otherwise sharp features.

Her tongue is sharp enough. She needs something soft to counterbalance it.

I reach out a clawed hand and pluck a few strands from the ground. The texture is unlike anything I'd ever felt—smooth, almost silky, with a surprising strength despite its delicate appearance.

I bring it closer to my snout, inhaling deeply.

The scent that hits me is unexpected, a subtle sweetness tinged with something faintly floral. It is a pleasant surprise, a stark contrast to the earthy, metallic smells that dominate my world.

Compelled by an urge I don't understand, I lift the strands to my mouth and take a tentative bite.

The taste is... interesting.

Not unpleasant, but unfamiliar. A fibrous texture with a hint of the same sweetness I smelled earlier. Before I can fully process the sensation, a sharp voice cuts through the air.

"What the fiery pit in the ground do you think you're doing, Drasuk?"

I blink, startled, the offending pink strands dangling limply from my maw. I must look utterly ridiculous, a mighty Maj'Ra chewing on a human's hair.

"I... I..." is all I manage to stammer, my voice uncharacteristically thick.

I clear my throat and try to recover my lost dignity

"I was just... examining it."

The lie tastes as foreign in my mouth as the hair, though decidedly less pleasant.

Kira stares at me, her expression a mixture of disgust and amusement.

"Examining it by eating it?" she deadpans.

Heat creeps over my chest and I don't know how to get her to focus elsewhere, let alone explain what I was doing and why.

"It... smelled pleasant," I mumble, feeling a small prickle of unpleasant emotion, but becoming more confident.

I've decided it was definitely an excellent idea all along by the time Kira snatches the remaining strands of hair from my grasp.

She scowls with an intensity that could curdle a vat of energon sludge, using the tip of her knife to dig a shallow hole in the earth. The implement isn't designed for such ill use, the metal groaning in protest as she pries loose clumps of dirt.

Finally, with a triumphant grunt, she deposits the hair into the makeshift grave and buries it with a flurry of displaced soil.

"That was a perfectly good snack you're wasting there," I rumble.

She doesn't seem to be fooled by yet another one of my foul-tasting lies.

Kira's face contorts in a look of disgust that threatens to curdle my insides.

"Good snack?" she chokes out, the single word punctuated by a series of dry heaves.

Her glare is sharp enough to pierce through my thick hide, making me instinctively shrink back.

I clear my throat. "All the best snacks are stolen ones."

"Stolen hair snacks?"

The silence stretches, thick and uncomfortable.

My attempt at humor backfires spectacularly, leaving us both floundering. Kira seems to be wrestling with herself, her mouth opening and closing like a fish gasping for air. Finally, she gives up the fight with a frustrated sigh that sends a stray strand of her newly shorn hair fluttering from her cheek.

"I don't have a response for that."

Then she simply gets up, stalking toward where the dead genali is lying in its own blood. I move to join her, coming close just as she finishes stripping the puddle of anything useful.

Then she walks off, continuing in the direction we were headed before, I hurry to catch up. When I get to her, she takes a long breath, clearly ready to speak.

Hopefully not about hair snacks.

"Look," she begins, her voice laced with weariness, "There's something you need to know..."

Her words trail off, and she squeezes her eyes shut, rubbing at them with her small hands for a moment as she moves.

The awkwardness presses down on me, suffocating. Part of me, a basic, drak instinct, urges me to break the silence with some witty retort, some display of dominance. Another, quieter part urges caution.

This human, this Kira, is different. There's a vulnerability beneath her bravado, a flicker of fear that resonates deep within me.

Finally, after what feels like an age, Kira speaks again, her gaze settling on the forest floor. "We don't know where this 'drop zone' is," she says, her voice barely a whisper. "And until we do, we need to..." She trails off again, searching for the right words.

"Need to do what?" I prompt gently, the rumble in my chest softer than usual.

She lets out a tired huff. "Look, Drasuk," she starts, then stops again, her frustration evident. "We need to find others. More women like me."

So she does have more information she's been keeping to herself. I had suspected as much, considering how guarded she always is.

"More pets?" I ask, the question slipping out before I can stop it.

Her head snaps over to me, and her eyes narrow into slits. "Pets?" she spits, the word dripping with venom. "No. I knew it was a bad idea to bring it up. You are disgusting."

Now that we are back to flinging insults, I feel much more in my element. I let out a rumble of relief.

"So, they're bigger and less squishy?" I prod, unable to resist.

The look on her face could launch a spaceship. For a moment, I think she might actually lunge at me, new little pink claws bared.

"No," she mutters between clenched teeth, her voice strained with a mixture of anger and something else, something I can't quite decipher.

My amusement bubbles over, erupting in a series of guttural guffaws that echo through the trees. The sound, a rasping rumble that falls somewhere between a boulder crashing and a volcano bellowing, surprises me with its power.

Kira, however, simply stares at me, a look of bewildered exasperation etched on her face.

The sight only fuels my laughter, the sound resonating through my chest.

With a final, earth-shaking tremor, I manage to get my laughter under control. Kira, however, isn't quite so forgiving. She snatches the hilt of her knife from an odd little pocket, the one she hadn't used for the hair-burial ceremony, stands up, and with a practiced flick of her wrist, sends it flying through the air.

The dagger, a dull, utilitarian blade more suited for survival than combat, finds its mark with a satisfying thud, landing squarely on the top of my foot.

I stop walking, staring at it.

The pain is negligible, a mere pinprick compared to the battles I faced on Maln'Kril. But the sheer audacity of the attack is enough to silence my laughter.

At least for now. I feel it lurking right at the edges.

Kira stands there, arms crossed, her chest heaving with a mixture of anger and something else, perhaps a flicker of amusement mirroring my own.

"See if you find that funny now, *lizard* brain," she says, her voice laced with venom.

I stare at her in silence for a moment before I resume laughing.

"You're impossible," she mutters, but there's an answering mirth in her tone that lets me know she isn't immune to my charm.

25

Kira

Drasuk's laughter, a sound like boulders clashing together, rumbles through the forest.

Loud as always, the dummy.

Despite myself, I can't help the small smile tugging at my lips. This weird lizard-dragon companion of mine is impossible. Absolutely impossible. His eye-squinting expression, something he does when he laughs, is almost endearing.

Almost.

It would have been better for me to handle retrieving all the women on my own, and Drasuk's response didn't exactly make me feel confident. I regret sharing now, but he doesn't seem to want to harm them.

I'll just have to keep forging ahead and hope they don't hate me for having Mr. Insulting tagging along, questioning their status as free agents.

I snort at him. "Since I crashed in the desert, there's a possibility that the main ship itself also crashed nearby. They are probably still in it. Do you think you could track the scent?"

Drasuk, still chuckling, tilts his head thoughtfully. "Yes, but we should also look from a height. We should travel along the boundary between desert and forest. That way, I can climb the tall trees at intervals and get an elevated view of the area."

I mull it over. It's a solid plan. "Alright, let's move out." I gesture forward, and he follows.

We walk in silence for a while. The only sounds are the crunching of sand beneath our feet and the occasional rustle of leaves. The tension of our earlier conversation lingers, but it's manageable.

My mind wanders, and boredom sets in.

An idea strikes me, and I decide to branch out with my insults. Experiment a little.

I try to say *prick*, testing the Drakonid translation. It comes out as *poking cock*.

Drasuk rumbles with amusement, which blends with the crunching sounds of our feet. "I would, but you refuse to tell me where."

I groan, rolling my eyes. "How is that anything like the same? It's an insult, not a description. Whoever made this translation program fornicated it up."

He starts to reply, but his words die in his throat. His body tenses, and he stops dead in his tracks. I follow his gaze, the hairs on the back of my neck standing up.

A thunderous sound erupts from the desert sand, and something huge bursts out with force, spraying hot sand everywhere. I barely manage to dodge to the side, instinctively doubling back to Drasuk, my gun raised, curses tumbling out of my lips.

The creature before us is a big, nasty thing with six legs and thick, rough brown skin marked with ovals. It raises on its front legs like a caterpillar, its skin thick and mottled everywhere except along its back and tail, which is covered in long, spiked white hair. Its many eyes glisten ominously, and it's even bigger than Drasuk's beefy nine-foot frame.

The creature speaks, its voice a guttural growl. "You look delicious," it says, its words translated perfectly by whatever changes the slimes made to me.

I swallow hard, trying to speak its language, which sends the usual spike of pain down my throat. "We are not food," I say, the words feeling strange on my tongue.

The creature doesn't respond, its eyes continuing to rove over us like we are a tasty treat.

"Don't bother with that," Drasuk hisses out. "Prepare for a fight."

We stand there in a tense standoff, the air thick with anticipation. My heart pounds in my chest, and my grip tightens on my gun, not wanting to be the first to attack just in case this can be settled without violence. Drasuk's claws flex, his body coiled like a spring ready to pounce.

The creature growls again as it sweeps its gaze over us, hunger clear in its gaze.

The creature's growl sends a shiver down my spine. Its many eyes lock onto us with an unnerving interest. Drasuk and I stand our ground.

It makes me wish I had a better knife, dammit. Not to mention a better gun.

My heart pounds in my ears, adrenaline coursing through my veins as I mentally catalogue how to reach other weapons, ready for whatever comes next.

With a blood-curdling half hiss, half screech, the creature closes in on us, shattering any hope for a peaceful alternative, its movements surprisingly swift for something so massive.

I aim and squeeze the trigger, the gun's report echoing through the forest. The bullet strikes the creature's hide, but it barely flinches.

Its rough skin must be tougher than it looks. Just like Drasuk. Ridiculous and fucking unfair.

With a sudden flick of the end of its long body, the creature whips me away like a rag doll. Pain explodes in my side as I'm sent flying through the air.

I hit the ground hard, skidding across the rough terrain before slamming into the base of a tree. My head spins, and for a moment, I can't breathe.

The world is a blur of pain and disorientation.

An angry bellow from Drasuk cuts through the haze. I struggle to push myself up, my vision swimming. I can barely make out Drasuk grappling with the creature, its massive form towering over him. The thing has its tail wrapped around his throat, lifting him off the ground. He claws at it, but it looks like he is barely patting the thing.

It doesn't match anything I thought I knew about him. He's just letting it strangle him.

I force myself to my feet, my vision clearing as I stumble forward. The creature is focused on Drasuk, giving me a chance to act. I raise my gun again, my hands shaking, and fire. The bullet strikes one of its many eyes, and it howls in pain, its grip on Drasuk loosening.

I run toward them, my legs feeling like heavy weights. My vision blurs again, but I blink it away, focusing on what's in front of me. Drasuk manages to break free, gasping for breath.

He just stands there, muscles tense, like he is having some sort of internal battle.

The creature quickly recovers, turning its attention back to me, recognizing that I am the bigger threat.

"Fornicate, Drasuk. Fight!"

He just stands there, trembling.

As it closes in, the creature's many eyes glint with malice. I shoot again, aiming for another eye, but it's too quick, dodging to the side. It lunges at me, and I barely dodge out of the way, its claws swiping through the air where I stood moments ago.

Drasuk charges at it, his powerful legs propelling him forward.

I assume he intends to slam into the creature, knocking it off balance, and some of my panic eases.

Instead, he swerves at the last moment, his momentum making him hit a tree with a loud crack. The creature swipes at him and this time Drasuk manages to hold on to it.

I can't understand why he isn't using his claws to tear into it. Instead, they grapple, a tangle of limbs and tails. I take advantage of the distraction, moving in close and firing another shot.

This time, the bullet hits its mark, striking one of the creature's eyes dead center.

It screams, a high-pitched, keening wail that makes my ears ring. It thrashes, trying to dislodge Drasuk, but he holds on, his claws digging into his own limbs, leaving long scores.

He's lost his fucking mind.

I fire again and again, each shot taking out another eye. The creature's movements grow more frantic, more desperate.

But it's not done yet. With a mighty heave, it throws Drasuk off, sending him crashing to the ground, then swipes at him, leaving long gashes on his neck. It turns its attention back to me, its remaining eyes filled with rage. I back away.

My gun is almost empty, but I refuse to show fear.

It charges at me, and I dive to the side, barely avoiding its snapping jaws. I roll to my feet and fire again; the bullet hitting one of its few remaining eyes. The creature roars in pain, but it's not enough to stop it.

It lunges again, and I have no choice but to meet it head-on.

With a burst of adrenaline-fueled strength, I close the distance, dodging its claws and teeth. I slam the barrel of my gun into one of its eyes and pull the trigger. The creature's roar of pain is deafening, but it's still not dead.

I keep pushing forward, using my gun like a club, bashing at its eyes with all my strength.

Finally, the creature falters. It stumbles, its many eyes reduced to bloody sockets. With one last desperate effort, I shove the gun into its largest eye and fire. The creature convulses, its death throes shaking the ground beneath us.

It collapses with a final, shuddering breath, its body twitching before going still.

I stand there, panting, covered in sweat and blood. My entire body aches, but I can't rest yet. Drasuk needs help, if he's even still alive. I move to his side, pushing the creature's bloody corpse off him. He's breathing hard, blood seeping from wounds on his neck.

"Are you okay?" I ask, my voice hoarse.

Drasuk winces. "I'll live. Thanks to you."

I help him to his feet, supporting his weight as best I can, which is pretty much not at all since he's massive. As we move away from the creature's corpse, I feel a sharp pain in my stomach. I look down and see the creature's spiked hair embedded in my flesh, blood flowing down the thin black suit.

"Great," I mutter, gritting my teeth against the pain. "Just what I needed."

We find a relatively safe spot and collapse to the ground. I dig into my pack for medical supplies, pulling out a spray container. I experiment with it for a moment before using it on the gashes on Drasuk's neck. The spray hisses as it comes into contact with his wounds, but it seems to help.

"Hold still," I say, trying to keep my hands steady.

My vision blurs again, and I blink rapidly, trying to clear it, then shake my head when it doesn't.

"Something wrong?" Drasuk asks, noticing my discomfort.

"It's nothing. What the fiery pit in the ground happened back there, Drasuk? I thought we were a team?"

"I... I don't know, Kira. It's like I couldn't attack it. Every time I tried, my body betrayed me. The most I was able to do was try to hold it down."

"You were able to attack me. What the fornicate?"

"Yes. And I killed genali before finding you."

"Probably another one of the ways they modified us. They said something about prey not being able to harm each other when they were talking about this place. They must have skipped that little upgrade for the sand eater over there. Fornicate. I hate the genali."

"I heartily agree, little human."

My eyelid twitches at his insistence on insulting nicknames, but I don't call him on it. For the first time, there isn't any jesting in his voice. No arrogance either.

It's scary as fuck.

He looks vulnerable for a moment before my vision blurs again. I reach up a hand and use the back of it, the only part of it not covered in grime and blood, to wipe at my eyes.

"Tell me what is bothering you," he demands.

"I don't know," I admit, blinking again. "Can you see what's wrong with my eyes?"

Drasuk leans in, his slitted pupils narrowing as he examines me. "You have a nictitating membrane," he says, his voice filled with curiosity.

"A what?" I ask, confused.

"A second eyelid," he explains.

"Like one of the slimes? Fantastic," I mutter, shaking my head. "Just what I needed."

Drasuk chuckles, the sound deep and rumbling. "You did well, Kira. Very well."

I blink at the praise, unsure how to respond. This new rapport is making me wish he'd go back to insulting me.

I know how to respond to that. Maybe not in the most grown-up fashion, but it's familiar ground at least.

I don't have a ready reply.

Instead, I focus on being busy, pulling out a replacement clip for the gun and clicking it into place, then grabbing medical supplies to tend to my wounds. I only have one more clip after this one and it makes me uneasy.

The road rash on my arms and legs stings, but I grit my teeth and clean them as best I can. The pain in my stomach is worse, but I manage to remove most of the spiked hair and bandage the wound.

As I work, I can't help but reflect on the fight. It was brutal and exhausting, but we made it through. Barely. I glance over at Drasuk, who's watching me with a mixture of respect and distress.

"Thanks," I say finally, my voice soft. "For having my back."

Even if he did leave me with all the work, aside from providing a bit of distraction.

Hell, I can handle all of this shit without him. If I haven't proven that by now, especially after fighting something straight out of a monster compendium, I don't know what would.

It feels good, but the sense of pride is fleeting when I glance at him again.

He looks defeated. I realize this is the perfect time to ditch the arrogant fool. Something tells me he wouldn't resist right now.

I huff out a breath. No, that wouldn't be right. I made a promise. Besides, he's useful. There's no sense in being upset with him for a limitation the genali put on him. He did what he could.

His expression is vacant now. Something tells me he isn't as forgiving of himself.

I'd just started getting used to his jokes. I don't like him like this and the urge to cheer him up is strong. To let him know it wasn't his fault.

My world shifts again. I'm not exactly known for being magnanimous.

I've had too many changes recently to analyze that one, so I return to treating my wounds and bite my tongue. It's probably temporary.

It fucking better be. This place will eat me alive if I go soft.

26

Drasuk

The battle hormones begin to fade, and I settle into a state of watchfulness as Kira tends her wounds.

I've never hated the genali more than I do right now. I was just saved by a tiny creature as I failed to uphold my half of our agreement. A Maj'Ra can't simply stand by while someone else defends them.

It isn't done.

I'm just as shocked she isn't pointing out my failure as I am outraged by my impotence. She should be reaming me with all kinds of insults about cowardice. I know she has a creative insult for any possible occurrence.

I would have earned every one of them.

I'd feel a lot better if she did. This is far worse. Instead, she patched me up and thanked me, and now she's acting like nothing happened.

Like I didn't just put her life at risk because I couldn't fight, which makes me feel sick on a whole other level beyond self-reproach. Some foreign sort of fear I have never experienced that centers around needing her to remain with me.

What does it mean?

I don't know what to say now.

The hiss of the spray container fills the air as she applies it to her stomach, where the creature's spiked hair has embedded itself. She winces, but keeps working, determined and focused.

Suddenly, Kira lets out an battle-fueled laugh, a sharp and unexpected sound that startles me. I don't see what's so funny about barely surviving that fight, and I can't help but tilt my head in confusion.

"Strange pet," I mutter, more to myself than to her.

I'm desperately seeking some sort of normalcy, which apparently involves poking at her to see if she'll be mean to me again.

I'm disgusted with myself.

She bristles, her eyes flashing with irritation. "Since I can't get rid of you, you might as well stop calling me a pet and just call me Kira."

I rumble out a laugh, amused by her defiance, grasping on to it like it's my last hope. "Very well, Kira. Then you can stop calling me a fumbling fornicator and use my name, too."

She smirks, mischief in her eyes. "I'll think about it."

I scoff, then fall silent, the pain in my neck minimal now thanks to her ministrations. It didn't really need to be dressed, but I enjoy the feel of her hands on me, so I said nothing.

My mind shies away from that pleasure and what it might mean.

Once she's finished, Kira suggests we move out of the area and find a place to wash up. I agree, and we head deeper into the trees, leaving the divide between desert and forest behind us. The thick foliage provides some cover, and the air is cooler here, a welcome relief from the desert's oppressive heat.

We walk in relative silence for a short while, my ears pulsing as I listen more intently to avoid a repeat of the last encounter.

I'll need to kill something, preferably brutally, to get the foul taste of failure out of my mouth, but for now we should nurse our wounds and get our focus back.

The silence stretches on, punctuated only by the rhythmic crunch of our feet on the damp forest floor. The dense foliage overhead creates a dappled light, casting swirling shadows on the mossy ground.

I'm startled when she starts speaking again. "Your wound is already closing. Do draks really heal that fast?"

"Not naturally. We have excellent regeneration, but it's helped along by nanites."

She grunts. "Did they put those in me? Because I'm healing faster than normal."

I look over at her, reminded again of just how little she knows about the wider universe. "From the way you look, I would guess there are billions of them in you, doing things I didn't even know were possible. Plus, of course, your translator."

"Is that why my throat hurts like a fiery pit in the ground sometimes?"

"Yes. It's been used for millennia and has always been painful."

She mutters some more of her human curses but doesn't continue the conversation.

Flight-capable creatures call out to each other, and the rustling of leaves creates a soothing backdrop. The path we follow is uneven, the ground covered in roots and fallen branches, but it's manageable.

We descend into a small valley not far from from the forest's edge, the air thickening with humidity as we delve deeper into it.

Impatience niggles at me. The oppressive quiet is grating on my nerves. "I have to admit, Kira," I rumble, breaking the silence, "your fighting instincts are impressive."

She shoots me a sideways glance, a look etched on her face I haven't seen before. "Just my instincts, huh?" she snarks.

"There's finesse there," I concede, "a certain efficiency. Not what I'd expect from such a fragile creature."

There's a flash of movement as her hand darts out, the middle finger extended in what I assume must be an obscene gesture.

"What's that mean?"

Kira rolls her eyes, the exasperation evident. "Never mind," she mutters, shoving the offending digit back into the company of its brethren.

I frown, the movement shifting my forehead spines together. Did I offend her?

My gaze flickers to the bandages wrapped around her stomach, a silent reminder of the creature we just faced. Perhaps I was too blunt in my assessment.

Or maybe it's that little episode from this morning, the one involving a dull knife, a rather dramatic haircut, and pink threads dangling from my mouth

It seemed like the right thing to do at the time, and the memory of it brings back the tantalizing scent.

Feeling a pang of something I can't name—an unfamiliar and unwelcome sensation—I decide to give her some space.

But apologizing? Not a chance.

My pride, an age-old trait baked into the very ground of our planet and culture, forbids it. Not for this, at least.

Besides, what do I even apologize for?

For the hundredth time since we were thrust together, I find myself pondering the enigma that is Kira.

This small, seemingly fragile creature harbors a wellspring of aggression that would put even the fiercest Maj'Ra to shame. How can something so physically delicate possess such a potent fighting spirit?

Natural evolution truly does work in the strangest of ways.

An irritated huff from beside me snaps me out of my internal monologue and I pay better attention to our surroundings. I can hear and smell water.

Maybe if I pose my compliment like a question, it will be better received.

"Where did you learn to fight so effectively?"

We walk for a while longer and I keep myself from adding any more. She'll answer if she wants. When she wants. The path grows steeper and more treacherous, and we choose our steps more carefully.

Finally, the dense foliage parts, revealing a sight that makes my hide shiver in appreciation. A clear stream cascades down a smooth rock face, forming a deep pool at its base. Sunlight glints off the surface of the water.

The sight of water is welcome. Maybe it will wash off the last of my unease.

Kira heads toward it, breaking the silence. "I was born to military parents," she starts, her voice steady. "Most of my childhood was spent moving from one active war zone to the other in a state on the brink of collapse, so my parents didn't have much of a choice when it came to good schools or hatchling care."

She snorts at the last sentence, and I blink, I didn't find it particularly funny, but for some reason she did.

Were all humans so desensitized to violence? You'd think their evolutionary path would better equip them for such a lifestyle, since they seemed to love it so much.

She continues, dragging me out of my reverie.

"My parents loved us and loved each other, but we sacrificed a lot for the sake of peace that was ever-elusive. It seemed like the more we fought, the more battles there were. Eventually, my father was killed in action. My mother mostly held it together until the last of us left home, but she was never the same. His death broke her."

I blink, absorbing what that means, and not only because of the sadness that would have caused her.

She is from one of the species who form deep, lasting bonds. A thrill passes through me, and then I stamp it down, another wash of shame rising on its heels.

That should hold no interest to a drakonid. None at all.

"I attended military school all the way to *academy* level and became a *corporal* for the *American Marine Corps* stationed in *Maine*. Soon enough, we were granted clearance for international operations."

A lot of that didn't translate, but I think I understood enough. I'm afraid she'll stop talking if I interrupt, so I let it pass.

She pauses, her eyes distant as she recalls her past. "I fought countless battles and moved up the ranks until the disastrous day we raided a bio-terrorist cell in *Antarctica*. The raid started off successfully, but it all went to a fiery pit in the ground. There were fornicating cyborgs."

Human civilization already had access to cyborgs? Interesting. Slaves are usually taken from the more primitive planets.

"No one believed me about the cyborgs."

That explains it. They must have been purchased from an outside force. Probably genali or braceaaer.

"I lost my entire battle-group, so I wouldn't say I learned how to fight all that well, would you?"

She stops speaking, her heart clearly constricted by the memories. I give her a level look, feeling the weight of her story.

"You have lived a warrior's life," I state bluntly.

Kira glances at me, her eyes shadowed by grief and resolve. "Yeah, I guess I have."

"Sometimes that means you are the only one left alive."

She doesn't respond, but I can see that she is thinking over my words. "Surviving is often the harder route," I add.

It's a fact only a warrior would truly understand.

After a moment to let her ponder, I decide to share a bit of my own story.

I don't imagine it'd be fair to hear a warrior's struggles and pain and not share one of my own.

"I was born on Maln'Kril. It's a relatively small planet in drakonid space, protected by warriors like myself. From a young age, we are trained to fight, to survive. It's in our blood, our very essence. My clan, the Raskhar, is known for its ferocity in battle."

Kira listens intently, her eyes fixed on me. "So, you've been fighting your whole life, too?"

I make a rumble of agreement. "Yes. But it is not just about fighting. It's about honor, loyalty, and protecting our kin. Every battle is a test, a chance to prove oneself."

I take a deep breath, recalling the countless creatures we must fight off constantly. "There are many dangers. One of the most formidable is a giant creature with an affinity for electricity. Its body can generate massive electrical storms, making it incredibly dangerous. Then there's the xylanth, a large long-bodied species capable of flight. Their skin is as hard as any metal, making them nearly impervious to our weapons."

Kira gapes at me, her eyes wide with shock. "No wonder you evolved to be built like *tanks*. Everything you fight off is insane."

My spikes drift together in my confusion. "*Tanks*?"

She waves a hand dismissively. "An armored vehicle. Never mind. But seriously, how did your planet end up with such monstrous creatures?"

I feel a hint of embarrassment as I explain. "It's not something we talk about very often, but most of the predatory swarms we have to fight off are the result of our own actions. Before we colonized the planet, we bombarded large swathes of the planet during nuclear and antimatter weapon tests. This had the unintended effect of triggering a volatile evolution in the formerly single-celled organisms that existed on its surface."

Kira stares at me for a moment, making me uneasy.

Then, she laughs at me. I grumble in irritation, feeling the need to defend my ancestors.

27

Drasuk

"They were a bit reckless with their weapon tests," I admit hastily. "A lot of the planet is considered 'no life zones' because of the constant devastation from energy and biological weapon, but they did it to make sure we had effective weapons to defend ourselves."

She continues to laugh, clutching her sides, and I sigh in exasperation.

"It's not funny," I grouse.

When she finally stops laughing, she wipes a tear from her eye. "It's just... it's such a cosmic joke. Creatures that evolved to be so dangerous ended up creating their own predators. Why would you test weapons on a planet you planned to live on, Drasuk?"

"Well, we didn't plan on living there. We thought it would simply be a forward base, but then our manticorid overlords decided to become pacifists."

She devolves into another laughing fit, and I huff as I give up and let her have her fun.

Her cackling at my expense eventually tapers off.

"Giant creatures that shoot lightning? That sounds terrifying," she finally says, her voice tinged with awe.

I rumble a sound that's somewhere between a chuckle and a growl. "The ak'thor are fearsome. Their bodies crackle with raw electrical energy, and their roars can shake mountains. A single one can lay waste to an entire battle-group if you're not prepared."

"And the snake-people?" she presses, her curiosity piqued.

"The xylanth, xhasa in the old tongue," I clarify. "They're a race of winged serpents, soaring through the skies in massive formations, raining fire and death down on their enemies."

"Fire?" she echoes, a frown creasing her brow. "But they're serpents, wouldn't that hurt them?"

I ripple my hide to let her know I don't have much knowledge about it. "They've adapted. Their fire is more like a super-heated venom they spew from their fangs. It burns with an unnatural intensity, capable of melting rock."

"From the looks of you, I would have thought you would be the fire breather."

My spines shift in confusion. "Why?"

"You sort of look like a *dragon*, but not exactly. Something from legends."

I let out a snort. Who knows what messed up views she has of me based on her own species mythology.

"No. We are mostly impervious to fire because of our planet of origin, but we are nothing like the xylanth."

She whistles, a low, impressed sound. "I can see why you talk so much about being precise and calculated. Your planet is more dangerous than mine. We have predators, but nothing like that."

"Well, it has its uses, since it keeps us from being too soft. Long before the manticorid pacifist movement, even the more bloodthirsty families of the Darangul Clan had been bled dry of the urge to act on our age-old urge for conquest. The manticorids left a power vacuum we were in no position to fill, and so we remained on Maln'Kri. The thirst for violence is still there, but thanks to evolution, we drakonids are a very unambitious race."

"You are saying conflicting things, Drasuk. You are either violent or not."

"What I mean is there is violence and then there is a need for conquest. We have the former, but lost the latter. We are peaceful in the galactic sense, but our old ways haven't been forgotten. We are at the farthest reaches of drakonid-dominated space. That isn't to say we are left alone, though. Far from it."

"Genali and braceaaer?"

"Mostly genali. Our body parts are sought after."

"Maternal copulators," she grits out.

Odd wording, as usual, but I appreciate the sentiment.

We stand in silence for a moment, the weight of my words settling heavily between us.

"No wonder draks are all about fighting," she finally mutters.

I let out a huff of air, a sound that could be interpreted as either agreement or amusement. "It's in our blood, the need to protect ourselves," I state simply by way of agreement.

"Right," she concedes, her voice thick with sarcasm. "Because what better way to ensure your new home is safe than by turning all the cute, cuddly, single-celled organisms into lightning-spewing monstrosities?"

I open my mouth to retort, but she holds up a hand, silencing me.

"Alright, alright," she says, a hint of sympathy softening her voice. "I get it. You were young, you were scared. We all make mistakes."

I scowl, the sting of her words unexpected. "We were not scared," I growl.

She sighs, a weary sound that seems to carry the weight of her own battles. "Look," she says, her voice softening, "I'm not judging. Just pointing out the irony of it all."

There is a truth to her words that I can't deny. A truth that has always left a bitter taste in my mouth. In the mouths of all Maj'Ras.

She turns away from me toward the water.

"That's beautiful," Kira breathes, her voice filled with appreciation and her gaze fixed on the inviting water.

The sight of her standing there, bathed in the dappled sunlight, sends warmth through me.

I like it.

"This is perfect," she says, a smile gracing her lips. She unclips the straps of her backpack, her movements fluid and practiced.

I watch, mesmerized, as she shrugs it off and drops it to the ground. Then, with a swift movement, she wades into the water.

Without a word, she moves deeper and deeper, the sunlight glinting off the droplets that cling to her.

"If this place has fornicating *leeches*," she mutters, her voice barely a whisper, "I'm going to kill something."

The unexpected humor in her words snaps me out of my daze. I let out a startled snort, and then a surprised laugh.

"*Leeches*?" I ask, the word unfamiliar to me.

"Blood-sucking worms," she explains with a grimace. "They're not a threat, just annoying."

A satisfied sigh escapes her lips as the cool water envelopes her up to waist level, sending shivers down my hide.

I watch, transfixed, as she swims toward the center of the pool, her movements graceful and powerful. The way the water clings to her curves sends a jolt of desire through me.

Why... why can't I look away?

My breath hitches as the top half of her dark leathery skin falls away, revealing a form I hadn't dared to imagine.

She isn't covered in a black hide, as I had assumed. Instead, smooth, brown skin stretches across her body. The water cascades down her in damp waves, clinging to the curves I hadn't noticed before.

Heat flares in my belly, an urge that surprises me with its intensity, causing a stirring and tightening in my belly.

28

Kira

The cool water seeps into my skin, washing away the grime and sweat of the fight. It feels heavenly, a contrast to the searing pain in my side. Wincing, I turn to inspect the damage.

The creature's spiked hair embedded itself deeply into my flesh, leaving behind angry red welts and a trail of drying blood.

Awesome.

I need to clean it better than that field rinse.

The sleek black suit that clings to my body like a second skin offers some protection but hinders access to the wound. I close my eyes, picturing the suit peeling back just over the affected area.

I assume it's made of nanites, since Drasuk says I have a bunch of the little robots.

Maybe they'll respond to a direct command.

"Open," I murmur, focusing on the area around the embedded hair spikes.

Nothing.

Frustration bubbles up. Maybe it only responds to spoken commands in English, or genali, the language it was programmed in.

I think back to the pod I woke up in and remember I didn't use my voice.

Fuck. How could that possibly have been only yesterday?

I sigh, picturing myself reaching up and pulling my shirt over my head. This triggers a response. The familiar buzzing sensation fills my ears as the top half of the suit dissolves into its nanite form.

I wonder if it retreats into my skin or simply compacts. I shudder when I imagine the former.

I don't want to know.

Either way, here I stand, suddenly naked from the waist up, the cool air sending shivers down my spine.

This is ridiculous.

I can't just stand here exposed. Glancing over my shoulder, I see Drasuk watching me, his amber eyes gleaming with something I haven't seen in them before.

My cheeks flush.

"Are you even less protected than I thought?" he rumbles, his voice a deeper rumbling of rocks than usual. "I thought the black hide was your natural skin protection."

"Stop looking, hand fornicator," I snap back, immediately regretting the childish insult.

It didn't translate properly, and judging by his expression it's another amusing moment for him.

"Hand fornicator?" he echoes, the spines along the top of his head betraying his confusion.

Or at least I'm beginning to make that association.

"Ugh," I groan, burying my face in my hands. "Never mind. Just... don't stare."

"Your hands or mine?"

"I'm not answering that, Drasuk."

"Definitely yours, then. They are small, but I'm sure you would make up for it with enthusiasm," he quips back, a sly tone in his rumbling voice.

My jaw clenches. As always, he is infuriating and enjoying any sign of discomfort.

When will I learn not to show it?

I ignore the part of my mind telling me I like it and try a different approach. "Hand fornicate off. Stop fornicating with me."

The words come out harsher than intended, but to my surprise, the nanites must have picked up on the context. The phrase translated partially, at least.

"You have that out of order," he booms. "We need to start having sex—which I have decided is a great idea—in order to stop. But how about we skip the stopping part?"

My eyes widen.

This conversation is spiraling out of control. I'm not sure if it's residual adrenaline from the fight, the cool water, or the sheer absurdity of the situation, but there's a newfound energy coursing through me.

No need to let him know I like it.

"We are not having sex," I shoot back.

My voice is surprisingly steady when I go on. "And even if we were, which we're not, there's no way it would involve whatever you're implying."

"Why not?" he challenges, his eyes twinkling with mischief. "Seems like a perfectly logical solution to our predicament."

"What predicament? But to answer your question, because," I mutter, searching for the right words. "Because sex is for... for..." I trail off, unable to think of a single reason why two mismatched species from different planets would have sex in the middle of a jungle.

"For pleasure?" he supplies helpfully, a suggestive glint in his eyes. "Isn't that what you said before?"

"Well, sure, of course sex is for that. I just didn't agree to doing anything with you."

"Are you sure? You seem to suggest it every few minutes."

I throw my hands up in exasperation. "Look, Drasuk," I begin, forcing myself to take a deep breath. "We don't even know if we're compatible. And besides, there are more important things right now, like cleaning this wound and figuring out how to get back on track with the mission. Save the women. Save the world."

I snicker at the pop culture reference, fully aware he won't understand it.

"True," he concedes. "But procreation is a fundamental instinct for most life forms. How can you resist the natural urge to continue your bloodline?"

"Ugh," I groan, pinching the bridge of my nose. "This conversation is officially over."

Knowing I won't win in a war of words, I move on to my original task.

Focusing on my body, I picture the nanite suit reforming around my torso, leaving just a small opening around the wound on my side. To my relief, the suit responds immediately, closing back up and encasing my arms and chest once more.

A flicker of disappointment crosses Drasuk's face, but I ignore it. Dunking myself back under the water, I scrub at the wound as best I can, wincing with each touch. The embedded spikes are stubborn, refusing to budge.

When I resurface, I move to a large rock at the water's edge and start picking at the spikes, hissing when they cut my fingers.

"You're going to hurt yourself more if you keep doing that," Drasuk says, pushing his way in and taking over bossily.

"Hey, I can handle it," I protest, but he ignores me, his large, oddly shaped hands surprisingly agile as he begins to remove them.

His touch is gentle, and despite myself, I relax a little, though I'm not done protesting.

All I needed were some decent gloves. I would have figured it out.

I try to push him off, but there's no real heat in my effort, and he refuses to budge. Eventually, I give in and let him help.

We fall into a tense silence as he works. The rushing water is a soothing counterpoint to the pain he is inflicting with each tug. His hands move with dexterity, each spike coming out with a precision that belies his size.

I watch him, fascinated despite myself.

"You're good at this," I admit grudgingly.

He glances up, his spines shifting to show his approval.

"I've had practice," he says simply.

I don't ask what kind of practice; I don't need to. The scars on his body tell their own story. Instead, I let the silence stretch, the tension between us shifting into something more complicated.

As he works, I find myself studying him, his features sharp and alien, yet somehow familiar. There's a strength in him that I can't deny, a resilience that mirrors my own. And beneath the teasing and the banter, there's a connection that's hard to ignore.

I'm not sure when his overbite of fangs stopped looking weird. Now they just look attractively deadly.

There's an answering throb between my legs as I soak in the sight of him. And a warmth in my chest when I see how focused he is on his task. He's annoying as hell, but pretty useful.

That doesn't mean I want to be horny right now.

Man, fuck those slimes, I groan internally.

29

Drasuk

The last stubborn spike comes free with a satisfying pop. I toss it into the water with the others, watching it disappear in a swirl of bubbles.

Relief washes over me, doing nothing to crowd out the desire that simmers beneath the surface each time I brush against her.

Kira, still submerged in the water, is a vision of raw vulnerability.

Her face, usually adorned with a mask of defiance, is etched with pain, her breathing ragged. Yet, even in this state, she exudes an undeniable strength, a quiet fire that burns brighter than anything I've encountered on this terrible planet.

As I reach out to offer her a hand, a niggling urge takes hold.

My fingers, rough from years of combat, brush against the cool smoothness of her exposed stomach. It's a fleeting touch, almost an afterthought, but the jolt that runs through me was immediate, a spark igniting a bonfire within.

So much for finding relief.

Kira's breath hitches. Her eyes shoot up to meet mine, a mixture of surprise and indignation flaring within them. Before she can protest, I retract my hand, the phantom warmth of her skin lingering on my fingertips.

There is a satisfied cant to my spines, I'm sure of it. It isn't just the thrill of successfully navigating the treacherous terrain or the adrenaline rush of the fight that still pulses through me. This is something altogether different.

A yearning that goes beyond mere survival.

Something forbidden.

"There's a lot more of you I wouldn't mind seeing cleansed," I rumble, a playful lilt to my voice.

A snort escapes her nose, half in pain, half in amusement. "As much as I appreciate the offer, *lizard man*, I can handle the rest myself."

Despite her words, her eyes hold something else in them I don't know how to interpret.

I lean closer, relishing the earthy scent that clings to her damp skin. "Are you sure? You seem to be having quite a bit of trouble with remaining clothed."

My teasing only serves to deepen the flush creeping up her neck. "Don't push your luck."

The growl that escapes her throat, however, isn't entirely devoid of heat. It sends a delicious shiver down my spine.

Here is a woman who wasn't afraid to show her teeth, to meet me head-on. And for whatever reason, I keep seeking more.

"Rear wipe," she mutters, then her eyes widen. "Finally," she growls out, throwing her head back in laughter. "Something that properly translates. Well, sort of translates."

"It only took you an entire day. It's a simple language, Kira. Very straightforward, and yet you still manage to approach it like... What was your phrase? A fumbling fornicator."

My amusement falters at the icy glare she shoots my way. "Fornicate in your own hole," she hisses out.

"We clearly need to discuss our roles and holes. I know you have one. I can smell how much it wants me to fill it," I respond, my tone playful yet edged with seriousness.

She squirms away from me, grabbing her bag and knife with a determined look. Her movements are quick and precise as she cuts her hair again, the strands falling into the water. I watch, fascinated, as she tosses the hair into the stream.

I cannot help but make a game out of it, splashing into the water and attempting to catch and eat the floating strands. She stares at me, her expression a mix of incredulity and amusement.

"You're crazy," she mutters, shaking her head. "Do you want some of the rations instead?" she asks, a hint of concern in her voice.

"I will eat again in a few sun cycles," I say, dismissing the notion with a wave of my hand. "Food is not what I hunger for right now."

She narrows her eyes at me, but then softens. "You looked like a hatchling just now. I bet you were a terrible listener and drove your mother crazy."

"She was out protecting the city. Drakonid aren't raised by their parents, but in broods watched over by aged civilians. Hatchlings who show interest and ability later go to Maj'Ras veterans with an interest in young warriors. I was taught to hunt by the elders. Our prey was fierce and cunning, much like you."

I wiggle my spines at her, enjoying the way she rolls her eyes.

"I grew up as a military *brat*," she shares. "My parents were always moving, always training. By the time I was ten, I could shoot better than most soldiers. It wasn't an easy life, but it made me strong."

Our eyes meet, and for a moment, there is an understanding between us.

"Tell me more," I urge, wanting to know everything about her.

She hesitates, then continues. "When I was thirteen, we were stationed in a war zone. It was the first time I saw real combat. My parents were on the front lines, and I was left to fend for myself. I had to learn quickly how to survive, how to fight, and how to protect those I cared about."

"Why would the young be so close to combat?"

She huffs out a breath. "It didn't use to be like that, but things are more desperate every year. I think they hope it will mean more of us will be warriors, and my parents agreed to it."

She smirks. "Believe it or not, it's also where I learned my first life skill."

I keep my gaze on her. "And what would that be?"

She snorts with amusement, "It's where I learned to cut my hair. It was a necessity. Long hair can be a disadvantage in a fight..." she tapers off, suddenly gaining a faraway look in her eyes.

"I, uh, learned that lesson the hard way after..." She shakes her head, letting the already regrowing pink threads fling water about. "It doesn't matter how. I've kept it short ever since."

I assume there is a very interesting story behind that, but I figure now is no time to pry.

I imagine how adorable she would be scrapping with someone and shrieking at them as they pull her threads.

Then my grin falls. Perhaps viewing this little human as cute is not a fair assessment.

Tiny as she may be, she was also raised into combat and pursued the same line as she got older. Just as I was, though in radically different environments.

"You are admirable," I say softly, then berate myself for saying something about such an obviously weaker species.

Why is she an exception? She is even weaker than a braceaaer. A genali, even.

She looks away, uncomfortable with the compliment. "I'm just doing what I have to do to survive," she replies uneasily.

"And you do it well," I say blithely before almost choking on a mix of my own words and a distressed groan of pleasure as an all too familiar sweet smell clogs up my airways.

It's that scent again. It might be the end of me, taking away my breath, causing a hitch that leads to a harsh cough that overtakes my body.

30

Kira

I watch, bewildered, as Drasuk's amusement curdles into a choked gasp. His chest heaves, clawed hands scrabbling at his throat.

Panic jolts me.

"What's wrong?" I blurt, concern momentarily overriding my simmering annoyance and almost boiling over arousal.

He throws a hand up, dismissively waving away my question. "Nothing," he rasps, his voice strained. "Just a little something caught in my throat."

The haughty dismissal grates on me.

This arrogant lizard nearly choked to death and now he acts like it's a minor inconvenience?

My hand instinctively tightens around my makeshift dagger, the urge to launch it at his smug dino face a very real temptation.

He is infuriating.

But logic intervenes. Throwing the dagger would accomplish nothing more than shattering it and potentially giving him a minor scratch. Besides, right now, cooperation is the only thing keeping us both alive.

Not to mention, I recognize that my rage is unfounded. He gets under my skin, and I don't like it.

Right now, that dislike is channeling into anger. It feels more comfortable than the story swapping, anyway.

I've told him more of my life and fears than anyone I can remember, and even after hearing his stories, I know almost nothing about what makes him tick. He's essentially a stranger, and I'm telling him personal things.

It's weird and I don't like feeling this way.

"Well, whatever it is," I say, my voice clipped, "get it under control. We need to move."

The sun dips behind a veil of thick clouds, casting the clearing in a cool, dappled shade. The oppressive heat recedes slightly, offering a reprieve.

"Speaking of moving," I continue, hoisting my backpack onto my shoulders, "where to from here? We can stick to the forest, avoid any more, uh, surprises like that last one."

My voice trails off, the memory of the giant creature still sending a shiver down my spine. "Maybe stay close enough to the border in case we need to cut our losses and head back to the desert."

Drasuk's spines shift in a way I know means he's amused. "Scared of a little sand now, are we, little human?"

I grit my teeth. This insufferable creature. One well-placed rock might be the answer to all my problems.

And wouldn't that be poetic justice?

With a flick of my wrist, I launch a pebble in his direction. It finds its mark with a satisfying *thunk*, landing squarely between his eyes. The annoying cant of his spines changes, replaced by a surprised blink.

"See?" I say, unable to suppress a triumphant smirk. "Not so invincible now, are you, lizard man?"

He groans, rubbing the spot where the rock connects. "A violent little thing, aren't you?"

"Says the nine-foot-tall killing machine," I retort, rolling my eyes. "Come on, before you decide to turn me into lunch."

For a moment, a flicker of something unreadable crosses his features. Then, with a dramatic sigh that ruffles the surrounding leaves, he rises up out of the water, considerably cleaner now.

He blinks again, and I watch his eyes warily to see the gears turning in his head before he reaches up with a sharp toothy snarl to rub the spot where the rock made contact.

"Seems the little human has a good throwing arm," he mutters. "I have surprises."

"That has been made quite evident," he chuckles, a deep rumbling sound that sends shivers down my spine despite myself.

I flip him the bird, the childish gesture feeling strangely empowering in this alien situation. He throws his head back and laughs, a sound that echoes eerily through the trees.

Standing up, I sling my backpack over my shoulder and head deeper into the forest. No point in waiting for Drasuk to decide when we move. He can follow or not, but I'm not babysitting a giant, reptilian pain in the neck.

Maybe he'll just stay here.

To my surprise, he doesn't tease or complain, but he certainly follows.

He falls into step beside me with surprising ease, his movements silent despite his size.

Was he stomping around making noise on purpose earlier just to annoy me? His stealth this morning makes it seem likely. That seems suicidal, but I wouldn't put it past him.

I steal a glance at him—his features are unreadable, his expression a mask of neutrality.

Part of me wishes I could understand him better, what goes on behind those slitted eyes. But another, more cautious part, knows that might be a dangerous path to tread.

We walk for what feels like hours; the silence broken only by the rustle of leaves underfoot and the occasional shriek or rustling of small creatures. The only fun comes in the form of watching him climb trees to look for glinting bits of silver.

The forest canopy grows denser, sunlight struggling to penetrate the thick layer of leaves overhead. The air turns even more humid and stagnant, carrying the smell of damp earth and decaying vegetation.

"You know," Drasuk finally breaks the silence, his voice low and almost hesitant, "back on my home planet, brood watchers are much less aggressive in their disciplinary methods."

"You lost me. What brought that up?"

"It's the only thing that might explain your continual rage."

I snort. "My parents were fair. We earned any punishment they doled out. I think you have this backwards. Maybe your brood watchers need to be harsher on draks, since you have an entire planet trying to kill you. An increase in rage doesn't sound all that bad in that context."

He lets out a sound that's somewhere between a laugh and a snort. "Perhaps you have a point, little one."

The way he keeps calling me *little one* grates on my nerves, especially when it makes my stomach do a little flip.

Fuck that.

I clench my jaw and force myself to stay silent.

As the day wears on, the landscape shifts subtly. The towering trees give way to smaller, hardier shrubs, the ground beneath our feet becoming drier and sandier. The air grows noticeably warmer, the humidity replaced by a dry, baking heat.

We reach a clearing, and I stop, squinting into the distance. The rolling plains of the desert stretch out before us again, an undulating sea of sand shimmering under the harsh afternoon sun.

"Well, this is it," I say, my voice tight. "The edge of the forest."

I always was a master at stating the obvious. As if we haven't been walking parallel to it for miles.

Drasuk stands beside me, his gaze fixed on the endless expanse of sand. "So it is," he rumbles, his voice tinged with awe.

I glance at him, surprised by the emotion I see flickering across his spines. "You've never seen a desert before? It's literally all we had to look at for hours before we went into the forest."

He rumbles out his disagreement. "I don't know if you've noticed, but I've had my eyes on you most of the time."

The sudden explosion of heat all over my body, and especially my face sends me into a sputtering mess. One he ignores now as he keeps his attention on the rolling sand dunes ahead.

So much for never looking away from me.

"To answer your question, a good deal of my planet is a desert. I say we continue along the edges of the forest," he weighs in, rousing me from my thoughts.

Huh. Must have completely misinterpreted that look.

I raise a brow before turning my eyes westward where the line between desert and forest continues, reminding me a bit of the intersection between two walls. I shrug.

"Well, there's no sense heading out into the desert where we'll be starved of supplies. Not to mention big bad uglies you seem to like to hug."

He ignores my joke and barb about the sand creature. "Then it's decided."

He resumes walking, a noticeable lilt in his step. I raise a brow.

"Well someone's in a good mood."

31

Kira

The forest hums with life as we trek along the biome divide, the transition between the dense, lush greenery and the barren, sandy desert still jarring to look at.

Hours have passed since we left the stream behind, and it has been a challenge to resist the temptation to cross over to the desert biome.

The open expanse, free from the tangled underbrush and relentless shrubbery, beckons. Yet, the memory of that subterranean horror we encountered keeps me rooted firmly on the forest side.

The last thing I need is another close call with a creature from the sands. Just thinking about it makes my skin crawl.

And itch. Damn, so much itching. I might go crazy.

The place where the embedded spikes were is a constant torment begging me to scratch at it. Even worse, whatever allergen or poison was in those things has spread to my entire stomach. From my bikini line to the bottom of my breasts, and around my sides is one big burning itch.

I glance back at Drasuk for a distraction, his massive form lumbering through the foliage. He bulldozes through the shrubs and vines as if they're mere cobwebs. I roll my eyes.

Typical.

My thoughts drift back to Ree and the genali ship. The cold, hard reality of our situation gnaws at me.

I'm hesitant to feel optimistic about their chances of surviving the crash, but then again, if I could survive being flung around in my pod and end up near a part of the ship that broke off, maybe they had a fighting chance, too.

Unwilling to let my mind spiral into a pit of worry, I decide to strike up a conversation with Drasuk. "Tell me what you know about the pink aliens that captured us," I say, my voice cutting through the silence. "The genali."

He turns his head slightly, his eyes flickering with something I can't quite place.

"The slimes, as most of us call them," he begins, his voice a low rumble. "They are a weak race, at least physically. High intelligence, though. They used it to trigger their evolution multiple times. They're still weak, but not as much as before. Even a drak hatchling could take out multiple non-modified genali in combat."

"Really?" I say, feigning nonchalance. "Doesn't sound like much of a threat."

Drasuk lets out a snort. "Don't underestimate them. They have a violent view toward females of all species. And they've become the newest conquerors of the universe. Joined forces with the braceaaer at first, but eventually struck out on their own once they improved their evolution and technology."

"The braceaaer?" I ask, curiosity piqued.

"You killed one."

"Oh, I called it a Graylord. I clearly played too many video games when I was young."

He grunts, then continues. "A similarly violent race. Stronger than they look by several factors. No smarter than the genali. The balance of power between the two has been shifting rapidly in favor of the genali, though I don't know why."

"So the genali are the major players? Weird, but okay. They don't really look like a species that would want to go out and conquer the universe. More like something that would be content to remain hidden in a swamp."

He lets out a mirthless laugh. "If only that were the case. While the genali's home planet is marine-based, most of them become scientists, politicians, soldiers, or, like those who captured us, cabal-sponsored bandits and species traffickers."

I absorb this information, trying to wrap my head around it. "So, they're the ones responsible for this mess. All of it? Not just sex trafficking."

"Yes," he says simply.

I walk in silence for a moment, processing. "What about the manticorid? What are they? The genali didn't share much about them."

His demeanor changes, a hint of reverence creeping into his voice. "They are a superspecies in the truest sense. A felidae-based race with remarkable strength, durability, and a healing factor that makes even drakonid recovery look slow. They have uncanny abilities, like gaining immunity to toxins and poisons after being exposed to them once. This immunity spreads to the entire population."

"Wow," I breathe, genuinely impressed.

Drasuk continues. "They were among the first species to begin an expansion effort, covering more than fifteen galaxies over five millennia. They held their territory until they began to demilitarize and pursue other fields instead of combat. Their decline allowed the xarxisi, then the braceaaer, and subsequently the genali to rise."

"They sound like something out of a myth," I say, half-joking.

"They're real," Drasuk replies, his tone serious. "They were the ones who triggered my species' evolution to assist in their wars. When they stopped their expansion, they granted us independence."

"You sound like you idolize them," I tease.

He nods without hesitation. "In a way, I do. They are worthy of respect."

The sincerity in his voice takes me by surprise. This infuriating creature is capable of genuine admiration.

It's a strange thought.

He lets out a rumbling huff, and when he speaks again, his tone has shifted dramatically. "I also resent how little they have done to deal with the threats we all face."

"What? They just protect their own and leave you to rot?"

"Even worse. They barely protect themselves, too worried about losing their principles. They are going to go extinct when they could instead rise again and radically decrease so many atrocities."

I glance over at him and note that his spines are slumped in a reflection of the heavy topic.

He speaks up again. "It shouldn't have been possible for them to capture one."

"Why not? If they were deities among felines, they wouldn't be in danger of extinction."

"No, no. They aren't invulnerable. I'm shocked to hear it because they destroy themselves in a primal rage if someone tries to contain them. Well, the males do, and of course they chose a male."

"What the fornicate? Their women can't fight?"

"Of course they can, but they don't have venom, and genali keep them as slaves. At least until they die of containment sickness."

"Fornicate. I hate those pieces of excrement."

"I agree with your sentiments, if not your word choice."

"So, we should be looking for a manticorid, then? Not just the rest of the women."

"Absolutely." He lets out a dark, rumbling chuckle. "Clearly the slimes have become over-confident. A Maj'Ra and a manticorid in the same hunting season? They are either suicidal or incredibly stupid."

I let out a low hum in response. "I am loving the sound of this, Drasuk."

He turns to me, raised spines shivering. "I am too, Kira."

We are both grinning like fools as we keep walking, though I'm pretty sure his is a promise of incoming pain, not an actual smile, since he communicates that through the many spines and spikes.

I glance back. Yep, that's a threat, not a smile.

Huh, I guess a lot of my smiles are that too.

As we continue our journey, the forest gradually thickens, the underbrush becoming more tangled and difficult to navigate. Drasuk's presence, while initially a nuisance, now feels reassuring.

Despite his intimidating size and gruff demeanor, he's proving to be a valuable source of information. And also a steady, clever companion.

Even if I don't want one of those.

"So, what do you know about this planet?" I ask, hoping to learn more about our current predicament.

Drasuk pauses for a moment, scanning the surroundings before answering. "I've researched a bit about hunting grounds in my spare time. It's a bit of a forbidden topic and, officially at least, they were outlawed a few generations ago. But that's just political speech for 'this council does not want to get on the genali or braceaaer's bad side.'"

I blink. "Council?"

He lets out a grumble, "It's a loosely allied confederation of sapient races that came together to police the universe during the decline of the Thorisian Empire, of the manticorid, I mean. Emphasis on the term 'loosely allied'."

I nod, unsure of what to do with this new bit of information.

"Information on hunting grounds like these is limited, but from the little I could glean, they are fundamentally terra-engineered to be diverse worlds, split into multiple biomes. The forest and desert are just two of them. There's also a tundra on a northern island, and a small pleasure island between them, according to the official template used in building them. Each biome has its own unique challenges and dangers."

"Great," I mutter sarcastically. "As if surviving the forest and desert weren't enough."

He grunts in agreement. "It's not an easy place to survive, but it's not impossible. You just need to be smart and cautious."

"Good thing at least one of us is taking that little caveat seriously," I grumble as he stomps through a thicket and announces our presence to whoever or whatever is within range.

So much for his quiet steps near the stream.

He doesn't rise to my bait. Or he assumes I was talking about myself. Yeah, the latter.

I roll my eyes and keep walking.

We push through the thick foliage, our progress slow but steady.

Despite the challenges, there's a certain beauty to it all, a sense of being part of something larger and more complex than myself.

My thoughts drift back to the rest of the women. The uncertainty of their fate weighs heavily on my mind. I can't shake the feeling of responsibility, the need to do something to help them. But here, in this strange and dangerous world, I'm not sure where to even begin.

"Do you think the others survived?" I ask, my voice barely above a whisper.

I don't know why I let the question slip out. I don't know why it came out in that tone either, but I freeze up internally, mortified at the underlying implication of the question.

Hard-headed bitch I might be, but one of the few behaviors I can accept is lying to myself.

Since when did I start seeking reassurance from anyone other than myself?

Even worse, why an incorrigible lizard?

Drasuk doesn't answer immediately.

When he does, his tone is surprisingly gentle. "It's possible. Survival often depends on a combination of luck and skill. If they are resourceful and determined, they might still be alive."

It's not exactly the reassurance I was hoping for, but in all honesty, I am happy that it's not. The need to comfort more often than not comes with the need to lie.

That said, they could be alive.

I cling to that small glimmer of hope as we continue our trek.

32

Kira

The silence after our conversation is stretching heavy and awkward. I'm kicking at rocks, sending a spray of dirt scattering in front of me.

The illogical part of me, the part I usually shove down ruthlessly, feels a strange pang of... disappointment? Am I enjoying listening to that lizard ramble on about galactic politics and outlawed hunting grounds?

Damn, the answer is yes. A huff of breath leaves my nose at the thought.

I like it when he speaks.

It isn't just the oppressive desert heat wafting into the forest making my skin prickle, though.

The sound of his deep, rumbling voice, a low, almost hissing quality to it, sends shivers down my spine that have nothing to do with fear.

Ugh, Kira, get a grip, I scold myself internally.

This is Drasuk. A giant reptilian killing machine, or so he says, who nearly choked to death on his own arrogance not two hours ago.

I've yet to see him do anything but play cat and mouse with me or hug that giant caterpillar thing while it tried to fucking kill him.

I let out a snort of amusement. Now that some time has passed, it's pretty damn comical when I picture it and the look of horror on his face. I have to hold in the laugh that wants to explode out of me to avoid looking deranged.

Well, more deranged.

My reaction to him? Not nearly as funny.

Needing a distraction, anything to break the awkward tension and quell the unwelcome arousal simmering beneath the surface, I blurt out the first thing that comes to mind. As usual.

"So, uh, how good is your sense of smell?"

Drasuk's head snaps toward me, his forehead spines quivering in confusion before moving back to their normal position.

"My sense of smell?" he repeats, his voice laced with amusement.

"Yeah," I mumble, feeling the stupid heat creeping up my neck again. "Like, can you smell things from really far away?"

He stares at me for a long, uncomfortable beat of silence. My cheeks are burning under his scrutiny.

Is there something on my face?

Does a giant space lizard have telepathic abilities that I'm not aware of?

"Is there something wrong with your inquiry, human?" he finally asks, his voice devoid of its earlier amusement.

"What? No," I sputter defensively. "Why are you looking at me like that?"

He twitches the spines along his back, which I've come to realize is his equivalent of a shrug. "It's an unusual question, wouldn't you say? Not a typical topic of conversation amongst humans, is it?"

My cheeks are flaming even hotter. "I was just trying to make conversation, okay?" I snap, my voice laced with irritation.

Drasuk blinks, his eyes studying me for a moment.

"Conversation, you say?" he rumbles, his voice tinged with something that sends a shiver down my spine. "An interesting choice of words, considering the implications such a statement could have on my home planet."

My breath hitches.

Implications? What implications? My mind is conjuring up a series of horrifying images, each one more outlandish than the last.

"I-I didn't mean anything by it," I stammer, backtracking as fast as possible.

"As far as I can tell, most of your words don't have meaning."

A growl escapes my throat before I can stop it. I'm spinning on my heel and storming off through the undergrowth, the sound of rustling leaves masking the frustrated tears welling up in my eyes.

The nerve of him.

Here I am, stuck in the middle of nowhere with a giant, condescending reptile, and all he can do is mock me?

I would make far better time and would be far stealthier without him. His intermittent bellows and crashing steps probably let everything in the region know about us.

It's a miracle we haven't been attacked again.

And if we are, what's he going to do? Hug them to death?

Suddenly, a deep, booming laugh is echoing through the trees. I whip my head around to see Drasuk lumbering after me, his massive frame shaking with amusement.

"Wait!" he yells out, his voice laced with laughter.

Case in point, right there. He is a lumbering oaf.

I glare at him, refusing to budge. Why won't he just go away? The jerk.

He finally stops a few meters behind me, his laughter subsiding into chuckles. "Alright," he rumbles, wiping a tear from his eye—or at least, what I assume is a tear.

It's hard to tell with his oversized features.

"I apologize for the amusement at your expense, human. But your flustered state is rather entertaining. Endearing, even."

I grit my teeth.

Endearing? The last thing I want to be to this bumbling lizard is endearing.

"Look," I say, crossing my arms. "If you won't simply leave me alone so I can sneak around instead of announcing to the whole fornicating forest that we are here, can we just move on? Before one of those things we fought earlier decides to make a snack of us?"

Drasuk's expression is softening, and a flicker of seriousness crosses his features. "As you wish," he rumbles, his voice regaining its usual depth. "Though, I must admit, your question about my sense of smell was a curious one."

I sigh. Here we go again.

"Well?" I prompt, a hint of curiosity peeking through my annoyance.

He tilts his head, his slitted pupils scanning the forest floor. "Our sense of smell is far superior to most," he explains. "We can detect scents from quite a distance away, depending on the wind and the potency of the odor."

"How far are we talking?

"I can still smell the wreckage."

A glance behind us confirms that I can't even see it anymore. We took a detour into the forest, before looping back, but I'd say it has to be a good ten klicks away.

"That far?" I ask, surprised.

This is worse than I feared when it comes to my raging arousal, and better than I hoped for locating the women.

"Yes," he confirms. "It's a valuable tool for hunting and tracking prey. It also allows us to detect danger from afar, such as approaching predators or changes in the environment."

"No excrement, Sherlock."

"Sherlock?"

I ignore his question. "I was in a pod when I woke up."

"A cryogenic chamber."

"Okay, a chamber. There were nine other women with me. Do you know what a chamber would smell like, and can you use my scent to scan for the women?"

"Yes. I have already been doing both, Kira."

"With your super nose, right. So, like a giant bloodhound?" I tease, a sliver of a smile playing on my lips.

"You'd have to define that for me to say."

"An animal known for a strong sense of smell on earth."

"I have no point of reference to reply intelligently."

I let out a guffaw. "Drasuk, that isn't what's stopping you from sounding intelligent."

He whips his tail around and I yelp as it smacks into the back of my thighs.

"Ingrate," I mutter as I rub them to help take away the sting.

"Should I start comparing you to mere animals from my planet? There is, in fact, a type of furry creature that likes to screech at you and throw rocks whenever you get near it. If you get close enough, it defecates and scurries away. I think there is—"

"Alright," I interrupt, not particularly interested in knowing what traits of mine he is going to dredge up in comparison. "You made your point."

"Good. Then let me just say that we don't just rely on scent. Our sense of smell is just one of many sensory inputs we utilize for navigation and survival."

All that arrogance really must have left him with a giant head, which explains why he tramps around like an elephant.

In spite of it all, I smile.

We continue our trek, the silence no longer as awkward after our banter. The revelation about Drasuk's heightened sense of smell sparks a new wave of questions in my mind, though.

"Can you smell, uh, me?" I blurt out, the question catching even me by surprise.

He stops abruptly, his gaze meeting mine. My cheeks flush again, a traitorous warmth spreading through me.

Why do I keep asking him such personal, obvious things?

"Of course I can smell you, human," he says, his voice a deep grinding. "Everything has a scent. Yours is a curious mix of sweat, fear, and... something else."

"Something else?"

He leans in closer, his face mere inches from mine. My breath hitches in my throat, my heart hammering against my ribs. The air is crackling with energy, a tension that is both exhilarating and terrifying.

"I believe that 'something else' might be defiance," he rumbles, his voice a husky murmur.

Then he just keeps on walking.

My mind is reeling.

Defiance?

Is that really what he thinks that "something else" is? Is he fucking with me? Because I know there's more going on here, something I don't really have the confidence to voice.

Which is completely unlike me, and I loathe everything about it.

My usual response is anger, but that quickly bleeds away as no justification for lashing out presents itself.

Maybe I'm growing up, then. It's not like I needed a justification before. Except I don't want to drive him away. Not really.

It's a terrifying thought. I hate it.

Not to mention Drasuk seems to like it when I get angry, which is crazy. No man I have ever met has liked it. Plenty have told me my anger is outright unattractive and unfeminine.

As if rage is only for men. Fuckers.

There's a lot to be pissed off about on Earth, especially with the rapid diminishment of overall respect and the insane ability for most of the world to completely ignore the suffering and injustice all around them.

Except when it impacts them, of course.

There's plenty to be angry about here, too. For instance, why won't my skin stop itching? I rake my nails down myself again, but freeze when I feel something rough.

A prickle of unease skitters down my spine, morphing into full-blown panic as I register a foreign sensation. My skin feels different. Rougher, thicker.

Heart hammering a frantic rhythm against my ribs, I split the upper half of my suit off me in a single, jerky motion. The material tears with a satisfying rip, revealing the source of my growing unease.

My skin, once a cinnamon-hued canvas, smooth and soft—my personal trademark, thank you very fucking much—with the occasional dark freckle smattering has been replaced by strange, oval markings that spread across my stomach and sides. They resemble the spots on the creature Drasuk tried to hug into submission.

Numbly, I poke one of them and it's a texture not too dissimilar from what I imagine a rhino would feel like.

A strangled cry escapes my lips, fear clawing its way up my throat.

"What the actual fiery pit in the ground?"

My voice, usually laced with a sardonic edge, is a high-pitched squeak.

My frantic gaze darts around until it lands on Drasuk. He's up ahead, partly turned, frozen mid step. His spikes are twitching in what might be concern, which may or may not have made me happy in normal circumstances.

This is not normal.

Instead, I want to verbally eviscerate him. Except no words will come out of my mouth.

"I must say," he rumbles, his voice a low vibration in the quiet cave, "that's an improvement over that soft squishy hide you had before."

The audacity of the beast.

"Improvement?" I ask, the word tearing from my throat like a wounded animal.

I run my hands over my stomach, then confirm that it extends around my sides, the rough skin beneath my fingertips sending a fresh wave of nausea washing over me.

Drasuk holds up his massive, clawed hands in a placating gesture. "Calm is needed to figure this out."

"Calm down?" I choke out, my voice regaining some of its usual fire. "Don't patronize me, lizard. Those pieces of excrement genali did this to me. They made it so I would change into whoever purchased me."

I have never before wished so hard that my enemy was in front of me so I could smash them into plops of sad gray goo. Instead, I have to channel my rage at the only alien in front of me.

"You have to know more about what's happening to me. You're a fornicating alien," I hiss out.

He sighs, a sound like wind rustling through ancient trees. "Kira," he starts, his voice dropping to a soothing rumble, "I honestly don't know what's happening. Maybe the genali tampered with your DNA, trying to turn you into one of their mindless drones, and this is some unintended side effect."

I glare at him, my anger warring with a flicker of morbid curiosity. Could that be it?

The thought is repulsive, but it also holds a sliver of logic. Drasuk, sensing the shift in my mood, decides to lighten the tense atmosphere, a foolish endeavor on his part.

"Besides," he continues, his spines twitching, "why all the dramatics? You keep denying you're squishy, yet here you are with not one, but two very ample pillows adorning your chest."

I lunge for him, fueled by a potent cocktail of fury and something else entirely—a surging possessiveness over my suddenly altered body.

He easily dodges my clumsy swipe, his booming laughter echoing through the forest and out into the desert.

Normally, I'd have countered with a witty retort, laced with enough venom to silence a viper. But right now, all I can manage is a strangled sound, a mixture of a growl and a frustrated whimper.

This is no laughing matter. My entire body feels alien, a constant reminder of my precarious situation.

Drasuk finally sobers, a hint of concern flickering in his eyes. "Alright," he rumbles, his voice losing its playful edge. "We can save the squishy debate for another time. I truly am sorry. I know you want answers, but we have no way of knowing what caused that."

He gestures toward my mottled skin, his forehead spines oriented in what seems like genuine puzzlement.

I sink down onto the ground, my skin shifting in ways that are utterly foreign, the rough texture a constant scratching against my newly sensitive skin. Frustration gnaws at me.

Here I am, stranded on a godforsaken alien planet, my body morphing into something I barely recognize, and all I have for company is a giant, condescending dino-dragon who offers unhelpful observations about my bust.

Taking a deep breath, I force myself to focus. Panicking won't solve anything.

"So, what do we do?" I ask, my voice hoarse. "Do you have some alien doctor on speed dial who can diagnose interspecies cooties?"

The flippancy of my words feels hollow, but a sliver of dark humor is all I have to cling to right now.

Drasuk chuckles, a sound that rumbles deep within his chest. "If I understood that correctly, despite the untranslated words, the answer is still no."

"Great," I mutter, burying my face in my hands. "Just fantastic. So, I'm stuck looking like a walking camouflage pattern with no way to reverse it."

A fresh wave of despair threatens to engulf me.

"Like I said, don't make any conclusions yet," Drasuk says, his voice gentle. He lumbers closer, carefully placing a large hand on my shoulder.

It's not repellant. It might even feel... nice... like I want more.

Before I can form a coherent response, Drasuk pulls back, his expression unreadable. He clears his throat, the sound echoing in the stillness.

"We should continue," he says gruffly, turning away and resuming his lumbering walk.

Left speechless and bewildered, I make myself get back on my feet, tell my suit to fix itself, and follow behind him.

The forest seems to hum with a newfound intensity, the rustling leaves and chirping insects taking on a whole additional dimension. Is it just my imagination, or is the air charged with what has been left unsaid?

I need to gain some space and no way in hell will I get by being slower.

I shake my head and stomp past him, not minding the fact that I shoulder-tackle him on the way by.

Well, more like bounce off him. Fuck.

Stupid iguana.

33

Drasuk

I bellow after Kira, my voice echoing through the dense foliage, "Slow down, little human! You'll twist your tiny feet in that undergrowth, and then who gets to carry your soft, squishy body back to the nearest medical facility? That's right, me."

She throws a look back over her shoulder; the scowl etched on her face deepening with each syllable I utter.

"There are no fornicating medical facilities here, hole in rear."

Her hand flies up, the middle finger extended in a gesture I've come to recognize as a non-verbal insult.

I assume it's the equivalent of a drak flicking their tail dismissively at someone they consider beneath them. Yet, there's a nuance to it, a human complexity I haven't quite deciphered.

Part of me wants to call out, to ask her the meaning behind the strange gesture, but she's already forging ahead, pushing through the undergrowth with a ferocity that both impresses and unnerves me.

Her defiance is a constant presence, a tangible thing that hangs heavy in the air between us.

It's delicious.

My frown deepens as my thoughts drift back to her earlier question. Her inquiry about my sense of smell left me struggling to maintain my composure.

I hadn't lied, not exactly.

Back home, a female in heat will often approach a potential mate with a playful question—how keen is his nose? It's a coy way of asking if he could detect the subtle shift in her pheromones, the undeniable signal of her readiness.

The sheer absurdity of the situation strikes me, yet again. The thought that she, a human female, could possibly possess such knowledge initially left me speechless. Relief washed over me when her flustered reaction confirmed my suspicions.

Humans clearly lacked such exotic social cues.

Still, that nagging thought remains: the fact that she is demonstrably aroused, even in this hostile environment. A traitorous part of me dares to wonder—is it me? I quickly dismiss that thought.

Arrogance is a luxury I cannot afford. Not here, not now.

Pushing those wayward thoughts aside, I focus on what's in front of us—navigating this treacherous forest. The air is thick with humidity; the silence broken only by the incessant drone of unseen insects and the rhythmic pad of Kira's feet against the damp earth.

The dense foliage offers little respite from the unrelenting sun that beats down mercilessly.

If we went farther into the forest, we would have shade. A glance at her and I revise my statement. She is shaded thanks to her small stature.

The wind shifts and I detect a faint, musky scent on the breeze. It's unfamiliar, not a creature I've encountered before.

Caution thrums through my veins, urging me to slow our pace. I glance at Kira, hoping to catch her eye, but she's several paces ahead, her focus fixed on a point farther down the path.

"Kira," I call out, my voice low and urgent. "Something's not right."

She spins around, her brow furrowed. "What is it?"

"There's a new scent," I explain, gesturing with my snout. "I can't quite place it, but it's unfamiliar."

Her expression remains unconvinced, a flicker of annoyance crossing her features.

"Probably just some weird forest animal," she scoffs. "We can't exactly stop and investigate every new smell, can we? Wait, what am I saying? You're never careful about anything, it seems like. So, what do you detect?"

"This isn't like the other scents. This one carries a hint of danger."

She hesitates for a moment, then lets out a frustrated sigh. "Fine," she concedes. "I trust your judgement. But we're not waiting around for long. If this mysterious creature doesn't show itself in five minutes, we keep moving."

I give her a curt twitch of my spines, appreciating the concession, however begrudging. We stand in silence for a few tense moments, my nostrils twitching as I try to decipher the source of the smell.

It's faint, almost teasing, swirling on the warm breeze.

Just as I'm about to suggest we continue, a low growl rips through the stillness. It originates from somewhere deep within the undergrowth to our left, the sound guttural and menacing.

Kira's eyes widen, the color draining from her face.

I give her a look that communicates that she should have believed me.

She doesn't respond, her gaze moving back to the direction the rustling leaves originated. The growl comes again, closer this time, followed by the unmistakable snap of a twig underfoot. Battle hormones surge through me, propelling me into action.

"Stay behind me," I growl, shoving myself between Kira and the source of the sound as she moves her gun into position. My senses are on high alert, my instincts screaming at me to protect the strange little human at my back.

The creature emerges from the undergrowth with a horrifying grace.

It is vaguely felidae, sleek and muscular, with obsidian fur and claws that glint menacingly in the dappled sunlight. Its eyes, however, are the most unsettling feature—swirling red orbs embedded in its skull, devoid of pupils or whites. It lets out a hissing snarl, revealing a maw filled with jagged teeth, dripping with a bioluminescent drool.

Kira gasps, moving to get around me so she can get a clear shot. Before she can, the creature launches itself at me, a blur of dark fur and malice.

I rear up on my hind limbs, towering over the beast, and meet its charge head-on with a thunderous blow from my clawed forearm. The impact sends the creature skidding back, a surprised yelp escaping its throat.

A tingle of relief passes through me knowing that I am able to hit it. I never again want to feel the same sense of powerlessness as I did with that cursed sand creature.

My jarring strike isn't enough to deter it, however. With a renewed snarl, it lunges again, this time aiming for my legs. I sidestep, feeling the wind of its claws whistle past my flank.

Kira takes a measured shot, but misses. It's very fast.

I retaliate with a sweeping kick, catching the creature square in the chest. The blow sends it crashing into a nearby tree trunk, its body contorting at an unnatural angle.

For a moment, there is silence. Kira, who is crouched, looking like she was poised to take to take another shot, lets out a shaky breath.

"Did you get it?" she whispers.

Just as I am about to respond, the creature stirs. Its eyes, flickering with a renewed fury, lock onto Kira. With a guttural roar, it propels itself forward, a blur of black fur and glowing teeth. A scream tears from Kira's throat as she raises her gun and fires three quick bursts.

One hits it in the chest, but it doesn't stop.

I don't hesitate, lunging forward, a roar of my own erupting from my throat. The creature meets me halfway, its glowing maw snapping toward my face. With a flash of movement, I dodge its attack, feeling the putrid breath singe my neck. I slam my shoulder into its side, sending it reeling.

It lets out a pained screech, but before it can recover, I seize my opportunity. With a swift movement, I clamp my jaws around its throat, the tang of blood flooding my mouth. The creature writhes and claws at me, its fur slick with glimmering blood, but I hold on with a vice-like grip.

The stench of singed flesh and desperation fills the air.

A crack echoes through the forest, followed by a sudden stillness. I release my grip, dropping the creature's now lifeless body to the forest floor. A wave of dizziness washes over me, the battle hormones slowly ebbing away.

Kira stares at the scene before her, face a pale canvas of shock. I take a shuddering breath, tasting blood and the acrid slime on my tongue.

"Seems we won't be needing that five-tick investigation after all," I rumble, my voice raspy.

She finally tears her gaze from the creature's body, a faint flicker of amusement crossing her features.

"Well," she drawls, her voice strained, "that was certainly fun to watch. Although, next time maybe try not to get your dinner all over the place?"

I stare at her, momentarily speechless. Did she just make a joke? In the aftermath of a near-death experience?

I approve.

My spines twitch in an involuntary response, then I simply let them show my appreciation for her humor.

Strange little thing, this one. Strange little thing indeed.

A weak smile tugs at the corner of her lips before she speaks again. "The whole fight was less than three minutes. Well done."

My chest warms with the compliment, loosening a tightness that has been there since I failed to do my part in the last battle.

"Let's just keep moving," I finally say, wiping the slime from my jaws with the back of my hand. "Hopefully, there won't be any more surprises today."

"Ha," she guffaws without mirth. "I think you just *jinxed* us, buddy."

She moves closer to me, then whacks me hard on my shoulder. From the look on her face, it must be something humans do when they are trying to compliment you.

I'll have to remember that.

She also brings her pheromone cloud closer where the wind can't disperse it some for me. I avoid taking a breath, lest I end up choking again.

I twitch the spines along my back, ignoring the sudden heat that brings that annoying tightness as her scent fills my nostrils again, despite the burning in my lungs letting me know they desperately want me to breathe.

She speaks again, providing a welcome distraction. "We better get a move on before some other creature, with more curiosity than fear, decides to come to see what all the *ruckus* was about."

34

Drasuk

The jungle seems to hold its breath, the incessant drone of insects momentarily silenced.

The tension is suffocating, so I decide to break it with a touch of my usual humor, a playful jab that usually gets a rise out of her. "Seems your little scouting mission to find pets is turning out to be a little more exciting than you expected, little human," I rumble, a hint of mock arrogance lacing my voice.

She throws a glare in my direction, but it lacks its usual fire. "Yeah, well, thanks to you getting your *reptilian* freak on over there instead of avoiding things like that, which I'm pretty sure you can do, I almost became monster *chow*," she mutters, gesturing toward the creature with a grimace.

"Wouldn't want anything happening to that soft, squishy body of yours before we reach those other pets you're so keen on finding. I was just protecting my investment, but I like to have fun."

A flicker of a smile crosses her face, fleeting but genuine. "Hilarious, though I prefer other sorts of games," she deadpans.

The tension in her shoulders seems to ease a fraction. "So, what exactly was that thing, anyway? Some kind of overgrown jungle *cat* with a drooling issue?"

I ponder her question for a moment. The creature wasn't native to Maln'Kril or anywhere else I've been, that much was certain.

"No familiar scent signature," I rumble, wrinkling my snout in thought. "Definitely not something I've encountered before. Probably some mutated monstrosity cooked up for this cursed hunting season."

She lets out a humorless chuckle. "Just another delightful addition to our vacation itinerary. Let's hope the next surprise isn't quite so toothy."

I rumble my agreement, the playful banter fading as a wave of weariness washes over me. I focus on the path ahead, my senses scanning the environment for any sign of further danger.

There's a nagging thought that keeps circling in my mind.

Her heat; this arousal that she keeps denying. My senses let me know it's a weak lie, as does the way her eyes refuse to meet mine when I mention it.

At no other point has she been too shy to show me the defiance in them.

The very idea of a human female, especially this particular human female, being attracted to me is ridiculous. And yet, there it is, a persistent ember burning in the back of my mind.

Why else would she keep signaling?

The thought sends a jolt through me, but then I scoff at the absurdity of it, drawing a questioning look from Kira I pretend I don't see.

Drakonids don't mate with other species.

It's simply not done. Besides, Kira is, well, Kira. Stubborn, infuriating, and about as socially graceful as a drunken xicut. Hardly the ideal mate for a proud Maj'Ra.

Still, the image of her fiery defiance and the way her scent fills the air when she is close lingers in my mind. I clench my jaw, forcing myself to focus. This internal monologue is getting me nowhere.

Suddenly, Kira stops.

I glance at her, surprised. She's staring down intently at a patch of sunlight filtering through the leaves, a frown etched on her face.

"What is it?" I rumble cautiously.

"Footprints," she mutters, crouching down to examine the damp earth. They're large, much larger than hers, and unlike anything I've seen before. Three clawed toes, each leaving a deep impression in the soft soil.

"It matches the paws of that *cat*-like creature," she shares.

I hadn't bothered to look, and a flush of embarrassment follows that realization.

She is simply too distracting, though it's satisfying to see her demonstrate her knowledge and skills.

I look closer now, and note that there are several sets. All seemingly heading in the same direction—deeper into the forest. A tremor of unease runs through me. These aren't solitary hunters like the creature we just encountered.

This is a pack.

"Looks like we're not alone," I mutter, my voice low.

Kira stands up, brushing dirt off her knees. The playful defiance has vanished from her eyes, replaced by a steely determination.

"You have a penchant for the obvious, Drasuk. Great," she mutters, her voice laced with sarcasm. "Just what we needed. A pack of oversized mutant freaks."

"We need to find somewhere to hide," I say urgently. "Somewhere they can't easily reach us."

She scans the surrounding trees, her gaze finally landing on a cluster of thick vines snaking their way up a nearby tree, then moving on, as if she discards it as a viable option.

"Why not the vines?"

"Way up there?" she asks, pointing toward the vines. "Seriously? How high do you think we'll get using those?"

"I'll get higher than you can manage on your own two squishy feet," I retort, a barb creeping into my voice.

Before she can retort, I surge forward, falling on all fours as I propel myself toward the tree. After a burst of power to launch me up as high as possible, I scramble up the trunk, using the thick vines for purchase.

I reach the topmost branches in mere moments, the dense foliage offering a decent amount of cover. I peer down at Kira, who's struggling to get a foothold on the lower vines, her height working to her disadvantage.

With a sigh, I climb back down a bit before extending the length of my prehensile tail toward her.

"Grab on, little human," I rumble, sure to include enough of implied insult in my tone to get her riled.

She hesitates for a moment, then grits her teeth and reaches out, grasping the rough spines of my tail with both hands. With a grunt, I haul her up, bumping her along the tree as she curses quietly before hoisting her onto the same branch I was on before.

She lands with a huff, glaring at me but not bothering to voice a complaint.

We crouch low amongst the leaves, waiting, then we both tense and make our breath shallow when there is a crack of a stick breaking.

The rustling of the approaching creatures grows steadily louder as we wait. Soon after, I can see glimpses of the pack through the gaps in the foliage. There are at least five of them, each one just as menacing as the creature I fought earlier.

Their dark fur glistens in the sunlight, and their swirling eyes scan the forest floor with predatory hunger. They move with a chilling grace, their movements silent and deadly. Kira lets out a shaky breath beside me.

"Any bright ideas?" she whispers, her voice barely audible.

I rumble back a negative, a grim feeling settling in my gut. We're outnumbered, possibly unmatched, and with nowhere to run.

This might be the end of it for both of us.

Still, as I look into Kira's eyes, blazing with a mixture of fear and defiance, a spark of determination ignites within me. I may not be able to guarantee her safety, but if I fail, it won't be because I ran.

A Maj'Ra fights until death, and I can see the same fervor reflected in her pink-eyed gaze, a mirror of my aggression and determination, albeit in a diminutive package.

Nonetheless, both of us err on the side of caution, remaining still and hoping the group will simply move on to other prey.

Instead, they lower their dripping maws to the ground, and move closer, one of them already following the line of our movement toward the tree.

We glance over at each other, both asking a question and offering a response, then she breaks out into a gleeful grin that's reflected in my spines.

Squeezing her waist with my tail, I let out a low growl, a sound that echoes through the trees. The pack stops, their attention drawn to our hiding place.

A tense silence hangs in the air, broken only by the ragged gasps of Kira's breaths. Then, with a guttural roar, the lead creature charges toward the tree, its glowing eyes fixed on us. The others follow suit, a wave of black fur.

I clench my jaw, adrenaline surging through my veins. This is it. We fight.

For survival. For the sheer perversity of not going down without a struggle.

A feral snarl stretches across my face and my spines shiver. For the first time since arriving on this strange planet, a thrill of anticipation courses through me that reminds me of my days as a hunter.

We both need the other to make it through, and it feels good. Just like any Maj'Ra should feel knowing another Ra will throw themselves into danger until it has passed.

A pleased rumble starts in my chest until it shakes the branch we are on. Kira lets out a long, triumphant *oorah* sound a moment later.

It's strange, but the sentiment is the same.

We are in accord.

There are very few things that can compare to the ecstasy of a good fight, and who would I be to say no now that the predators in this place are deciding to make things more interesting?

35

Kira

I would have preferred to keep the element of surprise, but I must admit that Drasuk's guttural growl is damn inspiring.

Stupid, but inspiring, and it feels good to have him with me in this fight.

He makes up for giving away our location a moment later by launching himself out of the tree just as the lead creature gets to the base of it. Drasuk lets out a roar as he plummets. My heart is in my throat for a moment watching him, then I hear the satisfying crack of the thing's back as he lands on it with his big ass.

Talk about using your assets.

I'm impressed as hell and let out a whoop, then focus on my role. They're moving so fast I don't have a good bead on any of them, but I try a shot near the middle of the pack, anyway. A puff of dirt in the air lets me know I missed. The next shot hits, but it barely slows the thing down.

In a blink all four are on him, a snarling pile of fur, with glimpses of his blue skin and spikes.

The first one isn't dead yet, just making pitiful, mewling attempts to make its useless body respond. Good riddance.

I'm trying to get a clear shot as Drasuk bats them around, punctuating each blow with a roar. They are all so damn fast I don't think I can avoid friendly fire, so I wait.

I can tell he's being surprisingly cautious. From his movements, it occurs to me that his underbelly must be more vulnerable than his fucking bulletproof upper hide.

"Idiot," I bark at myself.

Unlike my usual allies, I'm not going to do him any harm if a shot goes wide, at least if I avoid his stomach and eyes.

I'd really like to just spray the mass with a bunch of bullets and be done, but I don't have an endless supply. I hope Drasuk can hold out while I'm choosy.

A moment later, he presents me with a perfect opportunity as he opens his maw with those sharp teeth and chomps down on a furry shoulder. He shakes the thing three hard times and then flings it away from him. It lands with a groan of pain and doesn't instantly pop back up.

I take a steady breath, aim for its forehead and gently squeeze. The spray of blood and bioluminescent slime is satisfying, but I don't take the time to savor it before I swing my weapon back to the remaining three.

Unfortunately, that shot finally caught their attention, and when I look back, one of them has separated from the growling, screeching melee and is bounding toward me.

"Fuck."

Drasuk tries to shoot out his tail and grab it, but the others pile on top of his back, knocking him off balance. He lets out an enraged bellow, but the other two are too attached to his upper spikes, riding him like he's the scariest fucking bull in the rodeo.

As terrifying as it is to have one of them barreling toward me, I steady my hands and use the time I have until it gets to me to choose a better target. Drasuk has one of the others pinned just long enough for me to shoot it in the chest.

It isn't a kill shot, judging by the screech it makes, but Drasuk takes advantage of its momentary distraction to rip its throat out.

Two left, I tally, then swing the gun down, trying to take quick aim at the one rapidly climbing the tree I'm in. My first shot grazes its shoulder, but it keeps coming. The second one goes wide as my vision suddenly blurs, and then it's on me, knocking the gun out of my hands as it swipes at my stomach.

I expect a searing pain and quick death, but instead it just feels like a punch. The wind rushes out of my lungs as I twist and pull one of my knives.

I stab it multiple times, but it just keeps taking swipes at my stomach, finally making a spitting cry I assume is frustration. After the fourth stab, it twists away from me, pulling the handle from my grip before I can pull it back out.

A darting grab of one hand reveals that my glass knife isn't in its usual suit pocket. All I feel is shredded fabric and bumpy skin before I give up on that plan and shift to the usual human backup plan: sheer desperation.

I push my back against the trunk of the tree the creature has me caged against, raise my knees toward my chest, screaming as the side of one thigh contacts its claws, then I kick out as hard as I can.

My jaw drops open in shock as it gives way with a hissing screech and then goes flying away from the tree.

There's another shift in my already fucked up reality as it seems to fall in slow motion, claws swiping the air in panic, before it makes hard contact with the ground.

It doesn't get a chance to get up again before Drasuk is ripping off chunks of it and flinging them in all directions.

I shake my head, the sudden clearing of my vision letting me know my new extra eyelids just retracted.

Drasuk tips back from all fours onto his back legs and bellows out his victory cry. He's covered in gore, and it should make me gag. Logically, it's disgusting.

Instead, he looks utterly magnificent. The deadliest being I've ever laid eyes on. A quick glance lets me know some of the blood is his, but he just had a whole fucking pack of rabid, giant mutant cats treating him like a scratching pole and it's not fazing him at all.

I'll admit, seeing him like this is a turn on. And not just because of genali tampering either, but because I've always been attracted to someone who could completely wreck me if they wanted to.

Damn.

Some of that arrogance is well-earned, it seems.

Not that he will ever hear me say that. I'll take it to the grave before I pump up his already inflated ego.

"Stop it," I mutter to myself. I need to stop drooling already.

A quick look around lets me know that none of my weapons fell in the tree, which means they must be scattered around the base of it, plus of course the one I need to rip out of the one Drasuk just killed.

I realize that it might be in one of the meaty chunks splattered all over the undergrowth and let out a sigh.

Climbing down is no problem at all. I've never felt stronger in my life. Clearly, some new change is afoot.

My glass knife is near the bottom of the tree, a few feet away from the paralyzed creature, which is still hissing and spitting at us. I stride over to gather up my weapon, then make the mercy kill.

After that, the only sounds are my pounding heart and Drasuk's panting.

36

Kira

The sun filters through the dense canopy, casting dappled shadows on the ground. One of the creature's bodies lies sprawled before us, a testament to our victory.

I nonchalantly wipe the blood from my blade on the forest floor, glancing over at Drasuk as he pokes the dead creature with an outstretched claw, his curiosity unabated.

"Fancy a bite?" I ask, my tone laced with sarcasm. "Seems like it could be a delicacy."

Drasuk makes a hissing cough, then a rumbling sound, his spines showing a mixture of exasperation and amusement.

As I pull out the medkit to patch up my leg, he puffs himself up and I recognize the precursor to an arrogant statement that's half joke and half insult. "Drakonids have more refined tastes, but I'm sure it would be perfect for your more primitive species."

Yep, called it.

"Don't be a wad of cum," I retort with no heat in my voice, turning back to the creature.

A glace back over to him and I see that he's shifted his spines again to show his humor. "Why so interested in my seed?" he teases, his spikes rising along his forehead. "You want some, perhaps?"

I give him a long, level look before rolling my eyes and storming off dramatically to clinch the joke, throwing up a middle finger behind me for good measure.

My lips quirk up, destroying the whole image when I hear his gravel-crunching laugh as he moves to follow me.

He's a good companion.

The thought stops me in my tracks. Since when?

And at what point did I start wanting a companion, anyway?

I think back over the fight. It felt good to be with someone who not only had my back, but was fucking awesome at it. I also enjoy his humor and teasing. I search for the usual aversion to company and overwhelming desire to be left alone, but I don't find it.

Huh.

"Did you throw that thing out of the tree?"

Drasuk's question pulls me out of my epiphany and the mixed feelings it brings up.

When I don't answer right away, he keeps talking. "I wasn't sure I saw that correctly. There was a lot of fur and goo in the way while I finished the other one off."

"Thanks for the visual. We need a bath again, Drasuk. We are so disgusting. Time to head back to the water."

"I heartily agree, but stop deflecting. Have you been keeping secrets?"

My hands are shaking now. I'm not sure if I'm ready to face just how much I've been changing. I mean, those changes just saved my life, but I still don't like it.

I don't want to talk about it. Besides, sharing isn't really my thing.

People get so fucking judgy.

I let out a huff of breath. I'm being ridiculous. Of course, he's going to tease me within an inch of my life about it. About everything, but he also sticks around.

Under all that arrogance, I have the strangest sense that I'm accepted for who I am. That I could scream at him, call him every foul name I could think of, threaten to decapitate him, even, and he would just let out that gravely laugh of his and keep following me like an oversized puppy.

I don't think I can shock him or run him off. It's so fucking infuriating.

And it's also one of the best feelings. Ever.

My eyes get full thinking about it, and I have to wrestle down my practiced response of tearing him a new one for daring to make me feel something so... big. Something so lovely and terrifying, I just want to run from it.

To deny it as I stick my fingers in my ears and say *la la la*.

Be an adult for once, Kira, I tell myself.

He's been uncharacteristically quiet, I realize. I'm pretty sure just the expressions that have been flitting across my face as the silence grew between us provided plenty of material to take a verbal swipe.

I glance over and his eyes and spines are so neutral it can't be natural.

He's waiting and carefully not pushing.

My eyes well up again, along with the usual unrelated, unearned anger, but I ignore both of them and speak. "I think I've changed again. I shouldn't have been able to do that. Human females, even most males, aren't that strong."

He waits a beat, then speaks. "It bothers you, even though it is an advantage," he observes.

"Yes. Humans don't like change, and I don't like giving up control. Especially of my own body."

He makes a rumble and once again passes up the opportunity to take a pot shot.

When I think back, he's never taken one when I felt truly vulnerable, only when I was acting like a little shit.

My most common mode, so there's been plenty of opportunity.

"You were exposed to braceaaer," he says, breaking me out of my musing, "and they are much stronger than they should be based on size."

A dark chuckle bubbles out. "I'm a fucking ant."

"I'm not sure what that is, but I do know you aren't that. You are Kira. There is only one of you in the whole universe and you will keep adapting right along with each stage of your metamorphosis. You'll figure out how to use every single change to make them wish they had never made the mistake of touching you."

There's something in my chest that hasn't been there since my parents looked at me with pride when I enlisted. It's more than just gratification. It's... hope.

War has a way of making you forget. Making you hard.

My nictitating membranes slide across my eyes and sweep out the welling tears. It makes me realize they stopped bothering me at some point. Stopped popping across when I didn't want them to, but protected my eyes when I was in the stream.

Hell, when I think back, they were over them during the fight in the tree.

I look down at the nanite suit I haven't bothered to command to fix itself and I see the long cuts made in it by the creature. The only reason my intestines aren't spilled all over that tree, along with buckets of blood, is the patterned hide from the sand creature.

"Just how strong are the braceaaer?"

"A factor of ten times their body weight."

I do some quick math. I used to deadlift about 210 pounds. So... what? I can lift a ton now?

I stand there in shock, briefly consider trying to lift Drasuk, then realize he's probably heavier than that.

Maybe not by much, though.

I shake my head. My curiosity isn't worth the awkward social interaction.

I pick up a rock, then chuck it as hard as I can. It pulps a couple of tree limbs as it flies up into the canopy and I don't even hear it fall, though I assume Drasuk heard it thump to the ground somewhere in the distance.

Okay, that is pretty damn useful.

Drasuk makes a sound of appreciation, and when I look over at him, his spines betray his surprise. "Very impressive, Kira. We might have to wrestle after we are done destroying every last hunter on this planet."

I tilt my head back and let out a laugh. "You wish, iguana breath."

When I look back, his spines have shifted toward confusion. "I'm not sure what was lost in translation. You always seem ready for a good fight."

I let out a snort. "Are you incapable of understanding double meanings?"

"Of course not," he huffs. "You just never make sense. I am perfectly capable of grasping nuance."

"Of course you are," I say dryly.

"I'm glad you agree."

"It's called sarcasm, Drasuk."

He snorts. "I've had enough human words for now. There is no need to keep discussing this since we agree that you are confusing, while I am adept at understanding."

I let out another laugh.

"Sure, you are."

"Is it common for humans to simply repeat phrases while acting like they are saying something pithy?"

"Oh, yes. I am adept at pithy," I shoot back, mimicking his arrogant tone.

"You are hopelessly opaque."

"And your manticorid overlords entered the wrong commands into the evolution machine."

He bristles, his spines shaking in the intensity of his affront. "You betray your shocking ignorance. We were from the same star system as the manticorids, already toughened by our lava-ridden planet, and over the course of millennia the early empire hastened our evolution. They took care to groom desired traits for loyal, vicious, and intelligent servitors, but they were our traits. We were the perfect shock troops for a first wave against the more resilient races. Drakonids have only improved since. When we spread our proto-wings to the greater universe at large after our independence, every single species held its breath until the clans finished taking whatever planets they wanted to subdue."

My eyebrows are both raised as he takes a ragged breath and continues his tirade. "We are evolution perfected. No mistakes were made, I assure you."

I blink a couple of times as he catches his breath.

"Whoa there, cowboy. It was a joke."

He grunts, his spines still raised in outrage. "You make no sense, human. None!"

He stalks aways and part of me feels bad, especially after he said so many nice things about me. The bigger, more childish part of me is what makes me jiggle my ass in an impromptu dance to finally be the one who gets a rise out of him.

I let out a couple more *oorahs* while popping my hips and then trot to catch up.

Time to make peace.

That way, the next time I get him mad, the victory will taste just as sweet. Besides, he's not the worst person to have on your team. I like our banter, and I want it back. I should go plant the seeds for another round of teasing once I inspire the return of his usual arrogance.

Hell, maybe I can teach him some dance moves. He's got a heck of a lot more ass than I do to shake, and not many humans can say the same.

I pity them.

37

Drasuk

"You aren't curious to know what a *cowboy* is, Drasuk?"

Of course I am, but I know she's baiting me, so I ignore her.

Judging by the sounds she made, she feels like she held some sort of victory over me. I liked that battle cry when I heard it from the trees. Much less so when used to taunt me.

"Alright, fine, *Mister* Grump Spines. Why don't you tell me some more about politics and let out some more of that manticorid *fanboying*."

I'm not sure what that last word means, but her tone seems genuine, so I assume she wants to fill in some of the giant holes of ignorance.

It must be terrifying to know so little.

I clear my throat, then provide her with more context. "After the decline of the manticorid empire, the rest of the more intergalactic conflict-capable races started an arms race to annex as much territory as possible under their respective claims. The braceaaer were the first to take advantage, mostly due to the fortune of being from a resource-rich star system. They had secured dominion over the greater portion of their home galaxy. They were looking to expand."

"How long ago?"

"Two millennia of standard cycles."

"Any idea what that would be in based on Earth?"

"Not without calculations."

She grunts back. "Well, this place seems to have a shorter day cycle than back home."

"Stop being vague if you want an answer,"

"So grumpy. It's not like I have a watch," she grumbles, adding a few curse words. "I'd say about fifteen percent shorter, but I haven't seen many days for comparison."

After asking her how many days are in her solar year, I take a moment to calculate. "That means roughly 2500 years, but with a 200 year margin of error."

"That was some fast math, *lizard* brain. I'm impressed."

"Human brains are not so facile?"

"Well, it depends on the human. Mine is, though."

I glance over at her. "I assumed as much, since you seem to have a very high number of nanites."

"Really? What's the connection?"

"Processing efficiency and neuron pathways. But you wanted to know about politics, not bio-tech. The xarxisi were the main competitors of the braceaaer before the genali ultimately toppled them to become the dominant race in their own stretch of the universe. As far as I know, they are extinct."

"What about your people?"

"Draks only focused on conquering planets in the Tayden galaxy, but as clans instead of a united force. As such, we were limited to whatever sparsely spaced planets whichever clan could capture. We didn't have the same drive to dominate as the manticorid, or much interest in the sort of large bureaucracy it took, so we never formed an empire."

She makes a low hum, then asks another question. "What about now? Is it just the braceaaer and genali who are the biggest threats?"

"Recently, murmurs have started about an unmarked species rapidly expanding its reach in the Zedill galaxy. There was a bit of evidence a few cycles back to support the claim of their expansionist efforts. Nothing very revealing. Just feeds of the few probe ships that have been sent out to explore the galaxy, but apart from blurry images of ominous-looking orbital weapons unleashing attacks on different planets, not much media makes it back before the probes are destroyed by unseen elements. We can assume someone is making a move toward being a new overlord in the galaxy, but no one knows who that someone is or if they plan to expand."

Kira shudders. "I don't think I'm prepared for the types of wars that involve orbital weapons. I prefer knives and guns, but that makes me a *dinosaur* by Earth standards too, so I recognize I'm deluding myself."

"Well, at least you recognize it."

She flicks her middle digit at me but keeps walking. "They've mostly left you alone, or what?"

I let out a rumble. "They pick at the edges. The braceaaer were the first to be bold enough to take a swipe at us. The more radical clans of draks decided to band together to end the madness. It wasn't long before they backed away with apologies alongside a generous convoy of interstellar carriers filled with gifts and innovative tech."

"Fiery pit in the ground, yes. Way to be, *man*."

From the sound of her voice, I think that was a compliment toward my species, but the words make no sense. As usual.

I haven't asked why depressions in the earth seem to have some sort of special meaning for her, but I'm still not interested enough to inquire.

"Another millennium and the genali started their own war, but unlike the braceaaer they employed pirate-like techniques to target choice, relatively isolated worlds. They never attack in force, just as bandits, and as you'd expect, any official communique for a cease and desist is moot given the certainty that all you'll get in return is a wet pile of lies."

"That tracks," she says, as opaque in her meaning as always.

Tracks what? I don't get a chance to ask before she continues.

"The genali seem particularly driven by greed."

"You are correct. When I was younger, I read a lot about the varying histories and philosophies of the different species we mapped back in the glory days. The one concept I have never really understood is the point of bloodletting over currency."

"What's not to understand, Drasuk?"

"Let me finish. I understand the concept of greed well enough. It is quantifiable as many concepts are, manifesting itself in different ways and to different severities across all sentient and sapient species."

"Alright, I'll bite."

"Bite what?"

"Forget it. You are being too literal again. I meant I'm ready to debate. What about food? How does it not make sense to be greedy about that?"

Do humans bite people they plan to debate? I eye her teeth, but they are just as blunt as always.

No threat there.

"It does make sense," I concede. "When in short supply of essentials, the need to preserve oneself can manifest as greed. It might be obstinate, but at least it is understandable."

"How about greed over land? Surely that is exactly what all your clans were when they claimed planets."

"This too I can appreciate. Your territory equals the area you can control. The subjugation of one's immediate environment is part and parcel of being a member of the intelligent species. It might be cruel, but it fits in with the way of things."

"Then you are contradicting yourself."

I scoff. "Don't be so limited. I am talking about currency. A literal fluid concept that is only as stable as your civilization. That is what makes little sense."

"I can't say I disagree."

"Exactly. Madness. Madness and then some."

"Well. Currency-related greed is pretty much the basis of every war I served in."

"Then your species likely has more insight into the actions of the genali than we do."

She stops abruptly and when I look at her face there is shock and anger there.

"What the fornicate, Drasuk? I can't believe you just..."

She lets out a strange growl and then picks up her pace, tromping through the forest in a rage.

I watch her go, confused by her reaction. I twitch my spines and follow her, my mind turning over the strange human's behavior.

Weren't we just having a philosophical debate? Where facts drive conversation?

A chilling thought worms its way into my mind: is she so sensitive to the deplorable social progress of her species she can't even bear simple comparisons? I contemplate catching up to apologize, hoping to put this awkwardness behind us. My pride holds me in place for a moment before I decide it is best.

I tip forward onto all fours and bound after her.

When I try to speak, however, she ignores me. We settle into a tense silence.

For a tenth of this world's sun cycle, Kira keeps up her brisk pace, her defiance fueling her steps. I fall behind again, hoping she'll burn through her anger so we can talk again.

She might speak utter nonsense most of the time, but she is still intelligent, clever even. I enjoy each exchange, I realize, even when it frustrates me.

I marvel at her stamina, wondering how such an aggressive species hasn't grown to join the league of planet-conquering races. Currency greed is a powerful motivator of technological progress, after all, even if it doesn't make sense to me.

There's no time to mull it over, though.

My nose twitches as I catch a stronger concentration of dry, acerbic scent. Braceaaer, and a lot of them.

Their stench has been all over the region and so I assumed we would encounter them soon enough.

I rush forward to catch up with Kira, my eyes scanning the surroundings. She's frozen mid step, her gaze fixed ahead. I follow her line of sight and see them—short, gray-green aliens with spindly limbs and aggressive facial features. The braceaaer see us, too, their expressions shifting to one of hostile intent.

Kira not-so-stealthily pulls out her gun and checks her clip, cussing under her breath.

"I'm low on ammo," she mutters.

"Stay back and cover me with whatever you have," I instruct, my voice a low growl. "I'll handle the rest."

38

Drasuk

"Now that's a plan I can get behind," she replies, her voice tight with her battle hormones.

They mix into her already delectable scent in a way that drives me mad. This disgraceful obsession has moved past occasional twitches to making my member swell against its confines. Not the best development when you are about to go into battle.

This female...

With a feral hiss, startling Kira as she watches my features sharpen, I drop to all fours and charge.

The first two braceaaer barely have time to react before I slam into them, sending them flying with a powerful sweep of my tail. They scream, while others belatedly grab at weapons and shoot at me, their projectiles grazing my tough hide as I close the distance.

The fight is a blur of motion.

I tear into them with savage joy, laughing as my bloodlust rises to the surface. Kira fires from a distance. Her shots are precise, dropping any alien attempting to shoot at me so none have a chance to take more than a few shots. More emerge from the undergrowth, seemingly part of a large hunting party.

The braceaaer are fast, but it isn't enough. I dodge their attacks with ease, my claws slicing through their thin bodies with little resistance.

One of them manages to land a strike on my more sensitive underbelly, a searing pain that shoots up my side, but I ignore it. My focus is on the thrill of the fight.

Kira's gunfire echoes through the forest. Each shot a reminder that she is watching out for me. I glance her way, seeing her kill another one of them with a headshot.

Her ferocity mirrors my own, and pride surges through me.

More braceaaer rush at me, and I revel in the challenge.

I leap onto a low-hanging branch and launch myself at them from above. My claws sink into their flesh, and I roar in triumph. The taste of their blood is metallic, mingling with the bioluminescent slime from the earlier fight.

The camp environment works to my advantage. I use the trees and underbrush to my benefit, ambushing them from unexpected angles. My tail whips out, sending two more crashing into a nearby boulder.

Their screams are utterly delightful.

Kira continues to provide cover fire. I see her take down another braceaaer, her expression one of grim satisfaction. Her presence is a steadying force, grounding me even as my bloodlust threatens to consume me.

The fight rages on, but we are relentless. I rip through them with a savage glee, my laughter echoing through the forest. Kira's bullets find their marks, each shot a testament to her skill. The braceaaer begin to falter, their numbers dwindling under our combined assault.

Finally, Kira lands the last shot, dropping the final braceaaer with a clean shot to its small chest. I take a moment to compose myself, letting the savagery wane. My muscles ache, and I feel the sting of multiple wounds, but we won.

Kira gives me a wry smirk, her eyes glinting with triumph and a glimmer of something else. I feel self-conscious under her gaze, the battle hormones still pumping through my veins.

"What is it?" I ask, trying to keep my voice steady.

She looks away, a faint smile playing on her lips. "Nothing," she says, turning to the braceaaer camp. "Let's gather whatever we can from here."

I watch her walk off; my eyes drawn to her oddly enthralling backside.

I rub my face, smacking myself lightly to stave off the embarrassing influx of emotions, then deliver a sharp whack to my midsection to stop the infuriating swelling. With a resigned sigh, I lumber off to help her gather anything of value.

The acrid stench of flesh and braceaaer innards hangs heavy in the air, a lingering reminder of the brutal fight. Stepping over a mangled corpse, I huff out a breath through my nose.

The camp is a disaster. Scorch marks mar the ground where blasts from where Kira's archaic firearm connected, and the remnants of their crude tents lay in shredded tatters.

"Looks like someone went a little overboard with the decorating," Kira quips, her voice laced with wry humor.

She gestures around at the carnage. "Though, seriously, who divides their enemies into quite so many... pieces?"

I snort. "It is no fault of mine that they're built like overripe fruit. Besides, who wouldn't want to relieve some stress after staring at your perpetually grumpy face for hours?"

She grumbles under her breath, wiping ichor off with her sleeve. My amusement abates a little. Seeing her frustration prickles at me in a way I don't quite understand.

But then, most things about Kira leave me perplexed.

We continue picking through the wreckage. The only sounds are our heavy breathing and the occasional squelch of feet sinking into the gore. My keen eyes scan the debris, searching for anything salvageable. Most of their equipment is collateral damage from our fight, but hopefully there are a couple of weapons I didn't destroy.

Plus, of course, the clips Kira is pulling from the crushed barrels of the others. Many of them intact.

My claws snag on a piece of metal partially buried in the dirt. I pull it free, brushing off the grime to reveal a battered but intact braceaaer gun. It should be a better option for her, since their hands are more similar to humans than a genali.

Relief washes over me.

From the scowl, I'd say she's about to point out my wanton destruction and start threatening me again. Hopefully a better gun is enough to distract her.

Beside me, Kira lets out a frustrated sigh. "I would have liked to gather more," she mutters, kicking a mangled hunk of metal.

"Here is this," I say, tossing the gun toward her. She catches it reflexively, surprise flickering in her eyes.

"Well, well," she says, a smile playing on her lips for the first time since the fight. "I would never say no to this little beauty. Looks like even a *lizard* with anger management issues can be useful sometimes."

My spikes shift at her tone. "Is that a compliment, human?"

"Don't push your luck, Drasuk," she retorts, but her tone is playful.

Further searching reveals a few more nutrient bars and I hear Kira cursing behind me and turn around just in time to swear out loud.

She's rubbing an ankle, and I assume she must have just hit it against something.

"Maternal copulator," she hisses, her voice filled with frustration.

I give her my deadpan stare. "So you are a mother?" I rib.

"What? No," she snaps back, noticing my attention on her.

"Then I don't understand how that relates to me making you scream out my name in pleasure," I quip back, my tone dry.

She glares at me, her cheeks flushing. "You wish," she shoots back, her voice tight with annoyance.

I chuckle, enjoying our banter. "I think I found a weak spot," I say, my spines twitching in amusement.

"You hit something, all right," she mutters, turning back to her search and gesturing around. "Lots of somethings. It looks like you fornicating rolled all over the camp, Drasuk. Just keep your eyes to yourself."

I can't help but shift my spines to show my amusement. She must not have been paying very close attention. It was more like pouncing and landing on my belly.

I couldn't help it. Braceaaer are just so delightfully squishy. And now she wants me to stop looking at her?

I don't think so.

"I'll try," I lie, my voice low as I keep my gaze glued to her form.

She rolls her eyes. "Just focus on finding something useful," she says, shaking her head.

I growl out my agreement, then return to my search. Despite the carnage, there are a few items worth salvaging. I find a small medkit, its contents still intact, and toss it to Kira. She catches it.

"Thanks," she says, her tone softer.

I don't reply as I savor the surge of warmth at her appreciation.

We continue our search in silence, the air between us charged with a mix of tension and unspoken understanding. Despite our differences, I know there's a bond forming between us, forged in the heat of battle and the shared struggle for survival.

As we finish gathering what we can, I glance at Kira, my mind turning over the events of the day. She's a mystery to me, this strange, foul-mouthed human with a sharp tongue and a fierceness that rivals my own.

"Ready to move on?" she asks, breaking into my thoughts.

That's when I see it.

Half-buried under a pile of braceaaer cloth, a glint of dark metal catches my eye. I crouch down and brush away the debris, revealing a long dagger with a blade the color of darkened zeltium.

It is more like a short sword at her scale, I suppose, the hilt intricately printed with what I assume to be some sort of braceaaer symbols.

Despite its obvious deadliness, there is an undeniable beauty to it.

Picking it up, I feel a surge of appreciation course through me. The metal feels warm in my hand, perfectly balanced. This wasn't some crude weapon these hapless braceaaer used to hack away at vines.

This was something special.

"What've you got there?" Kira asks, her voice closer now. I turn, the dagger held aloft, and my breath hitches.

She is bent over, rummaging through a braceaaer pouch, the top half of her body tilted forward. The movement offers a new view of her backside, encased in the tight black suit she wears.

Heat flares, fizzling along my spine and rendering me incapable of speech. My heart hammers against my ribs, and my mouth feels suddenly dry.

This fixation on a specific part of her anatomy is a new development.

A troubling one.

I know I've been staring for far too long, but the sight holds me captive. Memories of the countless battles I've fought, the countless lives I've taken, all seem to fade away, replaced by this... yearning.

It's incredibly unsettling.

Finally, snapping out of my trance, I quickly lower the dagger. "Just a little thorn, but made out of a very hard alloy," I mumble, my voice rough. "You can have it."

The little bit of fur above one eye twitches upwards when she looks at me, and I wonder how much of my feelings she can read in my spines. They ignore my attempts to shift them to something more neutral.

She takes the knife and runs a finger along the sharp end, not minding the line of blood that flows down the edge. "Pretty nice for a 'little thorn'. You sure you want me to have it, Drasuk?"

I grunt, not bothering to respond when I've already said as much, moving to continue our trek. My spines are shivering as I try to trample all these useless thoughts and feelings.

I look back when she makes a sound of triumph. She located the sheathe and is unsuccessfully trying to loop the too-small belt around her waist.

I swing my body back around and start walking away from the camp, Kira not far behind me as she makes annoyed grunts.

The sun is finally sinking below the horizon, having given us a day that felt longer than it had any right to. With it comes a shift in weather; a chill wind blows from the desert, making me bristle. It has a more profound effect on Kira and her teeth audibly chatter.

"Enough dawdling," I rumble at her. "Night is almost upon us, and I have a feeling that we want to be nowhere near the desert when it happens."

***

Kira sighs in relief when I tell her we can finally stop.

We are currently right in front of a large waterfall, having broken off the desert forest divide some time back to evade a swarm of pointy-looking desert beasts. I managed to snag one as we ran.

It smelled nice. Much-needed protein, all things considered.

I turn and Kira's face is slack as she stares at the waterfall with wide eyes. Something tells me that if it weren't for the situation she was currently in, she would stand for a long time admiring the nice view in front of her.

"Let's go," I tell her.

Then, I stride into the pool at the bottom of the waterfall, heading toward it.

"What are you doing?" she asks, confused.

I pause and turn. "There is a small cave behind the waterfall. We will use that for the night."

She looks like she might balk.

I suppose if I was her size I might too. The waterfall looks turbulent; she'll take a beating trying to swim through it into the cave behind, but she doesn't seem comfortable being out in the open, either.

After a huff, she carefully makes her way down the large slippery rocks into the pool. I continue on before glancing back to ensure she hasn't broken anything. Something about what I'm doing must be amusing to her, judging by the look she has on her face.

The water line comes up to my chest as I wade through it. Meanwhile, she must swim through the water to reach me, which is choppy from the violent pounding. She's an excellent swimmer but also tired, so she takes a while to reach me.

I wait off to the side by an area where the falling water isn't coming down as hard.

When Kira meets me there, I push through the cascade. She takes a deep breath and goes under the water. She kicks her legs and throws out her arms, going as far in as she can, trying to clear the roiling water, but it simply spits her back out.

I thought she gained newfound strength?

She pops back up, sputtering and cursing, then tries again. She might eventually succeed on her own, or drown, but I'm too impatient to find out. When she gets close enough, I reach out my tail, wrap it around her small waist, and pull her through the plunge pool.

She breaks the surface with a deep inhale and looks around. "Thanks," she coughs out.

39

Kira

It's quite dark in here. The moonlight barely breaks through the thick wall of water, but I can still make out Drasuk's large form a few feet in front of me. I watch as he steps up onto the rocky, solid ground.

The water is calmer than outside as I tread over to him. Once my feet can touch the bottom, I wade through it the rest of the way and step onto the cave floor. I'm shivering as I trudge over to a large dry mossy patch and sit down.

Today felt like a year.

I've rarely felt this wrung out.

I flop down, my head spinning, then take in a long breath. Even soldiering in ass-backwards regions came with more comforts than this.

I miss my apartment, as stark and impersonal as it was. At least there was a bed.

"Will I ever get back home?" I hear myself ask, then wince that I let it escape my mouth so it can lay heavy in the air between us.

Drasuk ceases looking around the small cave and comes closer.

"I won't lie to you, Kira. I doubt you'll find someone with the means who is willing to take you."

A pent-up breath bursts out of my lungs. "I didn't exactly envision myself ending up kidnapped by the universe's biggest galactic holes in the rear."

I really wish that would translate better.

I also didn't expect some sort of lust modification that made anything sapient I look at cause undesired lust, but I don't mention that one. Even though it's somehow worse than the original kidnapping.

He lets out a dark, rumbling chuckle. "Yet here we are."

I snort. "Here we are."

"That's an understatement for them," he says. "And in some ways, giving them too much credit."

My jaw drops open. Did he just join me in my endless cursing? If even by extension?

"Drasuk, my man, I might be rubbing off on you. How about we make it this, then? Genali are insecure little excrements with inferiority complex issues and overcompensate for their small packages. Is that better?"

"Define *package* in this context."

"You can't guess?"

"Should I be able to guess?"

"Reproductive organs, Drasuk."

He lets out a long-suffering groan. "How many different words also mean reproductive organs in your language, human?"

I start to do a quick count, but abandon it right away. I'd be tallying all night.

"A lot, especially names for food."

"That's disgusting."

I let out a braying laugh, my mind latching on to the humor at his appalled tone like I'm a starving woman, and his words are ambrosia.

Where are you when I need you, doves of Olympus? I could totally crush an ambrosia delivery right now.

I reply to him with a smile on my lips. "It is disgusting. It really is."

He lets out his own chuckle, probably more at my species' expense than I would like, but it still feels good.

I like his laugh. It bounces off the cave walls as if he's grinding down the stones. It isn't anything like the sick honking laughs of the genali. Nothing sinister about it, just a carefree rumble of appreciation.

"Got to hand it to you, Drasuk. You're funny without trying to be."

When I say his name, it sends a small shiver down my spine. As it often does.

His spikes twitch. "I'll take that as a compliment."

"Don't get used to it," I warn him.

My lips turn down when I think of never seeing Earth again. Well, I might not get home, but maybe he has a chance.

"Do you think you'll be able to get back to your crazy planet?"

I'm sad to see the amusement leave him, but for some inexplicable reason, the answer is important to me.

"I would like to give you a definite answer, but I can't. Right now, I think the important thing to do is to survive. And the only way for that to happen is if we kill any hunters we can find. Because as long as they are alive, we are not safe."

"No offense, but there is only one of you, me, and who knows how many of them. I don't know if you noticed and all, an excellent shot I might be, but I'm not exactly carrying around an army."

"That's why it's best I look for them before they come looking for us."

I wait a few moments to see if there are any other steps to his grand plan for planet domination.

Nope. He just keeps staring at me like he's Themistocles at war with Persia and he just solved all our problems.

"That's it? That's your entire strategy?"

"Some of the most effective are the simplest."

I can't argue with him. Not because he's right, but because my overtired brain isn't coming up with anything better.

A giant yawn overtakes me just thinking about it.

"I'm going to hunt for food. I don't expect anyone to find this hiding place, but if they do, I'm sure you'll make them regret the mistake of bothering you," Drasuk says.

"You say the sweetest things," I purr. "Don't take too long out there."

"Why? Missing me already?" he teases.

I snort. "Sure, can't you tell? I'm barely holding back a mountain of grief right now. Try not to get yourself killed."

Drasuk is still chuckling as he moves toward the waterfall.

His chest continues to rumble as he laughs, the sound dampening once he's in the water.

Once he's gone beyond the wall of falling water and out of sight, I shift my ass around on the soft moss to find a more comfortable spot, angling to take advantage of the dim light.

Using salvaged scraps, I spend some time creating a better way to secure the sheathe of my new ridiculous-looking sword. My fingers are slow and it's hard to see, but eventually I have the sheathe secured to a makeshift belt.

I pull it out to make sure it comes out smoothly, my right arm crossing my body. Satisfied, I move to sheath it, but instead find myself admiring the blade. The gleam of moonlight on the dark alloy makes me remember the joy on Drasuk's face as he completely wrecked that camp.

He kept me alive in that fight, then pulled this out, knowing I would like it, though I could tell it would have been a good weapon for him, too.

Was there something in his gaze when he handed it to me? Something soft and hopeful?

I shake my head, flinging off delusions and distractions. He was just being practical and increasing our chances of survival.

I sheath the blade with a decisive snick of metal against metal, then huff out a breath.

After that, I'm too dizzy with exhaustion to stay upright, so I compromise by propping myself up on my elbows as I pull the braceaaer gun up next to me, laying my hand on it where I can snatch it up quickly.

Then I close my eyes, just for a moment.

They burn with my need to sleep, but I resist, though the giant white noise machine at the entrance of the cave isn't helping my efforts to stay alert.

I lay back on the moss and wait for Drasuk to return.

I'm fighting a light doze when I hear a disturbance of something big exiting the water not far from where I lay. I snatch the gun up and swing it around, then let out a sigh of relief when I see it's Drasuk.

From the scent wafting toward me, he not only had a successful hunt, but took the time to cook it. I don't care what the thing is, it smells heavenly.

"I could kiss you," I tell him.

"What's a kiss? More violence?"

I let out a choked laugh. "Uh, yeah. Violence."

"An odd reaction, considering how much your stomach has been grumbling for food. Or I assume that's what that odd growling-screech was our entire walk."

"Yes, that's what it means."

He snorts. "Fitting, since that's how the rest of you communicates."

I flip him the bird, too tired to try to figure out an insult that actually translates. Instead, I focus on eating as much of the still-warm hunk of meat he hands me as I can fit in my stomach.

He happily gobbles up what I can't finish, and I equally gladly take him up on his offer to take the first watch. With no pressing need to stay awake, I'm asleep within moments.

✳ ✳ ✳

I'm running. My lungs burn with every breath, my heart pounds in my chest, and blood pours down my temple, blurring my vision. My left arm is useless. A gaping wound pulsing with searing pain, aching and twitching against me. I'm clad in my combat gear, boots pounding the rough terrain, trying to escape from something that feels like it's always just a step behind me.

The world around me is a chaotic blend of shadows and dim light, shapes that twist and contort in my peripheral vision. The ground beneath me shifts and buckles, making every step treacherous. I stumble, nearly fall, but force myself to keep moving. I can't stop. If I stop, I'm dead.

A guttural roar echoes behind me, a sound that sends a shiver down my spine. I glance back, and for a split second, I see it—an amorphous, monstrous shape with glowing red eyes, teeth gnashing as it pursues me relentlessly before it morphs into gleaming metal and skin. It's eyes the black orbs of a cyborg. The sight of it fills me with terror, urging me to run faster, but my body is already on the verge of collapse.

My foot catches on a protruding root, and I go down hard, the impact knocking the wind out of me. I scramble to my feet, but it's too late. The thing is upon me, its rancid breath hot on my neck. I turn to face it, my one good hand fumbling for a weapon that's no longer there. Panic sets in, a cold, paralyzing fear that grips my entire being.

The creature lunges, its claws slashing through the air, and I brace myself for the inevitable.

40

Kira

I wake up with a choked scream, my heart racing, my body drenched in sweat. For a moment, I'm disoriented, the remnants of the nightmare clinging to me like a shroud. I take a few deep breaths, trying to calm myself, but my hands won't stop shaking.

"Fuck," I mutter under my breath, cursing myself for overreacting.

I can't afford to be this weak.

I force myself to lie back down, closing my eyes and trying to will myself back to sleep. This is my opportunity for rest. It might not be the best accommodations, but my belly is full of whatever mysterious meat Drasuk brought back.

This is as good as things get here.

I squeeze my eyes shut and tell my heart to slow. It's no use. The image of that monster, a twisted version of the past and present, is tattooed on the back of my eyelids. Mixed in is the remembered terror and the pain in my arm that was once a constant companion. It's all too vivid.

Sleep won't come.

The sound of footsteps splashing through the water reaches me, and I roll my eyes, remembering Drasuk's superior hearing. Of course, he heard me.

He reenters the cave, his massive form silhouetted against the faint light of the waterfall.

"What's wrong?" he asks, his voice low and rumbling.

"Nothing," I mumble, turning away from him and trying to go back to sleep. "Just a bad dream. I'll take your watch."

He doesn't move. I can feel his eyes on me, expectant, probing. Damn it. I let out a frustrated sigh and sit up, glaring at him.

"I said it's nothing."

Drasuk doesn't budge, his expression unyielding. "It's obviously not nothing," he says calmly.

I resist the urge to throw something at him. Instead, I slump back against the cave wall, my anger draining away, replaced by a deep, gnawing weariness.

"Fine," I mutter. "You want to know? I was dreaming about my battlegroup."

Drasuk listens silently, his eyes never leaving mine.

"I was supposed to protect them," I continue, my voice trembling. "But I couldn't. I watched as they were torn to pieces. And I couldn't do a damn thing to stop it."

The memories flood back, the horror, the helplessness. I feel the familiar wave of shame and guilt washing over me, choking me. "I wasn't strong enough," I whisper. "I'm not a warrior anymore. Not after that."

Drasuk steps closer, his gaze intense. "You're wrong," he says firmly. "You are a warrior, Kira, even now. We're being hunted on an alien world by some of the most violent species imaginable, and you're still here. You're still fighting. Still looking for civilians to protect."

A bitter smile tugs at my lips. I quickly hide it, looking away.

"I was only protecting one person when they took me," I whisper, "and they were a terrible excuse for a human. I can't sleep well anymore. Every time I close my eyes, I see their faces. I see them dying all over again."

Drasuk's expression softens. "I understand," he says quietly. "I see the faces of fallen Maj'Ras every time I close my eyes, too. It's a burden we both carry."

There's a moment of silence, heavy and loaded with unspoken pain.

I meet his gaze, and I see a flicker of vulnerability in his eyes. "Would you stay with me?" I ask, the words surprising even myself. "Just... hold me? But it doesn't mean anything," I add hastily.

Drasuk makes a rumble of agreement, understanding. He lies down beside me on the mat of moss, wrapping a rough-skinned arm around me, pulling my chest to him and squeezing gently. It's comforting, though the peace doesn't last long.

My skin itches, and I scratch at it absently, trying to ignore the persistent irritation.

I'm not ready to face what I think it means.

"Thank you," I whisper, more to myself than to him.

His presence is grounding, a small anchor in the chaos of my mind, but sleep remains elusive, and I know this is just one more battle I'll have to fight on my own.

As my mind wanders, so do my hands. They hit a ridge of scars I've seen many times now, but never found the time to ask about.

"Where did these scars on your back come from? They're equidistant."

It almost looks like he was one of those stuffed toys you're supposed to try to get in that claw machine game that rips everyone off. As if he was the easy target nestled next to the sought after expensive gadget and someone used far too much force pulling him up in their rage over having to settle for a stuffy.

Well, if the machine used giant knives and rattled him around until it left two massive wounds and...

Okay, the comparison isn't holding up to scrutiny.

I don't come up with something better before he answers me.

"Those were my proto-wings."

"What?"

"Proto. Wings."

"I got that, damn the thing. Just not what that has to do with scars. Did you lose them in battle? That's terrible."

"No. I cut them off."

My jaw drops. "Say that again?"

"I. Cut. Them—"

"No. Don't say it again."

"You just—"

"It's just a figure of speech."

"As in writing?"

I blink, not getting it at first, then see how the translator fucked up again.

"No. Bad translation. What I meant was: why did you cut them off?"

"Then just ask that, Kira. Say the words you mean."

"I do say the fornicating words I mean," I hiss.

I let out a growl and refuse to admit that I just underscored his fucking point.

Dammit.

"To answer you, now that you have decided to make sense, the Maj'Ras cut them off because they are useless as soon as we grow too heavy as adults. They get in the way. Most civilians keep them as drapings and a show of prestige."

So, there are rich dudes getting to waltz around with the equivalent of fancy suits made out of their useless wings because drak like him fight.

Sounds familiar.

"Wait. You could fly as a hatchling? Uh, kid?"

He lets out a grumble, but answers. "Yes."

I absorb that new info as I try to wrangle the giant surge of jealousy crowding my chest and throat into something more manageable.

Draks have all the damn fun.

"You don't miss it?"

"No. Jet packs are more responsive and don't come with an energy drain."

I absorb that new information, confused.

"Let me see if I have this right. You're advanced enough to make fornicating jet packs, but a surgeon can't amputate your outgrown wings without making it look like an animal gnawed them off."

"As usual, you aren't listening to my clearly communicated words. I. Cut. Them. Off. But you are somewhat right, it did partially involve claws."

Holy shit, Batman.

"I have no words."

"Is that all it takes? If only I had known before. Go to sleep, Kira."

"But why would you—"

"Sleep."

"—do that to—"

"Kira."

—yourself?"

He turns to stone beside me and refuses to speak anymore.

I briefly consider poking at him some more, but just the mention of sleep has me yawning.

I can't help myself from reaching up and running my hands along the scarring again. I assume their wings aren't bullet proof either, if he was able to slice them off with his fucking claws.

Weird.

It makes zero sense why he would've cut them off himself, unless it's ritualistic, but I've got to give it to him.

That takes a brass pussy.

That reminds me. I haven't spied any balls on him, not that I've been looking or anything. He's stark naked but without any sign of genitalia.

I guess other species recognize what human women have always known: keeping all those important bits on the inside is a great fucking idea.

He lets out a long sigh as I continue to run my fingers along the dips and grooves of his mutilated skin.

Since it's clearly soothing for both of us, I just keep going, enjoying the vast variety of textures and the rumbles of appreciation he makes as I stray close to his spines.

The feel of his rough skin and the intermittent evidence of how battle-hardened he is sends a thrill through me, but I'm too tired to resist it or to be shocked by it. Right now, we are just two people who had a really shitty day.

Besides, I like touching him, so I just tell my brain to stop analyzing or freaking out over it.

Soon after, he shifts his giant body so he can return the favor, running one of his large, chameleon-like hands down my back in repetitive, soothing sweeps. Starting at the base of my neck with a gentle squeeze, then with steady pressure down by back, and over my ass before starting again.

I let out a long sigh of contentment on the fifth pass and keep moving my hands, mapping the spines and scars along his side.

As the long minutes tick by, the weight of our journey presses down on me. We can't stay in this cave, not with the genali still out there and a bunch of defenseless women to help. But for now, in this small moment of respite, I allow myself to find a shred of peace in Drasuk's steady presence.

The thrum of the waterfall lulls me into a semi-conscious state where dreams and reality blend together. I see flashes of my squad mates, their faces twisted in pain, their bodies broken. I see the cyborgs, merciless and unyielding. And then, I see Drasuk, standing between me and the darkness, a silent guardian.

His words echo in my mind. 'You are a warrior, Kira.'

Maybe he's right. Maybe there's still a part of me that's capable of taking up that role again. It's not like my body is a limit anymore. Maybe there's still hope.

I take a deep breath, and for the first time in what feels like forever, I allow myself to simply believe in something.

* * *

Sunlight streams through the gap in the rocks above the waterfall when I wake up, painting dancing patterns across the damp cave walls.

Unlike the previous night, a sense of peace has settled over me, and for once sleep wasn't a battlefield of nightmares. Hell, even before that, I couldn't get any rest.

It feels... wrong. Suspicious even.

With a hesitant groan, I crack open my other eye, blinking away the remnants of sleep. The weight of my combat fatigues feels strangely foreign, a constricting layer against my skin.

Wait. I'm not wearing fatigues.

I shake the sleep from my mind and focus on my body. I had just started to get used to the new way the thick hide on my stomach moves compared to my skin. Now it feels like it's extended to my back, up the back of my neck, and down to my knees.

When I shoot into an upright position, it startles Drasuk, and he rises with a hiss, which makes me tumble off him. So much for a relaxing morning using him as a giant pillow.

He is sniffing the air and swiveling around trying to figure out where the threat is.

"Sorry, it's alright. It isn't a hunter. I think I changed again."

He lets out a grumble. "Your communication is as deplorable as always."

"Back off, man. I was still half asleep, and I panicked."

I raise a shaking hand to the side of my neck. The skin is thicker than it should be, but the texture is different than my stomach. I keep sliding my hand around to the back, and then I feel the spikes.

They extend up and continue to the crown of my head, mixed in with my hair, which has grown quite a bit since my last haircut. A quick pass over my face and the front of my neck feels normal, but when I lift my arm so I can feel behind me, I can tell the nubs and spines continue downward.

I let out a puff of air. "Let me guess, I've got your blue spikes?"

"I can't tell from this angle."

Might as well get it over with. I stand up, pull the hair that has grown a couple feet so it lays over my chest, turn my back to him, and tell my suit to fully recede.

41

Drasuk

Even though she told me there wasn't a threat, I still can't stop my nervous scanning. I hadn't meant to go into my mid-level sleep, but something about her laying with me lulled me into it. Even I can admit it's been a long, exhausting string of events.

Usually there are plenty of other Maj'Ras to help share the responsibility, which is why once we are past proving ourselves, we rarely travel in groups fewer than four.

When she stands, grumbling out curses, it draws my gaze. Her suit recedes a moment later, and my body freezes as I stare.

She's beautiful.

Drakonid skin and spines cover her back and rise up into her pink hair. Her body tucks in at a small waist, then swells out again before transitioning back to her legs. My blue hide continues right up to the top of the globes of her rear, which are still her soft, brown skin.

Her hips are covered, though, and her new, far more protective hide covers the outsides of her upper legs down to the joint in the middle. My eyes dart back up to where the sand creature patterns blend with the blue.

Then they are right back to looking at her still very soft looking behind. The Maj'Ra in me would have preferred that was covered too, but the rest of me is very glad it isn't.

"Come on, Drasuk. You're killing me. What do you see?"

I tell her. Of course, leaving out my opinions about the soft globes. I also don't admit how much I want to squeeze them to see how they feel under my grip.

"Fornicate."

It takes me a blink to remember that it's a curse, not an invitation. I don't let myself dwell on my disappointment.

A question passes my lips before I can trample it. "May I touch you?"

I expect a quick rebuke and some sort of insult about my parentage, but instead her shoulders slump.

"Sure, why not?"

I take a slow step forward, unaccustomed to having an invitation to touch someone beyond teasing swipes, or the near-deadly blows of a skirmish. None of those included putting my hands on someone so fragile.

It feels different from the night before, when we were exhausted, and she had already lulled me into thinking it was acceptable to return her caresses. I hadn't thought about it beyond wanting to reciprocate how soothing her touch was for me.

Like nothing I had ever experienced.

There's a tremor in the pads of my outstretched limb when I open my opposing digits and slowly glide them along her back.

She feels just like a drak, and a breath in confirms she smells like me now, too. I flick aside an errant thought that I'd like her to smell like me for far different reasons, then focus on the feel of her under my hand.

I reach around her side, noting the differences in texture. I grab on to the front of her waist to hold her in place as I drag my other hand down her spikes.

I wonder if they will help me better assess her strange shifts in emotion.

When I reach the transition to her soft skin, I stop pondering and focus on sensation. I pause, waiting to see if she will tell me to stop, but all she does is let out a few panting breaths.

My hand continues its slow glide, reveling in the softness, not just of her skin, but in how pliable she is. I might have to stop using squishy as an insult. I had no idea just how alluring it could be.

As I squeeze one of the globes, she lets out a low moan. It makes things uncomfortably tight along my belly in response.

The scent of her heat surges, but she is also trembling. It is a sign of deep trust for a Maj'Ra to display vulnerability.

My chest fills with pride that she would offer that trust to me, but I don't want to push, afraid she will take offense. Afraid she won't let me do that again.

I don't like admitting to fear, and my warring impulses sicken me. Completely unacceptable for a veteran of my status.

I let out a long breath, then slide my hands off her and take a step back.

Before, her vulnerability might have disgusted me, but that was when I saw her as weak. Now I take it for the compliment it is.

A determination to be worthy of that trust crests within me, spreading out from my chest into my limbs, which twitch with a need to hold her again.

Not right now. She needs something altogether different from me now.

She turns to me as her suit covers her, though I do get another tantalizing glimpse of her chest. I'm sure it would be just as pleasant to squeeze. Her suit doesn't cover the spikes, just fills in the space between them.

Kira looks like she's anything but calm, even a little defeated. I have to remind myself to exude nonchalance, for both our sakes.

At some point, I'm not sure when, I stopped feeling unconcerned with her changes. I can no longer just focus on their utility but am now also wondering if they might be a threat to her health.

It's a shock, but I'm just as alarmed as she is. Showing it won't help her, though.

She has the genetics of at least four different species. It isn't natural, even to me, a species that has been heavily genetically modified. Ours was just an amplification of what already existed.

Not the traits of others.

I can't say I have a lot of practice at it, but I try to be a soothing presence.

"Don't worry so much," I say. "The only expression that really fits you is that mask of rage you like to wear so often."

Alright, I'm not very good at soothing people. It's always better to focus on your strengths, so I decide to needle her until she's snarling at me again.

She snorts, but the sound lacks its usual bite.

"I mean it," I continue, my spines shifting as my amusement builds. "This slumping doesn't suit you. But a visage that promises death? That's the Kira I know."

She glares at me, but I can see the faintest hint of a smile trying to break through. I keep teasing her, determined to get a reaction.

"Come on, bare those blunt little teeth at me," I coax, my tone light. "You know you want to, regardless of how impotent they are."

When she doesn't respond, I decide to take more drastic measures. I whip my tail around and whack her on the side, which elicits a nice growl and a firm hand on her sword in warning.

The next one lands on her rump, mostly because I wasn't nearly done touching it, but the outraged squeal I get is a different, just as inciting, reward.

"Stop it, Drasuk," she hisses, swatting at my hands.

I keep going, and finally, she gives in, laughing out loud. She lands a punch on my last incoming tail swat, but it's half-hearted, her anger replaced by amusement.

I let out a rumble of my own levity. "I'm glad we have that behind us."

She rolls her eyes, but I can see she's calmer now, the fear and panic receding, if only a little. I take a deep breath, preparing to tell her what I know, even if it's not much.

"Listen," I start, my tone serious. "There is a chance the modifications, or whatever is making you absorb armored skin plates, might not be permanent. If my knowledge of the genali's disgusting female trafficking is correct, they are always looking for new ways to please clients. This latest change is more drastic than I thought they could manage, but a manticorid might know more."

She frowns, absorbing my words. "So, this might go away?" she asks, her voice tinged with hope.

"Possibly," I say, not wanting to give her false hope. "It's all speculation on my part. But adaptability suggests change and change means this might not be forever."

She nods, a bit more comforted, though the uncertainty still hangs in the air.

"I need to prepare myself for it being permanent, but I do appreciate your words."

"And the tail whacks? Did you appreciate those?"

She scowls but doesn't respond. Of course she liked it.

I fall to all fours, stretching my limbs. "It's time to leave," I say, breaking the moment of quiet.

She packs up our supplies into the backpack, her movements more assured now. I watch as she places extra weapons and clips so they can be easily accessed. She checks her ammo, smiling at how many clips she has, then re-situates the zeltium weapon along her hip.

As we leave the cave and wade past the waterfall, my nose picks up a familiar scent. Dread fills me instantly. I never thought I would catch their foul scent again.

"I smell someone I know nearby," I say, my voice low and tense. "Let me carry you. It'll make the journey faster, and I feel like being nice to my pet today."

She gives me a flat look, then narrows her eyes. "I thought we had moved past the pet joke, Drasuk. What's going on?"

"You only thought we had," I reply with false amusement in my voice. I hope she hasn't figured out how to interpret the movement of my spines by now. They will betray me.

When I see her eyes dart up to them, I have my answer, though I continue to deflect. "I'm sure by now you know that your resistance to your pet status is futile, though I do commend your attempts."

She raises one of her delicate eyefurs, her face telling me she is suspicious, but simply gestures for me to go ahead. I scoop her up effortlessly, her weight barely noticeable. She grudgingly holds on as we move through the dense forest.

We travel in silence as I run, the forest around us eerily quiet. The ground is uneven, and the air is thick with the scent of damp earth and decaying leaves. The canopy is much thicker here, not allowing much light to filter through. The lack of ambient sound is unsettling.

We come to a large pond, its surface still and reflective like a mirror. I place Kira down without a word, not liking what I smell, then tip forward onto all fours and bound toward it. She hisses a curse out at me, but I can hear her running to catch up.

My dread returns tenfold when I spot the corpse of another drakonid. He's lying face down by the water's edge. His Maj'Ra armor is worn from extensive use and ripped asunder, useless now, a sight that sends a chill down my spine.

I rush to the body, my heart pounding. I recognize him immediately. Thukul. He was once a Maj'Ra like myself, though our paths diverged long ago. I stare at the tear in his throat as Kira catches up to me. She blinks at the sight, then starts scanning around us, her new rifle in her hands.

"Thukul," I whisper, my voice choked with equal parts rage and shock.

I kneel beside him, my hands trembling. His guts spill into the lake, the water around him tinged with blood. I close my eyes, taking a deep breath to steady myself.

"You know him? Who did this?" Kira asks, her voice barely a whisper.

"I do, yes. I don't know who killed him, but I do smell other draks."

Ones I dreamed of coming across again, but never in this sort of context.

My mind begins racing. "The rest of them are close."

"Judging by how you're acting, these aren't friends."

"No, they are not."

I don't expound, and she, rather uncharacteristically, doesn't press for more answers.

We stay by the lake for a moment longer, the gravity of the situation sinking in. Thukul was a warrior, one of the best, though he chose to throw away all his principles. If he was taken down, then we are in more danger than I initially thought.

I stand up, my resolve hardening.

"We need to move," I say, my voice firm. "Whoever did this could still be nearby, and we can't afford to be caught off guard."

She shoots me a look. "You sound worried, so I assume this isn't going to go well for us."

I sigh, before gesturing down at the corpse before me, "Maj'Ras armor is incredibly difficult to destroy because it uses very expensive alloys. There's a reason you have to earn your place as a veteran Maj'Ra, plus have political influence, before you get a set made for you. Whatever it is that could rip it to shreds is equally dangerous."

"A fellow Maj'Ra, but you don't seem to be mourning his death. Traitor?"

It doesn't surprise me that she figured that out. "Yes," I reply, leaving it at that.

Of course, that bastard Xar'Ar'ax and his crew would spend their time in these degenerate pits.

She nods, looking as composed as usual when a fight is imminent.

"Well then, it's about time we got the fornicate out of here, don't you think?"

I give her the flattest stare I can muster even as she pivots on the balls of her feet and begins walking in another direction.

Again, with the fornicating.

42

Drasuk

We've been on this hole in the rear planet for days now. I wonder why I didn't detect them before.

I let out a breath. It seems this foul-mouthed female has infected me with her speech habits. I better not let myself verbalize that phrase or she won't ever let me forget it.

As we move through the forest, we remain alert, even though the unspoken hope is to avoid running into anyone. Not exactly my usual approach. I haven't bothered to move us out of the way of the dangers I've detected so far.

That was before it was other drakonids who might be hunting us.

The initial shock of running into that group of monsters dims the longer we walk. Like any other emotion-intensive activity, it loses its impact with every hour that passes by. Not long after, the fear is all but gone, though the caution remains.

At least until I follow the smell of blood to the herd of xyxis floxis up a steep incline near a river.

Floxis are common domestic animals, usually stocked to run wild as a protein source on newly terraformed planets. They are stupid, but incredibly bulky things, engineered to provide as much meat as possible on one animal.

They are a more intimidating sight when alive, though I've never seen a group of them look so gruesome.

To say it looks like someone had far too much fun being incredibly cruel to this herd would be an understatement. They are all slaughtered. Someone drove them here, trapping them against a sheer drop down into a raging river.

That's when I know the traitors are still nearby. No honorable warrior slaughters entire groups of animals like this, especially those with females and young. They litter the ground, which is completely saturated by the animals' strange orange-colored blood.

I take a long breath in, but all I smell is the blood.

Kira looks like she is as disturbed as I am at the sight.

She gives me a level look. "Why do I get the feeling you have experienced dealing with whatever did that?"

She makes a sweeping gesture at the herd while cursing.

When I don't answer her right away, she speaks more forcibly. "I was mostly fine with you keeping things to yourself for a little while. But seeing this level of evil, I think you're going to have to tell me what's going on, Drasuk. Who was the dead drak?"

I tense up, not ready to answer the question. Not ready to think back to when Thukul had my respect, and then lost it. "I do not wish to talk about him, Kira. It's too personal."

"I get that, and I want to respect it, but his death really bothered you, which doesn't really make sense if he was a traitor. You haven't said a single arrogant thing for a really long time. As much as I've wished you would stop, I find it disturbing."

My gaze sweeps to her. "He was a terrible person. That's all you need to know about him. And now that he's gone from this life, the better off everyone is. If I could, I would have done it myself, but as it is, I am more concerned about what killed him. I can't say for certain, but I have a feeling it was the rest of the traitors in his group."

She curses. "How many?"

"I don't know. I only smelled a couple others, but that doesn't mean much. They are led by the drak outlaw Xar'Ar'ax. He was my brood mate. We completed our proving to become Maj'Ra at the same time, and he was easily one of the best warriors of my clan."

I take a pause, remembering, and she urges me on. "What happened?"

"Among other crimes, he was accused of killing civilians and selling their body parts to genali pirates in exchange for genetic modification procedures."

She curses, and this time I want to join her.

"Years back, I led the squad that destroyed their hideout, losing many good Maj'Ras in the process, but he was never found."

And now, he is on the same planet as I am. No doubt joining this season's group of deranged headhunters. I just hope I can get Kira somewhere safe before I engage Xar'Ar'ax and his group.

"We're taking them out, right?"

"I don't think you would survive the encounter, Kira. It is my responsibility, not yours."

She glares at me. "What happened to being a team? I don't know if you noticed this, but this world is huge. Plenty of places for them to be. What's your plan? Split up? What if they find me instead of you finding them?"

"They are close. This blood is fresh. I'd rather run you out of the area and then stalk back in."

She lets out a laugh. "And you think I would agree to that? You drive me crazy, Drasuk, but I don't back out of my oaths. We are allies, and if you need to take out a threat, then I will be there with you."

"Even if it means dying?"

She rolls her eyes at me. "Let's avoid that part, but I'm not leaving you."

Kira opens her mouth to say more, but lets out a startled yelp instead when a shot hitting a nearby tree throws bark at us. She drops to the ground, then rolls onto her back with her rifle in her hand. She's back on her feet the next moment, moving for better cover.

I move to a better location as well, trying to figure out where the shot came from.

I feel my skin prickle. I should have smelled or heard them.

I take a quick glance over to where I last saw Kira, but don't see any sign of her.

Keeping my senses sharp, I turn around when I sense someone coming up behind me. I quickly whirl around to face them.

Standing before me is none other than Xar'Ar'ax, the very traitor who betrayed our clan to a lesser race all for the purpose of feeding his sick pleasures.

His brother Mar'cte moves in from the right, and, to my horror, Mar'cte has Kira in his arms. She struggles hard to get out of the crushing grip that holds her pressed back into his front. He's a deeper red than his brother, and also shows signs of genetic tampering.

His eyes are no longer drakonid. If they weren't extinct, I would swear they were xarxisi. They were known for their silver eyes with glowing streaks of bright yellow that were forever changing shape and orientation.

I have a feeling they might have some answers for Kira about her own changes, not that they could be trusted to tell the truth.

They are both covered in floxis blood, which explains how they were able to get so close without me knowing. Did they butcher the whole herd to cover their scent? Just one of them would have provided the requisite blood.

"This is quite a surprise," Xar'Ar'ax says, with a hiss in his voice that doesn't match my memory of him. "I never imagined that, out of all the possibilities of worthy prey we could've found, it would be you, Drasuk."

The large red drak is just as intimidating as I remember him, with the same disdain in his voice as always.

Part of Xar'Ar'ax's prestige back on our home planet came from his impeccable genes. He is bigger than most drakonids, and many females sought him out for their heat. He was consistently more athletic and stronger than most of us.

He also had the early realization, compared to those of us who reached the same conclusion much later in life, that a fight was no place for fanciful moves.

There is no honor in letting someone else draw blood, but he took efforts to avoid it to a different level than the rest of us. He was open to all methods and tricks that came with dirty fighting. That, coupled with his already impressive size, made him out to be the sort of opponent you wouldn't want to run into if you could avoid it.

And now he has further added to his menace. His impressive height has gained an additional boost in the form of new bony spikes. His skin is a brighter red, with odd streaks of silver. He is completely covered in armor and weapons.

All in all, a sight designed to inspire unease, if not terror.

I narrow my eyes at the traitor. "I hadn't expected you either, but I can't say it is a surprise considering your usual terrible choice of company and allies. You clearly have always had more in common with slavers and pirates."

Xar'Ar'ax chuckles. "I don't know what I enjoyed more. The cries of the female you caught me raping and killing or destroying members of the Maj'Ras as I escaped. Both were quite pleasurable."

I snarl in disgust and anger. "You truly are a vile creature. I almost pity the winds of death when they come to receive you upon your death."

My attention snaps to Mar'cte when I hear Kira cry out. The traitor has his hand around part of her throat and lower jaw. Fear is ever-present in her eyes as he squeezes her. Xar'Ar'ax laughs and follows my gaze to his brother standing next to him with the small female.

"I can thank you for at least keeping our prize safe for us. I thought she may have met her demise with one of the many beasts here. Instead, we find her in your presence."

I blink, confused.

He continues his pompous tirade. "Imagine losing a whole shipment of perishable goods like these over such a hostile planet. The genali traders really should be more careful with their ships."

"I assume you had something to do with it, then?"

"Of course we did. If they are going to charge that many credits, there really should be more hidden treasures to find."

Either he's lying, and they found out there were valuable slaves on the planet, or he shot down a ship just for entertainment. If they did the latter, they must assume Shentrea will never find out or they wouldn't take the risk.

The bastard's incessant rambling brings me back to the present.

"My brother and I will be taking her with us now. Tell me though, do you think she will be even tighter and more delectable than the young female you didn't save? From the size of her, we might only get one use out of her."

Mar'cte laughs at his brother's remark and responds to Kira's struggles by squeezing her harder with the arm he has around her chest. She lets out a pained groan and I hear the snap of a bone.

Disgusting degenerates, my mind screams.

I want nothing more than to take this despicable traitor's head off, but I'm dealing with a difficult situation here. If I make a move, they might kill Kira, just like Xar'Ar'ax did to poor young Nkisa.

My hands tighten into fists at the memory before I hastily push it away.

"Let her go. This fight is between you and me. Or have you become a coward in addition to a traitor?"

I glare at Xar'Ar'ax, my teeth bared in a snarl. "Let her go," I reiterate, louder this time.

Xar'Ar'ax cocks his head to the side. "Now, why would I do that? She's my prize. I found her."

"Slavery has been outlawed for millennia. You're nothing but a disgrace."

I hear the unmistakable sound of wrist blades being engaged and look over in time to see Mar'cte holding one threateningly in front of Kira's face. I growl a warning at him.

"Watch how you speak of my brother. He's one of the best warriors in our clan, and you and I both know it," Mar'cte growls.

"You are no longer of the clan. You will cease this disgusting banter and fight me. If I win, she goes free."

"I can fight for myself," she yells out, then lets out her usual string of curses.

Mar'cte's moves his hand up to her mouth to stop her.

Xar'Ar'ax reaches behind him to pull a weapon from his back. "I will fight you. No one else will be a challenge here and I have grown bored with squashing slimes and trampling prey."

Before I can begin the ceremonial acceptance, Kira takes advantage of the loosening grip, pulls her glass dagger and drives it into Mar'cte's unarmored hand. He lets out an enraged roar.

Xar'Ar'ax and I look away from each other to Mar'cte.

His hand bleeds as the tiny female pulls it back out and strikes several more times.

He lets her go with a snarl, then pulls his arm back and slams it into her. Kira lets out a pained grunt as his arm impacts her torso, throwing her back. She hits the ground hard and rolls down a small, steep hill toward the river.

Then the ground beneath her disappears, and she is free-falling into the raging river below, screaming all the way.

"Kira!" I roar.

I have longed for an opportunity to confront Xar'Ar'ax, but now I must choose: stay and fight or jump in after her?

For a moment, I want to turn to the big red drakonid and tear into his hide, as I have in many of my dreams. Then Kira's scream pulls me away from my role as a warrior. Pulls me toward the strange woman, with her bizarre phrases, and those beautiful, perfectly squishy globes I had in my hands as she made my skin catch fire with her touch.

So much for being immune to her heat. This is exactly why draks avoid attachments and speak derisively about manticorid bonds.

As badly as I want this fight, I make the weak choice and quickly give in, sprinting to the steep side of the cliff.

Self-loathing that I couldn't let her go and am instead fleeing a formal challenge fills my chest as I urge my body to greater speed, panicked over the thought of losing her.

The others don't stop me as I jump off and start falling toward the river. I tumble, catching sight of Xar'Ar'ax and Mar'cte approaching the side of the cliff to scan the water below before I right myself into a controlled plummet into the water.

43

Kira

I am struggling to stay afloat as the current rapidly sweeps me downstream. Drasuk is surprisingly not too far behind me, maybe twenty feet. He uses his powerful arms and legs to propel himself through the water, trying to get to me as quickly as possible.

I throw up my arms to make sure he can see me struggling to stay afloat.

"Kira! Hold on!" he shouts over the choppy water.

He keeps shouting my name as my body twists and turns in the turbulent water. I think I see a glimpse of him behind me, trying to swim over to me against the currents.

"Drasuk! " I yell, only to start coughing as water splashes into my mouth.

I am starting to tire and lose my breath as the current continues to pull me through the water. Every now and then, the choppy waves come crashing over my head, and I find myself completely submerged. The roaring water is loud beneath the surface as I continue to get pulled in every direction like a piece of flotsam.

I briefly see Drasuk again before the waves block my vision and another current pulls me under. This time, I am down longer.

I feel lightheaded from lack of oxygen, and my movements become sluggish as I try to claw my way to the surface. Just when darkness starts creeping in at the corners of my eyes, I feel a strong pair of arms wrap around my body.

My broken ribs scream out a protest as he kicks us hard against the current.

Once we break the surface, I greedily suck in air and start coughing my lungs up, each hacking cough a new agony.

I throw my arms around his thick neck, using his spines to help me keep my grip, and he continues to push his way through the current. Drakonids may be strong, but even he is getting thrown around by the current.

He shifts us around until he has me above the water, then curls up into an approximation of an upside-down armadillo. Just in time, too, because we enter a section of the river with giant boulders and his tough hide takes the blows instead of my skull.

He has more surface area than I do, and so the river pushes us at alarming speeds.

"Hang on tight," he tells me, while also keeping a protective arm tight around my waist.

I don't respond but tighten my grip as much as I can without passing out from the pain.

As we continue to rush downstream, I spot a downed tree up ahead off to our left.

"Do you see that tree?" I yell over the sound of the water.

He pushes us more toward the left side of the large, thundering river. I assume his tail must have something to do with it. Now we are on a direct path toward the tree trunk lying halfway in the water, its large branches jutting out in every direction.

After a few more minutes of being carried through the current, he latches onto one of the thick branches with his free arm, his chameleon-like hands digging his claws deep into the bark.

I grab onto one as well.

"Use the branches to start pulling yourself closer to the river's edge. I'll follow right behind you," Drasuk instructs.

"I don't think I can," I yell over the rushing water. "Broken ribs."

"This will hurt, then," he yells back, then I feel his tail go around my waist and tighten.

It does fucking hurt, but it also makes me a lot more confident.

I start the slow and challenging process of pulling myself to shore. It's hard because the strong current keeps knocking my body forward into the jagged branches and rough bark of the tree. I'm once again thankful for my new tougher hide, since only my chest, face, and palms take damage as I drag myself over.

Drasuk stays right next to me and makes sure my grip doesn't slip. I try not to think about just how easy it would be for the current to suck me beneath the surface and under the tree trunk. I'm not sure I would avoid drowning a second time.

It takes some time, but eventually my hands reach the pebbled ground right next to the water's edge. My feet can also touch the bottom here. I crawl out of the rough water and collapse onto my back, huffing out rapid, painful breaths.

A few moments later, Drasuk makes it out and sits beside me.

"How serious are those bleeding wounds?" he asks me.

"Nothing all that bad."

Mostly, I'm just exhausted and winded. I lay there for a couple of minutes, just inhaling and exhaling, trying to get more oxygen back into my body. My dazed eyes lazily move to the big blue lug.

He's breathing hard, too.

Once I feel some of my strength return, I push myself up into a sitting position next to him.

"Thank you, Drasuk. That would have killed me. Pretty sure you grabbed me right before I drowned."

Drasuk makes his pleased rock grinding sound. "I should start keeping a tally of how many times I need to save you because you aren't strong enough," he teases between breaths.

I weakly huff out a laugh. Even now, he's still making jokes at my expense.

The big jerk. I like his style.

Then I look around. We are still surrounded by dense foliage, but I also see what looks like a mountain range in the distance. "Excrement, how far downstream did we go?" I inquire.

Drasuk looks around. "The current took us far. We are quite a distance west of where we entered the water."

My head snaps in his direction. "How do you know that?" I ask.

"Wind," he replies simply.

I stare at him longer for clarification, yet the meaningful look goes over his head. Or he just ignores me.

Probably that.

"So, where do we go from here, then?" I ask.

"I'm not sure at the moment. Either way, we are definitely being hunted right now, and not just in the more general sense. Now that Xar'Ar'ax is aware of my presence here, he will continue to track us."

Too bad I lost both my daggers to that fucker with him. The first one when he grabbed me, and the second to get away from him. The gun is smashed against a tree somewhere, the imprint of my body probably in the bark like those Wile E. Coyote cartoons after getting tail-tossed into it.

A tail is a stupid advantage.

As a testament to their over-confidence, they didn't even bother to completely disarm me.

Still, we lost too much. The water tore the pack off me, though somehow the sword is still in its sheath, thanks to me having the foresight to add a loop to keep it in. I did it because I thought I would lose it while being tossed around. I hadn't imagined near drowning as part of that.

Redundancies are always part of the plan, though, which is why I can feel the pressure of a medkit, ammo, and rations against my body. Damn useful, this suit.

"What makes you so sure he will want to keep pursuing you, though?" I ask as I wring water out of my shoulder length hair.

Trying to cut it with a sword should be fun.

Drasuk snorts. "You don't know him as well as I do. Before he became a sullied traitor, we were bitter rivals. Always trying to best each other. Whether it be in a fight or who could obtain the most impressive accolades."

"Oh, look at you, an overachiever."

"I don't have the energy to figure out what you mean by that, Kira. As I was saying, no matter what the occasion was, we challenged each other. Whenever we fought and I won, he always took it personally, even if he won the fight before."

I let out a disgusted scoff. "I served with some of those. Everything they don't like about themselves is somehow your fault."

"Yes, exactly so. When I began rising swiftly in status, he became resentful. I believe he knew that the elders were planning to elevate my status to Elite. It's something he strived for but could never obtain because of his shaky morality and dirty fighting. It tipped him over some sort of edge and a lot of good draks died because of him."

I don't like how tired he sounds, or the haunted tone in his voice, so I try to lift his spirits by being mouthy. "Are you going to make me call you Elite Drasuk now? If so, you'll have to start calling me Corporal Kira."

He lets out a grunt. "I would, but I hadn't earned the title yet by the time I left. It takes many years."

I take a slow breath. "They'll just keep coming?"

"He'll not call off this hunt. Not only for the entertainment, but it's personal now. His main goal now will be to find me, engage me in combat, and kill me."

None of this information makes me feel better.

Not only is that giant red devil insane, but he has a personal grudge against Drasuk. And now it seems he will be relentlessly pursuing us until one or both of them are dead.

Great. As if the rest of this planet didn't already suck enough as it is.

I hate that I'm involved in this feud between them, but that's just my exhaustion speaking. That bastard had me involved from the moment he put his hands on me. Drasuk can have the red guy. I'm taking down his toady.

"Who was the one holding me?."

"That was his brother, Mar'cte."

"He's so dead when I see him next."

Drasuk lets out a subdued laugh but doesn't call me on my shit. Damn, he must be exhausted.

"How many did you smell?"

"They were covered in xyxis floxis blood to cover it, so I don't know."

"Are we talking hundreds here?"

"No, I doubt that. There are plenty of draks I wouldn't trust, but very few of them would fall this low. Xar'Ar'ax must provide enough financial incentive for the genali to outweigh the cost of his crew's body parts. If he had hundreds of draks he would be a target."

"Well, that is good news, at least. For all we know, they've been here a lot and know the terrain. Maybe even enough times to have found their own personal little caves or hideouts. But that can be to our advantage too. There are a lot of places for him to look, so we could keep moving and gather weapons again."

Drasuk lets out a grumble. "I don't plan on running or playing his games. While he's tracking us, I will track him in return. It's better this way and will keep us on high alert."

Why wouldn't we be on high alert, anyway? It's weak reasoning for someone who is usually so calculating.

There's history there, sure, but it doesn't his current state of uncharacteristic distraction. I'm still unsure because Drasuk refuses to tell me the reason why. A part of me believes it goes further than the two hunters being bitter rivals and Xar'Ar'ax turning to crime.

"Drasuk, I know you don't want to talk about it, but I need to know. What else happened between you and him? Because I can't help but feel this goes beyond what you've mentioned. Help me understand. If we are going to continue traveling together, I don't want there to be any secrets between us."

I pause for effect. "I need answers," I push.

He sighs and looks away from me. I hear a few clicks leave him before he slowly turns his gaze back to me. "Alright, I'll tell you. But not here. We're out in the open. You may not have noticed, but I have. There is a severe storm coming. And judging by how fast it's moving, it will be over us very soon."

He stands up and reaches down with an offered hand. I grab it, and he helps me off the wet, gravelly ground as I brace myself for a lot of pain. Instead, there is just a dull ache. Odd, but I'll take it.

I guess when I think about it, there's been a repeated pattern of my pain levels diminishing when I calm down.

Should have learned more yoga, I guess.

I look up and around and notice dark clouds upriver. We leave the banks, picking our way through the boulders and slippery rocks, and back into the foliage.

A gust of wind blows, making me shiver and I ponder the possibility of snuggling up for warmth to stave off the cold.

Best not to ask until he offers, I guess, but I admit that the thought of his hands on me is not the least bit repellant.

In fact, there's a pain in my chest that lets me know I don't just want it, but I need it. Fuck.

Whatever.

I suppose I should be irritated that I want to ask for reassurance at all, let alone anything more, but I'm over all the angst.

Everyone needs comfort sometimes and now I know laying against him is surprisingly pleasant.

44

Drasuk

Fortunately, it doesn't take long for me to smell a cave, and it's a quick run after I convince Kira to let me carry her.

Now we are sitting side by side in it as she eats a ration cube. She offered me one, but I lied about my hunger. I'll need to hunt soon, though cooking is much more of a risk now than it was before.

Something raw would suffice, but I'm not sure her species is robust enough to do that. I'll have to ask her when the storm passes.

I move my body closer to her to provide some warmth as we watch the storm from the entrance of the cave.

Judging by the tremors wracking her body, and how she keeps rubbing herself with her arms, Kira is suffering from the sudden drop in temperature.

If she asks, I'll pull her close to me, but I don't have enough space in my mind to make sense of any insults right now. Better to not risk her ire.

She leans a little closer to me and clears her throat. "Well, your one item plan is *foobahr*, Drasuk."

"What?"

"Your 'look for them first' one-step plan."

"I remember it, Kira, just not what your human word *foobahr* has to do with it. When will you figure out how to simply state what you mean?"

"It's a fornicating *acronym*, Drasuk."

"You are making even less sense than normal."

"Fornicate. An *acronym* is the first letter of the words in a saying. In this case, 'fornicate ascended beyond all recognition.' Excrement."

She makes a deep groan and then continues, this time speaking her own language. "*Fucked up...*"

She mumbles some more sounds with space in between, then lets out a growl. I assume one of frustration, since it's her usual state.

"Forget it. The letters and sounds don't line up. All I'm trying to say is your plan failed terribly."

"So why not just say that? You spent a small lifetime explaining something simple."

She holds her middle digit up at me with a look of murder on her face. As if her tiny pink claw could do anything against me. Plus, murder takes more energy than what she has right now, which she proves by how fast the expression drops from her features.

"If I knew what that meant, it might be one of the few instances of you using quick, effective communication."

"It means fornicate with you... except it doesn't."

"You are the most confounding being I have ever met. Let me see if I understand this. It's an invitation, but not an invitation? An insult."

"Yes. Exactly."

"Well, what if you need to actually extend that invitation, but now it's an insult?"

"You wish, *lizard* breath."

"Wish for which, though? Hold. Disregard that inquiry. I've had enough of Kira loops of insanity. We need a better plan."

"That's what I just said, hole in rear."

"No. All you communicated is how delusional you are and how very little you know about communicating that you're in heat."

"What the fornicate? I'm not a *dog*."

Next, she'll be explaining what that is, probably in ways that bring up more questions and confusion. "I don't need to know, Kira."

"It's a— "

"Hold."

" —four-legged, furry— "

"Enough."

" —animal with— "

I finally reach my limit and pounce, covering her ceaselessly flapping, incredibly confusing mouth with its useless teeth.

The fact that she's currently trying, and failing, to penetrate the much thinner skin of my hand with them as she flails in my grip is further evidence, not that I needed it. Considering how loose my hold is, since I don't want to hurt her ribs, she is well past the end of her energy.

I let out a huff and loosen my grip even more, since I suppose I do like speaking with her, even when she is confounding.

I'd also prefer not to be stabbed in my sleep, although that doesn't stop me from taking advantage of my current hold on her to move us farther back into the cave. It is just deep enough to provide protection from the howling wind.

Judging by the cracking and groaning sounds outside, there will be a lot of downed trees once it passes.

Kira continues to bite me as I walk her back, but I can tell she isn't putting much energy into it, otherwise she'd be trying to stab me with that sword. In fact, she doesn't even start cursing me when I let her mouth go.

Instead, she turns her body into my embrace and even makes a contented sigh when I situate her so she is tucked up against me, my limbs and tail ensuring she isn't laying on the cold ground.

The smell of her heat surges, and I take in a long breath of it. It feels like more of an invitation than it ever has now that she's communicating her intent with more than just her scent.

The time is not right, though, and something tells me that she wouldn't be interested in a drakonid version of ending a heat, that she wouldn't just be content with continuing her line and waving me away.

The idea of that both terrifies and thrills me, then I remind myself that I can't have the sort of deep bonds manticorids and humans have.

This moment will just have to be enough.

I'm content to have her against me, where I can stroke her fur and the spines on her neck and back. I'll simply let my warmth seep into her and let her presence soothe away some of the remembered horror from coming across Xar'Ar'ax again.

Once we've rested, I'll have to follow through with my promise to tell her more, but I don't want to think about it now. I just focus on the feel of her, pleased when her body stops quaking from the cold.

She pats the smoother skin of my chest, then speaks. "Nothing will be moving around in that storm, Drasuk," she tells me, her rough voice reflecting her exhaustion.

"I agree. This is our best opportunity to get some rest. We might not get another chance for quite some time."

She falls asleep quickly after that, but I stay awake for some time, my mind continuing to provide memories I had long since buried. None of them are pleasant, but some of their edges are blunted now.

Not just from time, but because of Kira, too. Because I know that, regardless of how much time we spend teasing each other, she will listen and understand.

That pleasant thought helps me settle into a deep-level sleep. My awareness surges back after one sleep cycle, but the storm still rages. I move into a mid-level sleep with the command for my mind to listen for any changes.

45

Kira

When I wake up, I'm deliciously warm and feel much better. It hadn't actually been very long since we woke up in the other cave and fell asleep in this one, but sleep has been hard to come by on this stupid planet. Apparently, it takes a giant wind storm to get us some rest.

I take a deep breath in and wiggle to check how far along my healing has progressed. Not bad, just a dull ache from my ribs now.

After a nice stretch, I open my eyes. And then scramble away as fast as possible.

"Drasuk."

He startles awake, instantly ready to kill whatever threat is in the cave.

"You're shimmering."

I look down at myself and let out a yelp. "I am too. What the fornicate?"

He lets out a breath and thumps down on the ground again. "We aren't shimmering. Let me see your eyes, Kira."

I look up and he grunts. "As I suspected. Did you see Mar'cte's eyes?"

"Yeah. They were super weird and gross looking. Oh, wait... Seriously? Fornicate! Swirling yellow on molten silver isn't an improvement over pink."

"How they function is the improvement, if they are, in fact, xarxisi eyes. Remember I told you there was a species that tried to replace the manticorids?"

"Yes. You said they were extinct, though."

"They are, but from what I've heard, they could detect living creatures, even through barriers, and they described it as a shimmer."

"Isn't there pretty much a living creature everywhere I look? Why wouldn't the whole cave be lit up with it? Instead, all I see is sunlight hitting the walls."

"I don't know. But you aren't seeing the sun. It's very dark in here, Kira."

My eyebrows raise. I can see everything in here. No problem. No weird green night-vision goggle issues, though I suppose now I'm stuck with staring at Glitter Lizard.

He looks pretty cute, actually.

"Alright, I'm picking up what you are putting down about these eyes being great."

He lets out one of his annoyed grumbles to let me know what I said didn't translate well, but I'm too busy looking around in wonder to restate it.

"Am I going to be blind outside in bright sun now?"

"No. I don't know all the details, but I don't think xarxisi were light sensitive."

"Alright, fine."

I let out a cackle, channeling all the terrible superhero movies I watched during my misspent youth. "I stole this from my arch nemesis. Round one went to Kira, you fornicator."

"You did stab him."

"Exactly."

"And then he threw you off a cliff."

"Close your dirty mouth, Drasuk."

His laugh echoes in the small space, and my lips quirk.

I turn my gaze to the outside of the cave. I can see where a number of mid-sized animals are hiding in trees to wait out the rain. Judging by the lack of smaller animals on my new shimmer radar, it must only pick up creatures of a certain size.

Good. I don't need to know how many thousands of bugs are around me at any given time. Some things it's best to remain ignorant about.

"Do you think the worst of the storm has passed? It might be a good idea to start moving before it stops raining. Maybe it will help hide our trail."

"It would diminish it some, that's true, but if they get close, they'll still smell where we went."

I put a cheeky grin on my face. "Well, we could always hop back into the river."

He grunts. "That's actually a good idea."

"That was a joke, Drasuk. I don't want to get back in that crazy river. Especially not after a morning of torrential downpour is swelling it even higher. I like living."

"True. But we also need to gain some distance from them so we can plan and find another braceaaer group or camp. This time I won't destroy so many of the guns so you can find the ones that fit you best."

I assume this surge of giddy glee about gun shopping is how some women feel about shoes.

"Maybe I'll even find some weapons that will fit my hands," he continues.

I look down at his tough pads with his double sets of opposing digits, realizing that they no longer look weird to me anymore. It doesn't even bother me that his hands and feet look exactly the same and I'm only calling them different names out of habit.

I shake my head to focus back on his crazy idea. Well, my crazy idea, I guess.

"Are you sure you can keep us from drowning?"

***

It's fucking freezing, but I'm still alive. Drasuk has kept us safe, if not dry. The rain stopped a long time ago, but the river is still raging. My body doesn't even get any time to warm up to the water soaking me before another icy splash hits.

I'm noticeably warmer where my skin has been replaced by thicker hide, but that's only about a third of my body. I let out a snort. Funny how survival flips the script from worrying about a third of your body changing, to thinking about how the other two-thirds aren't as robust.

What can I say? Practicality rules supreme.

We reach another calmer section and Drasuk relaxes in the water for a while. It must be really hard work keeping his armadillo boat position amidst crashing into boulders and deadly currents.

I pat his chest and rest, too, by flipping onto my back instead of clinging to his spines. I'm pretty sure my new ant strength is the only reason I haven't been ripped off him.

"Alright, I'll admit it, Drasuk. You are a beast."

"Your tone says that's a compliment. Your words say otherwise."

"I guess you'll never know."

His tail flings up from the water and whacks me across the thighs. "Stop that. I was just getting moderately warm."

"Well, you should— "

I tense up and look around when his voice cuts off. He takes in a long, deep breath.

"I smell a manticorid."

"Really? Get us out of here, then. We need some venom in our lives to take care of Tweedle Dee and Tweedle Dum."

He doesn't even bother asking me who I mean, just keeps reorienting himself and testing the wind. After a few breaths, he uses his tail to move us toward the bank.

When we get there, I fling water off and squeeze as much out of my hair as I can. It's to the middle of my back now, but there hasn't been a good opportunity to make Drasuk swear he won't cut my head off using the sword to cut it.

Actually, this might be a good time. "I think we should chop off my hair and toss it out into the river. Maybe they'll follow the scent or something."

"Good plan," he tells me, then simply steps over, grabs on to the wet fall of it and slices it off with his claws.

My jaw drops. "You let me struggle with a little knife this whole time when you could do that?"

"All you had to do was communicate intent, Kira."

I'm repeating the phrase back in a childish voice as he splashes back in to drop our red herring out in the water. Well, pink herring, I guess.

As I watch my hair drift down the river, I can't help but appreciate how Drasuk allows the space for me to be my own person, his very nature communicating his belief in me and his respect for my independence.

As if a fierce woman is a default.

Everything with him is face value, which is infuriating, but it also means that when he compliments me, he fucking means it. When he tells me he appreciates my strength and what I bring to this partnership, I can believe it.

It's mind-boggling. Too much to process right now, really, so I shelve it for later.

Then we spend a long damn time moving around in circles. According to Drasuk, the scent isn't coming from any one place and there are a lot of overlapping trails. Some of them designed to confuse.

He's confused, alright.

He didn't appreciate my sarcastic comments about his hunting skills, at least not once he realized I wasn't complimenting him. I wonder if his iguana brain will ever understand sarcasm.

Good thing he has me to train him.

A few nasty meals and one long nap in a tree later and he says he's convinced we're getting closer. I keep scanning with my new spidey sense. Shimmer sense?

We've bypassed a lot of opportunities to take out genali. That's how obsessed Drasuk is with finding this cat-man.

He's stalking along, his body rigid and his spines telling me what he thought of my joke about wanting to meet his maker. I tell myself it's his new shimmer that makes me keep looking at him, but I'm finding more and more to admire about him.

He no longer looks like a stupid dinosaur lug head. I mean, he is that, but what I see now is his grace. Appreciating how the cant of his spines can convey so much emotion. The nuance of which way they lean communicating better than his words sometimes.

Then there are all the scars. I want to know each one of their stories.

Then a thought occurs to me that has my brow furrowing. I don't have scars. If he has nanites healing him too, why does he?

"Drasuk?"

"I have no interest in your thoughts about things you know little about, Kira."

"Alright, sure. But I have a question."

"Didn't you just hear me?"

"This isn't about manticorids and how much you love and hate them. About nanites."

He lets out a long breath. "Ask."

"Why do you have scars?"

"Nanites don't heal scars, Kira."

"That's food excrement, Drasuk. I had hundreds of scars before the genali. Fiery pit in the ground, my fornicating arm barely worked because a cyborg crushed it."

"I'm tired, Kira. Speak clearly."

A groan of frustration rumbles up my throat, but then I rephrase. "I had scars before. I don't have them now."

He stops mid-step and turns toward me. "Show me."

I tell my suit to recede from my left arm, since it was a mass of surgery scars before. "Excrement."

It won't be much help as an example, though, since I'm not sure how I didn't notice, but it is now covered in dark red drak skin down to my forearms.

"I would have preferred more of my blue, but I still approve."

I let out an annoyed grunt. "Well, look at my hands, then. Completely scar free."

I turn them to all sides so he can see them.

"Regeneration is not normal."

"Is any of this," I pause as I gesture to all my new freaky additions to underscore my point, "fornicating normal, Drasuk?"

"Valid point. No, it is not. The best person to ask is the manticorid. If anyone made those nanite upgrades, it's them."

"Sure. I'll get right on finding them, since it's not like that isn't what we've been trying to do for a million years or anything."

Even my own eye twitches at the double negative, but I don't restate it.

He grunts at me in annoyance, then I switch to English and start belting out the best cat-man attractor I know.

"Here kitty, kitty, kitty!"

I keep yelling it louder and louder for a few repetitions and then stop. The pain switching back to his language is worth it.

"See? Useless."

"Are you sure? Someone just responded."

"No excrement. Are you fornicating with me?"

"I would never."

"I don't believe you."

"'Never' leaves little room for misinterpretation, Kira."

"No, I meant... This is not important. Who is it?"

"How would I know? I can't understand them. It just sounds like your curses."

"Mimic it, then."

He lets out a series of sounds I ask him to repeat three times before it sounds like *who are you?*

"They're speaking English, Drasuk!"

I yell back as loud as I can. "Kira. Who are you?"

I wait a beat, switch back to Drakonid, and ask what he heard. "What did they say?"

"'Ree,' I think. There were many, many more words than that, so I assume she must be human."

"Yes! I know her, Drasuk. Pick me up already and move those feet."

"Are you sure you can trust her?"

"Yes. Just go, glitter lizard."

He grumbles, but he does what I ask.

Ree and I keep calling each other's names back and forth, but it takes very little time to reach each other.

Probably because she's riding a giant orange cat thing like she's He-Man. A tiny, very excited looking female He-Man.

"Kira!"

It's all she manages to say because she's all choked up.

"Greetings, soldier Kira," the cat rumbles out.

A sharp pain and I'm speaking his harsh language. "Hello. I assume you must be the manticorid we've been looking for?"

Ree finds her voice. "He is. Did you really just use the cat dinner bell to find us?"

"Well, it worked, didn't it? Sorry I don't have any Fancy Feast."

We both start cackling at that.

She wipes tears from her eyes and speaks again. "This is Thivoll."

Then she slides off Thivoll's back and rushes over to me. I slip out of Drasuk's arms and then crush her to me in a hug and pat her back as she cries. I'll admit to spilling a few tears myself.

I never thought I would see her again. Not really.

46

Drasuk

Kira introduces me and then they talk about incomprehensible things for a while longer, and not because I don't understand the language.

"I only know a few words of Drakonid," Thivoll admits.

Typical.

"We can't keep speaking in a language he doesn't understand," Ree replies. "It's rude."

I like the manticorid's choice in mate. Not as alluring as Kira, but far more thoughtful.

Kira snorts out a breath weighed down with disgust, instantly providing a perfect example. "His language is ridiculously literal. You talk in circles all day."

My tail twitches at her continual insistence that my language is at fault.

She seems to find any possible way to disguise her message, so it's little wonder she doesn't understand the beauty of words matching their meaning.

I let them keep talking it over for a while, preferring them to choose my own language, but I can't add my thoughts without letting them know I can speak Manticorid.

The venom-beast should put some work in. Find some grit that extends beyond science, art, or whatever other soft career he had and learn my language. Far fewer miscommunications that way.

Well, as long as Kira never speaks again.

After a while, I get sick of their looping attempts to balance fairness with expedience and speak.

"I see the 'master race' is still looking down on servitors and not bothering to learn anything about them."

Everyone freezes, and I let out a rumble of satisfaction and humor at how stupid they all look as they gape at me.

The manticorid recovers first. "I do admit I don't speak Drakonid. Otherwise, I know as much as anyone can about your species. You don't reveal much."

"And invite more opportunistic predators to reap the benefits of your genetic tampering?"

His hide twitches at that verbal swipe, but he doesn't extend his claws.

Instead, he keeps talking in that annoyingly calm, sincere voice of his. "I would never think of you as a servitor, Drasuk."

I cough out my disbelief.

He continues speaking, ignoring my temper. "If I may inquire, why did you learn my language?"

The whole species is ridiculously ill-informed, it seems.

"Every Maj'Ra learns it. All of us know that one day you will stop being so obsessed with your Thela-cursed tails that you'll wake up to see the threat surrounding us."

It's immensely satisfying to see his whiskers twitch when I mention their ancient deity. Technically only the master race is allowed to use its name so flippantly, even though they long since stopped believing in it.

I continue, pleased to have made him uncomfortable. "We've known for millennia that we'll have to recombine our people. Or die out completely. That surety infuses every tenet the Maj'Ras are taught."

His whiskers drop down to his chest for a brief moment before lifting again, this time quivering. When he speaks, his voice matches the same excitement.

"We are stirring again, honored Maj'Ra. Abstainers were steadily losing their place in Session when I was taken."

I have never heard sweeter words, but I'm still unimpressed with every stupid one of the venom-dolts. "We will never accept a lesser role than an equal ally."

"I would stripe the hide of any fool who suggested otherwise."

A grunt escapes before I can contain it. I might decide to like this one.

Possibly.

"You two are fucking adorable," Kira breaks in.

When I look at her she has her tiny hands folded along her cheek, her head cocked to the side, and her eyes widened. Something tells me it's an insult.

A glance over to Ree, who's covering her face as her body twitches in apparent mirth, and it's confirmed.

Suddenly Kira throws out her arms to the side like something has shocked her.

I dart my eyes around, pulling in long breaths and listening for whatever threat she identified.

Nothing presents itself.

"Wait. Hold on, now, my people."

Even in Manticorid she sounds like she's trying to confuse everyone around her. I let out a grunt and stop scanning for nonexistent threats.

"Stop being such a fucking asshole, Drasuk. What? What? Yes!"

I open my mouth to point out that no one is bleeding so I was being anything but rude, but she just keeps talking.

"What the hell? Prick. Dick. Shut up. Screw you. Yes! Everything translates perfectly in Manticorid. Thank *Zeus* and his fucking sister-wife *Hera*. Thank you!"

She starts gyrating around, lets out an *oorah* while punching a stick arm up in the air, then suddenly stills and puts a deadly serious expression on her face.

"Fuck it, we are definitely choosing this as our language. It's decided."

I huff out a breath, not even bothering to ask about a species who mate bonds with their sisters.

I don't want to know.

"All because you are obsessed with fornication? Typical Kira reasoning."

"Every fucking thing fucking translates. Oh. My. Deity." She ceases flailing for a moment. "Ok, fine. Not that one, but I kinda like it."

Then she's back to flailing. "Fuuuuuuck yes! *Oorah*!"

I can't help it. My spines are shifting to betray my amusement.

I never really believed I would ever make use of the Manticorid I learned in my youth. I figured they would just die out as they clung to their ridiculous beliefs. That it would be a wasted skill I'd never have to worry too much about because I would be dead right along with them.

And as much as it irks me to abandon my native language for the tongue of such a short-sighted species, I have to admit I love seeing her happy like this.

Or at least I assume her gyrations mean happiness.

It becomes less and less obvious what the goal of all this is the longer she throws her limbs around. Now she has her head down, her hands on her knees, and is shaking her rear up and down. Ree is letting out trills and hopping around next to her, her long hair whipping around in her fervor.

There is no clear pattern to any of it.

I feel my spikes shifting as a reflection of my discomfort. When I look over at Thivoll, his whiskers are nearly flat against his chest, so he won't be any help unraveling the mystery of this strange ritual.

We exchange a look and I know he's thinking the same thing.

Humans are completely insane.

Thivoll's rough voice breaks in. "Is this the one you said grew up with a knife in her hand, Ree? I'm confused."

"Hush, *Superkitty*," Ree tells him in a breathless voice. "Just dance with us already."

He lets out a chuff at the same time a surprised rumble escapes my lips. They call this dancing?

I look over at the Thivoll and he shows me his teeth. After a startled blink, I realize he is mimicking the humans. It's terrifying.

And not because of his teeth, but because I am now surrounded by utter insanity. Then he proves it by bounding toward them. Next, he's twisting around in the air, kicking up his feet like a hatchling, batting his hands out to catch Ree's twirling hair.

I might have miscalculated, I realize.

That does look like fun.

Before I let myself think about it too much, I'm tipping forward and pouncing. The sound of Kira's laughter as I make the ground shake with my antics soothes something in me I didn't even know needed it.

47

Kira

Ree and I are laying in a heap, still giggling between pants. Our two scary beasts really put on a show, but you'd never guess it now. They are both doing their best to look like they don't remember hopping around the clearing like playful puppies. Both of them crouched in their respective protective poses like nothing just happened.

Too bad, because I'll never forget it. And if they won't join us again, I'll be sure to make sure they never forget either.

Either way, I win.

Ree lets out a contented sigh and looks at me. I give her a grin and I can tell the little dance party helped heal something for her.

It feels good that I sparked it in her. Really damn good.

Thivoll breaks the silence. "As I was about to say, Ree needs protection."

"Of course, big guy. We'll crush anything that tries to get near."

"Let me finish. She mostly needs protection from herself."

Ree groans and throws an arm over her eyes. My eyebrows lift. There's a story or two there.

"Alright," I tell him. "I've met her sort. I know what you mean."

She whips the arm away. "Kira! What about human solidarity? Help me out here."

"Nuh, uh," I tell her. "Pretty sure kitty cat knows you better than I do. I trust his judgment."

"Thank you, Kira," Thivoll says with a purr. "We need her protected so she can strategize and recruit."

"Well–"

I don't get to finish because Drasuk cuts me off.

"I think it would be wise to let those with the most combat experience make such important decisions."

Thivoll starts chuffing and then turns to me. "Has he not realized you are in charge of him?"

Now I'm the one laughing. I turn to Ree. "What did you do to the poor cat-man, girl? Withhold tuna? Sneak catnip into his food and hypnotize him while he was high? He's whipped already."

Ree laughs and flaps a hand to dismiss my teasing. "He isn't whipped. He just, uh, seems to think I'm the commander of a bunch of troops."

Drasuk lets out his rock scraping scoff. "You are even smaller than Kira. What kind of commander could you possibly be if anything here could kill you?"

Thivoll goes from relaxed and purring to standing with his fur puffed out in rage in a blink. I dart to my feet in response, spilling Ree off me. A grunt from her and Thivoll's tail is whipping around and Drasuk is on his feet with spikes in their most menacing position.

He's hissing from between all those scary sharp teeth as Ree calmly stands and brushes herself off.

"Drasuk. Thivoll." Ree doesn't speak loudly. In fact, she doesn't raise her voice at all, but it is deadly serious. "Stop acting like kits right this instant."

My hair's standing on end as the two of them immediately de-escalate. I'm pretty sure any one of us could break her over our knees in half a second, but her voice sends chills down my spine.

It's somehow soft, confident, kind, and pure fucking steel all at once.

I'm in awe.

Part of my brain is screaming at me to even consider being part of a squad again, but the rest is too caught up in being fucking impressed to resist where this is headed.

Thivoll turns to Drasuk with a purr. "See. Like I said. A commander."

"Well, fuck me sideways, Ree. You are definitely in charge," I tell her as I poke her in the ribs.

Thivoll puffs up his mane in outrage again. "She will do no such thing. She is mine, Kira."

"Keep your claws in your pants, kitty. It's a figure of speech."

Thivoll lets out a grunt as his whiskers drop. "I don't wear pants, but if I did, that would be a terrible place for my claws."

I turn to the only other sane person in this group. "What is wrong with the rest of the universe, Ree? Are they all so fucking literal?"

Ree makes a humming noise and pats me. "I see you, Kira."

"Of course you see her," Drasuk breaks in. "She is right in front of you."

Ree lets out a snorting laugh. "Wow, Kira. I thought it was bad for me talking in circles with Thiv, but Drasuk is next level."

"Oh, sis. The validation warms my heart," I tell her with a chuckle.

"As I just said," I drawl out with emphasis. "You've got command presence, Ree."

Drasuk lets out a rumbly scoff. "There is no way your talk of fornication meant that, Kira."

"Shut up, Drasuk. Oh, deity, that feels so damn good when it translates correctly. Anyway... command presence. Natural and strong. It's really rare, and I would know."

Ree's face has turned a deep shade of red. "Thanks? I don't like being in charge."

"That makes you a great choice, then. But, for more pressing matters, we're being hunted."

"Yes, we figured that out, too," Ree tells me.

"No, I don't mean just by usual riff raff. By drakonid traitors."

Thivoll is back on alert, pulling whistling breaths through the roof of his mouth. Ree does the same with a grimace on her face.

She got a super nose or something? Huh.

I look closer and notice her changes. Orange hair, black scales, then I do a double take when I realize she has claws extended.

"Wow, girl. Look at those beauties."

She looks sheepish as she retracts them.

"I want," I tell her, my tone downright lustful.

It makes me remember my questions about our changes. "Are these changes Ree and I are going through something your people came up with, Thivoll?"

He shakes his head, and I dart a look over to Ree. She's done a far better job training her dragon than I did. I should have watched that damn movie.

Not to mention cats are notoriously hard to train, so she really is next level.

"What about us not having scars?"

His whiskers drop to his chest. "You don't have scars?"

"So it's not your nanite healing upgrade in us either, I take it."

Ree makes her suit recede from one of her arms, then grunts. "We've been too busy to pay attention, but she's right. I don't have a scar where I was shot."

My eyes narrow at the news of someone shooting her. We really do need to exterminate all the bugs from this place.

"Maybe it's something your government made in secret?" Ree asks.

"No."

"How can you be so certain?" I ask.

"I'm not exactly a person of power, but my dam works with nanites. She's the best in her field and very overprotective. If we had this capability, then she would have injected me with them, even if it meant not telling me about it."

A quick glance confirms he has a ton of scars.

Drasuk rumbles out his discomfort, and his spines reflect the same, then he shifts his body, betraying his sudden excitement.

"Wait. Is your dam Thalvann dea Shelvoll?"

Thivoll nods. "Yes."

Drasuk makes a rumble and his spines shift in a way I haven't seen before. "She is very well respected, even among the drakonid. Is she as fierce as they say?"

Thivoll chuffs out a breath. "She certainly is. I am Thivoll dea Thalvann, her only kit."

Ree makes a strangled sound and we all look at her. "How did it not occur to me until now that we haven't even shared our full names?"

I bark out a laugh. "We've been busy, Ree, but let's just get it out of the way. I'm Kira Grayson."

"True. This whole situation is crazy. I'm Muriel Johnson."

We all look over to Drasuk, but Thivoll cuts in first. "Not to be rude, but how about the shorter version for now, Maj'Ra?"

Drasuk makes a hissing sound but starts speaking. "Drasuk celck Amelindaen flen Zisitrax stren Nievernna xent Alixueth Maj'Ra tri Raskhar."

Holy shit. There is no way I will remember that. "Damn, lizard brain. He said the short version."

Thivoll starts chuffing. "That was as short as he could make it without insulting one of his ancestors."

Drasuk huffs out a breath. "Names have power, but we need to focus. Who could be making these upgrades if not your dam?"

"I don't know," Thivoll responds, "but it scares me."

"Genali have been rising," Drasuk points out. "Maybe a genius among them?"

"Possibly, though they seem to lack the creativity needed for that kind of the leap."

"I don't like it, Thivoll."

"I am in accord, Drasuk."

I can't stop myself anymore and break in. "Awww, they're patching it all up. It'll be a bromance in no time."

Ree snickers, Thivoll's whiskers drop back down, and Drasuk's spines betray his confusion and annoyance.

"Look," Ree says with glee in her voice. "The same expression. That means confusion for Drasuk, too, right?"

I choke out a laugh. "Yes. Adorable, isn't it?"

Thivoll turns to Drasuk. "I have a feeling this human female coalition at our expense will continue. I will need an ally, Maj'Ra."

"Yes. I think a truce between us is wise, manticorid, lest we lose all semblance of pride as they grind us under their tiny feet."

"Bromance. I called it."

"She totally did."

Ree turns serious again. "We haven't come across all that many dangers here. Well, fewer than I would have expected, but they were bad enough. These drakonids don't sound like good news."

My brow furrows. "Really? Until today, it felt like it was constant danger for us."

Drasuk breaks back in. "Of course. We've been moving straight toward it most of the time."

"What? Are you crazy? I could have used a hell of a lot more naps, Drasuk. I thought you had super senses."

Thivoll makes a hacking sound. "That's typical drak behavior. Straight into the fray."

Ree growls at him. "Be nice, Thiv."

Drasuk lets out a rock-grinding laugh. "It is a well-known fact, Ree. No offense taken."

Thivoll lets out a chuffing sound I assume is his own version of a laugh, then speaks again. "Well, I would prefer to continue avoiding danger where we can. We should head back to our cave and get both of you some rest and armaments."

I perk up at his last word. "Hell, yes, kitty-cat. Weapons. You know how to extend a proper welcome."

Ree smiles at me, but then turns to Thivoll. "Are you sure we should leave a trail back to Amethyst?"

She turns back to us. "How far behind you are they?"

"We will have at least a sun cycle before they are in range, maybe more," Drasuk responds.

She looks up, thinking. "I suppose if you found us, I would assume they would recognize Thivoll's scent and also want to take him as a prize. By now we have left enough scent trails even I could follow them."

She nods. "Alright, fine. Let's regroup in the cave. It's better than them finding Amethyst while we are somewhere else. But after we take out this group, we are going to need to move her."

Something tells me that if anyone tries to touch Amethyst, Ree will make them wish they were never born. She is crazy intense now, when just a few moments ago she seemed all cute and fluffy.

"I assume she is still in her chamber if you don't know her real name?" I ask Ree.

"Yes. I want to give as many of them as I can the choice to choose their metamorphosis. Silver was badly wounded and just a little bit of contact changed her."

I let out a breath and my heart constricts. I got a quick glimpse of her on the ship. "You don't have her with you? Is she dead?"

"No, thankfully alive, but some stupid snake man took her and won't give her back," her hands clench and rage flits across her usually smiling features, but then she continues.

"Trust me. I've tried to convince his stupid face three times now. Navy died in the crash, I'm pretty certain. I have two other males out looking for more women, but we need to deal with this threat as quickly as possible so we can find the rest of them."

I nod. "Lead the way, Commander."

She shoots me a look and rolls her eyes, but simply walks over to Thivoll, climbs on and turns to us.

"Can you ride on Drasuk's back? I don't think you'll be able to keep up with Thivoll otherwise."

I let out an explosive laugh, then look over to see the look of absolute affront all over Drasuk's spines, and just keep cackling.

When I stop, Ree still looks deadly serious. "Let go of your pride, Drasuk. It has no place here."

I wipe the tears from my eyes. "Burn. Oh, I think I'm going to love serving under you, Ree. So. Much."

Drasuk takes a long, deep breath. "I never agreed to serve, but will consent to carry your soldier, small female."

I look over at him, my jaw dropping, then shake my head to clear the shock that he agreed. "You could always just carry me, Drasuk. Or maybe my new ant legs can keep up."

He lets out a grumble. "No, she is correct. I will need to be on all fours to match a manticorid's run and there is no point in exhausting you."

As I jump up and find a spot to park my ass between his back spines, I feel like I've entered some new, even weirder reality. I grab a couple spikes in front of me and squash down the urge to kick his sides and tell him he is a good little horsey.

Even I know when it's best to stay silent and let a person lick their wounds.

Alright, fine. That isn't what stops me. He wouldn't get the damn joke.

48

Kira

Not long after, we are scaling a cliff and entering their cave. It's full of lovely, lovely supplies. It only takes me a few minutes to bristle with weapons again. Once I am, I let out a sigh of relief and take a better look around.

There are two exits and two rooms that lead off the main one. Someone carved doorways and shelves a very long time ago. One of the rooms is obviously their bedroom, so I stay out, but I do take the time to visit Amethyst in the other one.

She looks peaceful.

Ree comes up behind me. "We can move her out to the main area so you two can be in here. It felt wrong before, but it wouldn't be fair to you."

She doesn't let me respond, just calls out to Thivoll and not long after they've set up a pile of blankets in here instead of a cryo chamber. I'd love to take a nap on them, but I want some more answers.

They may not know much, but Ree might have some insights into what's happening with my body, since it's clearly also happening to hers.

I go out to where she's working on getting Amethyst covered back up. Then she places a note next to her chamber. A quick glance lets me know its instructions to stay in the cave.

I'm not sure what to ask, so I just blurt out an observation. "You only look like you have Thivoll's traits. Why?"

Ree purses her lips. "Now that I think about it, I haven't picked up any traits from anyone else and I've had plenty of exposure. From the dull ache and itch on my lower back, I assume another change is coming, but I'm confident it will be one of his traits."

"Really? I'm a walking science experiment over here."

She stills, her eyes darting back and forth. I assume sifting through memories. Then she makes a sound that lets me know she's figured it out.

"One of the slimes covered this in an advertising-slash-torture session," she says as my lips quirk up at her voicing the keyboard function.

I can see why Thivoll is utterly smitten. She's such an interesting mix of softness, quirk, and spine of fucking titanium. If I was interested in women, I'd totally make a play.

I glance over at the giant cat-man. Okay, maybe not.

I like living.

Ree's voice pulls my attention back to her. "I'm pretty sure it's because Thiv and I, uh. Because we..."

She looks so cute with her face burning hot I almost don't bail her out, but bitches need to have each other's back, right?

"Because you made the beast with two backs?"

She chokes out a laugh. "Wait. Is that from Hamlet?"

"Close. Othello."

"Ah. Right. Well, yes. That."

She still won't say it, and my usual wicked streak won't let it go.

"Dipped the wick? Hid the sausage? Parked the yacht in hair harbor?"

"What the hell?" she chokes out. "Hair harbor? Just stop."

"Are you kidding? I'm a marine. I could do this all fucking day. And you can't even say a tame version."

I open my mouth to keep listing, and she lets out a little yelp, tears of mirth in her eyes. "Okay. Yes. We banged."

"Seriously, Ree? That's such a boring euphemism. I'll need to—"

"Stop," she chortles, holding her ribs.

I can hear Thivoll's purr from across the cave, and I glance over at him. From the look on his face, I just scored some serious brownie points for bringing her out of her usual state of self-sacrificing obsession.

Or I assume that must be her usual state, judging by his warning and the brief glimpses I've caught so far.

She wipes her eyes and then continues. "Once you ride the wild bull you—"

"Nice one," I interrupt, impressed with the growth she is showing already.

I'm a great fucking influence.

She quirks her lips. "Thanks. Once you ride the wild... drakonid I think you'll only pick up his traits."

I quirk an eyebrow. "Who says I want to?"

She rolls her eyes at me. "Anyone with half a brain could see where you two are headed. You were made for each other. Like some sort of swoony warrior-meets-warrior story."

I give her a non-committal grunt. I might not be totally convinced, but she's close enough I don't have a pithy reply.

Dammit, that alone says more than I'd like to admit.

She looks around the cave, then speaks in a whisper. "The perma-arousal will go away, too."

Well, that would be nice.

I whisper back. "I highly doubt Thivoll can't still hear us."

She gives me a grin and Thivoll's tail twitches as he looks away, pretending to give us privacy.

"So... I keep gaining traits in the meantime? Some of them are pretty damn useful. That isn't a great motivation for bumping uglies with the big idiot."

She shrugs. "That's for you to decide, Kira."

"C'mon, now, *Commander*. You're supposed to think strategically."

She growls at me, extends her claws, and flutters her hands around while pivoting her wrists like a demented princess waving to her adoring subjects. "Don't think I won't cut you, bitch."

I tip my head back and let out a roaring laugh. "Diety, Ree. I fucking love you."

She smiles at me, and then goes back to shifting around supplies. I take a moment to figure out her organization scheme, then move to help.

While I do it, I think things over. I have the traits of multiple apex species. At what point is enough, enough? I look down at myself. There isn't a lot left that hasn't been changed.

It might be time to be done. I let out a huff. Who am I kidding?

I just want all this sexual tension and non-stop arousal to be over. We have been heading in this direction for a long while, no matter how much we deny it to each other.

Then I look over at Thivoll. One more round of changes wouldn't hurt, though. Right?

I pace over to the kitty, then tell him my plan. It takes no convincing at all. He simply extends a claw, cuts into his forearm and lets me take a nasty little blood shower.

Ree just nods, her face showing her understanding. When Drasuk comes back from patrol, he makes a grumbling sound when he sees the horror show but doesn't say anything.

Gotta love being around a bunch of warriors.

I let the blood crust over while we plan, urging the little robots in me to give me some useful changes, not just the streaks of orange I see in Ree's long hair. How does she stand it that long? Bleh.

We decide the best move is an ambush, with the two of us leading them into it, but Drasuk points out their sense of smell.

Ree makes an excited sound. "I know the place. It's a hot spring, with a lot of sulfur in the air. They won't smell Thivoll or me."

Thivoll lets out a harsh hack. "You aren't going."

"I'll shoot from a tree, Thivoll."

"You will not. These are drakonids, not genali."

Ree starts to speak again, but I break in. "Have you not realized yet, Thivoll, that you are not in charge?"

He lets out a chuff at me turning the tables on him and stops arguing. At least for now. I have a feeling they aren't done with the conversation.

Ree darts me a look, then keeps speaking. "Like I said. I know the place. You two just need to get them there. And of course, you know, fight."

We spend another hour or so debating the finer details and then agree it's time to get cleaned up and get some rest. From the looks I get from the rest of the group, I'm the one they are talking about.

It's not as if I enjoy lounging around covered in purple blood. Sheesh.

Before we leave the cave, Ree pulls Drasuk aside. They speak too quietly for me to hear, but when they come back out, Drasuk looks more settled and Ree looks pleased with herself.

I raise an eyebrow at her, but she just shrugs.

It doesn't take long to run to a stream and get cleaned off. While we're there, Ree points out edible plants and I stuff them in my mouth gratefully. Nothing like ration bars and meat to make you appreciate your leafy greens.

Soon after, we are back at the base of the cliff.

"We'll let you get settled in while we patrol," Ree tells me from astride Thivoll.

"You don't want to talk more?" Thivoll asks.

She kicks out at his fluffy mane with one of her feet. "No. We are going to patrol. For a very long time."

She emphasizes the last three words and then gives me an exaggerated wink.

"Oh, I get it," I tell her.

"Of course you do, Kira. She, unlike you, is using very clear phrasing."

Ree lets out a guffaw. "Let's go, Thivoll. Kira needs to explain some things to Drasuk."

They turn and run away, and I assume Ree clues Thivoll into her plan because I hear loud chuffing as he bounds out of sight.

When I turn to Drasuk his spines let me know we've confused the hell out of him.
Poor little lizard brain.

49

Drasuk

Just when I thought being confusing wasn't a human trait, just a Kira issue, my hopes are trampled.

I carry her up to the cave, still puzzling over what extra layer of communication I must have missed.

Kira hops off and heads into one of the rooms. "Come on, Drasuk. We're getting it on."

"What on? You can't possibly fit any more weapons on your body, Kira."

She lets out a laugh. "I'm talking about your weapon, *lizard man*."

"None of these weapons suited me. As you well know."

"Drasuk. I swear."

"As I well know, female. You curse constantly. Stop being confounding and just say it. How about we speak Drakonid to make it easier for you?"

She comes back out of the room we were told to sleep in, puts her little arms on her hips and gives me a death stare. "No way. I like cursing. Listen. Are you ready for my very clear words?"

"As if you need to ask that, Kira?"

"Shut up. You are going to come in here and we are going to have sex, you idiot."

"I am not an idiot. Nothing you said would have led me to... wait. What? We can't procreate, so why would you want me?"

"Why wouldn't I want you? You drive me crazy. Literally drive me mad. But you also have my back, you never back down, you call me on my shit. I can't take you in a fight, which is my usual measure of hotness. See? Let's go."

She disappears into the room, and I stand there in shock for several long heartbeats at how quickly she is speaking in very different terms. I hear weapons thumping onto the floor, which makes me curious.

I follow her cautiously, waiting for her to tell me this is another of her jokes.

Apparently not. Judging by how naked she is and that she's patting the blankets next to her, I might have to conclude that she is serious.

"I didn't think you wanted... I mean, I haven't ever... A female hasn't..."

She sits up. "Wait. Have you never had sex, Drasuk?"

I let out a long breath. "There was once a female I thought would ask when she decided to enter her heat. Xar'Ar'ax was jealous. Nkisa was the one he killed. I spent almost all my time outside of cities after that. It just didn't feel right anymore."

I don't admit to her that it was like I lost something that couldn't be regained. Something that Nkisa wasn't even likely to give me.

Something I should never want.

She beckons me over, her expression softening. "Now I understand your obsessive hatred. I am so sorry to hear that, Drasuk."

I settle in next to her and she pets my spines. "It has been many years, and I didn't know her very well. It is more the idea of what could have been."

"I understand that, for sure. I was just surprised. Especially after how many times you joked about making me scream your name."

I let out a long rumble. "It was simply in jest. I knew you wouldn't choose me for your heat and once it passed, you would focus on your offspring. As you should."

She snorts. "Drasuk. I don't smell like this because I want to get pregnant. Like I told you, *lizard dork*, human women are different. We don't go into heat. We fuck who we like when we want to fuck them. Preferably a lot. What I'm telling you is I want you. Like, right now."

I am immobile next to her as I absorb this new reality, but then quickly reject it again. "We aren't the same species, Kira. It just isn't done."

"What about Ree and Thivoll? They made it work."

I let out a rumbling scoff. "Those two are anything but normal."

"And we are? Stop being arrogant and short-sighted. Are you attracted to me?"

My spines bristle. "Insults only—"

"Stop. Just answer the question."

I let out a puff of breath. I consider lying, but there's no point in it. "Yes."

"Well, despite all odds, I'm attracted to you, too. That's the starting point. So how about we just touch each other and see where it goes? If we don't like it or we aren't compatible, then we know."

I get a sinking feeling in my stomach when she mentions the possibility of incompatibility, but it brings up one of my greatest fears.

Since we are being honest, I decide to simply say it. "I'm afraid I'll hurt you. I'd rather never touch you, preserve the partnership we have, then hurt you because of the weakness of arousal."

She laughs, and I feel like a fool. She must see it in my spines because she places a hand on my arm and her face turns more serious.

"Drasuk. Let's make sure one thing is very clear. Arousal isn't a weakness. It can be, but only if you let it rule you. I think we've demonstrated our power over it, don't you?"

I let out a grumble to concede her point, and she continues. "There are many different ways to share pleasure. Will you trust me to tell you if something is hurting me? Can we agree to communicate our limits?"

I take a long moment to think it over. I'm not sure when it happened, exactly, but I trust her, and I know she trusts me. "Yes, agreed."

Then we sit there awkwardly, neither one of us making a move to touch the other. We just keep cutting our gazes over and then looking away.

She takes in a deep breath. "I came into this convinced we should just get a hard fuck out of the way, tamp down on the arousal, and move on with our lives... But that is the wrong approach."

My spines shift with embarrassment. "Because of my inexperience?"

"That's what first gave me pause, sure, and I think you're right about preserving our partnership, but that's also not why. I don't even know what it is, just that I feel like I'm missing some important piece you aren't communicating."

I know what the missing piece is.

What she is offering is exactly what my species does, except solely for hatchlings and we don't speak of the pleasure. Like it is something to be ashamed of. I should be thrilled to no longer have all the conflicting feelings stampeding around in my brain.

I'm not, though.

I feel sick with disappointment. Like there was a glimmer of something building I wanted to push away with vehemence and embrace all at the same time, and what she is offering is destroying it before it can grow into something amazing.

It's funny how it took being offered what I should want to make me realize I've been running away from what I absolutely need from her.

What I can only get from her.

"Kira," I start, then stop, not sure how to voice it.

She just looks at me intently, waiting, giving me the space to work through how terrifying this feels, quick glances at my spines letting me know she has sensed it.

"What you offer should make me happy. My species doesn't attach themselves to each other. In fact, although we are sure another drak is there to express love to our hatchlings, we think showing it to each other as a mate bond is one of the greatest forms of weakness."

Her above eye fur shoots up, but she doesn't interrupt me.

"I want more than that, Kira. I want what you said your parents had. What manticorids have with their mates. Even if it makes me an outcast among draks. I want that."

I clear the fear from my throat, then continue. "I want that with you, Kira."

She blinks several times, then her expression displays her own discomfort. "Thank you for explaining it, Drasuk. I'm not saying no, but you should know that I'm afraid of the bond my parents had. It killed my mother when he died. Maybe not instantly, but eventually. I'm already broken as it is. If I let you in... If you die..."

She can't finish. She just keeps making hard swallows and her eyes are full of the liquid that betrays big feelings in her species.

"First, you aren't broken, but we can leave the conversation for another time." I try to be gentle, but she needs a hard truth. "Would denying it make it any easier if I were to die tomorrow?"

She lets out a huff of air, then spends a few long moments thinking.

After a dark chuckle, she speaks. "I'm not known for getting attached. I've also never considered crossing the line to have sex with someone I served with. If you think of it that way, I'm just as inexperienced at this as you are."

That makes me feel better, and my body loosens. "I propose we don't have sex tonight, then. We explore each other and let ourselves enjoy each new thing. No need to rush."

She turns to me with one of her blunt-toothed smiles. "Except possible death tomorrow?"

My spines shift to show my own amusement. "I think we've both stared down imminent death enough times to know it can't make decisions for us. But you do understand what I am saying I want, correct? I would rather not do this if you aren't willing to at least try to form a mate bond."

"Yes," she tells me in a small voice, then repeats it in a stronger one. "Yes. Touch me, Drasuk."

She leans back and I take a long moment to simply enjoy watching her. Such a small vessel for so much fire. She looks soft now in a way I have never seen and never imagined possible.

I get a heady rush when I realize that softness is something only I will ever get to see.

I'm not sure how happy she would be to know just how possessive that makes me feel. Best to not let her realize just yet that I've decided that she is mine and only mine.

Forever.

I'll need to ease her into more things than simply learning each other's bodies.

For now, I shift next to her so I can easily reach out with one hand, then sweep it up her hip along the familiar feel of drakonid hide, up over the oval markings on her stomach, to where her brown human skin remains.

A gentle touch to the soft mounds on her chest and she lets out a moan.

"What are these called?"

"*Breasts*," she explains. "Those are *nipples*. And, yes, they are erogenous."

That's all the invitation I need to spend more time there, just like I've been longing to do since I first teased her about them.

Not long after, I know she likes when I alternate between them, and that the darker circle is the most sensitive place. She moans deeper and arches her back when I gently pull the rough pads of my hands across them.

Her response makes me bolder, and I squeeze one *breast* between my four opposing digits, the comparatively blunt ends of my claws creating divots in her flesh, then extend my long tongue out to taste her. When the forked tip touches her *nipple* she lets out a long groan.

She tastes like minerals and her personal scent.

I want more.

"Where else, Kira?"

She points to her neck, then opens her legs and touches herself there. I let out a growl and move toward her neck, knowing that once I move between her legs, I won't leave for a very long time.

50

Kira

This is surreal, but it feels right. My mind stuttered for a moment when I saw him extend that long blue tongue toward me, but one touch of the tip of it and all thoughts of how weird this all is fled.

Now, the juxtaposition between the rough pads of his hands and the gentle glide of wetness is sending shock waves down to my already soaked core. I'm clenching my thighs with every flick of split tongue against my taut nipple, my breathing already elevated.

I take a moment to re-situate myself so my new drak spines along my back are in a more comfortable position and then bring my own hands up to return his affection.

I'm not sure where his erogenous zones are and there's a tremor in my hands from the anxiety and excitement when I lift a hand to run it along his cheek.

His skin is surprisingly soft there, and once my mind moves past the soldier's assessment of it being another area he is likely vulnerable, I enjoy the feel of it under my fingertips.

Smooth stretches interrupted by bumps as it transitions to a thicker hide on his face. Then back to smoothness as I move my fingers down toward his overbite of sharp teeth. Touching them brings an extra thrill, as I recognize that it would take him a mere moment to end me.

Then another quiver follows when I focus on the gentle touches of his hand, far more gentle than I usually like. But even I can recognize my insistence on roughness with previous lovers was another form of creating distance.

Rough is fun, and I'll work Drasuk up to it, but right now the look of adoration and wonder in his eyes, and those soft touches that let me know just how breakable he thinks I am, is filling up something in my chest I didn't know was quite that empty.

I shake that thought off, not ready to face it, and move my hands up to the spines of his forehead. From the rock-grinding groan he lets out, I'm certain I just found a pleasure area, and so I make sure I explore every inch.

Judging by the shivers I see running across his hide and wiggling his spines, he especially likes when I swirl my fingers and hands around the base of each protrusion. The long groan he lets out when I experimentally flick one sends a fissure of satisfaction through me.

Those will be fun to explore with my mouth.

Then I let out my own moan of pleasure when he cups one of my breasts and squeezes it while lashing my nipple repeatedly with the silken tip of his tongue. As I thrash, a grin stretches across my face at how competitive we are, even in this.

A rumble of appreciation moves up his chest to his lips and then he speaks. "I want to taste you now, Kira."

My body is screaming out for it and my mind is completely on board as well, but it's my heart that tells me to wait.

I let out a long groan of pleasure and frustration all mixed together, and then reply.

"I can't believe I am saying this, Drasuk, but I want to wait. Jumping straight into that is exactly how I would usually do this. Move as fast as possible toward release, make sure you get your own in return, and then scramble away as fast as my legs can take me."

He lets out a huff. "My legs are faster. You would not get far before I captured you and had my tongue exactly where I want it."

I let out another long moan and clench my thighs hard. "Fuck. Stop it, you are not making this easier."

A rumbling chuckle tinged with his satisfaction rises, and his spines shift to show just how pleased he is to see me squirm.

The bastard.

"Dammit, Drasuk. What I'm trying to say is that if you want a bond with me, then I think we are going to have to do things differently. Which means we stop at second base and walk around with a bunch of raging lust. Like hormonal teenagers."

After a long blink, he speaks. "Repeat that in words that make sense, female."

"I want to leave oral sex for another time, even though I am ridiculously aroused and really want to know what your cock looks like and then make you cum all over me."

He coughs out a breath, his spines going wild as his hide twitches. Seeing him fighting for control is satisfying revenge.

After a long moment, he gains back speech. "I can't say I like the walking around with raging lust plan, but any path toward a bond is the right path, no matter how uncomfortable."

I let out a breath I didn't realize I was holding and feel something in my chest loosen. The fear of taking that road he mentions is still high, but having made the choice to walk down it to see where it leads, I feel lighter than I have in a very long time.

I don't bother analyzing it. I just enjoy the feel of his hands as he pulls me up against him so we are facing each other, then let out a long, contented sigh when he runs his hands along the spikes of my back.

I do the same for his side, not able to reach all the way around to the larger spikes. From the long breath he lets out, it is enough. We lay like that, letting each other know how we feel with our hands for a long time.

Eventually, I drift off, confident that Drasuk will keep me safe.

* * *

I wake up cocooned in the warmth of his body. I search for any regrets and find none. The raging arousal is still there, of course, but I'm glad we didn't do what I first proposed. Looking back, it would have been an empty moment.

I can tell by the way my skin has new areas of tightness that my little manticorid blood shower had its intended effect. I poke Drasuk awake, and he grumbles at me.

"Don't tell me what you see. I want to go have Ree tell me how I changed."

He cracks open an amber eye, then it pops open with a look of appreciation before roving his gaze over me. From the look on his face, I assume he approves, but he doesn't tell me.

It's surprisingly hard not look at your body when getting up, but I manage it.

Our movement must wake up Thivoll, because I hear him murmuring to Ree to wake up. A moment later I hear her screech out in alarm.

"It's beautiful, Ree. Truly lovely, you don't have to hide your face," Thivoll says in a soothing voice.

Oh, this is going to be fun. "Are you two dressed?"

A moment later, I remember our guys don't wear clothes, but Ree gets my point. "You can come in."

She's huddled up against Thivoll with a look of horror on her face. Weaving next to her is a tail. A quick look over to Thivoll confirms it isn't his.

"Thivoll's right. You are completely rocking that new tail, Ree."

"I would say more like weaving it, Kira," Drasuk offers in way of correction.

He mimics the movement with his own tail with a pointed look.

"Shut up, Drasuk. You have a Mini Me manticorid tail, Ree. Rejoice."

"You don't understand, Kira. I accidentally cut Thivoll when I got my claws. What happens if I envenomate him?"

Thivoll chuffs. "You won't have venom, Ree. No female ever has it, but even if you did, I'm immune. Drakonids are only slowed by it, so I assume both Drasuk and Kira would be fine, too."

"Are you sure about that, Superkitty?" she asks. "What do you think that is?"

We all look closer at where Ree is pointing. There is a spike extended from it now, dripping a light purple substance.

"Dear Thela..." Thivoll breathes out, stunned.

"Come on, big dude, catch up. It was your DNA that changed her, and you already admitted to not knowing how this works. She's now a human-cat-lizard-scorpion, and let me just say, it's a hot look, Ree. Speaking of, once you're over your little existential crisis, how about you tell me what new tricks I got from Thivoll?"

Ree lets out a laugh and looks over at me while I tell the suit to recede.

Drasuk makes a displeased grumble but doesn't stop me from baring it all.

Ree's eyes widen. "Damn, Kira. You weren't lying about the science experiment."

"Thanks so much, girl. I just called you hot, remember?"

She shakes her head. "Oh, you look hot, in a seriously scary sort of way."

I purr. Literally. After a blink to adjust to that, I respond.

"My favorite way to look."

She smiles. "To answer your question, you have manticorid scales over your legs and arms, at least up until the red and blue drakonid skin. They are also on the front of your neck, across your upper chest and up onto the sides of your cheeks. Can you turn your leg?"

I pivot for her, feeling like I'm showing off a fancy set of shoes.

"You have a claw on the back of your heels, and I assume from the way your fingers look, you have black claws there."

I can't wait any longer and pull my arms up to my face, giddy. They are beautiful, in a monster mash-up sort of way.

"Are his scales bullet proof, too?"

"No, he's been shot."

"Damn, that sucks. But why not? If your so-called servitors have a thick enough hide on their backs to deflect bullets, why not you, Thivoll?"

"We were only able to modify existing traits, and only so far. Our scales are thicker than they once were, but drakonids hides started out tough enough to withstand random explosions of magma on their home world."

"Alright, well at least I got kitty scratchers."

It only takes a simple thought of needing them to make my new ebony claws extend.

Ree grunts. "Extending is the simple part. Retracting them takes more practice. I, uh, think of the polite claws that Thivoll taught me."

He lets out a chuff. "I knew it. And you teased me about that."

"Polite claws?" I ask with a laugh.

"You will need another method for Kira." Drasuk cuts in. "Nothing about her is polite."

My lips twitch, but I'm too busy trying to think up something polite to disagree with him. I realize he's right and so I switch strategies and think of picking up a wiggling puppy. They snick back into place.

I snort. "Don't you get sick of being wrong, Drasuk?"

51

Drasuk

Finding them was easy enough this time. I simply followed the smell of floxis blood, which is now a sickly rancid scent, but still recognizable. And also still masking their smell, so I am unsure of their numbers.

"I see drak shimmers up ahead," she informs me, pointing.

We are slowly making our way closer, Kira near my side when I hear the distinct sound of a rock burst cannon being fired. I grab the small female, push her to the ground, and position my body over her for protection.

The ground beside us explodes with a near miss.

Another thump of the shell being loaded into a large chamber lets me know another shot will soon land. I quickly pick her up and move away as the shell hits where we just were.

I find a large hollowed-out dip beneath the roots of a large tree and shove her in it. Then I stand back up and scan my surroundings.

As soon as I spot the form of another drakonid in a tree a ways to my left, the one in charge of the cannon fires off a third shot at us. I growl in irritation and dart out of the way of that blast, too.

"You sons of pedigree-less yolks. Come out and face me," I yell at the hunter in the tree.

Instead of accepting the offer of a fair fight, the drak starts leaping from one tree to another for cover, which only further enrages me. Have they lost even the most basic sense of honor?

Now that they are closer, I can smell them, but I don't recognize their scent. Maybe they are from a different clan.

I follow his movements until he stops behind a tree to our right.

Once he peeks out and takes aim again, Kira is ready for him. Her shot knocks his weapon out of his hand and I'm charging toward him as he drops down to retrieve it.

I quickly lash out with my tail, knocking him off balance. With a growl, I launch myself at him, throwing up an arm to deflect his frantic blows. He is weak, and it doesn't take me long to flip him over so I can sink my fangs into his tender underside, tearing through flesh and muscle.

I assume he regrets choosing easy movement over armor.

He screams in pain and tries to push me away, but I dig my claws into his side, holding him in place as I eviscerate anything I can reach.

"Move!" Kira yells out at me, and I don't hesitate to leap away.

Another cannon shell explodes right on top of my victim, finishing him when he takes a direct hit to his vulnerable stomach. They are that willing to kill their own?

I glance over at Kira, then over toward what she's aiming. She's taking shots at the drak working the cannon. She must have been trying to hit their eyes because they have an arm thrown over their face and I see a shot ricochet off.

I take advantage of the distraction she is providing and tear through the trees toward him.

He's an odd patchy green and brown. Coloring and patterns I've never seen on a drak. As I get closer, I see the addition of bony protrusions that offend me on a fundamental level.

It looks like Xar'Ar'ax has been doing well enough to afford modifications to more than just his inner circle.

I resist the urge to bellow out my derision. They are fools to modify what the manticorids already perfected.

He pulls out a metallic spear, lengthens it, and holds it in front of him. Unlike this mixed blood, I don't need a weapon to win this fight, though I will happily take it with me.

I crush their cannon as they retreat from it, then turn to face them. I flick my tail menacingly and bare my fangs.

"Your move, you disgraceful piece of scat," I growl.

He screams out in rage and charges at me.

My spines shift in amusement at a Kira tactic working so well. If they are that easily goaded, this should be a quick fight.

I wait until the traitor is close enough, then sidestep at the last second and whip my tail across his back. He grunts and whirls around to face me with a snarl. He tries to jab me with his spear.

With each jab he throws, I dodge or deflect with ease as I analyze his attack patterns. He is not very good, and clearly hasn't worked to increase his stamina because his hits become sloppier.

Shortly after, I see the start of one of his repeated patterns, which allows me to time a swing of my tail at his head. I strike one of his eyes. The move stuns him briefly, giving me time to kick his leg out and slam my claws into his newly exposed throat.

He stumbles back and falls to the ground, his spear falling away. The traitor looks up with fearful eyes. He goes to get up, but I knock him back down.

"Wait. Stop, brother." he pleads.

I will hear none of it. "You are no brother of mine, you inferior piece of excrement," I growl.

I let out a huff of breath as I move to finish it. Kira's speech habits are clearly invading my mind.

In a desperate last effort, the traitor extends his wrist blades and swipes at me.

I take a light blow to my chest, and then move out of the way. It only takes me a moment to transfer his abandoned spear from my tail to an arm so I can drive it through a gap in his armor through his heart.

His body jerks and spasms as I pull the spear back out. Ready to face whichever new opponent has entered the fray.

When I catch another whiff of floxis blood, I know the rest have heard us, but it still takes considerable willpower to follow our plan and not let the rage pumping through me goad me into charging at them.

I have more than myself to think of, and Ree's plan is a good one, as loathe as I am to admit it.

Instead of bellowing out my challenge, I take the time to strip the traitor of wrist knives and the plate of armor over his stomach. It is far too small, but at least it will be some form of protection.

I get it buckled on loosely, then grab the spear, activate the button that makes it retract into a smaller baton, and then click it into place in the slot made to hold it on the belly plate.

The ill-fitting straps chafe my tender underbelly as I run back toward Kira, but I ignore it. When I get to her, she has a hunk of pink hair in her hand, ready to release strands of it as I run toward the hot springs.

"You were fucking amazing," she tells me in Manticorid, and my spines quiver in pleasure at the compliment.

I rumble my appreciation as she clambers up my back, her weapons thumping against my hide. "Your shots were as unerring as always, little one."

She's grumbling some nonsense about size obsession and overcompensation as I pick up speed.

Kira

I'm still replaying Drasuk's ferocity through my mind as we gallop through the forest, making sure I periodically let go of a few strands of my hair. Not too many, or it might be suspicious. Just enough to make them think they are the ones hunting right now.

I had almost forgotten how satisfying it is to rely on another person. Hell, to rely on a whole group and play your role so they can play their own. He did most of the work back there, but we would have been dead without my cover fire.

If those were the easy kills, then I know for a fact that we won't have a chance of surviving the rest without the help of Ree and Thivoll.

It's like having my squad back.

That thought sends a pang of panic through me and I let a larger chunk of my hair go than planned in my moment of distraction. My heart is pounding as I push that thought to the back of my mind as violently as possible.

Fuck no. The loss of them broke me. How could I even be thinking about having another one? I can't take that sort of pain ever again.

Never.

A slow breath in as I cling to Drasuk leaves me the mental space to remind myself that this is a situation where we can't win alone. I've already tied myself to Drasuk, and let's face it, Ree has so much empathy and charisma you can't help but attach yourself to her within a few minutes in her presence.

It's too late. I can't avoid the hurt now. All I can do is fight until my last breath to protect them.

Every single hunter must fucking die.

I let out an *oorah*, then go back to my job of leaving a bubblegum hair scent trail.

***

I've been sitting here concerned we are being far too obvious. That they will realize it's a trap. Just to have them bumble in here in a long row like they own the place.

Thivoll wasn't kidding when he said draks just go straight into the fray. Of course, there are six of them, and two of us, so we look like easy prey.

I let out a snort. I probably only count as a fifth of a person to them, if I'm counted at all.

With a shake of my head, I get back into my role, let out a fake scream of terror, fling myself off Drasuk's back and run into the trees.

From the rumbles of laughter that are still coming closer, they didn't catch on to just how terrible my acting skills are, but from the very quiet snicker I hear above me, Ree sure did.

I flip her off, not even sure if she can see me, then scramble up the rock I chose as my initial perch.

Drasuk made me promise to not start shooting until after he accepted a formal challenge, which is fucking stupid, but I can tell it's important to him, so I hold off while they exchange insults, my gun poised as I wait for the final sweep of movement he said indicates he's done playing Mister Knightly and Noble.

I pull in a few long breaths to steady myself, wipe my hands on my black suit, and settle into a comfortable position. I swing my gun toward Xar'Ar'ax, just to dream, but keep moving to another target.

I also promised not to snipe that bastard, although it is the obvious strategic choice to take him out when they are puffing up their chests and posturing.

Whatever. I swing the gun over to his brother, Mar'cte, then curse at myself when I realize that I don't want to make his death quick.

Hypocrite, I chide myself, but then move my aim to one of their cronies.

I pick the largest one, at least. A big, dark-blue freak that looks like he had the genali mutate him into a bloated caricature of a drak. His spines are hard to make out among all the added muscle, but from what I can tell, he has even more arrogance than Drasuk.

Impossible, I know.

When I see Drasuk move into the last stage of accepting Xar'Ar'ax's challenge, his tail sweeping in an intricate pattern, I stop pondering and start shooting.

One careful squeeze and all that muscle is useless because the bloated fucker is stone cold dead with a shot through his eye.

Shots from Ree and Thivoll ping off two others, missing anything vital, but they do provide another opening for me as one of the smaller draks, a purple and black bastard with half his tail missing, roars out his rage.

He doesn't seem to like a bullet down his throat a moment later.

And six become four, three of which are now barreling toward us, leaving Drasuk and Xar'Ar'ax to their fight.

We keep shooting, but they are on to us now, slitting their eyes mostly closed and keeping their mouths shut. I shatter a few of the larger green one's teeth just for fun as they run at us, but know the time for guns has passed.

The smaller green one is the fastest, which means he's the one that dies when Thivoll drops out of a tree, thumps on top of his back, whips his tail around and I assume pumps a load of venom in him because a moment later the drak is screaming.

Thivoll takes advantage of his momentary incapacitation to pivot his body, kick him onto his side, and then start tearing at his stomach like a giant, enraged tomcat. I shiver at the sight of it.

Big cats have always been terrifying to me and I'm glad he's part of my squad.

I yell out, taking shots of Mar'cte to make sure he's pissed off enough at me to not double-team Thivoll, or worse, figure out where Ree is.

Her tree perch isn't much protection against a drak.

The bigger green one reaches Thivoll a few beats later and without the benefit of surprise he has a much harder fight, but I can't focus on it because Mar'cte is almost to my rock, his eyes promising death.

A quick glance to Drasuk lets me know he's holding his own so far.

I take a few more shots at Mar'cte's teeth, making sure he loses a couple, then I scramble up to pull out my sword. Not exactly a marine's weapon of choice, but a dagger isn't going to do much against the enraged red drakonid.

He leaps at me, easily jumping up the dozen feet to the top of the rock. I stab out at the junction of two of his belly armor plates and the blade sinks in as I scream out to increase my braceaaer enhanced strength. Mar'cte roars in pain, but continues the swipe of his enormous arm, launching me backward off the rock.

After a few moments airborne, I land hard on my back, then struggle to get air back into my lungs. Mar'cte doesn't even bother removing my sword, just skitters down the rock, moving far quicker toward me than I have time to recover my breath.

A streak of black, indigo, and orange lets me know Ree definitely lied to Thivoll when she said she would only shoot from a tree. Instead, she is plummeting toward Mar'cte, her face betraying just how much she would like to scream out in horror.

She hits him hard, throwing him off balance just long enough for me to drag a ragged breath in and push myself up to my feet. I launch myself at the arm he is raising to swat her out of the way, terrified he will hit her before I make it.

I plant both my daggers in his arm before he has a chance, screaming out my defiance as he tries to fling me off. Then a moment later he uses his much greater strength, making my new ant power seem like nothing, to slam me down onto the ground.

My collarbone snaps, sending a wave of agony, then he's tearing at my belly, not yet realizing that he can't penetrate the hard sand monster skin. He's reaching up to tear into my throat when I hear Ree's scream and a thump.

A glance down lets me know she's used her new venom on a small opening in his armor. Mar'cte starts bellowing out his pain, limbs twitching, his claws still close enough to my throat to make long gashes in the black scales.

Thivoll said his venom would only last a few minutes, so I push past my agony, rise up with a screaming cry of pain and push on the end of my sword as hard as I can. It penetrates to the hilt, and Mar'cte's dead weight is suddenly crushing me.

"Kira!" I hear Ree scream out, then pull at one of my arms, but I'm not going anywhere, my lungs screaming out with the need to breathe.

53

Drasuk

I'm bleeding from multiple wounds, but so is Xar'Ar'ax, despite his better levels of protection. Armor only protects you so much and it also slows you down.

I've fought him hundreds of times in mock battles, so I know he has lost his edge. Whatever he's been doing out in the universe, it hasn't been a challenge.

I thought he couldn't sicken me more, but living a soft life after killing Nkisa and all the others of our clan somehow seems like the ultimate betrayal.

I realize I've been dragging the fight out for my own revenge when I hear Ree scream out Kira's name, terror infusing her voice.

A moment later, I use the latest of the dozen openings Xar'Ar'ax has given me to dart my spear forward into the small space left between his armor and his throat. I don't even bother to let any satisfaction flow through me to see his life blood pumping out of his heart or the surprise in his eyes.

I turn and sprint toward Ree's screaming. Thivoll is still trying to dart his tail at the belly of the large green drak, having to pull it back hastily to avoid the swings of the drak's giant axe. I push aside all thoughts of fair fighting and grab onto his green arms just long enough for Thivoll to envenomate him.

I leave the screaming drak to Thivoll's sharp claws, panicking when I see Ree pushing at Mar'cte's dead body. It only takes a moment to realize Kira must be underneath of him and my heart skips a beat as I speed toward them.

"Move!" I bellow out at Ree, giving her a moment to scramble away before I shift to where she was and lift the drak up and fling his body away.

The ragged breath Kira drags in, followed by coughing and pained keening, are the sweetest sounds I have ever heard.

Her throat is bleeding, and I would guess by the way she is simply laying there crying out in pain that she has broken bones, but she is alive.

Ree is back over, pushing against me to get by. "Oh my diety, Kira. I thought you were dead."

Ree's voice sounds broken, but her movements are practiced and her hands are steady as she checks Kira over. I move forward again, sure I can better care for Kira, but Thivoll's hand on my shoulder stops me.

"She's a healer. Let her do her work."

I look back to Ree and notice she already has wound spray in her hands, misting it across Kira's throat, and then is working to slow the terrifying flow of red blood pumping out of Kira's neck.

"Sit down, Drasuk," she barks out at me, and my body instantly complies.

The pool of blood continues to grow. Surely someone so small can't afford to lose so much?

"Fucking nanites!" Ree yells out, using her weight to push down on Kira's neck so hard I'm concerned she might kill her. "Work!"

With the fear rises the self-loathing. I was playing in my fight with Xar'Ar'ax while she lay here dying?

Never again, I vow to myself.

If she lives, I will never again let my inattention put her at risk. If I continue to run straight into fights, she will run into them with me. Always by my side, no matter the stupidity of the risk.

No more.

All these years, wanting my revenge, and it is simply a cold weight on my chest. Empty and useless.

An image of Kira's eyes empty of life makes me bellow out my grief. I feel a furred limb reach across my back, then Thivoll's mane and side are pushing up against me as he sits next to me and embraces me from the side.

This is why drakonids do not bond, but I have no regrets.

"Do not lose hope yet, Maj'Ra," he rumbles. "Your mate is strong."

Ree sits back and for a moment I am convinced it is because she has given up.

"She is, and the nanites have apparently healed her *jugular*. She'll be weak, but I think she's going to live."

Thivoll is purring now, and I don't feel the least bit embarrassed when I return his embrace, the surge of hope making me fling off any last vestige of pride.

"What happened?" Thivoll asks Ree. "I notice you are not in a tree, as promised."

Ree turns to him, her lighter colored face flaming a bright red. Nothing like the beautiful flush that spreads across Kira's darker skin.

"He launched her off the rock and was about to kill her. I jumped out of the tree."

Thivoll makes a hacking sound. "You are terrified of heights, which is why I thought you would actually listen. Foolish of me."

She's looking at the blood on her hands now, then moves her gaze over to Mar'cte's body. Her control instantly crumples, and I recognize the look on her face as grief and horror.

"I-I used my venom on him, Thivoll. It gave her just enough time to kill him, but then I couldn't get him off."

She's shaking now and Thivoll leaves me to go embrace her instead. "You did well, Ree, no matter what your body is telling you right now."

She looks up at him. "This lust pumping through me isn't right, Thivoll. It's sickening, considering what I just did."

I'm confused for a moment, then I remember that Ree has a softer heart. She is mourning that traitor, not that he deserves it.

I shake off the thought as I move over to Kira, needing desperately to touch her and feel the steady rise and fall of her chest. Her eyes are closed, and I need them to open again and pin me with one of her looks that promise murder.

I ignore their murmuring for quite some time, just watching her breathe, thankful she is still with me.

Someone speaking my name pulls me out of my trance. "We will patrol the area so nothing can reach you," Thivoll is saying. "There are supplies in that pack."

I look over to where he is pointing and nod dimly, once again no longer concerned to suddenly be acting far too human.

Why would using one of their expressions diminish me?

I have been foolish.

Ree speaks. "Once her manticorid scales shift to cover the wound, you should move her into a hot spring, but pick one that is only a little hotter than her body temperature. I don't know if he damaged her back, but there isn't much I can do about it anyway if he did. Just lift her carefully to keep it as straight as possible."

"I will," I tell her.

She comes over and places a small hand on my arm, and it helps pull me out of my daze. I look over at her, seeing her in a new light.

She's even smaller than Kira, with no evident training as a warrior, but she risked her own life to save my bond mate.

Now I see what Kira knew from the moment they met. She has the sort of focus a leader needs, and I lack.

"Thank you," I tell the two of them. "We brought this threat to you, and you did not flinch. I am honored to offer what help a Maj'Ra can, if you will take me."

She grins. "Of course we helped, Drasuk, and I'll take all the help I can get in return. It'll take everyone we can get to find the other women and protect ourselves."

I return to staring at Kira as they move away for their patrol. This time my eyes are trained on the slow shifting of her black scales. Urging them to close faster so I can do something useful.

54

Kira

I wake up to warmth, weakness, and less pain than I would expect based on my last memory of being a pancake under a red mountain.

"Kira," I hear Drasuk breath out as I open my bleary eyes.

It takes me a moment to realize he is holding me flat in warm water.

I try to speak, but only a rasp comes out I'm so parched. I clear my throat to try again, then feel the touch of metal against my lips and cool liquid against them.

I drink greedily, thankful it is clear, fresh water instead of that nasty blue stuff I swiped from that genali... three years ago. Hell, maybe a century ago based on the way my body feels.

"Can you move your legs?"

I focus on them, relieved when they respond.

"Good. I'm going to move you upright now."

I nod and he repositions me so I'm nestled up against him. Then one of the nasty cardboard rations are in front of my face and I am far less thrilled.

I eat anyway, the pounding of my head, and my dizziness letting me know that I need a lot of nutrients to make up for whatever miracle happened to keep me alive.

My world narrows to chewing and swallowing until he stops putting food in my mouth. By the time I finish I can already feel my strength returning, but I'm still completely wiped out.

It's a struggle to speak, but I manage it. "Where are Ree and Thivoll?"

"She checked on you again a while back, they rested here with us, and are now back patrolling. Go to sleep, Kira."

I don't bother resisting.

***

When I wake up, I'm still cocooned in Drasuk's arms. I'm starving again but feel much stronger.

Telling him this doesn't stop him from carrying me to a bush and then hovering as I hiss out curses at him when he won't leave me alone to pee.

After only a few steps to test my limbs, pleased to see they're all functioning, he swoops in again, this time ignoring my thwacking him on his stupid, thick neck as he carries me back to the hot spring.

I don't tell him that it's making my chest feel weird... cherished, maybe?

No need to tell him I like it. Or that the warm water feels amazing, and so do his arms around me.

Then he's cramming food and water in my mouth again until I have to hold both hands over my face to signal just how serious I am that I can't fit anything else in my stomach.

After I'm sure he's done trying to dote me to death, I clear my throat, then speak. "I will definitely kill every genali I see, with no plans to stop, but I do like the nanites."

Drasuk's laugh is muted, and I turn to face him, pleased that the dizziness has passed, and my head is clear.

There's a look on his face and a cant to his spikes I've never seen before.

"Forgive me, Kira."

My forehead wrinkles. "For what? Arrogance? It's permanent, Drasuk. I accepted that."

"No. I could have ended my fight sooner, but I let revenge put you at risk. I will never do it again."

I snort out my disbelief. "I wouldn't have changed anything. He was on me too fast. Did you make Xar'Ar'ax pay?"

"Yes. He realized in that last moment how far he had fallen and how weak it made him in the end."

"Fornicate yes, Drasuk. Wait. Why are we speaking Drakonid?"

When I look up at him, then glance to his spines I can tell he is still wallowing in his misplaced guilt, so I just give him what he wants.

"I forgive you," I tell him, still speaking his stupid language just to show him how much I mean it.

An itching, throbbing sensation in my lower back tries its best to distract me from my goal, but I ignore it. "Now that we have that out of the way, you are going to show me your cock so I know what we're working with here."

He lets out choking laugh, not prepared for my raging libido. "You almost died, Kira. It can wait."

I switch to speaking Manticorid, the sharp pain worth it so I can properly curse. "Fuck that, Drasuk. I have magic robots. I'm fine. What might kill me is not having you inside of me."

His spines quiver. "Well, when you say it that way."

"Ha. So, I can, indeed, speak clearly. You liar."

I plan to keep talking until he gives in, but then I see the hungry look in his eyes.

My suit recedes with a simple thought.

"Fuck, yes. Drasuk. Whatever you are thinking, do it."

Apparently, it involves spinning me in the water until I'm up against his chest, pinning my body to him with his tail, and cupping my breasts in his hands. He's not as gentle as he was in the cave, though I can tell he is still being careful with me.

Still, there is a possessiveness now that wasn't there before. Every squeeze of my breast brings a deeper and deeper moan because every one of them stakes his claim. Normally, that would have me running away, but I'm over it.

It's time to recognize that I don't want him to leave. That his bossy, taunting presence pushed me out of a deep loneliness I forced upon myself. We have already risked our lives and will keep doing so.

I'll risk the pain of loss in the future to avoid mourning the loss of this bond right now. Something I never thought I would agree to.

It feels right. And so, I simply tilt my head back over his shoulder and bare my neck at him, embodying that surrender.

As I suspected, he knows exactly what it means, and a rock-crushing grumble of satisfaction vibrates against me.

"Mine and only mine?" he asks.

"Yes."

He responds by closing those scary teeth over my shoulder and moving one of his possessive hands down from my breast to between my legs.

I shiver, the danger of his claws making it a heady experience, but as I knew he would, he doesn't harm me. Instead, he positions his opposing digits so the thick pad of one of them is placing steady pressure on my clit.

I let out a moan, then continue to let him know with my inarticulate cries what feels the best.

As with everything, he is a quick study. I'm cresting higher and higher, the feel of his sharp teeth against my protective hide and scales making me pant. His other hand is flicking gently against each nipple in a steady, alternating pattern.

My stomach clenches and I let out a cry, going limp in his hold. He responds by lifting us up and out of the water, placing me gently on my back, and then greedily pushing his large head between my legs.

His spines scrape against my thighs, sending jolts of pleasure up to my core.

A moment later, his long tongue is diving into my channel, which is still pulsing. A few moments of it flicking at my terminus and I am thrashing and moaning out from my second orgasm.

He pulls back and speaks, his voice concerned. "You are too small for me, Kira."

It's annoying to have to think about anything right now, but I do, and the question seems obvious. "Are you any bigger than a manticorid?"

"You don't need to know—"

"Stop being jealous. I mean that if Ree and Thivoll work, then we would, too."

He blinks, his amber eyes gaining back his hunger. "I see your point."

Thankfully, he doesn't continue the conversation, and his tongue is right back inside me. He has impressive control over it and learns just as quickly where the spots are inside that drive me wild, the sensation of the forked tip something I never imagined.

It's ruined me for anything else. Good thing he's all I need.

Well, once he gets around to showing me his equipment.

"I want to see where you are hiding this supposedly massive cock."

He gets revenge for my sass by writhing his tongue around, pulling another keening cry of pleasure from me as my limbs are taken over by a surge of pleasure.

When I come back to myself, he has tipped himself back and I watch in fascination as the long segmented skin along his belly parts and a glistening, royal blue member slides out. Standing proudly and twitching under my gaze.

My mouth drops open. He can be as arrogant as he wants about that beautiful thing.

It's oval shaped, instead of round, with nodules running along it in a swirling pattern, begging to be explored.

He starts to tip forward and I hold a hand up. "No way. Stay there."

I almost feel bad when his spines shift to confusion and embarrassment, but he'll figure out my plan soon enough.

I crawl forward, eager to touch him and find out how he tastes. He takes a breath, probably to ask me what the hell I am doing, but I'm too fast for him.

I take him firmly in both hands, pleased with the silken texture, as I fold my legs under me, then take a long lick from his base to his tip.

He lets out the most glorious sound. A mix of pain and rumbling of rocks and it spurs me on. I quickly find my rhythm, enjoying the tangy taste of him, the softness that glides over the nodule structure underneath.

The head of it continues down much farther than I would expect, and my tongue runs along the interesting ridge about a third of the way down as I ponder why it is there.

I don't get to think much longer because Drasuk barks out a command. "On your knees."

I resist the urge to balk at being ordered around, then move into position, my heart pounding in anticipation.

I'm not sure this is going to work, but if someone else can do it, then I can do it even better.

I moan when he grabs my hips, rough skin rubbing against my own tough hide. I was concerned it would lower my sensation, but somehow I can still feel each glide of his hands and the slight pinch of his claws.

Then I feel his wet touch at my entrance and my attention narrows to that slow, continued pressure. My body makes yet another handy transformation to allow him access, and I am loving every inch he gains.

55

Drasuk

When she takes all of me, I finally stop worrying about hurting her and focus solely on the pleasure. Her taste is still in my mouth, driving me into this frenzy, as I slide back out, her tight channel squeezing me just how I hoped it would when I mapped her depths with my tongue.

That pleasure was nothing like this. I take a long moment to simply grind against her, enjoying how, even in this, she matches me by pushing back, increasing the pleasure of the connection.

Then I glide out, and back in. Slowly at first, but she urges me faster. Then faster. And next harder, until I am holding her small hips in a tight grip, planting my back limbs to increase my power, and pounding into her.

Each collision brings a cry of pleasure from her that increases my own. Long moments of bliss later, I can feel my seed gathering, but I hold it back, continuing to pump into her until I hear a keening wail to signal that she is open for my seed.

Then I loosen my control, my movements becoming more erratic, my mind searing with the pleasure ripping up my tail and fizzling along my spikes until it bursts out of me. A roar bellows out with it.

I hold her to me, both of us panting. She shifts forward slightly, but I hold her tightly so she doesn't injure herself as my knot finishes expanding.

"Oh. What's... Oh, fuck. That's..."

She devolves into moans as I tie us together, allowing me the pleasure of caressing her spikes, enjoying the combination of red and blue, despite myself, without her trying to escape. Not that she seems to mind.

"Now I understand the shape of your completely amazing, totally worth being arrogant about, cock, Drasuk."

I rumble out my agreement. "Well, had I known this was what it took for you to see how right I always am, we would have done this a lot sooner."

"Shut up, *lizard dork*, and keep petting me."

"Did you hit your head, too? Even admitting to your pet status? I'm shocked."

She starts laughing and doesn't seem to be able to stop. A few breaths later, I join her.

Once my knot allows movement, I move us back toward the water, sliding out of her with a pleased groan.

We will have to do that again as soon as possible. I let a chuckle out at the thought of how little it took for Kira to convince me of her human approach to pleasure.

Maybe there is something drakonids have wrong. Even we can be mistaken about something.

Kira is limp in my arms as sit down in the warm water, my tail finding the same rock to wrap around for better balance. I position her so her legs are spread against my stomach and knead her lovely, soft rear.

She rouses from her stupor. "Oh, that reminds me. Do you feel a tail developing? Tell me it is so."

I reach farther up and confirm what I thought I glimpsed earlier. "Yes, you have a little hatchling stump."

"Damn. Not orange and furry, then?"

"No. It is blue. You will have my tail on you, and you should be proud of it."

She laughs. "Oh, I'll be proud. I just liked the idea of venom."

"I suppose I can't argue with your reasoning," I concede.

"Speaking of weapons, did we gather them from the draks we killed?"

She has one hand rubbing at her forehead and the other reached around to scratch at her growing tail.

"We didn't, but we can do that now. Is that an incoming change on your head?"

She pulls a face. "Probably your spikes, yeah."

"Good. Maybe I can finally make sense of what's going on in your mind if they shift."

She growls at me, but doesn't comment. "Let's go get weapons and track down the others."

It doesn't take long to return to where we ambushed the traitors. Scavengers have already been at them, but their gear is still intact. Kira lets out her 'kitty call' while I start stripping the bodies of anything useful, making sure to first retrieve Kira's sword.

Soon after, the two humans are chatting, mostly about tails, and Thivoll and I are figuring out how to repurpose some of the armor to fit his different anatomy. I'm ambivalent as I put on Xar'Ar'ax's Maj'Ras armor.

He no longer had a right to it, but this isn't how I would have preferred to regain my protective under-plating, wrist-blades, and spear. His neck was also shorter than mine, so it doesn't fit as well as my own set.

Lost to the slimes forever, most likely.

A glance over at Kira and the joy on her face as she mimics with her hands what she thinks she'll be able to do once she has a tail, and it suddenly doesn't matter.

This is all I need to protect her. I will make sure of it.

56

Kira

Drasuk looks delectably threatening in his armor as he and Thivoll walk back out of the cave, off to test their new gear against some unsuspecting hunters.

I can almost hear the screams of terror and it's so fucking hot.

"I gather you read a lot," Ree comments out of the blue and it catches me off guard for a moment as I try to figure out what gave her that impression.

I'm usually just spouting nonsense, though my snark kicks in just fine as I turn to face her.

"What, you don't expect that from a jarhead?"

She grimaces and seems to be grappling for a way out of how I twisted her words into an apparent insult.

I start laughing and she lets out a huff of relief, then gives me a weak smile.

She'll figure out my humor soon enough.

"Everyone thinks it's just a bunch of fighting and non-stop action. Most people don't realize military life is mostly waiting around. I used that time to edify myself. I'm partial to Greek and Roman mythology and military history."

She nods.

"Plus, plenty of smut, of course."

She lets out a laugh at that, then raises her eyebrows and quirks a lip in an *I see you, sister* look. Clearly, she's read her own fair share.

"I can't say ER work left me with much downtime or energy for that, but I had... shall we say, lots of unfulfilled urges when I was with my ex-husband."

"Pshh. Couldn't get it up? Glad you lost the dead weight."

A shadow passes over her face, and I force myself to become serious.

"Oh. That sort of dead weight."

She shivers and nods, arms rising to hold herself together after I unintentionally triggered her.

I reach out a hand and hold on to her elbow, telling her with my eyes that it's me who sees her now.

"Well, on the bright side, you couldn't get any farther away from him."

Her lips twitch, but I know I need to offer more to help her shift away from remembered horror.

"No need for me to be up on a murder charge, either. Look at all the fucking silver linings, girl."

She chuckles. "Something tells me you could joke your way right out of it. Or you know someone, who knows someone, who knows someone, who--"

"I get it, Ree," I tell her with a laugh in my voice. "A girl never tells, though."

Judging by comments on the way back to the cave, and her body language now, Ree still seems shaken from the fight, haunted by her need to help me kill. It's weighing her down still.

"You did well in that fight, Ree, but I can see it's still bothering you."

She lets out a huff. "I'm too soft for this place. I can't stop seeing the people I killed, even though they deserved it. Even though I would be dead if I hadn't."

"I would also be dead if you hadn't, Ree. And seeing their faces is normal. I'll never forget any of my kills. I assume Drasuk won't either. We just aren't as brave as you are to openly admit it. We bury our feelings about it so we can focus on what is right in front of us."

"I can't do that, it seems like."

"It's why we are soldiers, and you are a commander. It's not just your charisma, or that silver tongue Thiv was bragging about to Drasuk just a bit ago, but because you can be our heart. You keep us centered. I don't need to know what you told Drasuk, but that's what you did for him before the fight. Right?"

"Yes. He was torn between two motivators. I helped him see which one mattered most."

I didn't plan to pry, but now I'm too curious.

"Oh yeah? What did he choose?"

"You."

I'm confused for a moment and just blink at her.

"You, dummy. He chose you."

"Oh."

She snickers at me, but doesn't take the verbal swipe Drasuk or I would have. She's too nice.

It's adorable.

I let her get back to organizing. I spend a few minutes helping her before she shoos me to the cave opening to be our guard so she doesn't have to "face leak." Whatever that means.

From the smirk on her face, some mysterious inside joke.

I ponder what she meant by him choosing me as I scan for threats, not sure I want to know what it means. Hopeful that I do.

＊＊＊

The bromance seems to have deepened by the time our two beasts come back, but Ree simply interrupts them to say she and Thiv are going to go on another long patrol.

From the look of realization and shivering of his spines, I think Drasuk might have finally figured out what her winks and knowing, loud tone means.

I'm a bit sad that I don't get to point out to all of them that my tail is about three feet long now before they disappear, but the sadness disappears the moment Drasuk pounces on me.

Literally. He's rumbling out his well wishes for their safety one moment and the next he's taking a bounding leap at me, pulling a little shriek from my lips.

The need for revenge for causing such an undignified sound races up along my spine, my new tail perfectly following my commands to whip him within an inch of his life.

I fucking love every blue, bumpy inch of it, though it isn't having much of an affect on the big oaf as he carries me into our little room, pins me up against him and plops down on his back.

I cringe, thinking of how that must have hurt his spikes, but he doesn't flinch, just looks at me with hunger.

I finally catch on to where this fuck train is headed when he shifts me over his belly, my black suit receding just as his glorious cock starts gliding out to greet my pussy.

Still, I deliver a couple more blows to his side, at least until he darts one of his chameleon hands out to grab it. He wraps his tail around my waist to take my weight, then moves his newly freed arm up to wrap around my neck.

I'm already moaning when he moves me so I'm sitting right on top of his member, which is laying long and thick along the lighter cream color of his underbelly. His tail tightens, then starts drawing my wet opening along his length, then back down again.

Three strokes as he squeezes my neck and pulls on my tail and my orgasm bursts up from between my quivering legs, into my spine, and up into my skull.

I'm still throbbing as he pulls me back up again, the grip of his tail just on the edge of pain, and then repositions me so he is pushing at my core.

One hard thrust and he is all the way in, an answering keen crawling up my constricted throat. He lets go of my tail after the sixth thrust so he can move that hand to my bouncing breasts.

I take the opportunity to whip at his legs with it, making him groan and tighten his hold on my waist so he can slam me down even harder. I'm panting, the edge of panic about not being able to get quite enough air races through me, heightening the pleasure of each collision.

My stomach tightens more and more with each thrust and it only takes a glance down to see his intense amber eyes and his sharp teeth bared in a grimace of ecstasy to tip me over again. He slams me down onto him several more times, losing his rhythm before coming inside me with a muffled sound of breaking rocks.

We are both panting as he gently repositions me so I am laying on the soft expanse of his cream-colored hide. His tail loosens, moving to twine around my much smaller one, then back around my upper shoulder, between the spikes there, so we are locked together.

Then even more so as his knot expands, making my eyes roll back as he stretches me, shocks of another orgasm thrumming along with each expansion.

Definitely a case of not ever knowing what I was fucking missing. I let out a moan as another wave of pleasure starts, then let out a long breath.

He's still inside of me as I drift off to the soothing feel of his hands rubbing along my back.

When I wake up, it's to a throbbing pain in my forehead, and unfortunately, an empty pussy.

I groan out in pain and reach a hand toward it, startled when Drasuk speaks. "Careful, it's sharp."

My eyes pop open as my heart skips a beat.

"What is it?"

"Sharp, bony spikes. Just like Mar'cte had on his back."

I let out a snort. "Fucker didn't even try to use them on me. Ah, Manticorid is the best language."

With a push of my hands, I leverage myself up, figuring it's better to be upright if I want to avoid cutting a finger off with my new, unexpected shiny change.

I figured since Drasuk and I already boned... I snicker at my unintended pun, derailing my thoughts for a moment. We had sex, so why a change from someone else?

Oh, right. I guess I was trapped under the big red idiot while he bled all over me.

My fingers are shaking, this time with excitement, as I gently probe to figure out what I've got. Feels like two hard, bony plates on my forehead, covering my eyebrows. I can still move the muscles, but assume no one is going to see my snarky brow raises anymore.

Damn.

My fingers keep moving up past the ridge between them and they reach a row of spikes. He's right, the ends are wicked sharp and I assume there's some of my blood dripping down them by the time I count five of them.

Not a unicorn, then. Quinticorn?

I start snickering, which turns into a full on session of tears-in-eyes laughing.

When I take a breath, Drasuk breaks in. "I assume you like them. I hit one of those on Xar'Ar'ax with a metal blade and it did nothing."

"Fuck, yes," I growl out, turned on all over again.

I'm death walking, bitches, and I love it.

A glance over to him and the look of adoration and lust in his eyes and I realize I love him, too.

My smile drops instantly.

I do? Fuck!

I wait for the panic to rise, my body tense for it, but it doesn't. I feel... content.

Centered, grounded. I suddenly get why losing my father broke my mother.

Tears well up in my eyes when I realize something else. That I can finally forgive her for it.

"I understand now, Mom," I breath out in English, wanting this moment to myself. Just me and her, wherever she might be.

A smile lifts as I imagine the ass kicking she's likely doing there.

I focus back on Drasuk, who's looking at me intently, but doesn't pry, likely catching on that I'm feeling vulnerable, since he has that soft look he sometimes gets.

I'll keep it to myself, for now at least. I look forward to explaining to Drasuk just how much lighter I feel now that I've let go of the anger I didn't even realize I was holding.

And how he helped get me to that point.

Right now, I want more of that beautiful blue cock.

57

Drasuk

I can tell she just made some sort of important realization, and I hold myself still, pushing back the need to ask.

Or worse, the need to draw her attention back to me.

Not that I don't like it, but only the weak demand a female tuck in her tail and wings instead of taking up all the space she needs. Deserves.

It's enthralling to see her independence. Her aggression and fire. The pleasure of it shivers along my hide.

I especially love when she looks at me like she is right now, her expression shifting from introspective to voracious. It has my cock throbbing and pushing out again in mere moments. I move a hand to lift her, but she smacks it away.

"Overbearing Drasuk can play another time. It's my turn," she barks out at me.

I trample my answering aggression and need to display my dominance before it can rise to her challenge, intrigued to see what she has planned.

She wriggles down, I assume to return to our fun from earlier, but confuses me when she just keeps moving. Then her mouth is on me, taking me back to the brief touches of her small pink tongue I allowed before almost losing control of my seed at the hot spring.

I let out a hiss when she takes me in a firm grip, then a groan when she drags her tongue all the way up the length of me, swirling it along each of eddy of my nodules until I can't breathe. I barely hold back when her hot mouth opens and sucks on the tip, entering a trance as she alternates her movements to drive me toward release.

I try to pull her up to me with my tail, to ensure she gets her own pleasure before I lose control, but she growls at me.

"I want your seed all over me, Drasuk."

My forehead spines shift in shock. No female would ever agree to such a waste. It would mean extending the breeding contact.

Then I remember that she's not a drak and I'm even more thankful she's human. Small, fierce, and all mine.

Then she's back to sucking on me, her hands twisting along my member in the most delicious slide, ever increasing in speed. The vibrations of her moans are making me pant.

My head falls back, my neck no longer capable of holding it, my eyes shut tight as I feel the build of pressure right under where she is moving her dexterous, glorious hands.

It only takes a scrape of her teeth against my already swelling head to make me lose control. I manage to make my head lift just in time to see her position herself over me, so my seed pumps between the globes of her chest.

Then I lay there, dazed, as she wipes it across her breasts with one hand, then down her stomach. Her other hand is exploring the rapidly swelling expanse of my knot, while she bites her lips.

I never knew something so erotic and pleasurable even existed as an option, not that I've done much in the way of research.

I am very glad I didn't, since it would have taken away the satisfaction of such a pleasurable discovery. And the opportunity to see that look on her face. The one telling me just how superior she is feeling right now that she was the one who introduced me.

She earned that look of pride.

"I have no words, little Kira."

"Never," she retorts with a laugh. "I don't believe it."

I start to speak, proving the truth of her words, but a new color at the end of her now much longer blue tail catches my eye and the words die on my tongue.

"Huh," she comments. "I guess you are."

After a beat, she realizes I'm staring at her newly grown manticorid venom spike, and she follows my gaze.

"Is that—?

"Yes," I breath out, my chest filled with an altogether unpleasant sensation.

Envy.

I grumble out a wordless complaint, then concede that she needs it more than I do. "The most feared substance in the known universe, Kira."

She lets out a screaming cry I, after a moment of thinking she is terrified, realize is actually a reflection of how excited she is. Next, she's hugging it, petting the fur at the end like it's the pet we keep teasing about.

Now I'm doubly jealous and another grumble rises, this one echoing off the stone walls.

"Oh, be quiet, *Mister* Grumpy Pants. Get your own venom. Oh, wait. You can't."

Once she gets her laughter back under control and sees my mock death stare and it sets off more of her cackles, I join her.

She wipes the tears from her face, and I roll my eyes. After a moment of disgust that I've picked up another form of Kira communication, I decide to offer the compliment she deserves.

"Beautiful and deadly. The perfect pet, after all."

She chuckles. "I'm glad to know you aren't so choked up on your pride that you can admit to my fucking amazing utility. Now I will do an even better job, which has already been stellar, at protecting you with venom."

I raise my forehead spines, intrigued by her boldness. "I seem to recall saving your life on more than one occasion."

She smirks, a glint of mischief in her eyes. "And I seem to recall you needing my help just as often. Face it, Drasuk, we're stuck with each other. Might as well make the best of it."

"Stuck with you? That's a terrifying thought," I reply, my tone teasing. "I might just prefer the company of the predators out there."

"Is that so?" she shoots back, a playful challenge in her voice. "Well, I'm sure they'd love to have a bite of your tough hide. But you know what? I think you secretly enjoy our little partnership. You'd be lost without me."

I chuckle, shaking my head. "Enjoy? Maybe. But lost? Hardly. I've survived far worse than this. And let's not forget, I'm the one keeping you safe."

She rolls her eyes, but she's grinning now. "Yeah, yeah, big tough drakonid protecting the fragile human. Got it. But let's not pretend you don't appreciate having someone around who can think on their feet."

I can't help but acknowledge the truth in her words.

Despite her size and species, Kira has proven herself to be resourceful and quick-witted. She's not just a burden; she's an asset.

And every part of her has been claimed as mine.

My spines shift to betray my pleasure at this thought, but I go back to needling her. "Don't let it increase your already overweening confidence so large you can't walk anymore."

She grins, a triumphant glint in her eyes. "Too late. My head's already pretty big, thanks to you."

She turns serious, her gaze reflecting rare vulnerability. "I'm not like other women, Drasuk."

"I assume they speak more directly."

"Shut up. I'm being serious. I might never settle down or have kits."

Her lips quirk, then she goes on. "I like how translations in Manticorid assume you will be having kittens. But, seriously, I want to be stuck with you, but I'm not sure you want to be stuck with me."

I let out a rumble of displeasure at how she is speaking about herself. "You are perfect. Like a Maj'Ra female, except one I can hold at night. What we have is enough. Far more than I ever thought I would have. More than I could have ever dreamed."

Her eyes glimmer. "I love being stuck with you."

It's a strange concept, love, but I've decided I am willing to be an outlier. The drak everyone speaks about in whispers or in booming taunts.

"I love it, too," I tell her. "And you. I love you."

"Hold on, now. There's room for something else inside that *lizard* brain for something besides arrogance?"

I narrow my eyes and let her know with my spines that I expect a better response than that. Some day I'm going to have to ask what a *lizard* is, but I haven't yet been desperate enough broach the topic.

"What, you expect me to say it too? And sound like just as much of a fool?" she asks.

She lets go of her thunderous look and dissolves into laughter. "Alright," she says, her face looking as soft and sincere as I have ever seen it.

"I love you, Drasuk. You are the only one in the universe who could handle me. You take my fire and fill up something inside that I thought I didn't need. I'm glad you found me."

"I love heat," I rumble at her. "Burn bright, little one."

I pull her against me as she does the same and we both let out sighs of contentment.

I can't leave it at that, of course. "You'll have to be an inferno to try to match me."

She snorts out a breath and whacks me with her tail, for the first time making me hold my breath in fear that her spike might penetrate.

That would be highly unpleasant, even if it isn't deadly.

"I repeat," she deadpans. "How do you fit that enormous amount of arrogance in such a small brain?"

It seems like this conversation might need to end in violence. "We never did have that wrestling match," I point out.

She lets out a choking laugh. "Oh, it is on."

"Didn't we just do that? Twice. But I can do it again."

"No, that was getting it in."

"You said 'getting it on' meant the same as sex."

"Not in this context, Drasuk, and I didn't use those exact words. I said 'it is on.' Now it means I am going to crush you in mock battle."

"You aren't ever going to speak clearly, are you?"

Her lips pull back, showing her blunt teeth and her eyes narrow. Her face looks almost... evil.

"What would be the fun in that?"

58

Preview of Citrine

Whroahk

"It's intolerable," I growl, my voice tinged with an echoing click of disdain.

Normally, scents hold no sway over me, but today is different. This one stirs something within me, awakening sensations I had never known. It's as if I can truly smell for the first time, and the effect it has on me is... unexpected.

Terrible. The smell is terrible.

I can't comprehend how something so foul could permeate the surrounding air so completely. It's vile. Hanging heavily and assaulting my senses. It feels as though it has tainted the very essence of the world around me.

I shake my head in disbelief, trying to rid myself of the offensive odor that seems to cling to my skin like a suffocating shroud. But no matter how hard I try, or how many times I dip my body back down into the water, I can't escape it.

My stomach churns as I pull in each breath. It even makes me forget about my meal, which has never happened. My gaze darts frantically, searching for the source, but it remains elusive, hidden somewhere.

Then, from the other side of the stones, I hear it. A tiny grunt, barely audible over the gentle lapping of the waves. My eyes widen as I realize that I'm not alone. My meal, which fell from the sky in a streaking silver canister, is nearby, concealed from view by the rugged terrain.

Ignoring the smell, with a swift and decisive motion, I allow my tentacles to lift me from the water, propelling me upward with an effortless grace. The cool liquid trails behind me, droplets shimmering in the sunlight as I ascend the rocky outcrop.

Each jagged edge of the stone presses against my slick skin, leaving behind a trail of moisture as I scale the precipice. The rough texture of the rocks scrapes against my flesh. It is a sensation that is both exhilarating and uncomfortable. Nothing like the gentle buoying embrace of the water behind me.

I ignore the discomfort, my focus fixed on the mysterious, hopefully delicious, presence that awaits me above. This lake and its disgusting bounty of muddy creatures has driven me to take on unexpected new experiences. Never have I hunted on land.

What terrible creatures I would kill, crushing them to a pulp in my rage, for the chance to eat something properly raised in salt water. Finally, I reach the top.

With a surge of effort, I pull myself over the edge, my eyes scanning the rocky terrain for any sign of movement. And there, clinging to the top of a weathered boulder and just within reach if I stretch, is a figure cloaked in shadow, its features obscured by the dim light of the setting sun.

A thrill passes through my chest as I see the object of my hunt. A hearty meal. My tentacles are poised to scoop up the creature before me, but before I can reach out, bright yellow eyes meet mine, wide with terror. It slips from the rocks, tumbling to the ground below with a dull thud.

I study the fallen form. The creature is a female, I suspect. Though I'm not sure why that would give me pause. It never has before.

Bright yellow weeds are splayed around her, a bright contrast against the muted tones of the rocky terrain. As I study her, I notice the small, delicate frame of her body, far more curved than the females of my species.

Distinctly lacking in number and orientation of limbs to make her anywhere near as threatening as they would be.

Another whiff of wind drifts my way, carrying with it a stronger concentration of the unmistakable scent that invaded my senses earlier. I recoil, realizing with a start that it emanates from her.

An end needs to come swiftly, then, though I am disappointed that she will do nothing for my hunger. I lower myself down the cliff to reach her as I listen to her labored breathing.

Her body is delicate, almost childlike compared to the robust forms of my species. Even our young ones appear larger and more formidable than her. It's almost laughable how easily I could crush her with a mere flick of one long, twisting limb.

I lift a tentacle to do just that, excited to see her spill more of that red blood, even if it will probably make the air even more foul. I try to bring my limb down from where it quivers in anticipation.

I just... can't.

About the Authors

Please take a few moments to write a review.
They help immensely.

This pen name represents a collaboration with the goal of creating stories just like we prefer: spicy slow burn, strong character arcs, and all about the... shall we say delectably different.

Ky is our public face...

the one of us who posts on social media, who decided it was *smart* to get a PhD in History (and so now regales you with the book related historical mythology in our newsletter), who tends to have all the wild ideas, the writing voice we follow, and who keeps all of it moving (sheesh, that's a lot... thanks, Ky!)

On a typical day you can find Ky hanging out with her own Mr. Delectably Different, loving on her fur babies, or convincing her two kids that she really is funnier than they'll admit.

She's a musician, sculptor, graphic designer, and lover of weirdness. Most of the time, she's either working her 9 to 5, writing, or running out in the wild.

Join our free newsletter to find out more...
and to get access to exclusive content!
kylabreene.com

Legends Start Somewhere

Want to read more stories in the Alien Hunting Grounds Universe?

Join our newsletter for a free prequel short story! You can access it at kylabreene.com

Myth Awakened: Vimala and Jentoll

Vimala

I was once a courtesan for kings... until a rival sent an attacker in the middle of the night. One moment. One coward with a blade. I lost everything.

My beauty no longer sustains me, but I refuse to simply fade away. And yet it is hard to maintain hope after so much loss. Will this otherworldly avatar of Vishnu be my salvation?

Jentoll

I've given more than enough to my people. To my failing empire. I gave an eye. My tail. Pieces of my sanity... far too much precious time. And now it's crumbling to dust. Falling to a far different sort of rallying cry. One for peace.

Let the next generation bear that task. This is my chance to flee. To find a new home.

**Two wounded hearts, both seeking refuge.
Will they find it in each other?**

Join our newsletter to find out: kylabreene.com

www.ingramcontent.com/pod-product-compliance
Lightning Source LLC
Chambersburg PA
CBHW060436310726

48977CB00001B/207